DIGGING THE GOLDEN FUNGUS
THE SWIFTPAD INSURGENCY

"SwiftPad has now taken on a life of its own, spurring arguments between warring factions of opinionated phone addicts all over the world and, ultimately, spiraling out of control. This newly fractured international fearscape mirrors certain events taking place among real-world media outlets today, and raises the stakes for SwiftPad founders Kip "Chubby" Rehain and GG Oglethorpe. When America's leader—a trash-tweeting president taken over the edge by one too many liberal dissenters—paints a massive bullseye on Kip and GG's hometown of Portland, they'll have to assemble all of their allies to stop the city—and nation—from crumbling down upon itself."

DIGGING THE GOLDEN FUNGUS

THE SWIFTPAD INSURGENCY

BY

S. LEE BARCKMANN

BW

BARCKWORDS
PUBLISHING

Publisher: Barckwords Publishing

Paperback   ISBN-13 978-1-7352514-4-8
eBook   ISBN-13 978-1-7352514-5-5

1 3 5 7 9 10 8 6 4 2

TABLE OF CONTENTS

Cast of Characters ix

Prologue: Catching Up with Chubby xi

Technical and Historical Notes on the Evolution of SwiftPad . xv

CHAPTER 1:   A Visit to Reigny Deigh 1

CHAPTER 2:   The Ishpeming Statement 18

CHAPTER 3:   Chubby Takes Off After GG 38

CHAPTER 4:   Spence and Alison Surprise Each Other 50

CHAPTER 5:   The Story in Spence's Script 64

CHAPTER 6:   Kip Meets Nathan Schuette at Paula's
             Place in Haight-Ashbury 73

CHAPTER 7:   Spence's Script Story Continued 93

CHAPTER 8:   Kip Returns to Portland 96

CHAPTER 9:   Alice Learns of Kip's Return 100

CHAPTER 10: Chubby's Settles in Back in Stumptown 109

CHAPTER 11: Spence Rides Home after Drinking Beer
             with Alison 118

CHAPTER 12: Chubby Rides to G's House 126

CHAPTER 13: Spence Arrives at His House 131

CHAPTER 14: Chubby Arrives at GG's House 144

CHAPTER 15: Nate's Account of Events Leading up to
His Kidnapping 156

CHAPTER 16: The Board Meeting Continues 165

CHAPTER 17: Intruders 176

CHAPTER 18: Peggy Comes Home 182

CHAPTER 19: Aftermath 184

CHAPTER 20: Nate, Spence & Maggie/Peggy Eat Ziti 186

CHAPTER 21: Interrogation 191

CHAPTER 22: Spence Heads out to Meet Alison 198

CHAPTER 23: Back to the Hospital 203

CHAPTER 24: Gunfire on the River 206

CHAPTER 25: Goodbye 209

CHAPTER 26: The Great Escape 211

CHAPTER 27: Watching from the Shadows 214

CHAPTER 28: Incident at Couch Park 218

CHAPTER 29: Command Post Above the Kwikie Mart 229

CHAPTER 30: Signals 234

CHAPTER 31: Briefing at the Command Post 237

CHAPTER 32: Johnny Loves Ya! 249

CHAPTER 33: Live at the Moda! 259

CHAPTER 34: Peggy Sparks a Fire 263

CHAPTER 35: Ain't Nothin' but a Revolution 275

CHAPTER 36: Bugging Out 287

CHAPTER 37: At the Railway Station 290

CHAPTER 38: Mopping Up.. 297

CHAPTER 39: Goin' South.. 304

Coming Attractions 315

CAST OF CHARACTERS

Kip Rehain (Chubby, Cornelius Welles, K) – Cofounder of SwiftPad

Cynthia Oglethorpe (G, GG, Cindy) – Cofounder of SwiftPad

Jim Hunt (Jim) – Childhood friend of Kip, partner at SwiftPad

Walt Rehain – Kip's father, a rich logger

Alice Hunt – Jim Hunt's mother, Walt's sometime lover, and influential person in West Coast circles

Heber Young – Walt Rehain, Kip's and SwiftPad financial maven, direct descendant of Brigham Young

Kayla Holmes – Stanford Business school graduate, who is hired to manage Reigny Deigh Media

Spence Stromborn – The creative force at *Reigny Deigh Media*

Alison Aykroyd – Spence's colleague at *Reigny Deigh Media*

Nathan Schuette – Legendary writer

Margaret Stromborn (Peggy, Maggie) – Spence's wife, Nathan's former girlfriend

Gordon Lobetts (Gordy) – President of *Reigny Deigh Media*

Leone Humpkin – Influential editor, TV personality

Adele Humpkin – Leone's wife, and organist for the Jean Katon Express

Jean Katon – Lead singer in the Jean Katon Express

Gopesh Gupta – Billionaire inventor of C2B – the popular computer to brain technology

Paula Flayer (Pamela?) – Nathan's first love, a woman who seems pass through time unchanged

Ben Cadez (Guy Jumano?, Stewardo del Gente?) – Presidential candidate, former lover of Paula

Milana Shikshavalli – Kip's girlfriend from the Republic of Georgia

Nikoloz – Milana's Russian half brother

Elwood Taylor – (Elmer?) Longtime friend of Nathan and Paula's

Wally Cherry – (Walter?) Longtime friend of Elwood, Nathan, and Paula

Aldane Blyden – Kip's partner in some outrageous adventures

Hariet Miller – President of Cascade Sportswear

Hadley – Staff at SwiftPad, who has a crush on Kip

Archimedes Moropolis – The number 2 brain at SwiftPad (behind G)

Ted Henderson – Portland detective who has it in for Kip

Colonel Hassan Coleman – Mayor of Memphis, Tennessee, leader of the resistance against the RedHats

Senator (Retired General) Harvey Grennell – Leader of resistance

Telly Haines (Crocodile) – businessman, who had a big stake in Reigny Deigh Media

Johnny – Telly's bodyguard

Lew – Telly's lawyer

Moseley – a young soldier friend of Margaret's

Sequoia – Young woman refugee whom Nate and Margaret take in

PROLOGUE
CATCHING UP WITH CHUBBY

AS YOU MIGHT RECALL FROM THE LAST PAGES OF *Digging Up New Business: The SwiftPad Takeover*, we left Chubby in a drainage ditch, in a bittersweet mood, looking up at the rain. He had thwarted the homicidal kidnapping of GG in the Portland Rose Garden and then finished lopping off the serial killer's pecker after GG had nearly bitten through it.

Sometime after that GG left, taking off for Asia on her own, chasing Chubby's best friend since second grade, Jim Hunt. Jim, who helped both Chubby and GG create the most influential social media platform in the world, was chasing Macy, who herself was looking for the Chinese father of her daughter.

Kipling Rehain, Kip, a.k.a. Cornelius "Chubby" Welles (and soon to be known simply as "K"), let her go. He stayed on his father's compound up in the isolated Oregon Coast Range, west of Blodgett, east of Toledo, and north of Eddyville. His father, Walt, was dying and Kip devoted himself to the care of his father and came to a deeper understanding of "the meaning of life" as his dad drifted away. His earlier struggles with his father and their mutual misunderstandings suddenly became insignificant. He and his father shared a sweet sense of regret that they had not done it sooner.

During this time, *SwiftPad* was sold to Amazon for about $29 billion.

Heber renegotiated the original $8.7 billion deal that Kip had carelessly – but luckily – signed on the wrong page. Legally Heber was out on a limb, but Bezos really wanted SwiftPad, so he agreed, causing a temporary selloff of Amazon's stock that week. It enriched almost everyone involved, too: GG of course; Walt, Kip's father who owned most of the stock; as well as Chubby's best friend Jim Hunt. All of the original staff were now millionaires too, on paper at least. The company's Board of Directors and the other original investors such as Harriet Miller, founder of Cascade Sportswear, did well too.

At first, everything went smoothly, and no one looked this gifted horse in the mouth, but gradually there were lawsuits from peripheral players as well as from others who claimed that their shares were not adequately matched to their contributions. Heber, the Rehain family's consigliere, negotiated tirelessly and handled the distribution issues for the most part fairly, and soon the majority of the squabbling subsided. When Heber sat Kip down to explain the details of the sale and of the final distributions, Chubby quickly became bored, and just (carefully this time) signed the papers.

The SwiftPad crew founded and generously funded a string of related non-profit agencies for the homeless. These agencies were so well endowed, the energy so positive, and the management so savvy that they would have easily ended homelessness and various other kinds of economic misery in the city – if things had not gotten so much worse. But news of the programs only attracted more and more desperate people to Portland, and because of the dire general situation in the country, the numbers now began to strain the city to the breaking point.

That was all before the new Temp-Prez's "Thanksgiving Day Decrees" (TDD).

Although there were many high-profile arrests, particularly among Silicon Valley execs, it was the mass arrests and persecution of the Off-the-Grids (OTGs, people who had no social media or digital internet signatures) that really shocked the nation. A bill was introduced to make OTGs on par with vagrants, but it died in committee. Still, by order of the Thanksgiving Day decrees, it was essentially illegal not to be connected on at least one of the several designated Social Media outlets. The order was not enforced uniformly, but mostly targeted frequent posters and commenters who suddenly went silent, the assumption being that they must have had something to hide. This led to a huge black market in "burners," cheap smartphones available anywhere, to project a temporary image of connectedness. Privacy and public Off-the-Gridiness became the universal desire of the era. Virtually impossible to crack "one-time-pad" (OTP) encryption apps were extremely popular.

The new commercially available "privacy techniques" caused concern for NatSat, but Temp-Prez was too scared to take that issue on, at least not until the coming election. NSA was too overwhelmed to keep control.

Back in the Coast Range, about 25 miles as the crow flies east from Newport, Oregon, the common house that Jim's mother Alice was building was near completion. The recycled dark-green glass walls were mostly sculpted from a fortuitously unearthed trove of Olympia Brewing's quart bottles of Rainier Ale. The mostly subterranean, multipurpose gym/meeting and dining hall/guest hostel reflected the forest around it like a living emerald. The sparkle served as a cloak of invisibility that helped to hide the naturally camouflaged underground split level hobbit-like houses that spread out to form mathematically derived, naturally varying patterns of Mandelbrot's formulas. You might have known exactly where the hobbit lairs were located, but they would still be almost invisible, faded into the foliage around them, and soon, when the moss completely covered them, indistinguishable from the surrounding flora.

The construction continued throughout Walt's hospice care. Slow-moving, pony-sized electric-powered ATVs pulled soft-sprung wagons carrying dirt, the excavated earth that made way for subterranean dwellings. Several tunnels were also constructed among the structures for foul-weather mobility (and guerilla defense, if it ever came to that). The wagons hauling the dirt quivered like a spider on a web, and lightly bounced on very fat tires. These double-jointed, slinky-like moon-buggies crept about the forest floor carefully so as not to break up or muddy the permaculture topsoil.

Jim's mom, Alice, had once envisioned a community of the somewhat like-minded, who loved life in all its bizarre permutations, no matter how absurd it sometimes seemed. But more and more it was mutating into a defensive redoubt, a fortress in the woods. Fitness for combat slowly became a criterion for commune membership. Walt smiled approvingly. Walt had always hated the government, but never more than now. "You are finally learning..." Those were his last words.

Alice held her grief closely because her lifetime of knowing Walt was not easy to express with any single emotion. When he finally died, her grief mixed with a great fear of what was coming.

Kip felt that strange, sad, guilty sense of release that sons sometimes feel when their father dies. After a week of hiking through the dense, trackless Coast Range, he knew what he had to do. He had to find GG.

TECHNICAL AND HISTORICAL NOTES ON THE EVOLUTION OF SWIFTPAD

THE FIRST THING AMAZON DID WAS TAME THE *SwiftPad* Bots. But the next generation of bots designed themselves, and they slowly came back, more stealthy, scary, and harder to detect.

The app's Bots often got into arguments with other Bots and took different sides of real issues, trying to bait "blood-bags" (as the "Bots" referred to humans) into the fight. There were factions within factions among the Bots too. There were "Bot" issues, about which humans were unceremoniously told did not concern them. The Bots had been designed to fuck with humans. Bots would slightly lie about real users' input, the way real people do. They lied about other users' input (but didn't change it) to make an opposite point. The Bots lied and tried to pretend other Bots were the real enemy and that they were telling the truth. The Bots betrayed real users or other fake users (Bots that would then fake outrage). They would often switch sides in the middle of a discussion. Since it was impossible to tell who was real and who was not, this drove people to the heights of apoplexy.

People loved the *SwiftPad* app, and while they might not admit it, they really loved the way it drove other people crazy. They just wanted to make sure it was "fair" and was not being used by real humans (or foreign governments) to insert their agendas.

Amazon "cleaned up" all these controversial features, and simplified, with each post clearly marked; Beverly (bot) or Bob (bot) could be quite opposite in every aspect of their outlook, but the user/reader now knew they weren't "real." So that took a lot of the fun out of it.

Each user had his or her own input portal all laid out, like Elaine's apocryphal and colorful panties, inviting, daring, begging for engagement. Users joined groups and battled other groups while *SwiftPad* bots egged them on, or threw cold water on them.

The interface technology used to put real people into other scenes, news clips, and movies, and to put words in people's mouths, was abandoned by the app. But that same technology was improved and sold to high-end corporations and customers and lived on in hundreds of "fake histories" that were used to promote various commercial and political messages. For the most part, though, they had little influence. The country just didn't think about history, real or fake.

The Chooser interface still worked, so users could still create their own personal reality. But it took people to places they didn't expect and didn't want to be. The *Washington Post* discovered that this feature was no longer very popular. It was kept alive for gamers, mental patients, and believers of outrageous conspiracies who continued to alter their reality to match their imagined paranoid world. Knowing the identity of those users freed up many Justice Department investigators for more mundane tasks.

The actual platform, the "guts" of the application, was maintained by the *SwiftPad* staff. GG and Kip's company, SwiftPad Inc., remained in their old original headquarters on the northside, in the old industrial district. The crew updated the core product and worked on spec for changes.

The old lumber warehouse, the *SwiftPad* office, had plywood walls, old musty couches and beanbags chairs and still no wireless, you had to plug into a cat 5 cable to be connected. It was mostly a shell now that the App's technical work had been pushed out to the company's offices all over the world. It was the groodiest, (some called it the most disgusting) corporate office of a Fortune 50 company in existence. But no one wanted to change it. Many of the non-vested staff (the recent hires) had moved over to Amazon, so perhaps they didn't like it, but to the original crew, it was home. Heber Young, wanted to upgrade the building, and had a million practical reasons for doing so, but he could never get anyone else to agree, so eventually, he gave up trying. Heber, the company's consigliere, kept the company afloat while the rest of the crew took various kinds of holidays, flaking out, spending their new wealth. Heber, stayed with it though, and used aggressive legal action and innovative public relations tactics to keep the other "entities" out, be it NSA, Russian hackers, and other gawkers. Archimedes Moropolis led the tech crew and focused on keeping the secret sauce secret.

CHAPTER 1
A VISIT TO REIGNY DEIGH

7:00 AM, Friday, July 17, 2020

There was a now a huge permanent underclass of homeless Americans, way beyond anything previously, even dwarfing the Great Depression. The man in power, contemptuously called by one and all "Temp-Prez," had apparently flushed the previous President out in a surprise putsch, and then tried to assume his mantle by continuing his cruel and short-sighted policies. The "Real-Prez" had been on a golfing holiday, when he was somehow convinced to agree (no written agreement has ever been discovered) to "temporarily step down." His family then had him committed to a "psychiatric facility" in New Jersey hours later.

From *The Fall of it All – A History of the Big Dump*

"WHAT DO YOU KNOW ABOUT CYNTHIA Oglethorpe? Otherwise known as GG."

Kayla posed the question like a substitute teacher who had only just read the lesson plan. She scanned the room in a vain attempt to make eye contact with someone. Her eyes lingered on Spence.

Spence Stromborn, a.k.a. "Mr. Big Idea," the "Rainmaker," silently shook his head and stared out a 27th floor window that overlooked the north side of the city. Swan Island, the 405 bridge over the Willamette, the railroad yard, and even the cliff above the final westward bend in the river, all seemed incongruous with "weird" Portland.

Spence, who conceived and storyboarded campaigns for *Reigny Deigh Media (RDM)*, was meeting his new boss for the first time. Spence didn't invent "Portland quirkiness," but via *Reigny Deigh's* highly visible national profile, he helped shape and grow it in the online media petri dish that his company kept in the nation's mini-fridge. *RDM's* message – stony, Sasquatchy, gender-bendy, organicy, she's-in-charge-but-still-sexy, and Gen-Y (pronounced in house as "Jenny") drove many sponsors away, because how do you mass market something that has to be "local sourced"? But *RDM's* national profile, and its "bang for the buck" reputation, had brought in more clients than they could handle, even though the country at large was spiraling down the drain.

Spence, 47, as usual, had his Oregon State Beavers baseball cap on slightly crooked, his beard was scraggly and uncombed, and his dark framed glasses were sliding down his nose. He was getting thick in the middle, in spite of his nine-mile bike commute into Portland for work, and then back to Gresham. Sometimes he cheated and took the train in, with his bike, like he did today.

His wife Peggy did Pilates every morning, and they hadn't had sex in a couple of months, and looking down at his expanding gut, he wondered if that might be part of the reason. Maybe it was the great Oregon beer, even though the hops crop had been miserable last year, because it had just been too hot. It might also be the artisan pizza, and pasta, cheese, and the dumplings, and the peanut butter slabbed on apples and bananas. Well not lately, no bananas, not even in Whole Foods or New Seasons, or any of the other high-end stores. The apple crop looked OK for the coming autumn out of the Hood River. Spence was fit, he told himself. He could ride for hours without tiring. The spare tire around his waist was just latent energy, waiting for a reason to be burned off.

Looking at his new boss, and listening to her yammer on, brought to Spence's mind the fact that the rest of the country thought that the Rose City was full of overly sensitive, politically correct, spoiled, whiny androgynous narcissists. For the most part, it was nothing like that. That was just a silly stereotype, taken from a silly, out-of-date, cable TV comedy.

Still, it never paid to be too snobby about it. Spence had taken to heart the message of the film *The Man Who Shot Liberty Valance:* If the choice was between the truth and the legend – print the legend. The legend had made Portland a top-tier city, and reality had caught up with the legend. Excepting DC, LA and NYC, Stumptown was more influential, with more "soft power" than any other city. The popular KGW (Portland NBC) TV show, "Rose City Morning" had a huge worldwide following.

Since banning cars in the city proper, a long time drive-time commuter said, "People talk to one another now." Bicycles packed the bridges at all hours of the day and night. The Trimet, was called (by a famous Dutch architect) "the greatest mass transit system in the world." Safe, comfortable, and filled with amenities (like wine bars and classical musicians), it was a pleasure to ride around the city, whether commuting or just going out. The real "truth" was it really was "better" in Portland.

But everyone knew that the real driver of the "Portland Renaissance" was the mega-millions that *SwiftPad* had dropped into the city that had filled the coffers of every business and entertainment venue in town. Portlanders who had money made more of it. Some of it even leaked out to people who didn't have money. It was just considered incredibly bad form to flaunt it. *SwiftPad,* for better or worse, defined the nation's conversation with itself. Well, not the whole nation. In *RedHat* country Portland was Babylon personified. Temp-Prez had recently called Portlanders a "dirty, Godless collection of deviants". Real-Prez had said much worse, before his forced sequestration.

The river flowing through the city helped feed more than the ducks, fish, and otters. In a world that was drying up, River City was moist with life. The deserts and dry river basins to the south were emptying out and its people were headed north. Tents cities spread in all directions around Portland. More were coming, and even more were thinking about coming.

Suffering humanity was all around, everywhere, in fact, right outside the downtown building where Spence was working. Back in his yard outside of Gresham, two homeless families, eight people in all, camped in Spence and Peggy's yard. They used the kitchen and shower and, during the day while Spence and Peggy were working, they used their internet, and were welcomed in the evening occasionally as guests. It was a tricky balance but they all made it work, for the time being anyway.

Spence wondered if the burden of caring – constantly, unrelentingly – was ever going to go away. There were at least five other homeless families (using the term loosely) living in tents near his house who were mad at him and Peggy, and the "lucky" ones who camped in their yard. They even cursed Peggy as she was leaving the house once. Should they give it all away? Become homeless themselves? They had never had that conversation, but he knew it weighed heavily on Peggy too. It was a conversation that the whole city was avoiding.

A vagabond, a dirty young man, unkempt, in old torn clothes, was contemptuously showing a sullen cop an overflowing wallet; that was the premise of the viral GAP trailer, that RDM had recently produced. Spence, of course, had created it, and it was playing over and over seemingly everywhere. GAP sales skyrocketed. Spence cringed every time he saw it, and he regretted producing it.

But back to the question – who was Cynthia Oglethorpe? Most Portlanders knew her as GG, and most everyone in the room had met and talked to her. Cynthia was almost synony-mous with *SwiftPad*. When you thought of Portland, you thought of *SwiftPad*, then maybe Mount Hood, or the White Stag sign that overlooked the river downtown, or maybe the annual Naked Bike ride, or Nike, or Cascade Sportswear. It seemed impossible to live in Portland and not to know that Cynthia (GG) had been the brains and driving force behind the most successful company in the country.

Spence had once been a close friend of the other *SwiftPad* founder, Kip "Chubby" Rehain. He got sick every time that thought reared up, because he had turned down a place on the board of directors back when *SwiftPad* was little more than an idea. He had blown his billion-dollar chance and now he really didn't want to revive the memory.

The traffic on the 405 bridge over the river was backed up coming into town, as it usually was this early in the morning. Coming in, as Spence had gotten off the streetcar from the Max stop at Pioneer Square, he saw more young, very able-bodied refugees, two, three at a time, heading up the hill toward the tony enclave of Northwest Portland and beyond, into the vast primaeval Forest Park that overlooked the city. Some kind of con-cert? Oregon Burning Man? Raining Man? Rain Man?

Normally Spence would be pedaling into work on the Spring-water Bike Corridor at this time, but this morning he had brought his bike in on the 6:30 AM Trimet Blue Line train from Gresham City Hall to attend the new Creative Director's ridiculously early meeting. What was the question?

Oh, GG – Cynthia Oglethorpe.

"Wasn't she that GAP underwear model?" Spence spoke list-lessly, obliquely mentioning a big client who loved his work, just to let his new boss know with whom she was fucking.

Kayla continued to smile, but with more teeth, and without her Zoloft-like dreamy half-grin.

Charles guffawed into his hand and Joyce snickered.

Alison sat up straight, alertly blank-faced as usual.

Kayla had come from *Eastbay Productions*. She had a Palo Alto vibe going, with a laid-back Marin County style, but was still Stanford all the way, her hand up and homework done. Definitely not East Bay. Particularly not since the earthquake.

Kayla wielded a highly customized Android tablet like a pro, sliding her fingers over open applets, sometimes pulling one into the other, creating that mirror reflecting a mirror *ad infinitum*. The tablet projected onto a high def 60 inch screen, producing a "vision" video, mostly views featuring herself talking. She wore a different outfit in every scene. This morning Kayla wore a plain turquoise blue dress, held up with angel hair spaghetti straps, taken in under the bosom, and plaited down just below her knees. Her wild, dirty-blonde hair was half controlled by an antique pearl barrette, and her black hiking socks and blue Keen sandals gave her a tacky, retro-Portland nerd resemblance.

She was the kind of woman that Spence normally tried to avoid.

Spence was originally from Auburn Hills, Michigan, but during his junior year in high school, on a spur-of-the-moment whim, he decided that he wanted to move to the Northwest. Even though he loved literature, and was big in his high school Drama Club, performing a series of soliloquies from various famous science fiction novels at a school assembly, he chose Oregon State, the engineering and agriculture university in Corvallis. Being a bit of a math geek, and having a practical bent to his nature, he studied Civil Engineering, and minored in Computer Science. He discovered he enjoyed writing code too, at first in Perl and Java, and recently in more exotic languages such as SwiftPad-Script.

He married right after college, and he and Vicky moved to 40 miles south, to Eugene Oregon, where Vicky enrolled in a master's program for Ecstatic Dancing at the University of Oregon. Spence got a job at an engineering firm and she got involved in a theater group. About six months later, Vickie, and four other women performed a mimed play at the WOW Hall about patriarchal oppression. Spence had sat in the audience with other boyfriends and husbands who all applauded enthusiastically. Spence applauded too, but afterwards, he had one or two technical criticisms.

She left him soon after that, and then when he was testing the structural integrity of a concrete sample at his firm's materials lab, he dropped it on his foot, breaking his left cuboid bone. Even now, years later, his left foot still hurt sometimes. Those were some bad days, he thought.

Now, as he rubbed the top of his left foot with his right heel and looked at Kayla, he realized she had a certain symmetry with Vickie. No physical resemblance, just a resemblance of manner.

"A sparklingly fresh addition to *Reigny Deigh Media*'s collection of quirky creatives," an *IndieWire* report said about Kayla Holmes in the "New Faces" section. Quirky creative – the same phrase was also used to describe Spence on *Reigny Deigh*'s website. Spence thought about what it meant to be a "quirky creative." Maybe quirky creativity was a condition with the symptoms manifesting as Max Headroom–like spas-spas-spasms?

It was mid-July and the quiet but ubiquitous air conditioning was putting out an uncomfortable chill.

"Is anybody cold?" No one answered and Kayla looked around and theatrically shivered. Alison surreptitiously logged into the indoor environmental portal and tuned the temp down a degree. She turned her fone toward Spence as she did it, causing him to stifle a laugh.

Kayla had brought *Slashing Queens* to *Eastbay Productions* last year, just before the earthquake, and it was a coup, no question. The Eastbay studio, located in Berkeley, had caused a minor shake-up in the Indie entertainment industry, and Kayla had been its star producer. Second at Sundance, a big write-up in the *NY Times*. It didn't make much money, but carried a lot of "cred," and she had "relationships" with some of next year's big names, as well as the hottish newbies who often served as the third guest on the late-late night talk shows.

Spence had heard the rumors about Kayla. But neither he nor anyone else even slightly hinted, even in private conversations, how they all thought Kayla had become so successful. Most of her clients (and all of her bosses) were men and – she had that thing.... All this passed through his mind, in and out with no lasting effect. He was going to have to be careful, he thought.

Reigny Deigh Media (like Kayla's old shop, *Eastbay Productions*) was putting together deals – movie deals, celebrity partnerships, brand-building, creative "talent scouting," public relations campaigns, even high-end advertising campaigns for a particular set of indie outfits – bringing talent together, raising money from *nouveau riche* celebrity stalkers and the young money with Daddy or Mommy issues, mixing it up with West Coast–casual gatherings where wine was drunk out of small mason jars. Customers didn't flinch at the exorbitant number of hours that were billed for the simplest of tasks, and for the most casual of conversations. Those conditions, combined with the non-negotiable, non-refundable hefty earnest money down payment, weeded out everyone that might have an objection to the *RDM* experience.

RDM's founder, Gordy Lobetts, looked 15 years older than he was, and although he had a reputation for being on top of everything, rumors had him stoned (on what? maybe pot, but his occasional manic jags seemed to indicate something else) before and during work, which was only from 10 to 11:30 AM because he was usually out of the office every day before noon. Spence, who worked for stock incentives during the formative first six months of the company, still owned approximately 15% of the company – down from 30%, the difference of which he had to sell back to Gordy to pay Vickie's divorce lawyer.

Spence had met Gordy in Eugene at the WOW Hall – at Vickie's show. Gordy was on the board of directors, and used the venue to promote most of the out-of-town shows. Much later

Spence learned that Vickie had been fucking Gordy on a regular basis way before their final split, but by that time, he and Gordo were deep into some profitable business together and Spence had moved on and just let it go.

Gordy in the meantime got another gig managing talent at a downtown Eugene bar. He had one season of incredible success bringing in low wattage but highly regarded talent. He convinced David Lomberg – the David Lomberg, folk-rock–electric guitar legend – to sign, just after the release of his music video *Legend of Squidman*, and it was off to the races.

Once *Reigny Deigh* moved from Eugene to Portland, and became a brick and mortar operation, with an office downtown in the Pearl, Gordy practically disappeared. He sat in the back of the room for some of the get-acquainted meetings, usually for only the first 10 minutes. But beyond that, his company was the crew sitting around that table on the 27th floor of the RDM Tower, with its window overlooking the north side of the city. (Plus about 50 other "support staff" on the 25th and 26th floors.)

Spence had continued to run things at *RDM*, at least until Gordy introduced Kayla that morning. Spence was wondering if he was on his way out the door, and was sure, as he munched on a double chocolate croissant, that his new boss, Kayla, wasn't yet 30. Gen X (him) working for Gen Y. Why did this happen, he wondered? Kids born in the late '80s and early '90s seemed to have a clear agenda that included no nostalgia, or even much self-awareness, but only their own "bottom line." Gen Y, being that there were so many of them, like the baby boomers themselves, they had a feeling that history just didn't exist for them – or if it did, it was irrelevant for the Millennials because they would change history to fit their own needs.

Gordy made it clear that she was to run things, to allow Spence "space" to be "more creative" and to come up with the clever things that made the company what it was. It rang hollow to Spence, because even though Gordy gave Spence a bigger office down the hall from his, and kept him on all the memo distribution lists that Kayla was on, and insisting to everyone that he was the edgy, provocative, grungy, off-the-wall rainmaker he always had been, Spence was still mightily pissed at the new reporting arrangement.

Privately, Gordy told Spence to stop scaring the horses – meaning the money.

(COUGH, COUGH) Kayla continued her presentation.

"No. I am pretty – pretty sure Oglethorpe never modeled underwear, although…" she smiled, to let Spence know she was in on the joke, "I do think it would be an incredible GAP trailer."

"GG! Sure," Spence said, "She's the *SwiftPad* chick."

Kayla's Zoloft half-smile started to re-appear. "Yes. The *SwiftPad* chick. Anything is possible though. I mean, once upon a time – I did some modeling…" she said, pausing to allow them to imagine her in gold flaked bra and panties, "…but Spence – didn't you write the pilot for that TV show – what was it, Sparky something…?"

"*Sierra Sparks*," said Alison. Kayla turned toward Alison, who had said nothing up to this point.

"No, I didn't write *Sierra Sparks*."

Actually Spence was very involved in the development of *Sierra Sparks*. He wrote half a dozen drafts on the pilot script, in fact came up with the title *Sierra Sparks* – along with the name of the show's unreliable narrator, who was always just out of the frame. But when it got to production editing, it was clear Spence's vision of the project was never going to fly.

Sierra Sparks had a run a couple of years ago on A&E and then had a one-year deal with Showtime. It was now languishing on Netflix. The scumbags at *Beezyoo* put it together with some older, semi-indie actors and their Santa Monica millionaire friends. It was kind of a *Misfits in Mayberry*, a "quirky" modern Western with pick-ups driven by the bored wives of ranchers. Some of those ranchers were occasionally off on Brokeback Mountain holidays, or holed up in trailers with child prostitutes, or were

PTSD-affected war vets on the verge of suicide. The Indians on the nearby Rez were always outsmarting the rednecks, and a lone sheriff was always fighting for truth and justice. It had a loyal following, but the demographic was fiftyish and rural and they didn't buy the right stuff, so sponsors lost interest after a short burst of initial enthusiasm.

"Sure – great show. But no, I didn't really – write any scripts. I just consulted and in the end they didn't listen to me. However – I did bring Nate Schuette in and he wrote some incredible episodes."

"Wait a minute!" Kayla exclaimed like a lawyer who had just caught a hostile witness in a lie. "Schuette? The China guy? No one has seen or heard from Nate Schuette in years. Remember that *Vanity Fair* article – 'Looking for Nate in All the Wrong Places' – when was that – 8-9 years ago? Ended with the *VF* writer thinking he might actually be dead?"

"I was interviewed by that guy," said Spence. "I told him that Nate was very much alive, but I wouldn't help him find him."

"Wow! I was still in school then!"

Spence double-clutched, and shot a glance at Kayla. "I have not seen Nate since 2003. We did correspond through a website when we traded scripts and emails. It was just business. He did it for money. I payed him upfront. Getting the money from the producers was a hassle."

"I thought I read somewhere that you were his friend?"

Spence now gave Kayla a glare that could have burned through a concrete wall. Kayla seemed to lose a little color in her cheeks.

"Anyway," Spence, after taking a deep breath, continued. "Nate's scripts gave *Sierra Sparks* a boost – for about four episodes anyway. I mean – you know – it could've been...a great series." Could have been, if the Colorado River hadn't drained away. The American West was tits up, and no one wanted to be reminded of it by a "quirky Western."

"They made it too homespun...backlit with yellow, brown

dirt. Doesn't pop. The John Ford style doesn't really work in color, and certainly not on video," said Spence.

Kayla continued to look at him, waiting, as if she were giving him a chance to apologize for – for what? Spence was getting pissed off and he looked out the window.

"What you have to understand, Kayla," said Alison, "is that Spence is so old school that his ideas now seem new, and that is why it is so strange that his stuff always seems to work." The room was silent as she paused. Spence looked over at Alison with an enigmatic ponder.

Charles and Joyce, both old friends of Gordy, burst out laughing, then stifled themselves with their hands over their mouths.

In her late twenties, Alison was pretty, in a hard way, with spiky brown hair, faint eyeshadow, and understated, barely dangling earrings. She scared everybody, including Gordy.

Kayla lifted her upper lip and curled the corners of her mouth at Alison's explanation of Spence's situation. "Very interesting, Alice."

Spence smiled at Alison. She said nothing, so he said, "Alison..." and nodded at her. "Not Alice."

"Alison, yes, I knew that – just give me a day or so, I wrote it down here – see 'Learn their names.'" She held up a piece of paper and looked at Spence. "Thanks, Spencer."

"Spence is fine."

"Well..." again with a dreamy, squinty-eyed smile, that seemed like she was recalling the very first time she had actually enjoyed sex, "Cynthia Oglethorpe – GG as she is known by her techy friends – has just moved back to Portland and is pregnant with one of her *SwiftPad* colleagues – Jim Hunt. Her experience – what two, three years ago – when she was nearly killed by the madman serial killer – I forget his name – and was saved by then her boyfriend – Kipling Rehain was it? That is a story that is begging to be filmed. It is so..."

"Quirky?"

She looked at Charles, nodded and smiled.

Spence stifled a scream.

"And Gordy wants us to find – or as a last resort to write – the script and put a deal together. Then..." she looked around as if deciding who would get the booby prize, "we go find the money to make the – uh...."

"SwiftPad-C2B script," Gordy's disembodied voice reverberated Deus Ex Phonika. "Let's keep that – story – idea – under our hats – right? Everyone needs to understand – we aren't quite ready to – but we should know soon. There is something going on tonight that I need...uh," Spence was not surprised Gordy had been listening, but Kayla appeared a bit shocked. Spence looked at Alison. "Uh...if Spence is still there, could you have him come into my office?" Here we go, thought Spence. "You too, Kayla. Thanks, everyone, we will get back to this later today or tomorrow."

Kayla and Spence got in the elevator together and gave each other insincere smiles but otherwise rode in silence. They got off at the top floor and went into Gordy's office, but he wasn't there. Kayla looked confused, and then concerned. She gave Spence a conspiratorial look, which he sardonically returned. Gordy's face appeared on the 42" flat screen mounted just next to his desk.

He was in his car, and from what could be seen of Burnside street west of I-405 whizzing by, he was heading up the hill toward his condo next to Washington Park.

"Thanks for coming up to see me on such short notice. Sorry, I had to – uh – this uh, this – script we need to – uh – it has some...it is going to be...uh – it's – uh – Spence – well – we have a script request from Telly Haines – you remember Telly? Uh, he is being cagey, he is coming into town tonight, and he wants a meeting pronto. Like tomorrow afternoon. A Saturday! So fucking rude, but...we have that thing, Kayla, so we can worry about that later. After the thing."

"Right. Are you picking me up?"

"Uh – oh, pick you up? Right. Telly wants to talk about the Nate Schuette script. You've heard of him, Kayla? Schuette?"

She looked at Spence quickly, and looked back at the screen, nodded, and said, "Yes."

Gordy looked quizzical at her head movements. He took a deep breath, in an effort to pull himself together.

"Telly wants Nate Schuette who is…uh…who wrote it, I think. Honestly, I don't even know if there is a script! But if there is, we want it. I heard that Schuette wrote something about a Howard Hughes super weapon – involving telepathy or something like that. Maybe documentary style, I don't know. So maybe that can be a bone to throw Telly. Remember, we have to keep Telly at arms' length and when we land this real *SwiftPad* story, he must have no involvement – we cut him out. Financially and otherwise."

Spence looked at Kayla, wondering what the Eastbay wunderkind would say. She was staring at her fone.

"Schuette. Yes. He's – he did some stuff in the '90s, didn't he? Wait! Here," she said, fingering her fone. "Nate Schuette – China memoir – everyone knows about that – here – 'The Last One In Is a Rotten Egg,' a fictionalized story about Natalie Wood's death…"

"No, no. He actually wrote it in the '70s before he went to China," said Spence.

You mean before she…she drowned," said Kayla.

"Right," said Spence.

"How…?" Kayla began to ask, looking at Spence, to which he smirked, and which she pretended not to see.

"Schuette himself showed me his original notes on it." Spence kept his face neutral and unexpressive. "It was really about something that happened to someone else."

"Well, I am sure you two will – uh –"

"What about Telly? Who handles him?" Kayla looked a bit shell-shocked.

"None of it matters unless we get Schuette to write the real

SwiftPad story for us. You know – GG biting off whatshisname's dick – Spence –"

"Yeah," Spence said. "But what I don't understand is how Nate Schuette is going to know what to write. Even if he writes it, it would still need to be converted to SP-Script, if we are going to try and run it through the Neural Interface."

"Right," said Gordy, as if that were just a minor detail.

Fuck, thought Spence, I am the SP-Scripting guy. "I heard that they ran a little test and 19 out of 21 people who were wired up to receive a short SwiftPad-C2B program about snorkeling in Bermuda said they could actually smell the ocean, and they all described snorkeling with a school of yellow reef fish in stunning detail."

"See. I knew it," said Gordy. "It will be sensational!'"

"But three of participants, two middle aged women, and a man in his mid-twenties, came down with severe headaches afterward, and one of women is still hospitalized," said Spence. He really didn't want to do this.

"Oh…" Gordy stopped himself.

"How does the SP-script work?" asked Kayla.

"It is the same principle as the app's conversion from text to video – it has an AI lookup function – like an imbedded Google query – and then in real time it converts that to a "signal" that mimics the brainwave of the same image. So you either need to recreate that image in somebody's brain, and transpose it digitally, or have a library function that had been recreated previously. They still don't understand how the brain handles it. It comes out slightly different in everyone. There are only about 500 SP-functions available so far, so you almost have to craft new shit from ground zero. And then it has to be run through the C2B interface, which as we know causes problems with some people."

"But no one experiences exactly the same thing?"

"No. It is close, but different. Anyway, the library of brainwaves is growing," said Spence. "They are working on a simpler procedure to make new ones. That is the slowest part of the process. You can't predict what images or other reactions might occur."

"Spence, you will have to make the magic happen," said Gordy. "And somehow put Nate's name on it – Johnny loves Nate's scripts...It will be much more sellable with his name on it."

"Johnny?" Kayla mouthed silently. Depp? Malkovich?

Gordy held up his finger and widened his eyes, as though he were having a brain fart. "...and...uh – Kayla I need you to make him go away. You take care of Telly, OK? You have to use your magic right? But as far as Nate and the script stuff is concerned, Spence, you have control here. You, uh, have a relation – uh, you know him. So, uh... just – uh – run everything by Kayla, OK?"

"I haven't seen or talked to..."

"Look, bring in a script."

"A *SwiftPad* script..."

"YES! Of course. So we can plug it into the *SwiftPad* Neural Interface and then into the C2B! We need to be the first. This is like being DW Griffith. Birth of a Fucking Nation. This is the future."

"Amazon is humping the cheap C2B units!" Kayla was almost hyperventilating. "Six hundred dollars and you can pick up the simple telepathic broadcasts."

"But those things are as likely to burn out all your bulbs – still a science project. Nobody over at SP Central is commenting. Amazon is denying they have 'enriched the signal.'"

Kayla was gripping the desk. "I agree with Gordon. Even if it fails it will be – really big!"

"Exactly. Hold on. I got to pull into the garage." The screen went blank.

Kayla hit the mute button. She took a deep breath and tried to do her Zoloft smile, but she looked like she was getting her teeth cleaned. "Who's Johnny?" she asked.

"Johnny is this guy none of us have ever met. Gordy seems to run everything by him, he says. Myself, I don't think there is a Johnny. Who knows? Not sure it matters."

"Great," said Kayla. Gordy's head popped up on the screen again. She unmuted him.

"...build on it – two heads better, uh – you know." Gordy was not in his car, but sitting in what looked to be a fern garden. "Kayla, you need to touch base with me later, OK? If Spence works out the details with the tech people, fine, just – uh, the checkbook is open. The problem is uh – Telly is uh – kind of a loon, kinda right wing – he did that documentary with What-shisname – the guy – you know – anyway – it was pretty scary," Gordy started laughing and then started coughing. "He will want to use this – technique – to help his guy in the election, if you know what I mean."

Since the former President got "Sectioned Four-ed" (popular shorthand for the fourth section of the 25th Amendment), Telly Haines had suddenly become known as the media guru for the Acting P (Temp-Prez). That of course, was before the Temp-Prez got beat decisively in the Primaries last spring. No one knew which way Haines would jump now that Temp-Prez seemed out of the running.

"Anyway, even if C2B gives 10-20% of people who use it a headache, nobody is going to give a shit. The real money is going to be what we can do with it once this political shit is over with. Think of the possibilities! We could do some politics with it – sex it up, you know. What I want to know – me and everybody else – Will this *SwiftPad* Interface make you actually cum? I mean, can't we just somehow associate our candidates with busting a nut?"

Spence shrugged, which somehow Gordy understood.

"You two work it out. Bring in Schuette's script."

"Will do," said Kayla. "See you tonight Gorden."

Spence laughed. Maybe it would bring them all down together. Yeah, that might be fun.

CHAPTER 2
THE ISHPEMING STATEMENT

4:00 pm, Monday, January 13, 2020

"We now see that they require two different kinds of fungi and an algal species. If the right combination meet together on a rock or twig, then a lichen will form, and this will result in the large and complex plant-like organisms that we see on trees and rocks very commonly. The mechanism by which this symbiotic association occurs is completely unknown and remains a real mystery."

Nick Talbot, University of Exeter,
quoted in *Atlantic Monthly*

*How a Guy From a Montana Trailer
Park Overturned 150 Years of Biology,*
by Ed Yong, July 21, 2016

THE LANDSCAPE WAS A BOULDER-STREWN, BARE ASH and oak woods. Unseasonably warm for January. Peering out the tinted, bullet-proof windows from the backseat of a black GMC SUV, Nathan Schuette watched the automatic gate open. Two body guards, one in the front seat, the other to his left, both had sunglasses up on their head, and short barreled automatic rifles on their laps. Chauffeured through the trees for about a quarter mile, then wheeling to the right, in a kind of flanking maneuver, Nathan watched as they approached the house obliquely, crunching the driveway's rock gravel. They rolled up to the sprawling, single-storied, granite-hued hideaway. The house was larger than it first appeared. Schuette noticed that the rear of the fortress-like, lakeside "cottage" followed the contour of the sloping bank, stepping down two full stories, following the grade down almost to the edge of Lake Superior. The gray siding was spotlessly clean. One of the blinds on the half-shuttered windows flipped up, then back down. As the car rolled to a stop, Nathan heard the doors simultaneously unlock.

An unadorned, heavy oak door opened. A thick-set man who looked to be in his late 60s, wearing baggy jeans and a plain gray hooded sweatshirt, came out. He had a wan smile on an otherwise slightly pockmarked but impassive face.

Nathan Schuette had been famous 20-some years ago, when he wrote and published a book that came and went like a flash of lightning. Set in China, as it emerged from the Cultural Revolution, the memoir/novel was a cross-genre sensation, both supported and denounced by vociferous literary factions, of all stripes. Unfortunately, its title, *The Long Goodbye*, 龙再见, was a confusing and obscure play on the word "long," 龙, which is Chinese for Dragon. It flew over the heads of many Western readers, including some influential reviewers. Still, the book received great popular acclaim in North America and Western Europe, by the public and critics alike.

But soon after its high-profile launch, doubts about its "authenticity" began to circulate. Then, with pathetic self-destructiveness, Schuette poured gasoline on the smoldering controversy. While appearing flustered and visibly intoxicated on a mid-morning cable news show, Schuette insisted he had seen the stone tablet with Old Testament text written in Chinese, and that the tablet was unquestionably from Pre-Qin China. He also repeated an account (one of several that he said he had heard) of a Chinese nuclear strike, carried out in 1971. The implication being that it evaporated an elite unit of Soviet troops, as well as the Chinese soldiers they were then battling.

Schuette was quickly denounced as a fraud or a dupe by experts, commentators, and the Xinhua News Agency. The Chinese announced he was banned from China and soon after that, his publishing contracts were cancelled and his book was removed from circulation. Schuette became a punchline and a laughable disgrace.

For a while, Schuette continued to write. (And drink.) He went through a harsh break-up with his East German girlfriend, who then gave him the public heave-ho in a *Der Spiegel* interview, which led to an unfortunate mostly on-camera back and forth that embarrassed even the most tasteless of the entertainment news outlets.

He then made it worse by ranting on a conspiracy-mongering podcast that his career paralleled that of the blacklisted writer Dalton Trumbo, a claim viciously mocked by those few left who paid any attention to him. It was true that he had been paid in the low six figures for a film script about Natalie Wood's drowning (never produced), and he had pseudonymously drafted TV scripts for several episodes of a quirky, pick-up truck cowboy comic-drama (cancelled). But beyond that, he had vanished from public view after his brief moment of fame.

The guards got out and stood watchfully, one in front, the other in back of the SUV, while chauffeur grabbed Nathan's bag, and led him up to the door with a well-practiced professional smile. In the doorway his former college roommate, heavy-set, unshaven Leone welcomed Nate with a wry but serious look, and nodded to the driver as he took the bag. He made a slight grunt, closed the door after Nathan without a word, and ushered him into his house.

Gary "Leone" Humpkin, retired editor and publisher of the nation's most respected middle-brow opinion magazine, had had a storied journalistic career, and was simply (as Tom Brokaw once called him) "the gold standard of credibility." Bob Schieffer said that Gary (as he was known to the world) was America's closest living approximation to Walter Cronkite.

Until recently Leone had been an occasional guest on business cable shows, where he had often called for a "toning down" of the nation's ongoing cultural and political wars. His middle of the road approach to politics was a quaint trope from an era before the Internet. But lately he had stayed away from view, only making occasional technical observations on his *SwiftPad* feed about the failing economy.

The former maverick editor didn't look particularly healthy now, but then he never had. His skin was "rough" – a little pock-marked but mostly blotchy – areas around his chin and ears were a little redder than his cheeks. His once thick black hair was graying on the sides – a little too uniformly though, leaving lack-adaisical evidence of it having been retouched.

Walking down the hall, Nate glanced at the wall, largely covered with magazine covers and newspaper headlines of the past 40 years. They passed a full-length mirror in which Nathan caught a glance of himself. He involuntarily winced. He never traveled well, but he looked particularly terrible today. He was slightly stooped, paunchy, and walked with a noticeable limp from an Achilles injury that he hoped was not permanent. His once limpid blue eyes were rheumy, and his reddish hair was now thinning and brittle.

But his aging had not been a slow, steady decline. Nate had stayed a young man for thirty-some years after college, and then, suddenly had grown old with inhuman rapidity. Back around the turn of the century, with no fanfare, he stopped eating the Golden Fungus. In a mere month, he had transformed from looking and feeling as if he were still in his late-20s to bent over, flaccidly muscled, constantly tired old man, even though at the time he was still only in his mid-50s. No shriving time allowed, as Hamlet had once decreed.

He had stayed in bed during that whole time, getting up to drink water, eat soup, and pee. That month-long illness – from Nate's perspective it was identical to a long illness – occurred just before his (actual) 53th birthday. When he finally recovered, he was almost an old man, but oddly felt relieved to have finally joined his own generation. The change in his metabolism and the speeded-up aging had been the worst month of his life, and now nearly 20 years later, he still felt the effects, although he suspected that much of his agony was just the way all old people felt. His medical physicals had been normal, for his age. All and all he didn't regret the experience.

The Golden Fungus was a mythical "plant" (actually an eukaryote, which is neither plant nor animal) that was unknown and unrecognized by any of the established mycological conventions. It had no Latin name. Still the stories persisted, and those who could claim membership in "The Circle of the Golden Fungus" were honored, respected, and welcomed, particularly in the coastal rainbelt from Northern California through Oregon and into Washington, and up into British Columbia. People who lived in that climate knew the power of mushrooms, which also are eukaryotes. Among those very few initiates who could claim to have known someone who had eaten a golden fungus, or even to have seen it in a mason jar up on a hard-to-reach shelf in a rustic kitchen, they spoke in hushed voices of the great transformations that the fungus evoked, ranging from the power to perceive the thoughts and emotions that are swirling around all of us constantly, to bestowing on the imbiber a long, long summer of youth. No one ever called it "eternal"; it was understood to be an "organic process," one that ends eventually. Anyway, it was just a myth.

It was the myth of "The Circle of the Golden Fungus," a mystic fellowship of wizards who could control and move vast throngs of people, silently, and mysteriously, people who were "off-the-grid," and not connected to any of the software you could download, or to the mind-reading gizmos that you could buy on Amazon. The real humans, an "endangered species", as they saw themselves, believed in the fungus, although very few had ever encountered it.

Some cynics joked that the "circle" invoked the image of a ringworm rash. Nevertheless, Nathan was known, and welcomed, in many quarters, and if anything, he had actually ascended to a higher status, a leader of sorts, or would have, if the Circle had leaders. His literary successes and failures such as they were meant nothing, one way or the other, to the Circle. He was one of a very, very few who had actually been transformed by the fungus.

In actual fact, the "Circle" myth was just that, a myth. Nate had been there from the beginning. He was there when Paula and Elwood found the white tree fungus with the orange interior. (No one seemed to know why or when it became "golden".) Nate was pretty sure he knew everyone else who had eaten it. It was not a very long list.

Stories get started though, and that was why he was in Ishpeming, at this auspicious convocation. That and the fact that he had been Leone's roommate in college.

As they walked down the hall into Leone's Upper Peninsula home, Nate noticed Leone walked slowly and carefully too. Leone, who was a little younger than Nate, looked even worse than he did. Leone watched his own feet as he carefully stepped down into the huge, sunken living room. A roaring fire threw heat all the way across to the opposite back wall. He will be needing a cane soon, Nate thought, with a tiny bit of mean self-satisfaction. He wasn't jealous of Leone's success, just pissed at himself for blowing up his own career.

Nate looked around the room – a big flat-screen TV, and then stepping down again, a stainless steel kitchen. Two beige couches set on a huge beautiful green Persian rug covered the center of the room. Between the kitchen and the fireplace, a sliding glass door opened out to steps down to another section of the house, between which was an open but covered patio surrounded with heated torches.

Except for the Persian rug that covered about a fourth of the living room, the floor was bare, polished hardwood, and it reflected the soft light of the fire and the custom hand-painted Chinese lamps that were set in the corners. On the back wall was a vintage Hammond B3 organ.

"Help yourself to anything down in the kitchen. I am having dinner brought in. There are some cottages up the lake a few hundred yards that most people will be staying in. Your room is down the hall on the left," Leone said, pointing to the right. "You will have to double up with somebody once everyone gets here, but you can nap until then. Sorry – some business waits in my office down there..." he pointed to a corridor on the left, "...we can talk more once you are settled."

Nathan nodded and warmed himself in front of the fire. He looked up again at the big TV. A small camera was perched up on the corner of the ceiling, looking down on the room like a barn owl.

Even in college, he had always thought that Leone had some kind of dissociative disorder, what they now called "being on the spectrum." How was he able to seem so trustworthy on TV? Was it just acting or did TV project a bizarro image of what reality seemed to show? Or was reality itself in flux? Was he acting now? Leone's nationwide reputation would undoubtedly suffer if his association with himself were known. Why the hell had he come, he thought. He didn't fit the agenda, and even if he did, why would anyone listen to him?

Having slept through most of the long car trip, Nate didn't need a nap, and so he sat down on the living room couch. He took a deep breath and cleared his mind. No regrets – well, maybe some.

He looked up and saw a man who looked like a Bollywood soap opera star. He had walked in from the corridor to his left, wearing a brown sweater and khaki slacks. He was dark, thin, and had sparkling brown eyes. It was Gopesh Gupta. Gupta had been the one tech exec who had not spoken out against either the Real and the Temp Prezs. Everyone had assumed he was with them, but his presence here certainly belied that!

Gupta's product was the most mind-bending in history; but he didn't own a sports franchise or a fleet of private spaceships; and was the only major tech player not to be under the Temp-Prez's TDD arrest altogether. And yet, here he was, risking it all in this most audacious act of defiance yet.

"Mr. Gupta," Nate said.

"Please – I am just Gopee." He moved his head slightly side to side, a head wobbling *achha* that Nate found comforting for some reason. Millions of units of Gopee's C2B boxes had shipped recently. It was popularly pronounced quickly and with minimal enunciation, "seed-a-bee." The multicolored boxes and matching headsets were in offices and homes around the world. C2B was computer-to-brain interface technology. It had been on the market for the last six months and there were various models ranging in price and sophistication from $800 to $25K. See-to-Be Inc. public stock offering split at $50 a share three times in the first week it was offered. It was rumored he had developed his product with the help of over 100 transcendental yogis.

The issue however, for westerners anyway, was that not much C2B content was available for purchase or download. It was expensive and time-consuming to produce brain-dumps. There were regulations, currently under Food and Drug, that no one understood, and that had no enforcement provisions. A number of lawsuits had been filed, just from the first trials. Congress and the President also had expressed concerns for other reasons. But demand continued to outpace production, in spite of the downsides.

On paper, Gopesh was the second richest man in the world.

"Nathan Schuette," Gopesh said, reaching to shake his hand. "It is truly an honor to meet you. You are a great pioneer!"

"Oh, ha ha, well, coming from the man who flipped the Turing test, the honor is mine."

"How do you possibly mean?"

"Well – the Turing question was designed to test whether a thinking machine was distinguishable from a human. C2B brain dumps seem to be indistinguishable from human thought. So actually you flipped the Turing question by asking if human thought was actually machine-driven."

"Yes – yes – very good. But your discoveries were much much more significant. You have united the histories of the East and the West."

"Well, India still stands alone."

"Oh, gosh no – Alexander the Great came to India almost right after the Bible came to China. We have always known about the universal connections throughout history! You have proved to the West that they have the same history as the East. Unfortunately those capable of understanding this are not the ones who need to learn it!"

"Perhaps. You are very kind."

Gopee nodded, his eyes bright and probing. He smiled warmly with a look of inner contentment that Nathan had learned to recognize from close observation. The eyes really are the windows to the soul, he thought, and Gopesh's soul appeared to be content and at peace.

"Mirror mirror on the wall..." Nate turned, and there she was, Paula Flayer.

His memory still blazed with erotic gymnastic scenes from when she was a graduate student and he was a college freshman. Later, he had pulled her out of a crack that had opened up underneath her as the earth itself had tried to swallow her up and bury her forever. The memory of her climbing out of that hole was also seared forever into his consciousness, even more indelibly than any of the many nights and afternoons they had spent together in bed. Nate had always supposed that her dark-haired Latin lover had not made it out of Managua, but recent events had sadly proven that that was nothing more than wishful thinking. The fireplace flickered out its warm and wavering light. Paula and Nate continued wistfully and warily to gaze at each other.

"I'm glad to see you," Nate said, his voice quivering. Her bright eyes blazed with too many emotions to count.

Nate suggested with a slight gesture that they sit down. He looked at Paula for a long moment and she just blushed. She was the same! Still the same, a 30-something dream from his past, an image right out of an early Meg Ryan rom-com. So beautiful, but now so full of experience and wisdom. It was overwhelming. "What's it like?"

"It's the same – I mean – Nate! Come on! You know!"

"But what do you think?"

"How can I say? Compared to what? How would I know? This is the way I am. If I miss a day – I am sick. It is a lost day. I am trying to get used to it, but it is so hard! I need to talk to you. I am trying to get ready."

"For what?"

"I am almost out. Elwood says there is no more, anywhere. And I believe I will be OK, because of you and what you went through. But there is none left. You know Elwood would know, if anyone does. I have about four or five months left. I am going to try and stretch it, but as you probably know, that doesn't work."

"Yeah. If I ate less than a gram a day, it left me with migraines and stomach pain. Just like heroin. So what happens then – when it's gone?"

"I don't know. You quit so much sooner than I will. Stopping in my Mid-70s will probably be different than early 50s. I know I will get sick. If I stay sick – well – I doubt I will be able to take it. So it goes. Was it hard for you?"

"Yes. But in some ways it was a relief. The fungus hurt me. I was always queasy. Sometimes it gave me convulsions."

"Why didn't you stop sooner then? I mean before you ran out?"

Nate laughed. And so did Paula. As the old Indian Don Juan might have said, the fungus didn't like him, but he liked it. "He must still have some, doesn't he? Pretty boy. You know who he looks like?"

"Ronaldo – the soccer player."

"Yeah – almost to a tee. He hasn't changed either."

Paula shrugged and nodded. She looked up at the camera next to the TV.

Yeah, he thought. There was no point bringing it up, even here. It was all gone anyway. The best biochemists money could buy had tried to duplicate it, but failed. Well, that didn't include those guys at the Howard Hughes Institute in Houston. They had obviously come up with something, although there were clearly still manic side effects.

"Ronaldo" – or "Ka-Dez" as his rabid followers chanted – and Paula. Unless the fungus grew again, they were the last ones. Paula was 74 and looked about 30, if that. It would have been better for her, he thought, if she hadn't been so beautiful.

"Leone says you – teach high school..."

"I did, for over 20 years. Actually junior high school," she said. "I needed to do penance. Lately I am kind of an investigator – private detective – I find people. It pays the rent, and keeps me sharp."

Nathan laughed. "Really?"

"How do you think Leone found you?"

"Hmmm...OK. How do you feel now?"

"Good. I am healthy."

"How's your love life?"

"Are you kidding? How would that work?"

"Well – it doesn't have to be forever."

"Yeah." Paula said, laughing. "Anyway, you can't believe how stupid young men are. We – I mean our species – have degenerated in the last 50 years." She paused, and Nate let the uncomfortable pause linger. "I have been staying low. Get a new identity every 10 years or so. I don't think anyone ever noticed. My parents both died before it became an issue with them. So it doesn't matter. They aren't looking for me anymore."

"Until lately, that was probably true." Nathan and Paula stared at each other, neither daring to talk about what they were really feeling. Nathan had been young once, he remembered.

Leone re-entered the room with a statuesque, black woman with piercing eyes.

"Nathan, Gopesh, Paula – this is my wife, Adele." Of course. Adele, an ebony-skinned beauty who could have been any age, and as far as Nate knew, had never eaten the fungus. She played the Hammond organ in the Jean Katon Express, the hottest Reggae-Haitian group in the world. Adele had been a well-known studio musician for a quarter of a century, but recently had become world famous. She wore a long colorful African gown and an orange diaphanous scarf that wrapped as a turban around her head. Leone was in love with her, you could see that with your eyes closed. She nodded and smiled at Nate, while avoiding Paula, and sat at the edge of the sofa on the far end. Leone left them to make drinks, and Adele continued to side-eye Paula with suspicion.

"So you really know that evil shit Ben Cadez?" Adele finally asked. Adele kept looking back and forth at Nate and Paula.

"It was a long time ago. We were young."

"Young? You?" she exclaimed looking at Paula. "When was that?"

Leone brought in vodka gimlets and looked at his fone. "OK, they are here. I am going to go out and greet. Let's not get off track on little shit." He gave a warning look to Adele.

The bus was grimy and the Trailways logo showed faintly under the dirt. It was dented too, but clean and well appointed on the inside. It had brought 46 people to Leone's and they would sleep dorm style, in the main house and the cottages, for the next three days, planning, arguing, and coming to hard decisions.

The mayor of Memphis, and former Special Forces Colonel, Hassan Coleman, was the magnetic focus of the group. "Greater

Memphis" had expanded its political reach up and down the river, up north almost to Cairo, and south down to just above Vicksburg. The strategy hadn't changed much since the 1860's – hang onto the river towns, and split the South from the West. This time however, it was not the result of deep planning though. There had been a population shift over a very short time that had startling consequences. The RedHat's called it "The Great White Flight", while the Southern Christian Leadership Council called it the "March to the Promised Land".

Whole white neighborhoods turned into ghost towns with astounding rapidity. At the same time, black families listening to some call on the wind that escaped everyone else had relocated to Memphis and nearby environs, by the thousands. African Americans and many young whites moved to the north and south of Memphis, taking over dying towns, and abandoned corporate farms, which were run like Kibbutzim by the newcomers.

As has been said, it all occurred under the national radar with little to no overt organizing. It just seemed to happen. Most believed that a series of events closely related to the election of the Real-Prez had led to the "population swaps". Stricter abortion laws, massive defunding of public education (and the rise of all white "Charter schools"), and a series of "Stand Your Ground" killings against blacks who were deemed too loud, too assertive and in some cases, just too black all seemed to hit the south's black communities as too much to take anymore.

Most of the land swaps had been conducted through normal real estate transactions and land values while declining, remained somewhat stable, at least until the very end, when Memphis' controversial Homestead law made homeowners of thousands of squatters and renters.

Coleman declared Memphis and its surroundings a "Super Sanctuary," signaling a form of secession from the rest of the country. Colonel Coleman's appeal cut across all races and classes.

Coleman was funny, and smart, and did not pander to African

Americans, but he didn't hold back either, or wait or equivocate about overthrowing the vestiges of white patriarchy. Young white couples were nearly 40% of the new arrivals and most enthusiastically supported Coleman. He appointed a number of smart women to be in day-to-day charge of his administration and left no doubt that a tight band of bad dudes, (as Real-Prez had often called African Americans) ran things. Blues Town was an inspiration, and their music was everywhere.

Many of the whites who left headed to Arizona and Nevada, where cruelly they would soon find themselves out of house and home again, this time as refugees from a manmade "natural" disaster.

RedHats were now fighting among themselves to decide who would succeed Temp-Prez. No one thought their disunity more than temporary. The primaries were coming, and everyone agreed the newly installed Temp-Prez had no chance.

The former senior under-secretaries, and the NatSec and defense officials who came to Ishpeming surprisingly made no attempt to dominate the discussions. Three young, but virtually unknown union officials, two social workers, four or five public school teachers from deep RedHat country, a couple of economists, LGBTs who avoided talking to each other, leaders of food collectives, fiction writers, four Midwestern business types, some Latinos, a leader from a Rez, and an unknown but dynamic street corner rabble rouser also came. The Tech Business sector was for the most part under house arrest, but they made their support known.

Caroline and Rosie, the two leading contenders for the Presidential nomination were there too, and like the NatSec people, were mostly quiet, listening. They all suppressed their own leftist tendencies, understanding that eventually the country needed to find its way out of the mess. Rosie asked with a manner that was not retorically, How can we save democracy?

A former President and a Vice President both sent greetings, and vague words of support. It was diverse, and not unexpectedly, considering the nature of the national emergency, united in purpose.

Nate and Paula were both peripheral to the main event, or at least they felt that way. Leone introduced them as representing "The Golden Circle", a West Coast collective of great influence and importance, with access to tremendous talent and a lot of money.

In other words, *SwiftPad*. That was the real hippo in the gazebo. Paula was close to Alice Hunt, Jim's mother. Everyone of influence up and down the West Coast knew Alice, and that she could open doors that were behind the doors.

Yes, *SwiftPad* was very much the mastodon on the autobahn, the "outer Matryoshka doll" of the tech world. The rest would all pack inside *SwiftPad*, if the Portland software consortium decided to take the lead. SwiftPad had extended its influence far and wide, recruiting the cream of the tech world. Paula played it cool, but still claimed with authority and confidence that the Portland megatech company, and its technology and influence could be brought around.

She could not alleviate all of the nervousness. Everyone knew that the *SwiftPad* braintrust was AWOL, but at least they were not under arrest or in jail, like most of the other high-profile tech execs. Cynthia Oglethorpe, Kip Rehain, and Jim Hunt were all MIA, off on unsecured, untethered, vagabond journeys through the wild parts of Asia and who knew where else. It was well known that the social media app's source code remained under *SwiftPad* control, and would soon be integrated with several new technologies – in particular Gopesh's C2B, which in theory would allow SP content to be transferred directly into the consciousness. *SwiftPad* was the "Content Motherlode." It was a big deal, and there was no way to account for the uncertainty it brought to the political calculations.

Nate and Paula's past encounters with Ben Cadez were not discussed outside of a small group that included Leone and a few other people. It was a topic just too hot to handle at this point, and the fact that they even knew Cadez's secret, (and his access to the tainted fungus) needed to be kept top secret for now. Leone explained, in his avuncular style, that making an issue of it would trigger the religious wackos and that might in turn lead to some jihadi action that everyone agreed needed to be avoided. Religious wars made civil wars seem like tea parties.

They listened to presentations from security officials. The RedHats were well armed and mobile. Mounted .50 caliber machine guns on Ford F-150s were their go-to weapon, and their rallies featured thousands of them on parade through places like Birmingham, Tulsa, Wichita, etc. They brought their own guns, AR-15s or some other version of an assault rifle. Rallies with hundreds of trucks speeding across the fields in mock war games, sometimes precipitating bloody friendly fire clusterfucks that were illustrated in popular YouTube videos, much to the mocking delight of Blue country.

The Air Force was grounded, domestically. The Army too was staying out of politics, as required by law, a fact that the Pentagon held onto like a rope off of a life raft. So in any confrontation, strikes from high altitude would be unlikely, and there would probably be no tanks on the street.

Without a doubt, the armed tension in the country was triggered by the deployment of the bunker buster low yield nuke that emptied Lake Meade. The north plug in the Hoover Dam overflow channel, carved into the rock mountain that supported the sides of the concrete mammoth dam, had been blown out by a 2 or 3 megaton device, and Lake Meade had quickly drained, the deluge flowing around the dam itself. Officially it was still under investigation, but most believed it to be the reason for the 25th Amendment coup that had put the Real-Prez in the sanitarium in Short Hills, New Jersey. The Temp-Prez blamed the drug cartels for the attack. A group called *Equipo de Reconquista* had claimed responsibility, but nobody was really sure if the group actually existed. Apparently, whoever they were, a small band of commandos captured the dam at night, blindfolded and drove the staff offsite, and blew the concrete plug out of the north diversionary tunnel. No one was caught; no photos, or even physical descriptions, surfaced. In all it took less than a couple of hours. When the Army team arrived all they could do was watch Lake Meade drain away. This information, that was being shared at the conference, had never been released to the public. The two defense officials attending said that three different, and independent sources both confirmed that the autoradiographic signatures and spectrometric data from the blast indicated it came from the US's own stockpile.

"Sounds like an attempt to start a Reichstag Fire," said Rosie.

"We don't know that," said Leone. "Until we have more proof, we must not discuss any of what we know about this."

"The blast reverberated through the casinos like a thunderous rebuke". The denizens of Los Vegas rushed out of town almost as fast as the waters of Lake Meade itself. Phoenix's population soon followed. With little to no snowpack in the Rockies, the desert was quickly reclaiming the remaining human habitat. Like human divining rods, the Southwesterners were headed for water, which for most was the Pacific Northwest, even with the declining snowpack in the Cascades.

The previous season's hurricanes had wiped out Florida's Gold Coast, as well the South Jersey Shore from Cape May to Long Branch.

Russian icebreakers had been refitted to do commercial iceberg towing duty, bringing mountain-sized Arctic and Antarctic icebergs of fresh water to cities such as Melbourne Sydney, Los Angeles, and the Persian Gulf metropolises. The stock market bumped every time part of the ice sheet broke off, and the list of potential customer-cities was growing.

The summer had been horrible. Tornadoes and floods had devastated the RedHat Midwest even more than usual. The Zika virus had infected thousands of pregnant women with the expected sad and horrifying results. A mysterious meningitis epidemic had killed or permanently disabled 15–20% of the incoming freshmen at Ohio State University. And three separate mass shootings on the 4th of July alone had killed 278 people. The shootings elicited no comment from any congressman or the President, or anybody else for that matter, having long been assigned to the "shit you can expect to happen" category.

In spite of the various plagues and disasters of the summer of 2019, it wasn't Mother Nature that finally put Real-Prez out to pasture. After the draining of Lake Meade, and all the downstream destruction it caused, the "Big Dump" was the financial shock that reverberated from all the major insurance companies filing for Chapter 11 protection during the same week in mid-October. That was what finally woke the Real-Prez's party.

The Dems investigated, and what they found was horrifying, but the possibility of the government's involvement in the Hoover Dam destruction was buried, covered-up, and stonewalled. The closest vote for removal from office after the three votes for impeachment was 65-35 – two short, with a South Carolina senator keeping everyone guessing until the end when he announced his opposition for removal while standing next to a golf cart.

The close Senate vote was actually the final straw, although it surprised no one. The Thanksgiving Decrees were announced during the halftime of the Detroit Lions–Chicago Bears classic by the Temp-Prez – on behalf of the Real-Prez. Then two days later, on Saturday, came the news in dribbles about the so-called 25th Amendment Resignation/Intervention. He was suddenly out. Perhaps he had a stroke, said one report. Others speculated he had contracted some other condition; it was never spelled out. The actual details of the transfer ceremony were hazy too, from garbled audio or the unfocused shot-from-outside-the-doorway bedside video of the signing over of the government to the timid and feckless VP.

But in his first speech to the nation, the Temp-Prez made it clear he would wield the necessary repression to uphold the junta. The beatings would continue until morale improved. The country quickly discovered that the sycophantic former VP was just as cruel and even more hapless than the Real-Prez had been, just not as inflammatory.

The ouster of the Real-Prez was a confused and clearly contentious event, the details of which were still not completely known. That was quickly followed by a series of harsh measures that declared (in convoluted, formal language) that the government could arrest anyone for anything. ICE was reconstituted to deal with the "Homeless Crisis." Vagrancy was declared a scourge and would be "wiped out" with "Retraining Centers." Giant, corporate-run concentration camps were being set up in National Parks across the country. The Temp-Prez announced that one hundred thousand ICE [now to be called (V)ICE (Vagrancy, Immigration Control Enforcement)] workers would be recruited over the next three months. He declared a national emergency to secure the funding when Congress would not come across with it. The recruits were young, white for the most part, from hamlets that were politically reliable to the regime. (V)ICE was providing high-paying jobs, as jobs went, and applications poured in. Training consisted of rallies, with Eastern European goose-stepping added to the standard American style of para-military strutting.

So this secret meeting at Leone's place, on the Upper Peninsula, on the outskirts of the township of Ishpeming, came to be known as the The Convocation of the Ishpeming Fifty, and they produced the Ishpeming Statement. The statement was vague and very general, but still, it left little to the imagination. The people of the US would use all means to resist the unconstitutional attempts to undermine American freedom.

No attempt was made to justify this rebellious gathering of the Ishpeming Fifty in traditional representative democratic terms. There was no claim they were forming a Shadow Government. Everyone understood that unity was paramount. All efforts were directed to ensure a united opposition to retake the Government in the election that was coming in ten months. The statement emphasized that they intended to enforce a fair election, by any means necessary.

Additionally there was a secret codicil to the Ishpeming Statement. It created an action committee dedicated to armed resistance, if there was an egregious usurpation of constitutionally recognized local authority, with the cities of Memphis, Tennessee, and Portland, Oregon, specifically mentioned. Armed militias would be raised to protect these cities from Federal intrusion. Portland and Memphis would be defended. A working committee was formed to recruit and command for that purpose.

As the meeting broke up and the participants were secretly smuggled out in small groups, sometimes one by one, back to their homes, Paula convinced Nathan to come back to San Francisco and live with her in her apartment in Haight-Ashbury. For safety's sake, she said, because they knew that everyone who signed the Ispeming Statement would need to go underground. Their adventure had started together fifty years ago and in spite of their yawning "age" difference, they would make a go of it. Nate was surprised to find they still had a "thing" for each other. Since there didn't seem to be any reason not to, and after all she was young and beautiful, he decided to take Paula up on her offer, and move to San Francisco.

CHAPTER 3

CHUBBY TAKES OFF AFTER GG

September 2019

ALICE WAS IN CHARGE OF THE COMMUNE VILLAGE AT his father's compound, deep in the Oregon Coast Range, so Kip decided to head off on a trip. He was heading in a general direction looking for GG, Jim, and Macy; at least that is what he told himself.

Kip landed in Hong Kong, and took the train into Guangzhou. From there, he traveled across China, first by bullet train up north to Xian and then west along the old Silk Road, taking buses and hitching rides with truckers and various other travelers. At some point, exactly when and where he could never specify (even to himself), he decided that he wasn't really looking for GG.

He continued his travels, thinking consciously that perhaps he just might run into them, but he knew he wouldn't. When he did real "thinking" about it, which was not often, he realized he didn't actually want to find them. He knew any reunion, no matter how extraordinary or surprising, would only lead to heartache for everybody. Nevertheless, he could not help scanning crowds, or even asking at hotel bars if anyone had seen or heard of Cynthia Oglethorpe or Jim Hunt.

Sometimes he felt invisible, like he wasn't there, even though he stuck out like a hitchhiking thumb. The Chinese economy was severely contracting, and the crowds of beggars outside the train stations reminded him of black and white photos of China from the 1930s. He was only going in a general direction, taking what rides he could get and staying in little places sometimes for a week, enjoying whatever he found. This went on for about two months. When he exited China from Kashgar through the Tianshan Mountains into Dushanbe in Tajikistan, everything changed, even though it looked the same. His Russian finally began to be useful. The remnants of the Soviet empire flapped like a broken doorway in an abandoned street. He made his way over to Uzbekistan, then down to Merv in Turkmenistan, and was about to cross into Iran. Kip's Russian (the only subject he studied seriously in his various stints in college) was improving by the day, and as he sat in an outdoor kiosk in Ashgabat in lower Turkmenistan, he overheard a goat herder with a flatbed truck packed with hircine billies and nannies, telling anyone who would listen (in the worst pig-Russian he had ever heard spoken) about a mass hanging in a village a few kilometers ahead. He saw it from the roadside, a ramshackle gallows that looked like it was about to collapse from eight or nine men still twitching at the end of thin cords. All young guys he said, gropers, dopers, and backdoor pokers – village idiots and excess labor, a warning to the others – stay in line or you will end up on the end of one. None of them died quickly either; fucking Persians didn't even know how to tie the knots.

So Kip decided to skip the delights of Iran and caught a ride northwest toward Turkmenbashi. Stay in the old USSR, he thought, nothing bad can happen there, right? Central Asia was exactly as he expected, hardly changed since the Great Game, the long Soviet occupation only a memory.

Bouncing through the dead land west of the Aral Sea, he thought he was dead himself. Did his driver friend even know he was there? Was he still invisible? Kip was drunk most of the ride, and stoned to boot. Hashish was plentiful. Another reason to avoid Iran, because you dangled on the end of a rope if they caught you with dope.

It really wasn't as bad as one might imagine out there. There was no place to run to, but no one was likely to chase you either. Other than the scarcity of high-quality goods, things were seemingly normal. There was no anxiety on the faces, no panic like you saw in the wealthy cities of the West. Central Asia had been like this for centuries, which made it, in many ways, preferable to Europe and North America.

For Chubby, it was a blur, crossing the stinking, oil-polluted Caspian Sea on a sketchy ferry to Baku, then through Azerbaijan with some Ukrainian porno/heroin smugglers into Armenia, where he got robbed by some cops in Ashtarak. They only got a couple of hundred US dollars, but he had a couple thousand stuffed in the ears of his dirty, cloth Ushanka hat.

The Black Plague was back in Baku, and horrible bloated corpses were the only people you saw on the streets. Sometimes he saw movement behind the cracked-open shutters and fluttering curtains.

He caught a ride with a Russian long hauler, a big furrow-headed blond from up near St. Petersburg, and they rumbled through Vanadzor up to Metsavan, then into Georgia and Tbilisi. Kip taught him some English, and by the end they were toasting each other with vodka and repeating in unison, "What the fuck are we doing in this shithole?"

The truck driver had it memorized by the time he let Kip off in Tbilisi, where almost immediately Chubby was beaten up by again, this time by Armenians, who for a while he imagined were connected with the real estate salesman running for President – Douglas Turdashian. They took his fone and left him crumpled on the sidewalk. He got up and stumbled into a Tbilisi café, where he met a sloe-eyed beauty hidden under a lumpy babushka frock and pinned-up black hair that half covered her right eye.

Her full red lips invited Chubby with a brief pucker, and he sat down. She seemed to have been expecting him.

"I am Canadian," he said.

"North American, then," she said.

"But not from the United States." He pantomimed spitting and said, "Americans."

Whatever, she shrugged.

Her name was Milana, a half Chechen sculpture artist, and that she worked exclusively with pine. Her daddy was a Sufi warlord, fighting somebody...non-violently...she told him later, as they lay chastely in her encompassing feather bed. A couple of days after his arrival, an intense young man who she introduced as her brother, Nikoloz, joined them at dinner in an open-air Tbilisi restaurant. Said he graduated from Moscow State University about 10 years ago. Spoke Russian better than his sister, or any of the other Georgians he met. "No – not the Moscow in Idaho," Nikoloz said, a joke Kip never did completely understand.

Nikoloz told him the father-was-a-Chechen-Sufi-warlord story (Milana rolled her eyes as it was slightly different from her version), how their dad was on the run, wanted by everybody. Still, they both swore their father was a "non-violent" Chechen warlord. Hmmm. Different mothers, she later told him.

The three of them viciously pounded vodkas and talked about books, history, and conspiracies late into the night. Nikoloz said Americans were doomed because they had no experience with true suffering. Why does one need to leave the United States to get into a profound conversation, Kip thought. Why are Americans such shallow, small-talking navel gazers?

That night Milana ravaged him vengefully in the soft feather bed.

After that, Nikoloz disappeared. Milana said he was working in Sochi, as some kind of a ski instructor/security expert. Nikoloz was relatively light complected, unlike his sister. You never know about genetics, but something told Kip the difference was because of more than their different mothers. During his stay in the Georgian capital, Kip met lots of people in a lot of places – a mystery writers guild meeting, a street corner gathering of an anti-Russian graffiti gang, and a semi-annual meeting of an ancient society once dedicated to the assassination of Timur the Great (most of the original crew died horribly) – now more of a civic group – that sponsored soup kitchens, after-school programs, and Georgian book clubs.

Milana had interesting friends, most of whom seemed to hate all forms of authority. My people, Kip thought. Middle finger flippers without borders.

He bought a bike and rode to the Sioni Cathedral, then over to Stalin's birthplace 50 kilometers away in Gori. Milana and he even attended services on Sunday at that famous Georgian Orthodox church.

"You are not Georgian, you are Chechen, right?" he asked her as they listened to the liturgy.

"You are confusing me with Nikoloz," she said.

"But..."

She waved her hand at Kip and shook her head.

As the weather warmed in the spring, Milana and Kip left Tbilisi and moved to the edge of the Mtirala National Park, in a clean cabin with glistening hardwood floors and a window two meters high and twice as wide. In the western distance, the afternoon sun sparkled off of the eastern edge of the Black Sea and right below them, a stone monastery from the 15th century stood guard on the approach to their love fortress.

They met Nikoloz again, and after another evening of heavy drinking he asked what Kip was doing in "the Caucasus" as if it were all one big country, and the question clearly had nothing to do with his sister, if in fact he really was her brother. Kip thought that maybe somebody had fingered him as some kind of *agent provocateur*, but Nikoloz never came right out and asked, so he continued to just play along, seeming not to understand the real intent of his questions. Nikoloz said it was unusual to see an American in Georgia, and Kip was a bit too slow to correct him, and when he finally did say no, no – I told you I am a Canadian, from Vancouver...Nikoloz nodded matter-of-factly and said nothing more about it.

From then on Kip knew he was being watched. Nikoloz seemed to back off at that point, as though he was just probing for a weak spot. They talked trivialities, but Kip sensed something slightly sinister in his demeanor. The last thing he said was, "We will meet again, my friend." And then he showed him his fone. He held down his finger until all of the apps were blinking with "x"s above them. Then he pointed at *SwiftPad* and deleted it, and smiled.

He stood, shook Kip's hand, nodded to his sister, and walked out of the bar, followed by two men sitting at a corner table whom Kip hadn't noticed before.

Immediately after moving to the cabin by the sea, Milana had started hacking out a disturbing pine likeness of Kip, with hammer and chisel, catching his body in that exact moment when his muscles began their decline. You can see the effects of gravity on the fleshy wood, his chest and belly beginning their inevitable journey south, his cleft chin losing its prominence to his puffy cheeks. Kip saw it all, as though it were a mirror running on fast-forward.

"Wait until I varnish it," she said listlessly.

To stave off cabin fever, Kip rode Milana's electric moped down to Batumi, to the same bar he and Nikoloz and Milana had been at earlier. One of the drunks there said that Nikoloz was going to kill Kip for "dishonoring" his sister, which...well... as Falstaff said, what is honor anyway? There was laughter and pledges that it was all a joke, because that was how Georgian brothers were. Kip didn't correct him and say he was really Chechen, if in fact that was even true. It made him wonder just how safe he was in Georgia, since it was a pretty good bet that his secret was out.

Milana said all she wanted was help learning English; in other words, he shouldn't stress out about her becoming attached, that he was free to leave without emotional consequences if that is what he wanted.

Which was where it all stood when Paula showed up. Just a San Francisco private detective, she said, sent by Alice, Kip's best friend's mother, who as you know, was now managing his recently deceased father's compound.

Kip didn't want to leave, but Paula seemed to leave him no choice. *SwiftPad* was at risk of being hijacked. The software code they controlled and maintained was becoming the soft innards of the American news media, grinding out artificially intellect–ed manufactured "news" to augment the dry, unrelenting tale of folly and misery that otherwise seemed to be the generally agreed upon reality. It was taking the country toward a future no one thought was promising...after all, if *SwiftPad* is benign amusement and an eventual means to a more pure and direct democracy, run through a machine, controlled by...? Hmmm... what could go wrong?

There was something else going on too. This woman Paula had the demeanor of a mischievous avenging angel that hid behind a slightly raunchy, seemingly unsophisticated con artist, who refused to recognize what was waiting for her on the other side of the next day. But not today, not yet. Her eyes were deep, her soul was old, and her beauty was anything but fragile, yet Kip felt as though he had a responsibility to protect her, from – what? He wasn't sure of what.

Paula had showed up at their hideaway in the woods over-looking the Black Sea. It was just getting dark. They were about an hour from the nearest hotel, so she stayed. Milana was a per-fect hostess, fixing a couple of delicious Megrelian dishes – cheese breads, lamb stews, and eggplant salads – but then as the week went by things got a bit jiggy. As Paula talked about how she came to be looking for Kip, Chubby's "cover" as a Canadian was completely blown. And so was his cool. He could not take his eyes off of Paula. Neither could Milana. Paula seemed to have stepped out of a mythological legend. She tried to be ordinary and put off their stares of wonder with bathroom humor and even moody exhaustion, but it did nothing to change the impression she made on Kip and Milana.

How could she possibly be so young and yet know and understand so much? Her gaze pulled him in and pushed him out like two magnets together. She seemed to have arrived from the distant past, like Athena walking among the mortals. Milana said with no particular prompting, that the Colchian Grove, where Jason and the Argonauts, (with Athena's help) found and snatched the Golden Fleece was only a few kilometers west of the cabin. Interesting, Paula said, with a smile.

Kip went to a mirror, slapped some water on his face, and laughed at himself. Snap out of it, he said to himself. Deep down though, he knew this was the beginning, that he was about to start wading in some deep shit.

Both Kip and Paula discovered that their paths had crossed before, and that they knew some of the same douchey Silicon Valley tech executives. After *SwiftPad* was up and working, just before the Amazon sale went through, Kip went to an exclusive off-the-record conference in Los Gatos, and the Vice President flew in (not the now acting Temp-Prez, but the one before that) to lecture the tech execs about "responsibilities" – social and security related. Paula said she "did" security at that conference, and that she remembered Kip, and then reminded Kip of exactly what and how much he had drunk at that farewell dinner.

He laughed nervously. Who was this woman, he wondered? Paula said that she did a good business taking care of the Silicon Valley's dirty diapers. Said she extracted little brothers out of whoring tours, and daughters running off to be part of polygamous marriages in southern Utah – she had found them and usually brought them home with no fuss. Professional discretion, she said with a twinkle in her eyes, would not allow her to tell him what tipped her off, or even how she made her way to the Mtirala cabin.

Paula said she didn't care if he came back or not. She found him, job done. She took a selfie with him, emailed off to Alice, poof, she was done, proved she found him and delivered the message. Said she wanted to see a little of western Georgia herself, and then she would be off, leaving in the morning, promising to be back in a few days.

Paula slept on the couch, and snored like a growling prelapsarian monster, but was gone when Kip woke.

Kip and Milana spent most of that week hiking around or driving down to the seaside, chatting with the drunks and lounge lizards who presided over the little cafés and drinking establishments in the area. Those little visits were Kip's farewells even if no one acknowledged that. The crew slipped into the Georgian language, cutting him out of the conversation, switching into Russian as an afterthought, as if to say, "Are you still here?"

Milana was waiting for him to go, with her own particular brand of "are you still here?" attitude. Gradually he began to realize that there was no graceful way out, because Milana knew what Kip really wanted. At least her English had improved considerably. Kip asked her if she wanted to come with him, and she laughed and shook her head "no" emphatically.

A week later Paula returned, saying very little about where she had gone. That night Milana and Paula left Kip in the cabin and took off in Paula's rental jeep. It was nearly 3 am when they returned, both a little drunk but otherwise tight lipped about where they had gone or whom they had seen. The three of them got outrageously loaded, and pounded down bottle after bottle of Chacha, Georgian grape "vodka," technically a brandy, but clear and medicinal. They laughed their asses off for hours. They all woke up together in Milana's feather bed, and got up and had breakfast without another word. Then Paula left, for Istanbul, where she said she would wait for three days, and then fly back.

Driving back from the Batumi airport, Kip understood that even with the hideously oppressive political oppression that lurks in every city from Beijing to Tbilisi, life goes on, and that it is a gift wrapped up in fun and laughter, and that everything else is a waste of time. The panic going on in Europe and North America was nowhere evident out here. They had seen the worst, and now didn't seem all that bad. It wasn't that different than it had been before! The effects of global disruption were situation normal out here. Kip was really hating the idea of leaving as it became more and more inevitable.

And now, after having traveled across Central Asia and meeting a beautiful woman who licked the wounds of his rejection and of the journey – the gold standard of adventure – that was coming to an end as well. Should he stay or should he go?

You can only do this so many times in your life.

He had walked through the human bone–strewn field outside of the ancient city of Merv. Merv was one of the lost cities of Alexander the Great and had possibly been the most populated city in the world when it was conquered by the Mongols. The Mongols executed over a million people there. Down the road, at Geok Tepe, the Tsar's army had slaughtered the people of the city, men, women and children all, as they tried to run. Kip had walked where the still visible bones of the thousands killed by the Russians in 1881 were mixed in with the sand and rocks, and they were just the icing on a very deep cake of murdered humanity. But you felt it out there. When you looked at the faces, across the whole expanse, where the DNA evidence suggests that one in every twelve people was a direct descendant of Genghis Khan, the Mongol conquest came alive clearly and brutally.

The constant grime, bad food, and horrible tasting beer and vodka never bothered Kip. Every day mattered, and you were on your own. Death was omnipresent and certain, and was a little bit embarrassed too, because everyone out there laughed at it. Buried in the sands were the cities of the Silk Road, along with the headless skeletons of millions of victims of the Mongol hordes, and etching out a living in those sad backwater villages were the descendants of the raped daughters and sisters of those victims. But in fact, he realized that described all of us, that all living humans were the children of wretched survivors of horrible nightmares. Nightmares were coming that we all thought were over, but we had forgotten that night has to follow the day. No. He had to return home, and fight if need be.

The Mongols leveled Tbilisi too, but they never made it to the mountains and forest of western Georgia, to the wooded hills that looked down on the Black Sea. So it did seem like the edge of the world, almost like some Tolkien-inspired fairyland. Milana loved to sing, and he taught her his favorite song and she changed it even more profoundly than Jimi Hendrix changed it.

There must be some way out of here,

Said the joker to the thief...

For her it was a desperate cry of despair, a tear jerker of imminent loss. This was the edge of the world, the Kaçkar Mountains, the Watchtower. And behind them, coming from the West, the Greeks – Jason and the Argonauts – it was the sharp edge of the world, a sliver of land between the southeastern end of the Black Sea and the other side. Now he felt dread as he looked out across the Black Sea.

Before he left, he told Milana who he really was, and how rich he was. He told her that he didn't know when he would be back, but if Milana wanted to help him, she should tell any other investigators who came snooping and asking about him that he was still somewhere in Georgia or out there in the mountains of the Caucasus, or maybe out on the Jaxartes River with the ghost of Alexander – out here, somewhere.

He had strangers take some pictures of the two of them smiling and relaxing in a local hotel lobby, by the seashore, in front of a cathedral. He had a plan, he said. He told her to find a nice house to live in and he would fill her bank account when he got back home.

Milana sent him off with a bit more than just a kiss. She never let on that she doubted him, even though it was embedded in her bones to distrust him. She gave him some advice.

"Paula is a witch of some kind, it is true, but I think she has a good heart. Be careful, because she is very careless. I will wait – not in that way naturally – but I will let you find me, when you come back." Kip just nodded, and said, like he was reciting liturgy from a forgotten religion, that he hoped so.

He flew to Istanbul, and met Paula at the Hagia Sophia. After an all-day flight, they landed at SFO. Kip accepted her invitation to come into town and crash on her couch for the night before flying back to Portland.

CHAPTER 4

SPENCE AND ALISON SURPRISE EACH OTHER

5:30 pm, Friday July 17, 2020

THEY ARRIVED IN THE LOBBY AT THE SAME TIME, from different elevators.

"Skipping out?" Alison smiled at Spence, who shrugged.

"Yeah, this is early, isn't it," he said.

"Are you going to that party at Oglethorpe's house tonight?"

"No. I wasn't invited. How did you hear about it?"

"It's on Gordy's calendar."

"Oh," Spence shook his head. "Socializing with clients is probably more up Kayla's alley."

Alison shrugged. They wheeled their bikes out of the building and headed around the corner toward Northwest 12th Avenue.

"Actually," Alison said, upon reflection, "that is a perfect event for Kayla, don't you think?"

"Maybe it wasn't so stupid of Gordy to hire her. Gotta schmooze in this business. Want to get a drink?"

"Just one?" she asked. "Let's go across the river."

They rode down Lovejoy to Broadway and turned south past Union Station, past the "Transition Projects" or the

Homeless-to-Housing apartment complex that SwiftPad Inc. was funding. Both sides of the street were packed with wild- or empty-eyed people, some talking to themselves, some staring off with looks of hopelessness and pain that they seemed to know wasn't getting better. These were not the dispossessed refugees, not recently stable middle-class people whose homes were destroyed, or communities that had dried up, people who were mostly camped on the outskirts of town. These were the long-termers, people with all of the issues and disabilities that the modern world had infected in those who were only a generation or two away the simple drudgery of farm life or repetitive, muscle requiring factory work. Most had been waiting for housing and other services for years. Spence recognized many of them.

"Yuppie scum!" A tallish man pointed at them as they rode past. He combed his jet-black mullet down to just above his eyebrows. He had an anvil chin, a bare, old man's chest, and wore long camo shorts real low, just to the top of his ass crack. A thin purple tee-shirt hung from his thick, black belt. A short dark complected man, carrying a hacksaw, and a skeletal, bleached-out woman who yelled, "Cuntwads! Ass turkeys!" at Spence and Alison, strutted on either side of the Mullet Head. The shirtless Mullet Head stared at them. The three of them were walking in the same direction that Spence and Alison were riding.

They rode faster, and a block later they saw a very long line of people – all types and ages – standing outside what appeared to be a soup kitchen. Across the street a similarly long line queued up in front of a methadone clinic.

Spence and Alison pedaled even harder. It was high summer, and still hours to go before dark, and Old Town Portland stunk like rotting cabbage. The funky odor lasted until they got to Waterfront Park.

They pedaled south and then up to the Morrison Bridge, to the Eastside, Spence following Alison, who whipped around walkers and slow riders, over the Willamette River, then down the ramp toward Water Avenue. She rode another block south, turned left and pulled up to The Leaky Faucet, an upscale micro-brew pub, where they parked their bikes and went in.

They ordered beer, and Spence told Alison what happened with Kayla in Gordy's office and what he was expected to do.

"Gordy wants you to find Nate Schuette, doesn't he?"

Spence laughed. "You know my history with him?"

"No, not really. You are like a battered woman, Spencer. You do all the work, and then hide behind the man who steals the credit, who in turn gossips about your personal life."

Spence took a shammy cloth out of his wallet, and cleaned his glasses. "I never thought of it like that. Why? What did Gordy say?"

"I only heard part of it," said Alison. "Something about your wife and that Schuette guy. Look – *RDM* would be shit without you. Kayla is Gordy's bluff to keep you away from him so he can get stoned in peace. She was brought in to plan parties and give virtual blowjobs. You should just pretend she works for you, and see what she does."

The beers came, along with a bowl of pistachios and pretzels, and Spence had his brewski half down in one sip. He was already thinking about getting something really hoppy for the next one. Spence pulled out his fone. "OK – you want to know about the Schuette shit? There you are. This is your fone, right?" He showed Alison his screen.

"Yeah."

"I'm sending you a file. Check that out, it is my Nathan Schuette script – the one he claims I plagiarized."

"Got it. Can I read it now?"

"Yes! Let me tell you something about Nathan fucking Schuette..." Spence took a long pull of his pilsner, then thought for a moment. He let Alison read as he scanned the tables. He looked out the window. Sitting on a bench across the little plaza next to the Faucet was the old guy with the black mullet. He had his dirty purple sleeveless shirt on now. He had lost his hacksaw buddy and the blond tweaker, and was now attended by a couple of young men with big trail backpacks. He appeared to be haranguing them and they were listening intently. How did he get here so fast?

Alison was reading.

"Fuck – so this is fiction, right?"

"Of course. Although it parallels Nathan's story – which I have at home – where he used the real names. For example, in that one – Herbie – that is actually 'Nate' – in his version." Alison kept reading. Spence caught the eye of bar waitress and signaled another, pointing at a tap entitled Supernova. Alison drained hers and pointed at her glass. "After graduating and helping Gordy manage Tonegarten – I admit 'Floating Anchor' was a classic, but they were a one-hit band – my life fell apart. I split up with my wife – my first wife I mean – and I quit working for Gordy for a while."

"Are you bitter?" Alison asked. She kept reading, as she half listened to Spence. The beers arrived, and now, settled in, working on the second beer, they both took a deep breath, and slouched a little.

"Bitter? No. Gordy earned his money. He hustled and took shit and talked to people I wouldn't or couldn't talk to, in ways I never could. No. Well, maybe a little – bitter. That was when I ended up living above Nate Schuette's garage." Spence grabbed a pretzel, tasted it and made a face, and shook his head as though it was the memory of something shameful.

"Wow! I didn't realize you knew Schuette that well. Pretty weird arrangement, considering…"

"Yeah. The neighbors called me Kato Kaelin."

"Who's that?"

"Oh, yeah – he was OJ's tenant. You – won't remember that. Anyway, it used to be funny. Go ahead and read, I have to take a piss."

Nate went into The Leaky Faucet's john. A big screen showed a *SwiftPad* feed that was divided up into six screenlets showing the Temp-Prez giving a speech to investors, thousands camping on the Washington Mall, surging crowds running from shooting soldiers in Central Park, the funeral of Prince Philip, Charles and his mother sitting in a pew together, a local station's feed of thousands camped in Champoeg Park south of Portland, and a (V)ICE spokeswoman speaking in front of what looked like hundreds of corpses, the ticker feed saying were they were members of the Reconquista Terrorist group, killed in some raid in the Southwest. Spence lingered, watching it all as he washed his hands.

"Anyway," he said as he returned to the table, "We – Nate and I – were really good friends at first. I thought he was the coolest guy I had ever met. It had nothing to do with Gordy or *RDM*, at least not at first. Uh – my – my first wife…"

Alison looked up and laughed. "What a sad phrase. A veritable punchline." She continued laughing, and got Spence smiling too.

"Well – it was short."

"When was this?" Alison took a long pull and caught up to Spence. Spence caught the barwait's eye and she came over.

"Another?"

"Sure," said Alison.

"Me too…anyway, all that – marriage, first wife, ugly break-up – all that was before I met Nate. The idea for the shit you are reading there came from my head and my imagination. But – as Nate says, I must have stolen it from him, because what else could possibly explain it?"

"Stole what? His wife?"

"That's another story. Jesus, no, I am talking about the script – the script we are supposed to get for Gordy – remember? Well – not this script – anyway by the time I started it, Nate Schuette had already sent his version to his publisher and it had been rejected. There are a lot of differences between his and mine too, but – I swear discussions I had with him about it, if I had had any, which I am sure I didn't, I know that they couldn't have had any effect on my script. I used to think it is more probable that he ended up stealing it from me, but it appears that that couldn't have happened, unless he could go back in time. Not only that – he says his story is not fiction! He says it actually happened to him."

Alison picked a pistachio out of the pretzel/pistachio mix on the table.

"If you read his version – this was a hallucinogenic bud of some kind that allowed me – us – with the help of sensory deprivation and an advanced two-way electroencephalographic biofeedback machine..."

"Bet you can't say that three times fast!"

"It did real telepathy – and also – it was some kind of fountain of youth. Nate's story was a sixties style trashy sci-fi stoner memoir, interesting, but not really – you know – serious. No attempt to make it convincing or based in reality. I couldn't write that way if I wanted to. My script, as I think you will see, was a college hijinks memoir and I made up all that shit about the peyote and telepathy, all from reading *The Teachings of Don Juan*. I was trying for a – Holden Caulfield takes acid kind of thing."

"Wow."

"Yeah. Both versions were set in the early '70s, and for me – my story – the whole Howard Hughes thing, the plot to weaponize it all, was a pathetic imitation of Kurt Vonnegut meets Raymond Chandler...with all that going for me – my version sucked. His was better, more – I don't know...internally consistent."

"Get out –"

"No, it's true. OK – but listen – in this story, I did a lot of research on Watergate and I had Nixon's dirty tricks team steal the Machine, and the mutant peyote that caused the mind reading. Then the hero – my hero, Herbie – ends up in Managua, Nicaragua, in Hughes' suite in the Intercontinental Hotel. You know about that, right?"

"No. Well, yeah, I remember reading something about Howard Hughes in a hotel – but..."

"Right. Hughes went into isolation in the 1960s as his OCD and paranoia worsened. He lived in penthouses on top of big fancy hotels. For a long time he lived in Las Vegas, then, probably to avoid taxes and subpoenas he moved to Managua, where he could be protected by his buddy, the dictator Somoza. So, the story ends up with Hughes lying in a double sensory deprivation tank next to my hero – Herbie – who the fuck is named Herb or Herbert anymore? They have eaten the mind-melding shit – some kind of hallucinogenic shit – peyote and whatever – well – this is where history and fiction intersected. This is stupid – I mean – never mind..."

"No, no – I am interested!"

"OK – well this guy Herb – he's a – well like me – kind of a writer, provoker, and he is the one who figures out there is something strange about this weird strain of peyote. He is an experienced LSD type druggie; he hears voices and thinks nothing of it. So he has this other friend – they are in college, right – undergrads and not really serious about research – but this other guy has been playing with electroencephalographic biofeedback – EEG – it records the electrical output of the brain and graphs it. It's been around almost since the turn of the 20th century and was really refined in the 1920s.

"So this science-type guy – friend of Herbie's – sets it up so that the electrical signals are transferred from one person to another, syncs the signals up, so to speak, matching the frequency of the biorhythms. So you can feel or listen to the electrical activity of another person. In reality, it doesn't do much of anything, but it can have a disorienting effect, like a strobe light does."

Alison took a big sip of beer, keeping her eyes on Spence, and said, "You know what that sounds like? The movie *Brainstorm* with Christopher Walken and..."

"Natalie Wood. Right. That was the movie she was shooting when she drowned. It almost killed the movie's release – in fact it did for a couple of years."

"So what are you saying?"

"Well…" Spence stopped to take a pull on his pilsner. "…I need to say up front that that movie did not influence my story – I never saw it – not until recently – but there is another twist, that you are going to have to take my word for…" Spence downed his beer, and so did Alison. "The EEG and the brainwaves – and my characters – you know there is some stuff going on – petty jealousy, who is fucking who, etc. – but that is just the windup before the pitch, because eventually they built a sensory dep tank for two people – like a double tank – this is where it gets to be like that Ken Russell/Paddy Chayefsky movie *Altered States*, but I swear I had never seen that movie either, then, you know, before I got the idea for this novel. My novel is set in 1970–73 or so. But I wrote it in the late '80s."

"OK. This has something do with Nathan Schuette?"

"Am I keeping you from something?"

"No, I am sorry for rushing you, I was just wondered if you had lost the thread," said Alison. She had a wry grin, which Spence returned.

"No, I've got the thread. So this bizarre woman, a graduate student in psychology who had a weird affair with the character, and who seems to never get old – she stays young throughout time…"

"Like Victoria Wren in Pynchon's novel *V.*"

"Jesus! I hadn't thought of that! Yes! Exactly! Didn't you ever do anything except read when you were young?"

"I was all-state in basketball in high school."

"Could you dunk?"

"Touch the rim. Well almost."

"Anyway, for some reason that I never was able to write about convincingly – she – the woman, Pamela – she transformed from an 'Off the Pig' campus radical to a Nixon girl! She became a spy for one the Watergate guys – the guy who was actually taking directions from the Huston Memo. The Huston Plan – you know about it?"

"No. Well…"

"A nobody staff guy named Huston wrote it to suck up to Nixon. It called for massive violations of personal privacy, break-ins, kidnappings, the whole dictator playbook. Nothing anywhere near as fucked up as what the government is doing today, but still for the times – hell, even J. Edgar Hoover balked at it…"

"But, that was just a bureaucratic power play, nothing to do with ethics or patriotism," said Alison.

"Right – so you know what I am talking about."

"Of course. It was all done in total secrecy – Gestapo shit that would have ratfucked the Constitution. It was seriously discussed, and Nixon had to pretend to kill it, just to get J. Edgar off his ass."

"Right," said Spence. "But the Huston Memo became the basis for the real show – the real Watergate horror, not the Gordon Liddy, Howard Hunt farcus."

"Great premise!" Alison said. "OK, so what was this other operation?"

"This other 'plumber' was working a different angle – psychological manipulation. In my story, Guy Jumano, a young Seattle psychologist, and friend of Ehrlichman's, was given the Huston Memo and told to figure out how – to do it – get the goods on the leaders of the anti-war movement. The Huston Memo envisioned old-fashioned break and enter, firebombing, fake terrorism stories, etc. But this Jumano guy, a PhD in Psych, was to set up a program that figured out – other ways. He was never caught, or even named in any of the court filings and indictments against the President's men. All books written about the era, from *All the President's Men*, to *Will* by Gordon Liddy, none ever mentioned him, or hinted that the crux of the Huston Plan had never been cancelled.

"So, in spite of Hoover's disapproval and feigned ignorance after the fact, a clandestine program and psychological dirty tricks against students was begun. It was the most secret of the secrets."

"Hmm," Alison was smiling at his story.

"The targets would be selected students, and of course the pros – Abbie Hoffman, Tom Hayden, etc. And they needed to do a test run, a limited pilot project. Jumano met Pamela at an academic conference and talked her into helping psych out the leftists that she would ID on her campus. How that happened – what caused her to switch so drastically – well – I didn't – get that."

"This Pamela is the Victoria Wren character, right?" asked Alison.

"Right. And as we learned from Watergate, the Plumbers and White House guys were amateurs. They never investigated her past, which was that she was big in the anti-war movement itself. Double psych! She would have been a target if she hadn't joined the enemy. And she – Pamela – really does falls for Jumano…the guy is very good looking. I guess – sexual attraction can be blinding."

"Believe me, that happens," said Alison. "Sometimes the simplest explanation is best."

"Well – first she fucked Herbie – but that was just radical chic fucking for the revolution shit. They had a brief fling, but she moves on, because Herbie is just a goofy, teenage undergraduate looking for a good time. They traveled in different circles."

"OK," Alison said. "You want to get something to eat? So then what happened?"

"No. I really gotta go soon." Spence pulled his wallet out of his pocket. He really wasn't sure that Peggy was teaching tonight. He wanted to have dinner with Alison, and that was what was scaring him at the moment.

"OK, OK," said Alison, motioning him with her hands to slow down, "I love what you have so far. So this Pamela has betrayed Herbie to Nixon's guys…"

"Right. Because – she thought that Nixon's guy, Jumano, who she was now fucking, would be powerful and she would get lots of grant money or whatever for her research.

"Again," Spence continued, "I left things foggy when I got lost. So she – that is all blah blah you know. He was offering her power and she betrayed her principles for it."

"No, no – I can see it." Alison was shaking her head. "That is – that is one of the oldest stories. Happens all the time. One more beer?"

"Yeah – but that's it, I gotta go." Spencer pointed at Alison and himself and rubbed his thumb with his fingers and the barkeep nodded. Spence downed his mug and said, "Fuck, this is good beer, on a hot day. Shit, it feels good. I could stay here all night and drink."

"Yeah," Alison agreed. "Want to hear some music this weekend? Jean Katon is playing the Moda tomorrow. I have been dying to hear her live. Why are we working on this *RDM* shit anyway?"

"Money," said Spence. "She is really hot, and what a band! That sounds like it might be fun. Maybe."

"OK. What happened next?"

Well – the Feds take the machine away, destroy the sensory dep tanks, and – Pamela – gives them some of the wacky cactus – some kind of mutant stuff, maybe not even peyote, I don't know. It ends up at the Hughes Corporation – and Howard wants it for himself. He hires botanists to try and grow it in the lab but that fails – so they bring it to his hideout on top of the Intercontinental Hotel in Managua. Herbie is arrested – really just kidnapped, he is never booked – and is put on a plane to Central America to show them how it works…follow?"

"Kinda – yeah."

"So they hook Herbie up to Hughes with the EEG, in the sensory dep tanks. Herbie is on the receiving end of Howard's brain waves when – boom – the great Managua Earthquake of December 1972 hits. It was huge. It really did happen. Thousands died. That was when Roberto Clemente – the baseball player – died in a plane crash taking food to the victims."

"Fuck," Alison was half-grooving to the grunge-rasta music of "The Mane Shakers" playing on The Leaky Faucet speakers. She smiled at Spence. "I'm listening!"

"In real history, or what passes for it," Spence paused,

"Hughes' aides put him on a stretcher and got him out of the city. But in my story," Spence continued, "they were right at the point where Hughes' 'mind' – his memories, and thoughts – had seeped into Herbie's mind when the quake happened. So Herbie stumbles out of the sensory deprivation tank and down the fire escape and out of the Intercontinental Hotel into the after-shocking Managua. Herbie was stuck – half Hughes – half himself. In a total fog with memories of Hughes' youth and of all his romantic conquests – Jean Harlow, Marlene Dietrich, Bette Davis, Katharine Hepburn, Gene Tierney, Olivia De Havilland, Ava Gardner – the list goes on, and on, all of them, he was the ultimate 20th century cockmaster..."

"Don't forget the severe OCD and depressive paranoia. I think he was..."

"What?"

"Nothing – go on..." Alison was enjoying it.

"Hmmm – Herbie had Hughes' memories, and it was almost embarrassing as well as massively discombobulating because Hughes was a terrible lover; in fact in many ways sex disgusted him, which is what you were going to say, right?"

"No – I have heard stories about a lot of those women – and I think maybe some of them might have been lesbians. Dietrich, Hepburn, maybe others. And Hughes might have been turned on by that?"

"Really?" Spence looked at Alison. Her hair was swept up from left to right, and was spiky at the part-line. She had on a light blue, plain tee-shirt covered by a cheap, snug Adidas sport jacket. Her eyes held nothing back, but were not flirting either – just straight ahead. "Yeah – I can see that. Definitely. In my original story it was pretty erotic but – that makes sense. Hmmm."

Alison smiled to herself and took a more dainty sip than previously.

"So to finish this up – Hughes – I mean Herbie – remembers it all, plus the plane crashes, the movie *Hell's Angels*, and his business with mobsters and Nixon, etc. It was the secret history of the 20th century and it was all there in his head. But jumbled too, because of Howard's mental illness.

"Hughes and his team take off – for the Bahamas, to another hotel where he will stay for the next couple of years until he dies. Herb wanders away from the hotel, and thinks he sees his old flame Pamela with Jumano, her Nixon operative lover, sucked into a crack in the earth – because of the aftershocks or something – at least that is what he thinks he saw – remember, the wacky peyote along with Hughes' memories is still coursing through his head – and he somehow catches a ride with some kind of pilot – maybe CIA – and Herbie makes his way back to Hughes' childhood home in Houston and wanders around and..."

Spence looked at his beer but only had a sip left, so he continued, "That is as far as I got with the story – I mean I had a bunch of endings, but none of them worked. Everyone dies, or else they live happily ever after, who knows? Is Pamela really dead? I don't know. And the other thing – when I got to that point in writing it, I was like this guy Herbie – confused, dazed, with memories that he wasn't even sure were his."

"Wow," said Alison. "That should be the script! It's got everything – it's techie, full of possible conspiracy, nostalgia."

"It could be that – this mind-reading apparatus in my story is like *SwiftPad* connected to a C2B. The neural interface that is supposed to be coming out and work with SP-Scripts. I talked to what's his name – Arkie's guy –?"

"Lester Lucas."

"Yeah – he is looking for somebody to help test it," said Spence, nodding and looking out the window watching the Mullet Head walk away. "I could work *SwiftPad* into the story – years later – only now *SwiftPad* is the wacky cactus and C2B is the EEG machine – hmm – that is what would make this story come together – thanks, Alison."

"For what?"

"I needed a break after that meeting with Kayla. Gordy is deluded. Telly Haines will crush *RDM*. He is out of his mind if he thinks he can push Haines out."

"Did he say that?"

"Yes. To both Kayla and me, just this morning. I am getting tired of Gordy's shit. Even if we can pull something out of our butts to make this happen for *RDM*, even if this half-assed script that Nate swears is his – only his version is supposed to be better than mine – because his actually happened, and he was there, so he says! Fuck. I went through the same shit with him with *Sierra Sparks*. Even then – in the end, Gordy is going to try and fuck me – us – and then I am sure he will get fucked himself and lose it."

"To Telly Haines."

"Right," Spence said as he and Alison smiled at each other as if they had come to an understanding, which neither of them completely understood.

"Why did both you and this Nate guy, whose wife you stole, end up writing the same story?"

"Both? Stole? Shit. That is the mystery. Why did we write the same story? Why did I make up a story that he says actually happened to him? Because we ate some shit that made us think the same thing. Or one of us read the other's mind. That is what he says."

"The wacky mushrooms!"

"Something like that."

"Why did you eat it?"

"Because it was Saturday night! Why are we..."

"Just a minute." Alison pulled her phone out and looked at a text.

"Fuck. We gotta go."

"Who is it?"

"Kayla."

CHAPTER 5
THE STORY IN SPENCE'S SCRIPT

December 1972, Lawrence, Kansas

THE COLD HEAVY NIGHT HUSHED THE BACCHANALIA, enclosing the riotous, juvenile din like a mother's womb. The delicate, unique lace-like complexity of the dancing, glowing snowflakes visibly vibrated as they entered the sharply defined street-lighted border against the night.

Lenny, Herbie's roommate, talked up the Sense Dep Test on his campus radio talk show. Every hour for a month on Friday nights, he would announce Elmer's address on Tennessee Street and the hours – usually between 7 pm and midnight – and on Saturdays from 9 am until noon – when they were looking for volunteers. It would never last more than an hour and was rare when both participants would both stay in for the full time. Usually one or the other would be pounding on the plywood lid, yelling, in a panic because sensory deprivation was scary for certain people.

Sometimes couples would come, looking for that connection, that soulmate spark that would confirm their feelings one way or the other. Most were friends of Elmer's, science undergraduates, some from the Psych department. Then afterward, if they made it through the whole session, usually an hour, Gail and Kathy would "debrief" them, separately of course, asking a set of questions looking for common "mental" experiences. And they had tape recordings, which caught their comments while in the tanks.

"Elmer designed it so half of the electrodes record and the other half transmit," Herbie said, as he followed her out. "So our goal is to put people on the same 'wavelength.'"

Pamela's goal was different. Herbie, drunk, gently pawed her, and she walked out on the porch to get away from him. She was done with him and all the others. No more. Different wavelength. She had found her soulmate.

"We've never done it in the snow."

"No," she said.

"Pam," she turned and looked at him with silent coldness. "OK. I –- I appreciate you – for getting me off – am I off? Or just out on bail?"

"You're on bail, but it's just a formality. You are out. Off." Pamela laughed.

I'll pay you back."

"Forget it. I didn't raise it; the fund is there for situations like this. Don't sweat it. You are off." If only he knew where the money came from, she thought, he wouldn't be so appreciative.

"Situations? What situations?"

Herbie had been hauled down to the jail on charges that went back two and a half years, to the night he – or Walt – threw a rock that crashed through a cop car windshield. They caught Walt that night, but Herbie had gotten away.

It was early in the morning when the warrant was served. Herbie yelled "Go away!" but they broke in the door. Joan sat up as Herbie was ripped off of the bed and brutally thrown against the wall.

"Are you fuckers done?" They stared at Joan and did nothing as she sat up, naked. She wrapped herself in a blanket and sat on the edge of the bed. They left her alone and let Herbie get dressed in silence before they took him away.

Two hours later Pamela brought "Kid" Wendel, a local drug

attorney, downtown with her, posted bond, and sprung him. It was the first time Herbie had seen her since the summer of 1970, over two years before.

"I don't understand how you just showed up?"

"We knew what was happening."

"We?"

"Yeah. Your experiments, over at the Tennessee house, have drawn the attention of some people I know. We want to put this together so that you and Elmer can make a company or be a division of a larger company, or just sell it to his company after you graduate. It is real, Herbie. That is why we sprang you. We want to put you in business."

"We..."

"We – people I know – just leave it at that..."

"Well – I can't speak for Elmer."

"Don't worry."

Kathy came out on the porch with Lenny, and from the look on Kathy's face, it seemed for the same reason Pamela had come out, to get away.

"It's great out here, oh, it's so beautiful, come out everybody." Looking off the porch at the snow piling higher by the minute, muffling all the usual noise of the night.

The idea of trial and court costs had made Herbie a little ill. The good life would have been gone. The prosecutor said he would have asked for five years, as he slammed his briefcase, shooting daggers at "Kid" Wendel.

Bail money, lawyer, entertainment...he remembered when they met, how stingy – downright larcenously cheap – Pamela had been on that trip across the country back in January – 1970 – two years ago. He hadn't a clue what he was going to do. Medieval history – grad school? Who was he kidding? But at least he would not go to prison.

Kathy pelted Gail with a snowball, and in no time, a free-for-all started. Pamela and Walt went back into the house.

"Herbie still thinks I blew the whistle on him, doesn't he?" Walt set what was left of the wine on the counter, and began scrounging for a couple of semi-clean cups.

"Ignore what he thinks. They'll drop the charges against both of you."

"How do you know?"

"Wendel knows – they are overwhelmed and only go after the easy cases. My colleagues have friends. Don't worry. You are off the hook now, and they will never pursue this."

Pamela left Walt in the kitchen and saw Herbie standing on the porch drinking and talking to at least 10–12 people who had heard about the early morning bust and now, 12 hours later, were welcoming him home.

"Kid" Wendel was cutting lines of coke from a massive mound of snow-like powder. The snow itself had released some pent-up frustrations and anxiety, along with the fact that the semester and finals had wound up that afternoon.

"Come on, Herbie, let's go find Elmer," Pamela directed.

Herbie finished his drink and found his coat, and he and Pamela slowly walked out into the soft, white night. They walked in the road on the tracks of the lone car that had been through that evening, crushing the neatly fallen six inches of snow. Pamela reluctantly let Herbie put his arm through hers. They crunched on, down to Tennessee Street, and up to Elmer's place. He had the top floor of an ancient house that was over 100 years old. It had been rebuilt right after Quantrill's bloody raid on Lawrence in 1862. It creaked, and didn't seem perfectly plumb, either.

They didn't knock. "Hey!" Herbie yelled up the narrow staircase.

"Just a minute." They climbed, then walked into Elmer's bedroom. Joan sat on the edge of the bed again wrapped in a sheet. She twisted her mouth as she looked at the ceiling.

Elmer slowly sat up, laughing. "Hey. You got a warrant?"

"This is the second time today!" Joan pulled her hair out, combing it up with her fingers.

"Sorry," said Herbie. "Me and Pam want to get in the tanks and hook up EEG."

Joan put her head back and laughed. She jumped up without a stitch of clothes on and put her head against Herbie's and knitted her brow.

"Ommm!" she hummed mechanically.

"Why am I hearing static?"

She rolled her eyes. "It really works, Herbie! I just tried it with Elmer. It works!"

Herbie looked at Elmer, and he seemed a bit sheepish. Herbie smiled at Joan. He hadn't seen her since earlier that morning when he had been arrested. He and Joan had been following a pattern since September. It was like a Mexican soap opera. Joan enjoyed the drama probably more than she enjoyed sex. Mornings were awkward. It was a hell of a way to kill a weekend. Before the Christmas holidays they had vowed to stop seeing each other and until last night had succeeded, when they were interrupted by the cops. So in a way, finding her with his friend and partner Elmer was a relief.

Elmer, already dressed, had quickly retreated to his garage lab, and was soon joined by his three guests. Joan claimed the best chair near the corner, and Pamela and Herbie sat on the edge of the tank. Joan stretched, although she kept Elmer's robe pulled up over her.

"We want to get in the tank," Herbie said.

"But," said Pamela earnestly, "if something bad happens you have to get us out!"

"I will be right here, watching your vibes on the screen. This – is our EEG signal screen – you will be in tank A – and Herbie will be in Tank B. See."

"I don't want to get my underwear wet," said Herbie, "do you have any..."

"No – just go in naked. Take a shower first. It is expensive to change the water – so don't pee! Make sure you go first. But let me clean this place up a bit first," said Elmer.

"First?" asked Pamela, in a flash of sobriety. "What's second?"

"Strip, both of you."

She sat down and began taking off her boots.

Joan tidied up the area in back of the tank, sweeping and moving various discards from the construction of the tank.

Elmer turned the heat up and cleared a path to the bathroom. He leaned his whole torso into the open hatch door of the tank. The water lapped softly against the sides of the enclosed walls.

"Where's your friend?" Elmer asked Pam sarcastically. She smiled weakly. "Got rid of him, huh?"

"No. Not even a little bit. He is probably back at the hotel. Why, what did he say?" she asked firmly. Herbie looked at Elmer.

"He wanted to talk money, and I said I needed to talk to my partner."

Pam looked at Herbie, who shrugged.

"Every time we change the water we have to use about 800 pounds of epsom salt for buoyancy. So no pissing."

"You already said that," said Herbie, "good thing we got that grant from the psych department."

"You're welcome for that too." said Pam. "Do people actually piss..."

"Well, people tend to lose themselves in there. I imagine it's a little worse when you've been drinking."

"I know you helped us get the grant, Pamela. Thank you. This clean tank is dedicated to you, Pam."

"Is it like a waterbed?" asked Pam, undulating her body like a snake.

"Sort of. The buoyancy keeps you floating right on top of the water."

"Totally soundproof, but it's subject to vibrations in the floor. So..." Elmer walked back into the kitchen. "Herbie, come out here and give me a hand with this." They walked out of the garage into the back door, which connected to the kitchen. In the corner next to the refrigerator was a cubic box, three feet on each side, with an instrument control panel.

"This thing – this EEG machine – is just a piece of shit, Elmer," whispered Herbie. "Has it ever worked yet for you?"

"Well…it's hard to tell. I am still trying to figure out how to calibrate…"

"Come on. It's just a reproduction of electrical garbage coming out of the neurons. These things have been around since 1924. It's nothing. There is no mind-reading potential."

"Just – let's see what happens", said Elmer. "We don't have to…include the buds."

"But she knows about it. Shit, she tried it with you, back…"

"I know, but – let it ride. Come on, help me pick it up. We might be able to make some real money with this."

They carried it out the door, down the steps.

"Pam, could you get the door! Look out!" Herbie and George carefully brought the modified (and bulky) electroencephalograph back in and set it next to the tank.

Pam held the door open, but still looked as if she wasn't ready to go into the tank. Her hair glistened. Her mouth took on the shape of an off-centered oval, dilating and contracting apparently at the thought of the tank or brainwaves.

Herbie began to take off his clothes. Pam, with no outward reluctance, followed his lead. Elmer pulled the electrode headset off the bench and brought it over to Herbie. He explained the next step was to assimilate the brainwaves together into one composite and create an integrated electrostatic field of those integrated signals around the headsets.

"By constant repetition we should get closer and closer to the composite. At that point all your energy should be vibrating at the same frequencies. It's like biofeedback, and it should happen naturally, so just let it flow. If there is such a thing as synchronicity, it should exist at that point."

"Wait a minute," said Pam. "You mean nobody has actually – has this actually worked yet?"

"Well, Joan and I just did. Right, Joan?"

"Uh huh."

"You remember the crazy cactus that we ate on our road trip to Arizona?"

"Yeah," she said.

"Remember how we felt? Like we were having the same thoughts?"

"Well, that was two years ago. It was – I don't know. It's hard to remember."

Herbie finished drying, and Elmer wired up him up while Pam showered.

Pam got out and after drying, didn't bother to wrap herself with a towel. "Let's do this," she said.

Joan sat in the corner, reading *Psychology Today*, and said, "It's getting hot in here!"

Elmer brought over a mason jar. Pam and Herbie sat on the shag rug–covered platform leading up to the tanks. He pulled out a bud and carefully cut it into three more or less equal parts.

"I will be the 'control' participant," Elmer said. He popped one of the soft dried pieces into his mouth. "Since I am not in the tank, maybe we'll see if it is different when not sensory deprived. I'll take notes. Both tanks are miked. Two tape recorders. See?" Under the table were two Sony cassette recorders. "To record, you have to speak. This is the only way to measure. Someday maybe they will have instrumentation that tells what is going on in the brain."

"So," Pam said, "we just say whatever is happening, when we sense it, whatever visions, or thoughts, just say it, anything. Just babble."

"It will pick up both your voices. If you both talk at once, I can slow it down and catch what you are saying, but it should be no trouble. We need to capture precise timelines. We'll compare notes afterward. But the slightest sensation – try and describe it – OK?"

Both Herbie and Pamela were buck naked with a crown of wires leading to a single thick coax cable that snaked into the EEG machine. George had jacked up the thermostat to 85 so it was warm in the garage.

"I'm going back to bed," said Joan.

Herbie climbed into the tank first. "Oomm a few bars for me, Herbie," Elmer said.

Pam got in the tank without ceremony, and closed the hatch. "Oooooommmm. Check, check, check!"

"Loud and clear," said Elmer, nodding to himself.

CHAPTER 6

KIP MEETS NATHAN SCHUETTE AT PAULA'S PLACE IN HAIGHT-ASHBURY

Monday, July 6, 2020

Doing abstract work while staring at a computer was about the only thing that paid anything anymore, and much of that had been outsourced to low wage intellectuals on the Indian subcontinent – until their war. But even with the loss of the outsourcers, the pool of cheap labor was deep and was now moving into the northern province of the recently united Korean peninsula.

But in the States many, if not most, people were unsuited for abstract employment. Fones had destroyed the nation's attention span.

And some of course, just preferred freedom to digital slavery.

From *The Fall of it All – A History of the Big Dump*

CHUBBY KNEW THE BAY AREA, AND HAD SEEN REPORTS of the earthquake, but seeing it up close was a jaw-dropping shock. The "cab" they had taken from SFO was an armored SUV, with a pop-top roof, and a hydraulic mount that could quickly push up a medium-sized "minimi" machine rifle on a swivel mount, but the guy in the front passenger seat, riding "shotgun" (who actually had a shotgun on his lap), said he had only deployed the "minimi" once, and that only to shoot over their heads.

Coming north from the airport, the catastrophe was not evident until just off 101 as you first came into the city. The Portola District was practically flattened. Homeless people picked through the rubble. It was like springtime in Berlin, 1945. All along, the streets were filled with hollow-eyed people pushing shopping carts filled with blankets and various other personal items.

Paula had insisted the cab take the long way, to show Kip the city, since he was planning on leaving the next morning. They drove around the Embarcadero, which, judging by the clean, smooth pavement, had just been rebuilt.

"The geologists say that a fissure a half mile down collapsed. Nothing to do with the San Andreas fault. Popped like a bubble, and then when the bay rushed in, that was it – North Beach wipeout. More people died than on 9/11 in New York. A lot of people survived the collapse of those apartment buildings, but then ended up drowning. After the first shock, people in the Financial District all ran down here to the Embarcadero when whoosh – the bay came in. None of the buildings up there even cracked, much less came down. Very strange."

"And it looks like they are rebuilding in a hurry."

"Yeah," said Paula. "You can do anything with money."

The next morning, the sun woke Kip up. He pulled a pair of shorts and a tee-shirt out of his backpack, and made his way out of the little guest room and into the living room, and then out the front door. As Kip came out on the porch, he smelled smoke and human shit. Paula reclined on a beach lounger, snug under a fleece blanket that doubled as a robe. Paula was drinking coffee on the porch above Fell Street, overlooking Panhandle Park, in San Francisco's Haight-Ashbury district. The earthquake had passed by the

Haight and it was like an island that had been shaken but still was standing; there was very little damage to the neighborhood.

The fog was still clinging to the sky like lint, and it was chilly. Kip didn't notice an older guy was sitting in the chair next to hers, until he nearly sat on him. The old guy's eyes, still half closed, cracked open. He wore maroon sweatpants, flip flops, and an old blue sweatshirt. A candy apple red Beretta 9mm sat on the table next to him. Early as it was, still, there were many people already in the park, some who had crawled out of hidden nooks to continue sleeping safely, and others just sitting in the patches of sun that broke through from the east.

A (V)ICE cruiser, or Crush, or ICY (the nickname used on a wildly popular vlog entitled "The Vagrant Sluts of Sector Nine"), crept slowly across the park. The front driver's side of the ICY's darkened window was down and a dark-clad, commando-styled crew-cut blond dude was leaning out, clearly enjoying the panicky effect he had on the people in the park. The cruiser, with just-for-show spoilers jutting out of the armored hood, was a modified Ford Sandcat, SUV-like, armored all around. Mounted on its roof was the standard issue unmanned big-ass gun that purposely swiveled around, automatically following the crowd. People quickly hopped up off the grass, some just leaving their sleeping blankets, moving, some fast, while others stood rooted in place. Others gathered their stuff into old packs and bags, some posing with defiance. Nobody got out of the (V)ICE truck.

"Wooh!" Paula said, holding her nose, while checking the drama in the park. "Fog's almost gone this morning – kind of weird actually. Sleep OK? Did you feel that aftershock earlier?" She threw her fleece robe off, revealing an oversized red pullover and blue knee socks. The old man with wild bushy, straw-like hair, who was sitting in the lounge chair, looked at Kip briefly, smiled and nodded. He was munching on a half-eaten bagel and a slice of hard white cheese. Kip looked at the little blue Beretta 70 strapped on Paula's ankle. His and hers, patriotic colors.

"If they see you packing, they keep moving," she said, noticing Kip eyeing her piece. "It is awful we have come to this. I have never had to point it at anyone." She knocked on the wooden doorframe. Kip shrugged, and looked over at the guy next to him, who reverted to half sleep.

"There's a batch of scrambled eggs in the kitchen – help yourself. This is Nate."

The old man slowly reopened his eyes.

"We get aftershocks pretty frequently. But hardly had any damage in the neighborhood – yet. You saw what it did south of here." Kip gave a quick, disturbed glance at the old man, who was staring off into the oddly sunny morning. "I slept well," the old guy said. "Not too foggy this morning, huh?"

Kip watched the people in the park while stretching and twisting. It was the first time he had slept in the US in over eight months. Where had he seen this old guy? "Yes! I was dreaming, but I definitely did feel something last night, dreamed I was floating – drifting on top of the waves. I am glad the house didn't fall on us."

Actually he had dreamed about Paula and Milana all on a big rubber raft. But the whole thing was indistinct and – foggy – and the shaking came at a peculiarly auspicious moment.

"Just a tremor. Kip, this is Nathan, my…roommate. Well…"

"I'm her boyfriend. She just uses me for sex, but I am fine with that. Maybe you've read my autobiographical novel of China…"

The China memoir! Yeah, Kip had read it, maybe a quarter of a century ago. Kip looked at the old man closely now – Nathan Schuette! Holy shit, he used to be so young…he had once been one of Kip's heroes, back in the '90s. On the cable talk shows, discussing all the hubbub about China back – years ago, maybe right after Tiananmen, or maybe before, it was a long time ago; that was the last time Schuette had been on Kip's (or anyone else's) radar. Two foreigners murdered in Beijing, and then a spate of stories linking Nate to them, and then – nothing. "I remember you," said Kip, shaking his hand. "I mean, I remember the...the China story..."

Schuette turned with some difficulty to face Kip. "It is heartening that you read, although you could pick better writers. China no longer seems to exist in America's consciousness. Since Real-Prez's tariiffs, trading has practically stopped. But one and half billion people are still there." Nathan took a sip of coffee. "I know you too. Tech billionaires are a dime a dozen, but *SwiftPad* is different! And here you are, crashing on a couch in the Haight. Exactly as I would expect! The famous Kip 'Chubby' Rehain, the Steve Jobs of Portland, the creator of *SwiftPad*! I guess what they write about you is true. Paula says you two just got back from the Black Sea..." Paula was grinning.

"I wasn't the creator of *SwiftPad*...just – sort of the midwife."

"It's good you're spending a day or two here before going back to Oregon," Paula said as she poured Kip a cup of coffee. "We are in some hurry, because your dad's accountant wants us at the upcoming *SwiftPad* board meeting, very soon and there are many things to arrange, as well as..."

"We need to explain some things," said Nate.

Dad's accountant? Heber?" What did she mean – us, thought Kip. Paula made a little face he couldn't decipher. "Yeah."

It began to concern Kip how much this woman was creeping into his life. What did she want? She had ripped him away from a good life, a life he was sure to which he could have adjusted. She just showed up in Georgia and he ended up leaving with her.

Now he was back in the fucking shitshow. This woman had a grip on him – in that mother-sister-wife-mistress way. But now, something about her was...different... And Nathan Schuette, the writer who opened a bizarre door into the history between the West and China. Her boyfriend? Clearly he was old enough to be her grandfather.

Out of the country for eight months, more or less incommunicado, in the wastes of Central Asia, and then finding refuge on the Black Sea, when Heber sent Paula to get him. Why send her? Didn't she say she was Alice's friend? Too strange to be a coincidence, Kip told himself; take a deep breath.

"I am going to jump in the shower," said Paula.

Old man Schuette stared at Kip watching her walk away from behind his coffee mug, and then said, "The grossest, most bottom of the barrel aspect of any matter related to people will always override and blot out everything else. It's the universal Gresham's Law. The bad drives out the good. Gossip and trash beats beauty and facts. It is getting worse. We are in the garbage dump of history, the stinky hole at the end of the road that we have always hoped to avoid."

"Oh?"

"Yes, yes you are. You poor fuck – how old are you?"

"Forty-seven."

"Gen-X! Mr. X-Man. Sorry, you got the shitty end. Now it's all about to turn to shit. We have arrived in the time of dread. Sorry, sport, it's your burden, mine too, but not anything like yours. I am, as you can see, old. Nobody listens to the old and we get to get out, to exit before the curtain falls. Most of you X-people blame us. Sorry. But that won't help; you can't run from it anymore. We didn't run, but just got rolled, in slow motion. I suppose if we had fought when the times were good, and we were young and strong, we could at least say, 'Hey we tried to warn you!' Which we did, some of us, but not very seriously, or in a direct way, not loud enough, obviously. That is on us, but saying so does you no good, sport. Sorry, It's time."

Kip looked at Schuette, but didn't say anything.

"No," Nate continued, "you are going to have to spend your best years dealing with the shittiest things in life. Sorry, but I don't make history, just report. These should be your best years, and it is going to suck. As I said, sorry."

That seemed like a pretty rude way to start a conversation, thought Kip. "I don't believe in the guilt or innocence of 'generations.' People are just bounced by the forces of history. From the past and future it seems obvious, but not as it happens. That human nature is a fixed variable. You guys tried to pretend it wasn't fixed."

"Well, you may have something there." Nate nodded his head in agreement. "My best years are back there. You can have what's left, but..." Nate drifted off for a few seconds. "Ever since they overthrew whatshisface, or whatever it was, we have been pretending and acting as though everything was OK. Section 4 – the 25th amendment saved us from all the drama and we thought, shit, maybe it is turning around. Yeah, half the world becoming rubble, or parched, or broke, or just plain unlivable, but we wanted to come back from commercial break and find it all to be OK."

Kip nodded. From what he had been able to gather from Georgian TV reports (especially after the Русски E-invasion that took over all the media everywhere east of Potsdam), the former first family had drawn the curtain, occasionally releasing a picture of the Ex (or the temporarily recuperating Real-Prez, depending on your preferred narrative). When they showed him in the media, some evidence of the date was always displayed, such as a TV news crawler reporting a recent event, like a note from a kidnapper proving his victim was still alive. Then, when @Real-Prez notes appeared like rocks thrown from a prison window, they sent out his first wife to give funny interviews about his dottering dementia, to satisfy the need to avenge the two and a half year national nightmare.

But now his replacement, Temp-Prez, had been emasculated in the Republican primaries, and everyone thought it was going to finally be over – that it would get better.

"But we are in the same spot, only we are starting from a much worse position than before. Nothing has changed." Paula shifted in her seat, and her robe opened just a peek. "Your foundation is thinking about getting involved with money – and maybe even – fine-tuning the *SwiftPad* Machine, to maybe put your thumb on the scale, if you catch my drift."

"Slow down, you are way way ahead of me." Kip stood up and slowly poured himself a cup of coffee. "Who and why..."

"There are some things you should know..."

"And what do you mean, my foundation?" Kip knew they had a few billion lying around looking for something to do, but didn't realize they had a "foundation." "I really have no idea. I have been out of the country and...I..."

Kip had read Nate's China story years ago, about the discovery and then the loss of the physical evidence of the Old Testament in China, hundreds of years before Christ. It was all too heavy, the implications so bizarre that it was rejected by just being ignored. The world just didn't want to hear how interconnected it really was. China was a mythological place, with no reality for the West; it was almost like the time before Marco Polo had returned.

Kip picked up the tablet that lay between them on a table and read the open tab.

According to voices friendly to the Temp-Prez, (FOX News) the Hoover dam was blown by the "Geronimo Unit", which was actually a consortium of the drug cartels, revenging air attacks by the US against them inside Mexico. Speculation is that they bought the bomb from Islamists, who stole it from Pakistan. Lake Meade was now completely empty, along with much of the Southwest's water supply.

"It is not even clear who the 'commandos' were who destroyed the dam. (V)ICE claims there were no survivors, but that's just the administration's explanation. Rumors say the bombers all escaped. I can tell you one thing that only a few people know – it was an inside job. The bomb was made in the USA."

Kip said nothing.

"Doug Turdashian picked up the most of the idiots who put us here in the first place, and then some," said Paula. "Cadez wants to take the next step – round-ups of opposition – any opposition." She had fire and anger in her voice. She looked hard and angrily at Nate.

Nate paused to sip his coffee, "Yes, Cadez is scarier. He doesn't scare you though, does he, dear?"

Paula pointedly ignored Nate's comment. Kip looked at her and back at Nate, but neither would give him a clue as to what he meant by that, or why he didn't scare Paula.

Kip knew almost nothing about the recent politics, other than that Temp-Prez got crushed in the R primaries. His first thought was he was being hustled for a big donation by a bunch of scam artists. Sometimes he forgot that he was extremely rich. Now it dawned on him that Heber controlled his fortune.

"The *Post* is trying to control the *SwiftPad* phenomenon," said Nathan. "They are riding a tiger they can't get off. They don't dare switch it off because it's a drug, feeding the *Post*'s bottom line, and sedating the country's anxiety."

"The persuasive power of *SwiftPad*," said Paula, "has overwhelmed the circuits. Everyone knows that this app is fucking with the public opinion in ways that no one understands, but they are so afraid of it, no one is suggesting it be 'shut down.'"

"Your fucking application is a monster," continued Nate. "The *Post* thinks they control it, but really it is controlling them. *SwiftPad* has a mind of its own. You guys should never have sold it – you should have deleted it. But obviously the money..."

We have a way to shut it down, Kip thought.

Paula looked at Kip as he was thinking this, and stared. Kip stared back, so she continued. "Hmm. Well." They stared at each other, and neither said a word.

"The money..." interrupted old Nathan, who suddenly had a coughing fit that went on for a while. "You need to find a way to fix this – with money!" More coughing. "I don't know if you can do anything else, but at least you have money. I have a feeling just talking to you that -".

"That what?"

Nate smiled. "You don't seem too keen on fighting to keep your company. If you don't someone else will. I am asking what are you going to do about it Mr. Rehain?"

"Well..." Actually, Kip hadn't given it much thought. He and G had talked about it some back before they built it and released it, about the various meta features of the app. One was a destruction or self-destruction function. It would delete itself and then remain in somnolent alert to prevent it from being relaunched. It required a zombie system that wakes, attack, and passes on the function to another zombie. It was just theoretical then, at least for him. But he knew G had designed that "feature" into it. He knew how she worked.

Nathan just stared, trying to recover his respiratory equilibrium.

Fuck, Kip thought, he had to talk to GG and figure out how to shut *SwiftPad* down. They could do it, but he didn't know how. First he must convince her that it had to happen. Need to talk to G. Kip realized he didn't really know how the backdoor was activated, only that it could be done. He tried to remember what she had said.

"You know something that you're not telling us, don't you?"

Kip stared at Paula. She would not break him like she had done by the Black Sea.

"What do you two have in mind?" Kip asked. "I know Ben Cadez will actually be competent at taking us the rest of the way into some kind of permanent fascism. He is smart and will jail or kill the rest of us. His cold bloodedness flies out of every pore when he is on camera. We all know he will do it. But knowing it and doing something about it are two different things."

Paula looked at Nate, who was smiling and breathing slowly to keep from coughing. "What do you think, Paula?" Nate said theatrically. "Is Ben Cadez really that bad?"

She glared at Nate. "Back at you," said Paula sharply. "How

far will you go to stop them? That is the question we all have to ask ourselves."

Kip sensed an odd vibe between them. "What is going on? Do you two know Cadez?"

"Yeah," said Paula. Nate smirked and shook his head and silently pointed at Paula. "Yeah, we do. But answer me, how far? Or are you just in it for the glamor?" Paula asked again.

It was a point of honor that he held his ground for now.

Kip looked back and forth at them. "How do you know Alice?"

"Alice," said Paula with a wide smile. "I met her right after her husband ...your...friend Jim... when his father...died."

"What! That was 40-some years ago. How have you have known Alice that long?"

Paula laughed, and looked at Kip closely. "I remember you and Jim coming in from one of your adventures on the Mary's River. You were both scamps, intent on some mischief, that was plain. You don't remember me, Kipling?"

"No, I – maybe..." The vertigo hit Kip again. That funny feeling he had about her in Georgia suddenly came back. A weird, color-strobing dizziness came over him. His perception of Paula began to shift as through a prism. Oh shit, he did remember her! He remembered feeling when she showed up in Georgia that she was old, much older than himself, much older than she appeared. But he hadn't believed his own perceptions. And still didn't.

He looked closely at her. With well-toned skin and clear sharp eyes she looked like a woman in her thirties. Early thirties really, maybe even younger. He looked at her hands. They were the hands of a young woman, a teenager. She smiled.

"I think you should listen to Nathan's story...if you want to understand – all this," said Paula, almost in answer to his own doubts. "It is not just his story...and I know there are things you want to ask me."

Kip grabbed a bagel and said, "Yeah, let's hear it."

"OK," said Nate jumping in. "but I have to start at the

beginning. I am in this story," said Nate, "so you have to make allowances. Fifty years ago, wasn't it…" he looked over at her, as she laughed and nodded with a fresh sparkle in her eyes. "Yes, fifty years ago last January."

~~~

I was a freshman at the University of Kansas, just having finished the fall term, and was home for Christmas vacation, in New Jersey.

January 1970 was cold. I had the phone number of a guy who lived on Long Island who was headed back to Lawrence. Elwood was his name. He lived in my dorm, but, as I said, I really didn't know him. He said to meet him at a shopping mall in Paramus, New Jersey.

My father drove me, and I told him not to wait around, but it was cold so we sat there, in the gray early morning, Dad with the window opened, smoking. It's one of those scenes in your life that sticks with you for some reason.

An old AMC Marlin pulled up. The driver was a woman wearing a black stocking watch cap, brownish blond, mid-twenties. In the passenger seat was a tall, burr-headed guy, Elwood, who I vaguely recognized from the dorm. The Marlin was two-door, white on dolphin blue, a hatchback with a pretty cramped backseat and barely any room in the trunk.

The driver lit up my eyes, even bundled up in a thick blue peacoat. My dad saw her and I could see the smile on his face as he got out of his Caddy to help.

She opened the hatch door. I had two bags, and there wasn't room for both of them.

"We still have to pick up Wally," said Elwood.

"I'll ship one of them to you," Dad said, then turned, smiling at the woman. "What's your name, sweetheart?"

"Why? You gonna call me up for a date?" She looked at my dad over her granny glasses. My dad gave her a Jack Benny shrug, but kept smiling at her just the same. Her eyes were piercing, certain and clear. She didn't flinch. And she was older too – at least 23, maybe 25. I had only turned 18 the previous October.

"Well, son," Dad said, still half smiling at the woman in the black stocking cap. He reached out to shake my hand, probably wondering if I understood what I was getting into. "Have fun." He clapped me on the shoulder as I climbed in the backseat.

"Please get that suitcase shipped," I said. "I'll need those clothes."

My dad nodded with an annoyed look, waved as we pulled away. I don't think he ever took his eyes off of her. So we took off, down the Garden State Parkway, where immediately she hit us up for cash for the tolls.

Paula let out a stifled laugh.
"She thinks it's funny. Am I lying, darling?"
"No. Not yet."

Anyway, the engine didn't sound all that good, and we got on the Turnpike near the Raritan Bridge and then headed down toward Pennsylvania where we had to pick up Wally in King of Prussia.

I sort of knew Wally from that first semester in the dorm, better than I did Elwood anyway. Funny guy, always up for going on a toot, ready to get high or drunk anytime of the day. It was lunchtime when we got there and Wally's mom invited us in for kielbasa sausages and perogies. Finally after a while, Wally said we had to go, and he had even more stuff than I did. He was determined to pack it, and what didn't fit was crowded into the small space we had in the backseat. My knees were up to my chin and I was not looking forward to driving 1200 miles like that, but we all agreed we would rotate seats often so no one had to sit back there for too long.

There were four of us in the Marlin. It was probably a 1962 or '63 model, honestly I can't remember. I was at a low point in my life, stuffed in that sputtering piece of shit Marlin, wondering how to get off of academic probation, or even if I really wanted to go back to school. Sitting in that goofy car, mile after mile, I started to fall in love with her. I was still an unfucked virgin, you understand.

"You are making me blush, Nate!" Paula smiled.
"Yeah – right."

We headed west on the Pennsylvania Turnpike. It got dark early, and we made a wrong turn and ended up driving toward Pittsburgh, where we ate dinner. By the time we got back on the road, we were way behind schedule and it was about one or two in the morning, somewhere past Zanesville in eastern Ohio. I was in the back seat, wrapped up in my heavy coat, settled into the journey across the frozen wastes of the heartland, innocently expecting to be snug in my dorm bed by late afternoon–early evening the next day.

Then a desperate cry of fear and horror suddenly woke me, a screaming plea of terror blurted out like a long island– accented DEATH RATTLE!

"The wheels are falling off! The wheels are falling off!"

The car was shaking and there was a sudden lurch, and we were hurtling off the freeway at 70 mph, into the deep and still accumulating snowbank.

It took us two hours to push the car back on the highway. It was so fucking cold. I was shaken out of a very deep sleep, slashed to the bone by the shock of getting out in the biting polar predawn, and pushing that heavy Rambler out of the snowbank, somewhere deep in the Ohio woods. Fucking torture. Elwood continued to swear that the front wheels had been shaking violently and driving into the snowbank was the only thing he could do.

Wally took over the driving and said it was steering fine. But, in fact, it would take us four more days to make the trip to Kansas.

Wally got a speeding ticket somewhere around Columbus and we had to pay fifty bucks to the cop right there or he would have run us in. Wally only had about twenty, so the rest of us had to cough up the remainder. We spent almost all of our money and I didn't think we had enough for gas for the rest of the trip. We pushed on. She said she had a friend in St. Louis, so our plan was to see if we could get some cash there.

All this time I was dreaming about her, wondering if I could somehow get naked and – I was going nuts, couldn't stop thinking about her.

"Kind of like now, right, baby?" Paula was laughing.
"Exactly! How about you?"
Paula shrugged her shoulders.

Anyway, I would have masturbated to those dreams, but it was crowded in that Marlin. She was so good looking, and so seemingly unmysterious, clean, direct, with a tomboy femininity, and me being six months out of high school, thinking she was somehow – it is hard for me to understand my 18-year-old self from the vantage of 70, but, well I believed in "purity" back then.

The Marlin made it to Vandalia, Illinois, less than two hours out of St. Louis, and bang. I was driving and I went to pass a truck, when, as I said, Bang! The sound of the piston rod breaking through the engine housing jarred my teeth. The Marlin coasted to a stop. Dead.

We would end up spending three days in Vandalia, and

two nights in the local Fayette County jail, Vandalia being the county seat.

We had the car towed. Wally and I both negotiated with the owner of the garage, an old blind man named Wiley, who just yelled and slapped his cane on his desk, saying he wasn't taking any shit from a bunch of rich Easterners. Wiley said he had a young guy who was "a damn good mechanic for a retard." The mechanic was one of the most handsome men I had ever seen; he looked like a young Montgomery Clift.

Monty's girlfriend had a horrible case of acne, and something was wrong with her hip. But she was smart and relentless, walking Wiley and us through every imaginable repair scenario, figuring every way imaginable to get us on the road.

We tried to push off the decision to our lady friend in blue peacoat and black watch cap, but she insisted the Marlin belonged to a former boyfriend, and that she was fine with getting rid of the last vestige of him.

Anyway, the four of us finally got out of Wiley's garage to talk it over and decided to head out to smoke a reefer somewhere. We walked east until we hit the edge of town, and wandered past the last house when we found a path into a wooded flood plain. I was walking with her and she seemed to like me, but I didn't know how to act on it. My mind could not get away from what she must have done to get a car from a guy, who she apparently no longer cared about.

We wandered into the woods, and the crunching untrodden snow. As we got closer to the Kaskaskia River, the trees thinned out. When we got to the edge of the embankment, we fired up a fat one, and passed it around.

It was cold and although it was only about 4 pm it was already getting dark. It would be another night in the Fayette County jail. The deputy at the desk there had said we could stay one more night, but that was it. The stoniness hit us all about the same way, and we just stood there on the frozen riverbank, smiling and shivering.

Elwood, who was still pre-med then, and eventually a botanist, saw some frozen white fungus on the bark of an alder tree. "This is pretty cool looking," he said. He picked it off and broke it apart. Inside, it had an orange peachy color and it appeared to be growing on a number of trees on that embankment. Elwood put it on his tongue. "Wow. It's tangy."

"How do you know it's not poison?" Wally asked.

"I don't think so. I think it's kind of a sulfur fungus." He took another bite. "It's pretty good."

"You're fucking crazy eating that tree shit."

The Marlin woman in the blue peacoat took a bite too. "Wow – I bet this would be amazing cooked. What the fuck, right?"

Wally and I looked at each other and shook our heads. "It's fucking freezing, let's get out of here," he said. We all headed back into town to claim our free, heated cells in the Fayette County jail.

As we walked back, I tried to hit on her, it was pathetic really, and what made it worse was she seemed to think it was cute. I remember she kept saying, "Wow" and "Wow." But it wasn't about me. I was still an unfucked freshman, as I might have mentioned, and she was a graduate student, a complete mismatch. She was nice, and stared at me, and I thought it must have been the pot, but we had been smoking the whole trip, and it had never affected her in the way she was acting now. She seemed to be giving me encouragement on my awkward approach, which I kind of appreciated in a resentful way. I mean I wanted to get naked with her, but I had no idea how. It was so fucking cold for one thing. And she was sleeping in the women's section of the recently painted jail, while Elwood, Wally, and I held down the men's side. They took our shoes and belts. Elwood wasn't talking, only smiling and also oddly saying "wow" over and over.

The next morning our plan was to explore the town, and after a cheap lunch head over to Wiley's Garage to see if Montgomery had fixed the car. Elwood and Marlin girl seemed to be having a moment and somewhat mysteriously headed off together, back toward the river, while Wally and I wandered around and found ourselves in a two-story, white-shingled building that had been a meeting house way back in the early 1830s.

Vandalia used to be the capital of Illinois. Abraham Lincoln, then in the state legislature, hated the town, and used his powers of persuasion to get the state capital moved to Springfield, where it still is. The Vandalians, the ones we met anyway, still blamed Abe for consigning their town to Backwatersville. Apparently some Illinois politicians would congregate in this old house and discuss the future of Illinois or some such backwoods issue or the other. A couple of old ladies who volunteered there eyed us with distrustful suspicion as we looked over the exhibits. I asked them, "Golly gee, ma'am, this sure is an interesting building, did Abraham Lincoln really work in this place?" Later I would wonder if Lincoln had eaten the tree fungus while living in Vandalia.

"Yes. I understand it is of a peculiar historical interest. To my mind he was the worst president we ever had," she said as if it were my fault he had ever risen so high in the world. "He ruined this country and we are paying the price for it even now." The old lady looked at us and ended the tour when Wally started laughing at her. I asked why she thought the country was going to hell, but she ignored me.

I was a little jealous of Elwood, wandering off with the woman in the blue peacoat. I had neither the experience nor the imagination to come up with a move that would have led anywhere with her.

So while Wally and I negotiated a deal to let Wiley keep the Marlin in exchange for some kind of transportation on to Lawrence (a short run really; we were almost to St. Louis, and then it was just across Missouri, 250 miles, and we were practically there). Paula and Elwood roamed the streets, looking and acting ecstatic over something that had happened between them. They were tight lipped, and I assumed they had found a warm, dry place to get it on.

When it came to buying gas for the remainder of the trip, she was tapped out and insisted we (Elwood, Wally, and I) had to come up with the money. So finally Elwood and Wally worked out a deal for another car (the Marlin had thrown a rod, and was basically only good for parts) that Montgomery's girlfriend insisted would easily make it to Kansas. Her retarded boyfriend Montgomery, who was doing all the work, giggled, and I think he might have been smarter than Wiley gave him credit for.

So off we went, in another piece of shit car, down the highway, Wally driving. It was just getting dark as we left and it was cold. We got about five miles away when we realized that the exhaust was blowing through a hole in the floor of the car. We opened all the windows and were driving 70 mph, the temperature well below zero – note to rest of the world, zero Fahrenheit is minus 18 Celsius.

I'm in the backseat with her, and all four of us are laughing. There was no way we could make it to Lawrence like this, hopeless. Yet all laughing, and her snuggled up against me and I so happy. Even though I was soon to die of carbon monoxide poisoning or freezing, I was ready to go.

But then the car coasted to a stop. Another dead car. After an hour, a state cop pulled up behind us and listened to Elwood blurt out the tale of our auto adventure in Vandalia. He heard Elwood say we bought a car from Wiley with no legal plates.

Broke, soon to freeze if left on the road, we got a ride in the cop's Crown Vic back to Greenville, and he took us to the jail.

The next day the same cop brought Montgomery's girl-friend to Greenville (Janice, and she called him Luke) and she begrudgingly gave us enough bus money to make it back to Lawrence, while Monty would go back to finding bro-ken-down cars on the highway. The cop told us there had been complaints about Wiley and his gang before, although to be honest, other than "impounding" the Marlin, Wiley had done nothing wrong.

We all slept on the bus the whole rest of the trip, not talking at all.

When we got to the bus station in Lawrence, a long-haired, bell-bottomed guy came and picked up the woman in the peacoat. She wrapped her legs around him like a snake, and he carried her to his van. She waved to me as she got in.

"So that is how I met her." Nate looked at Paula, who shook her head, laughing.

"So this all happened 50 years ago?" Kip asked.

She smiled. "Your taxi is here."

"If that story was supposed to explain things, I have to tell you, I am more confused than ever."

"Think about it," she said.

Kip looked down on the street and saw a tall black guy get out of a Prius. A white guy was next to him holding a shotgun.

"I'll finish the story when we see you next week," said Nathan.

"For the Board of Directors meeting," said Paula.

"Yeah. Yeah. OK." Chubby was ready to get back home. "I'll get my stuff. You really are coming up for that meeting?"

"We'll be there."

CHAPTER 7
SPENCE'S SCRIPT STORY CONTINUED

December 1970

HERBIE WAS IN THE TANK FOR AN ETERNITY. HIS mind had exploded with detailed and specific colors and pictures from his life, past and future.

All of his friends, his lovers, his enemies peered back at him, but when he approached them, they ran away like cottonwood seeds in the wind, and Herbie chased after them, but one by one, they flew away. He was alone and grappling with an existence that, relentlessly, only existed in the moment.

After a while Herbie was in the desert, drinking from a muddy well. He could taste the gritty sand in the water, but it tasted sweet, like dried, crusty brown sugar. A mirage in the distance glimmered like the Taj Mahal, and to its right he saw a man on a camel approaching. He took another drink from the well and suddenly the sand turned to moist verdant grass, and he was sitting under a tree, on a grassy knoll, overlooking what appeared to be a peaceful and domesticated countryside. About ten meters away, a large calico cat, the size of a leopard, lay on its stomach with its paws out, staring at him. He saw the delicate hand of a woman petting the cat. She did not face him. In the distance

Herbie saw a man riding a horse. The cat got up, stretched, and walked slowly toward the man and horse. The woman turned to him. He watched the rider chasing the cat, clearly playing, back and forth as if practicing jousting or polo while the cat alternately lunged and turned away at the last minute.

Pam said to him, "If you are coming, now is the time."

~~~

Then the lid on the tank opened, and the man (who Herbie saw sitting on the horse) stared at him as he sat up and steadied himself on the side of the tank.

"Well?"

"Who are you?"

"Jumano. It is time to decide." Pam was behind him, dressed and combing her wet hair. Elmer sat on a bench near the door, bent over printouts, comparing one to the next.

"You can't – this is amazing. We have to immediately reconstruct this. We need to pull out detail. This was fantastic. We need to document this now! Fill this in. It was a 100% – you – we – all had the same – thoughts – very specific thoughts, unusual, uncounterfeitable. All at the same time. They were dream states, which makes it – I don't know – more unlikely to be some experiential common thing. I was on a camel and saw you stealing water – at the same time you saw me. Then, the camel turned into a horse, and I was chasing a cat."

"We want you and your machine." Jumano was tall, dark, thin, and moved gracefully. He had wide, bulging black eyes, bright and feverish. His nose was sharp and prominent, his hair dark and wavy. "Would you spend your Christmas in a luxurious Caribbean resort if we paid you $5,000?"

"I can't go," said Elmer. "But if you want to go, great. I'll take my cut now."

Herbie was exhausted. Pam looked washed out. The experience in that tank left him with a blank – he had nothing left.

"When?" Herbie asked.

"Tomorrow night. We will have a plane waiting for us at KCI."

"Before we sleep we need to debrief. This was the most successful session we have ever had! The three of us. We repeat and listen – fill in as much detail as we can." Elmer was insistent. "We should do it separately first and then talk. Here, listen again to what you said, sleep, and tomorrow, try and reconstruct memories, while it is fresh. This is fucking amazing. I need to figure out how to build variables, but I bet it is a million to one against any of this being just coincidence."

"We need the money now," said Herbie.

"Yeah," said Elmer.

Jumano looked at Pam, who smiled, and looked about to nod off.

"No reasonable offer will be refused," said Jumano.

"OK. Let's go," Herbie said.

CHAPTER 8
KIP RETURNS TO PORTLAND

Tuesday, July 7, 2020

KIP FLEW TO VANCOUVER, BRITISH COLUMBIA, AS HIM-self, intending to sneak back in, to confuse customs and other agencies of the government. On the flight up the coast, thinking about his time with Paula, acknowledging Paula appeared to be in her late 20s or early 30s. But her "boy friend" who looked 75 said she was really around 75 too, well, he wasn't an idiot.

The fact that he could conjure her up in his memory of childhood was disconcerfting, but really didn't prove anything. He was sure he remembered her sitting, drinking coffee with Jim's mom, in their trailer outside Philomath, when he and Jim, "scamps," as she said, were about to head out to play by the Mary's River. A pretty lady, Alice's friend. Could he trust his own memory? Was it a real memory, or just something he himself invented to make the story fit? He wondered if she was a time traveler, picked up by a light-speed traveling space vessel, who left and returned, unchanged 30 years later.

It was either a hoax or some strange juju from an unknown but possibly natural source, like what Nate seemed to be suggesting; that it was the result of eating some midwestern tree fungus. He rejected all supernatural explanations; he had seen and felt Paula's body up close – REAL close when they were drunkenly rolling around on Milana's bed back in Georgia, and she was tight, in all the right places.

It was most likely a hoax, he decided, and his memory of this Paula was muddled with or by some other memory.

Maybe Nate Schuette and the mystery woman named Paula were trying to get at *SwiftPad* by freaking him out. A bullshit story, a gas lighting scam, yes, that was the only thing that made sense. He decided that that was what it probably was.

Kip normally didn't dwell on problems. It was a survival trope that had always worked for him. He put Nathan and Paula on some back-burning element in his mind, and was half asleep when his plane arrived in Vancouver.

He had to find a way to hide if he was going to live in Portland – how the hell was that going to work? No proverbial penthouse with the other rich people. Stay on the east side of town, away from City Hall, away from the hip-rich scene in Northwest Portland and the West Hills and the Pearl, and the media. A difficult trick. Friends aside, stay out of the public glare and away from the suck-ups, gawkers, and starfuckers who were stalking him. Don't hole up in a fortress with staff, guards, and cameras and all the other crap that turns rich and powerful people into prisoners.

He hiked at night through a private, swampy duck-hunting preserve just outside Abbotsford, BC, then hiked around the shore of a swampy lake, then another five miles. His buddy Aldane Blyden, met him at a designated cross road, and then drove him to Bellingham, WA. He was illegally in his own country.

He and Aldane spent another night in a motel there, cut and shaved his brown hair skinhead-short, and trimmed his month-old chin growth into a passable Vandyke. The next morning he rented a car and drove back to Portland, a new man, so to speak.

He called Gina, a young woman whom he had personally promoted (over Heber's mild objections) as a public relations executive (she went from intern to exec with no change in her situation other than salary). After establishing with some difficulty that he really was Kip Rehain, majority stockholder of *SwiftPad*, he got her to help set up some interviews. Kip Rehain, business savant and tech business guru, had left the building, he was gone from Portland for good. He had flown back to the Black Sea from Canada, and was now on the far side of the world – in Georgia, the former Soviet Republic in the Caucasus. A beautiful young artist and graduate student on the Black Sea coast had stolen his heart, and he decided to move to Georgia. His "fiancée" Milana Shikshavalli, a brilliant sculptress and scholar, was working on her PhD in history (focusing on the Mongol occupation of Georgia) at Batumi State University. Kip planned to live with her in a modest house on the Black Sea coast. Pictures of the two of them relaxing (from his fone) popped up on internet gossip sites.

Gina figured out quickly what he wanted and within an hour he was doing an interview from "an undisclosed location" with a local Portland anchor, discussing his new life, and the love he shared with his Georgian girlfriend, whose name, unfortunately, sounded similar to the Real-Prez's most recent former wife. Milana "just wanted peace and quiet" to write her thesis at BS University. Kip was "officially" moving to Georgia.

With Kip out of the country, his new name was "Cornelius Welles" (his high school alter ego). He had long been preparing for this transformation. Over the next three days he collected the necessary IDs from his "documents guy". Gina would ensure Cornelius Welles' bank account was just barely above the waterline (maintaining the fifty-dollar minimum for free checking) at the end of every month. The article from his fone interview earlier was picked up by the online *Oregonian* and prompted an editorial bemoaning the city's loss of the "visionary entrepreneur."

All signs indicated that Kip Rehain was leaving for good. Even the online *Wall Street Journal* picked up the scent, in a long Tech section feature.

Enter "Chubby" Cornelius Welles, private dick. It had been his dream from long before he and GG's founding of *SwiftPad* to open a detective agency. He wanted to be Philip Marlowe or Sam Spade, with a sporty hat over his tightly shaved head (shaving his head every morning would undoubtedly become a problem, as his bathing habits left something to be desired).

Eventually he would hire a gum-chewing secretary who would sit in his office on the second floor of a dilapidated office building along the eastside waterfront. Settle into the role first.

He knew his old friends would be hip to his disguise. How was that going to work? How he would maintain his "Chubby Welles" facade in the face of all the interest that Kip Rehain's fake departure would generate, he didn't know.

Chubby's main goal in life now was to not be imprisoned by his money, and to stay as anonymous as possible. Set up shop and let life and adventure come. He wanted freedom from his own astounding good fortune. One step at a time, he thought.

CHAPTER 9
ALICE LEARNS OF KIP'S RETURN

Wednesday, July 15, 2020

While the details of the putsch were still secret, rumors and unattributed sources said they had done it without actually using the 25th Amendment section four, but rather section three, "Whenever the President transmits to the President pro tempore of the Senate and the Speaker of the House of Representatives his written declaration that he is unable to discharge the powers and duties…" The Democrats had the House, barely, but the Speaker insisted she had neither seen a note nor received a call about the matter from the former President. The Republican President Pro Tem of the Senate said that he had shown it to her, and she said he didn't, and they had a pissing match about it for about a month, but by then the Temp-Prez had moved into the White House. The House had sent up endless bills to alleviate the situation (conflicting bills which were as confusing as the situation itself), some of which the Senate, occasionally and barely, approved. But they all died on the Temp-Prez's desk.

From *The Fall of it All – A History of the Big Dump*

THE LONG, WINDING, UPHILL ROAD TO THE COM-pound was watched very closely, as were all other more informal approaches – the foot and elk paths as well as ancient and now unused logging roads. Alice was checking out the modest command center, where two young mothers took turns watching each other's infant while the other monitored the radar, radio channels, video cameras, and audio descramblers that pulled in feeds from the entire perimeter.

Alice had a tight operation now and she depended on the nearly 100 new people who had moved in – some small families, and others – racially mixed millennials mostly, quite a few former military guys, including an Army Ranger. A diverse crew. The movement was spreading, especially on the West Coast. The sense of solidarity was new to this generation, but they took to it and began to bond in a way that hadn't happened to a generation since the late 1960s. She had interviewed all of them and had rejected many – gently, usually with recommendations for better fits elsewhere, because the movement was growing. The main criterion was – smart, racially diverse, no addiction to social media, physically fit, and a commitment to freedom for all and to the concept that America was an idea, and not a *folk*. As the culling went on, Alice began to choose hard people, fighters, ex-military people, because to maintain a "hard" posture, it needed some hard-assed people.

Alice sat on the porch with Paula, who was lying back on the goose-down cushioned chaise longue, wearing a wool hat with a heavy cover pulled up to her chin. She had only arrived the day previously, but insisted she was feeling better. Doctor Nivel, a 32-year-old internal medicine specialist, and homesteader, concurred. She was tired. Something else, more ominous, was happening to her.

Her long-time friend and former lover Elwood was there too, grinning infectiously as he always did, the 6'8" mycologist, until recently a professor of biology at Washington University in St. Louis. He had spent his life living in and around the backward and boring southern Illinois town of Vandalia, Illinois, teaching biology and chemistry. He had recently been hired as a (35-year-old) chemistry and biology instructor at Vandalia's "New Approach" alternative high school. He had been graying his hair for years, but finally realized that questions as to his youthfulness were beginning to stir in the eyes of his fellow faculty at Washington University. As one of the leading mycologists in the country, he had a certain latitude for eccentricity. He drove the 75 miles to Vandalia and the surrounding area every couple of months. He tramped through the woods and the river banks of southern Illinois and Missouri, looking for the tree fungus that had changed his life, on that trip across the winter landscape of middle America 50 years earlier.

Paula had reduced her daily dose of fungus to about a quarter gram, and it was taking its toll.

"Wally is in St. Petersburg, can you believe it?" said Elwood. "He started a software company, and is – well – rich."

"Did he give up his citizenship? Is he working for the Russians?"

"I don't know. Sometimes he is so forthcoming, and other times, nothing. Silence."

"He never ate any, that I remember," said Paula.

"I know. He must be old."

Paula laughed. "I bet he doesn't feel as bad as I do now."

"Get used to it," said Alice.

"I have spent my life protecting and hiding the fungus from the world," said Elwood. "But now it is gone. Except for the lab in Houston, which completely fucked up the strain, I don't think there is any left. Warm Midwestern winters have killed it."

Paula was quiet. After they stole the EEG and grabbed the stash, the Hughes people tried to reproduce it in the lab. They built a huge warehouse, kept at -17 degrees Celsius. Something in the Kaskaskia River basin was different – they managed get something to grow in the lab, but it kept mutating. But they never got it right. Wally had hacked their data and sent it to Elwood.

"I am pretty sure what they grew in that fucked up Summa lab was what finally drove Hughes around the bend," said Elwood. "It is toxic shit."

"And that is what Cadez is eating," said Paula. "Do you think it was a mistake, Alice?"

Alice sat in a rocking chair next to the chaise longue, wearing khaki shorts, hiking shoes, and a green pullover. Her brown hair was pulled back in a ponytail and she looked like Jane Goodall. She started to answer, then shook her head to herself. Which mistake? "You mean how we got here? This whole thing? Of course – I just don't know what started it and if there was anything we could have done about it."

"Well, I know what I did wrong. In fact, I probably could have stopped it in its tracks. – I mean…" Paula mused.

"I don't exactly remember when we met. I think it was in the '70s at some music festival."

"It was the Oregon Country Fair. In '77 or '78…"

"Yeah – my first husband had just died – he drank himself to death up in Alaska. Jim was about five or six and staying with my sister. I wanted a complete break with the past."

"And so did I, although…"

"That is the part I never understood – you were pretty…"

"I was drunk and stoned and fucking any man I could."

"I was pretty and you know – well the revolution was pretty much a man's thing – unless you were willing to be a plaything – which I was to a certain extent. I was smarter than they were, and I ended up making most of the decisions."

"You never told me any of this," said Alice.

"Well – I was ashamed. And I was hiding, on the lam. You could find old pictures of me on post office bulletin boards all over the country. Before all that – when I was still a graduate student – I met Nate here."

"She could have been arrested for statutory rape," said Nathan.

"You were eighteen!"

"Barely!"

"I met BF Skinner and was pretty excited. I managed to stay in school and stay focused on the anti-war movement, for a while. Nate was just a kid – I was doing graduate work then and he was a goofy freshman..."

It was a beautiful summer day in the Coast Range. Alice, 70-something, looked her age, but sitting on the railing of the porch drinking tea, she appeared to be a picture of health. Paula, whose unlined face and lustrous hair looked to belong to a woman approaching her 40s, did not look healthy.

"How did things go at Ishpeming?" asked Alice.

"Just be ready. I swore – to keep my mouth shut. I don't know the details – but there is a rebellion brewing, and (V)ICE is going to land hard there very soon. Just be ready," Paula warned.

Nate looked around; would they try to storm the compound? It was an eventuality Alice had been preparing for over the last year. On the surface there didn't seem to be any reason why they would. Taxes were paid up to date, and she got along fine with the Lincoln County Sheriff, as well as the people on the Siletz Reservation. And the place used to be owned by Walt Rehain, a well known right wing old coot.

Paula was covered by a heavy wool blanket, even with the summer sun shining on her. She stared out at times listlessly, but then would appear to wake up and seem to focus. She was aging fast, and feeling the effects of it in real time.

Paula told Alice about how she went to work for Cadez, who used to be Stewart Gent, short for "del Gente". Stewart did contract consulting for the CIA and then the White House. He was later brought into the Plumbers. Never heard of him? Well, Gent was from Seattle and was a buddy of Egil Krogh, who was in law school there. There was a program that never surfaced in all of the many investigations of Watergate, mainly because it was funded by Howard Hughes.

"After the spring of 1970, I left Lawrence, Kansas, and moved to Ann Arbor, Michigan," said Paula. "Moved around a lot. I dropped out for a while, worked in a grocery store in this little town up on the south shore of Lake Superior, not too far from Ishpeming, actually – spent two winters up there with this guy – you would know him probably – a writer. No I can't tell, not that it matters a bit, but we vowed to each other, solemnly, no matter how safe or trivial it would seem, that we would never admit out loud that we had every known each other, or reveal each other's names."

"You keep getting stuck with loser writers," said Nate. "Should I tell them who?"

"No!"

"He's pretty famous."

"No, Nate. I don't know if he kept his word, but I am keeping mine. It's too embarrassing. I smoked pot and just watched TV when I was not working. We lived in a trailer court. Doublewide, at least. I swear, remember that scene from *The Shining*, where Shelley Duvall sees that Jack has typed hundreds of pages of 'All work and no play makes Jack a dull boy'? Well I found three pages of action dialog followed by three 81/2" × 11" pages of exclamation points. Typed – this was 1972.

"Spring came and I moved to Ann Arbor, reconnecting with my old friends, a lot of them 'selling out,' getting straight jobs (like what I just left) – anyway I was always very forgiving. I tried to get it back, but everybody in the movement was fucked up in some way. I did meet with some of the Weathermen who knew me from the old days, summer of 1970, after I met Nate. They were just getting started and said I would be their 'Mistress of Information.' So by October '72 I was done. Completely through with the whole Radical thing. It was really the constant expectation that I would fuck some or all of them that got me invited." Paula leaned back in the chaise longue and took a deep breath.

"I didn't, but the hostility and meanness I endured from those guys was never-ending." She looked at Nate, who looked down. "So this thing came up, related to the Panthers in Oakland, who actually, of all the groups, were the most solvent. They had money, and were looking at partners to help launder it. For which I volunteered (saying to those rich boy Weathermen that a white girl could get whatever she wanted from dem mother fuckers). Anyway, I was flying to the Bay Area, where I figured I would just vanish – just get off of everybody's radar and start over. No more winters in the woods with insane 'writers.' No more secret meetings with whack jobs." Paula looked at Nate, who was grinning as he looked at his fone.

"Then I got busted – I had a weird route, through Houston, a layover then reboard. I was pretty drunk from the long session at the airport lounge, and somebody rat-fucked me. It was probably the Feds, although for a long time I thought otherwise. But somebody planted a bomb in my luggage. I am not even sure it was a bomb; it could have been a mockup.

"Once they got me in the van, they put a bag over my head, drove me around for a while, and put me on a plane. I still am not sure where I went, but it was a very long flight. I must have taken off at Ellington Air Base, which is just south of Houston. Anyway – Latin America somewhere – probably Bolivia. I found out later it was part of Operation Condor, the US-funded promotion of right-wing military dictators. This was just before Allende was overthrown, and at the time I thought it was probably Bolivia, where Hugo Banzer was in charge. Later I changed my mind. I am sure it was Somoza's Nicaragua.

"They drugged me, pushed me under the water until I couldn't hold my breath, revived me, questioned me, made me tell everything I knew about the underground. It was amazing how well informed they were; in most cases it was obvious they were just using me to confirm what they already knew. All of the interrogators were Hispanic with accented English, but I am pretty sure they were Americans – little things they said, very inside stuff you needed to know the culture to catch, like one of them replying sarcastically to what I was saying, 'So – that's the way it is!' in a deep almost Cronkitean voice. Then I was isolated – days, saw no sun, I had no place to cover my shit, which piled up and was the only way I had to measure how long I was there. I was raped – with the bag over my head. I remember being so scared that this would be a constant gang rape, but it stopped after one time. And then, some days later – well – bag over my head mind you – a guy with a southern accent came in and apologized, took me to a room, took off my bag – he was wearing a headbag but with eye holes – and said, they would 'make things right.' He took me into a concrete cell, and made me watch them beat to near death and then castrate the man they said did it – raped me – claimed he was one of the guards, but – I am pretty sure he was just another leftist.

"The southern guy said something like, 'OK then,' as though that settled the whole matter. As we walked out of that observation room – well that is where I met Steward del Gente."

"OK," Alice knew a bit about "Stewy", because that was a story she had heard a number of times before, in fact had heard it told from different points of view by people who could not have possibly known the other people who repeated the story.

It went like this:

Steward takes her back to the US. He plays that he is the real victim of the system, even more than she. Yes, he knew what they had done to her. Yes, he knows it was horrible what they did. It was a mistake. They somehow mis-identified her with another young woman – a terrorist, he said – a former compatriot (Argentinian) of Che Guevara, a girlfriend of Pombo. She fit Paula's general description, and then of course they had her well-documented political statements and lots of film starring her at rallies. So they jumped the gun, and honored an extradition request.

"Doesn't that have to go through a court?"

"Extralegal extradition, to be more precise. This was right when they were planning the coup in Chile. Thousands were being treated worse than me," Paula said. "Yes, of course. Later, in Managua, I learned the real reason I had been kidnapped," she went on, "that the kidnapping was only a way to soften me up. It became apparent."

She went on.

"He said, 'you have to work with me.' 'What, why,' I asked? 'Work with you?'

"And so he laid it all out, told me he was with me, that together we could change things from deep inside the monster. We could help my friends – other people they were going after. They needed me to keep an eye on Nate and Elwood. He treated me really well. He didn't just release me; he nurtured me. He debriefed me."

"Weren't you suspicious?"

"Of course I was. I knew he was bullshitting me, but he didn't try to fuck me. He protected me. I had nowhere else to go and he – I was still in shock, from the prison – and utterly empty. He showed me evidence that they had not one but three agents deep inside the Weathermen, that they had ratted out my mission and anyway, we became friends, and then – lovers. That was later and that was on me, he didn't give me any trip about it, tried to nicely avoid it, but, so. We became partners. Me and Stewardo."

"And that was when he sent you back to Lawrence."

"Yes. Right away actually. He knew all about my thing with Nate, back in 1970. And that was when – he told me about what he and Elwood and Wally and a bunch of other people were up to in Lawrence – something so fucking amazing that Howard Hughes wanted a piece of it."

"We have to leave tomorrow and get up to Portland for the *SwiftPad* board meeting," said Nate.

"I know. I am coming up with you, but not to the meeting," said Alice. "I'll visit with Jim and Cynthia later. Make sure they are taking care of my soon-to-be grandchild. You sleep."

CHAPTER 10

CHUBBY'S SETTLES IN BACK IN STUMPTOWN

July 10–17, 2020

L ATER, A FEW DAYS AT MOST, KIP RENTED A PLACE above an Albina neighborhood convenience store, the "24 Hour Kwikie Mart," two blocks off of MLK in Northeast Portland. A Pakistani named Ranjit ran the store downstairs and rented him the apartment.

Chubby wanted to be in the old Eastside business area, but for now this would do. He set up his desk looking out into the street. The apartment was huge, stained hardwood floors, and almost no furniture. It was an old building with a thick floor separating the upstairs from the store below, right on the border between Portland's old black neighborhood and the new hipster village in NE Portland. The last tenants had been a couple of young lesbian dancers, who had used "the space" as a studio.

He bought a burner, a one-time-pad (OTP) "talk & text flip-fone" at a kiosk in the Lloyd Center. Take it slow, think, rebuild and renew. Break the old habits of "Kip"; figure out how "Chubby" is going to live.

It was a hot July day, no air conditioning above Ranjit's store, and he imagined that in August, while sitting around in shorts and a Marlon Brando tee-shirt, listening to reggae and fusion jazz, he would languidly swat flies away from an ice-cold watermelon. Either that or be working on a case. He reminded himself that the first thing he needed was to get some business cards. He had to figure out how to get a Private Investigator's license, as well.

But he needed to get his identity established. He didn't want to be pulled back into the *SwiftPad* melodrama.

He had saved his SIM card in his wallet all these months, so he slide it into his new flip fone, connected to his voice mail and listened to a message from Heber, who told him that Jim and G had finally returned from Asia, together, actually. They had bought a house in the Woodstock neighborhood in Southeast Portland and were having a soiree on July 17, and it was important that he come, because they had business to discuss. It was a fundraiser for *Caroline for President,* as well as an informal *SwiftPad* board meeting. Heber gave him the address for Jim and G's place, and said something about "the new team," but wasn't specific. Chubby, reluctantly, decided he would be there.

Jim and G's place? Chubby had seen the sparks when they met. After the now fabled "encounter" with the serial killer in the Portland's Rose Garden (where Chubby saved G from the murderous rapist and cut off his dick), G and Chubby gave it a last shot. It wasn't clicking, so GG left Oregon (and Chubby) over a year ago.

Now she had returned to Portland with Jim, Chubby's best friend since childhood.

It was almost 11 am. Chubby was hungry. He remembered a couple of places up on Mississippi Street, so he walked over there, and eventually wandered into the Kajun Klam. He saw Aldane sitting at a table by himself, halfway through a plate of beef ribs.

Aldane was a reggae bard from Chubby's other world, away from the money and prestige of *SwiftPad*. Lately Aldane was doing weekly gigs on the public radio jazz station, where he played all kinds of island music, from calypso to the Icelandic band Hjálmar.

Originally from St. Thomas, Aldane had come to Portland after meeting Chubby in a bar in Charlotte Amalie in the late '80s when both were still teenagers. They went "Full Rasta" for a few months, yachting up and down the Antilles, looking for King Solomon's jewels, stolen from the "Lion of Judah," Haile Selassie, the Emperor and direct descendant of Queen of Sheba and Solomon. A Cuban soldier who fought with the rebels that overthrew Selassie told Aldane that after the Emperor died, he and two other Cubans, bailed on Fidel and became Rasta in order to serve Jah. They stole a trove of rubies, diamonds, and gems from a hidden room in the Emperor's palace in Addis Ababa. It was part of the mythic treasure of King Solomon.

Aldane and Chubby, hitching rides on various boats, from yachts to inter-island barges, as well as a dope plane, followed the trail to the jewels, finally to Jamaica. Aldane and Chubby set up shop, living in ganja splendor, up in the hills above Kingston. Aldane introduced Chubby as an heir on the run, which was true. They knew they were close, they heard the rumors, and conflicting stories, even saw and held a sample of the ancient treasure trove when the shit came down.

On September 11 (an auspicious day), 1987, their neighbor Peter Tosh (the greatest reggae artist of them all) was killed by some stone-cold evil dudes who, as no one then or now knew, were really looking for Chubby and Aldane. They knew though, and they ran, up higher and deeper into Blue Mountains above Kingston. Sleeping in the lush tropical vegetation near a tumbling waterfall, they met a couple of beautiful, young Danish hikers. That cushioned the blow, and for a couple of days, Chubby forgot about King Solomon's lost treasure.

Ten days later they snuck back to their now totally trashed hootch, with a warning scrawled on the wall in what looked to be blood – Stay Away from the Lion of Judah!

Chubby left that very night, hightailing it to the Kingston airport to wait for the next flight out. Aldane stayed on, not wanting to give up the search quite yet.

Weeks later, Aldane showed up at Chubby's place out in Canby, Oregon, south of Portland, looking a little scared and very cold, still wearing his island clothes in the chilly, wet Oregon November. He stayed on Chubby's couch for a few days, bitched about the rain, but within a week Aldane had put together a salt and pepper band of Rastas and soon had high-paying music gigs in Portland, Seattle, Eugene, and Vancouver, BC.

Kip told Aldane about his recent adventures in Asia and his father's death, and that G had returned to Portland with Jim.

"So you gonna go see her tonight?"

"I kind of have to – business and all," said Kip.

Aldane shook his head. "She gonna be likin' dat – havin' bof a you on da string. She way too smart for you two." Chubby shrugged, and ordered a regular breakfast, grits, biscuits, with eggs sunny side up. Having subsisted mostly on fruit and nuts, as well as not having gotten up early enough to call any meal he had taken lately as anything other than late lunch or supper, it was his first real American breakfast in months, if you didn't count the bagel in Frisco on Paula's porch.

"Look ower dar," Aldane nodded his head toward a table near the front. "See! Man, dat's wrong," Aldane shook his head, as they watched a young white couple walk, minding a three-year-old boy with blond cornrows and a baby dashiki. "I rather they do what they gonna do, and childproof the whole damn place, than trying be what they ain't. Just don't be pretending. Sheet!"

Chubby nodded, not really understanding what he was talking about.

"This restaurant is seriously out of whack." Aldane said "whack" very softly as if it were an outrageous blasphemy. "Kajun Klam? You don't start 'C' words with a 'K' – you know what that sounds like? In a black neighborhood? Even a gentrified one like this?"

"You're eating their ribs for breakfast. Can't be that bad, can it?"

"I figgers you oughta like dat. Like be sucking on a manly dick." He pulled the nearly bare bone through his teeth getting the last of the meat off it. Aldane laughed deeply. "No. Dey close to da bone, but fo true, dey get better later. Wait too long, at night, dey too crispy. Dese could use some more heat." Aldane threw the bone on his plate, pushed it away, and wiped his lips with a paper napkin. "I don't know, it's all too..." he wiped his mouth with the paper towel again. "See – look at dis here shit. You never see a paper towel napkin in any of those restaurants downtown. It's insulting. What dey trying to say? Is this how people eat? Tink putting a couple of bloods out front make it legit?"

The black bartender looked for just a second, then turned away just as Chubby caught his eye. Aldane's impromptu review of the tavern moved the barkeep to the other end of the bar, where he ignored everyone and started moving bottles around on the wall. The bar was packed with people trying to get his attention, and people were sitting on the benches outside waiting for a seat.

"You gonna eat that white bread toast?" asked Chubby.

"You wanna to get a big skin again? What's you think dey call you Chubby fo?"

Kip was hungry though, and his order was slow coming. "I lost 35 lbs so I got some – cushion."

"Cushion? Sounds like you lost da cushion!" Aldane laughed hard and loud at the thought. "I'm just bullshittin' ya. What's going on, Kippy! You been gone a lang time right? Now you got to get right, find a woman and forget that goblin-girl you been so sweet on. She gone! You dah richest motherfucker in town – and you live like a – I don't know – like you keep your clothes in a shopping cart? You worry me serious, mon."

"I changed my name. Cornelius Welles."

"Cornelius! I like it. What's you hidin'?

"Just me. Hiding out."

"Hidin' from what? I tink it's time you be needin' real security man. Shit, every crazy motherfucker look at you and the money – they cut off ya pinky and send it to the goblin-girl. You know how many crazy motafuks are out here. I am gone. Soon. I am moving to Nairobi before this election shit is over. Maybe Memphis, first. They some stone cold motafuks there, playing the blues with AKs and RPGs. RedHats scared a dem niggas! Anyway, you white motafuks soon be shooting at each other like crack punks, no matter who win. I seen em up in da hills ober the city. You know how many body-boys Bill Gates have? And they still found him and locked him up last Thanksgivin'. Gobermint just another gang now, you got to be prepared!"

Chubby shrugged. "I really don't want to have this conversation. If it's a problem, I'll move and let you have my apartment. Nairobi? Where you going get pussy like you got right now?"

"Pussy! It's everywhere, you know dat! Let me have what?"

"Above Ranjit's, off of MLK."

You mean above Abboo's badego? I would-nuh live inna dat dutty yaad!"

"It's an island in a sea of troubles, my friend. Just what I need – maybe you too."

"Maybe? Nairobi not 'xactly – but Goin' home. Get back to the Island in yo' sea of trouble. Sheet! Memba when you run like a bitch from Kingston cause you tink you heard a shot?"

"Shot? It was a firefight! Come on – I was the only white guy anywhere near there."

Here Aldane laughed, almost hysterically. "Yeah! Yeah! Here! Here you just anotha lost white dude, in a sea of 'em. You don't fit here eder!" At this point they were both laughing. "No – I don't want yo tinky apartmin. I stay up inna hills with de lady. I dey only blood in dat neighborhood and I don't need to be runnin' eder!"

"You hearing a lot of gunshots in the West Hills?"

"Sometimes. Sometimes. Yeah. And lots a dudes, all kinds."

"Just dudes?"

"No – women too. But it ain't what you tink! Not like dat

on dey island, man! A lot of big-assed guns, and people out in the woods, building shit. Mr. Mercedes – with dey Cali plates be givin' me shit all da time – don't like me – he be yelling – 'Go back to LA, OJ!' I ain't seen him in some time. Dem don't bother me or my ol' lady. But near everybody else dey scared like house cats!"

"Called you OJ huh?" Chubby laughed.

Aldane gave Chubby the "tiny" sign with his thumb and forefinger. "You tink I'm bullshittin'? You gonna tink again real soon. They up dar, up to sompon. So, what's going on down wit you?"

"Me, I thought G and I were good, but…"

"There you go, acting like a little pussy. G and you weren't right. Maybe Jim and her end up taking yo dad's place. You tink? Then his money. You be living all-time above the tinky store for sure. Maybe you run the Abboo's store someday." Aldane was laughing deeply at the thought.

Chubby looked at Aldane. "I don't know. Maybe we were a bad idea, but – it was good for a while – that's when it got weird."

"Ebey ting a bad idea if you give it da time. It all turns to shit. And even shit it's own self ain't forever." Aldane ordered another bloody Mary.

"Gotta get right in my head."

"Yeah. Good. Just let it go, Cornelius, you got bomb shelters down dar…we gonna need to hide when the next crazy man moves into the White House. Maybe you can get me a place at you Daddy's farm."

"Yeah. Sure. After the election?"

Aldane shook his head and waved his hand, evidently no liking the idea on second thought.

"It's the other dude you got to worry 'bout – the Somoza dude – Cadez. We know all 'bout him down-eyeland, mon."

"What do you mean Somoza dude?"

"Just shit I hear. De eyeland man got to stay in tune."

"I don't know." The both sat quiet for a minute. 'I ain't gonna to work on Maggie's farm no mo,'" Chubby sang.

Aldane made a face, and shook his head laughing. Actually, they both remembered, but didn't allude to the fact, that Arlo Guthrie was playing for free in the gazebo bar along the quay in Charlotte Amalie when they met, and he sang that song. Chubby was in St. Thomas scuba diving during one of his "Spring Breaks" from college, breaks that sometimes lasted six months – his usual way of leaving school.

Aldane drained his bloody Mary. "So now you moved back here to help push up rents so that my cousins have to find another place to live, right – gentrifying!"

"Yeah – with all the little white kids with cornrows – gentrify it all up. Would you even live here otherwise?" Chubby was trying to get a rise out of Aldane.

"I don't live here now, I tol you I'm living up ober in the hills."

"With your lady and the bad dudes with big guns, right?"

"Shit. Dey gonna be rocking soon, you see!"

Chubby nodded seriously, and Aldane stared him down again. Aldane had chopped his dreads and moved back to Portland when *SwiftPad* was starting to take off about a year ago. After almost thirty years – thirty years of coming and going, living on the road, spending winters in the islands, and touring (mostly internationally) as the "spaced out Rastafarian on vibs" with The Mane Shakers, a Grunge/Rasta band with their own special sound, now, finally, Aldane seemed to have decided to stay in Stumptown, dreams of the Motherland aside. Anyway, the three big hurricanes last year pretty much put the kibosh on returning to the islands.

Aldane did about 20 hours a week on a public radio station jazz show, but his DJ gig didn't even cover rent. But they could work when the wanted, and the money was good when they did. He was staying low in the West Hills with his lady friend.

"Come with me to Jim and GG's tonight?" asked Kip.

"Can't."

"I need backup, Dane." Aldane looked at Kip, and shook his head. "I need some cover if things go south. Like you said – security."

"South!" He laughed. "No, mon, I don't think so. Not tonight, mon. I don't want to see your soul get crushed. Not tonight. I'll take da check some other time."

"Listen, Aldane, seriously, I think something is up, I need you. Anyway, I owe you for picking me up at the Candian border."

"Forget it. You gotta get your shit together," Aldane got stone cold serious. "Your friend stole the goblin-girl. She gone. He still your friend? I can't help you. Look, anyway I ain't going over to no tighty-whitey wine and cheese party tonight. Just nerdy girdies with the big glasses – they good fucks and all, but they all got too many problems. I can't be dealing with dat, I got shit to do. You take care of your own, cause I got mine. Call me when you got something definite."

"So what are you doing tonight?"

"Rehearsing. Got a gig coming up."

"Gig?"

"We opening for Jean Katon tomorrow night."

"Shit, I want to see her. You are opening?"

"The Mane Shakers baby!"

"Wow, getting the band back together!"

"We never stopped. Might be touring with her too. I am getting out of here. So I don't need yo' money."

"Something definite is coming."

"That's what I been tellin' ya! Problee out of the hills up above town. Crazy motafuks up there. I ain't shitting. Just tell me when you got da plan. I ain't saying yes to something that you don't even know what it is. Call me when you figure out where you at. Just not tonight." Aldane got up and gave Chubby a left-right combo, and pulled him for a hug.

CHAPTER 11

SPENCE RIDES HOME AFTER DRINKING BEER WITH ALISON

7 pm, Friday, July 17, 2020

SPENCE AND ALISON WALKED OUT OF THE LEAKY Faucet together, and Alison still listening intently on her fone. As they got to the bike rack, she clicked off.

"Weird. Sounded like she was with Gordy. She bailed on me in mid-sentence, said she would call back."

"Maybe she was about to fuck him?"

"Who knows? Three beers on an empty stomach! Woo!" Alison said as she fumbled to unlock her bike.

"I had to get going anyway," said Spence. "You don't live far, do you?"

"No, I...so you converted that to a SwiftPad-C2B Script?"

"Yeah, well – kind of," Spence said as he wrapped his locking cable around his bike seat. "But I have not tested any of it yet."

A muffled vibrating sound interrupted her and Alison held up her hand and again she pulled her ringing fone out of her backpack. "Hey." After about ten seconds, she shook her head. "Yeah, OK. When? OK. Yeah." She held her hand on the phone and mouthed Kayla! "OK. Is Spence coming?" She looked at Spence and pointed at the phone, then down her throat as if gagging. "Oh, I was just wondering. Yeah – yeah. OK. Alright. No, I'll try and make it."

Spence looked at Alison, grinning.

"I guess Kayla and Gordy are at Oglethorpe's house, and (here Alison did a spot-on imitation of Kayla's rich girl valley speak) 'Everything is going great!' Then there is a meeting – with Telly Haines – at Gordy's condo to talk strategy. Tomorrow morning, around ten."

"And she doesn't want me there."

Alison shook her head. "Some bullshit about separation of tasks, and loss of focus, but yeah, it sounds like she doesn't want you there. Or me at the meet and greet, just at tomorrow's meeting with Telly."

"Umm. Yeah. Good. They're at Oglethorpe's, huh? What a liar! 'Just schmoozing a customer.' Right! Gordy will do anything to keep me away from the big customers. Probably serving fish heads and haggis."

"I bet it's better than that," Alison said.

"Well, I wouldn't advertise that you and I are friends now. We are friends, right?"

"We better be! Look – I am not going to get pulled into her show, even if I have to pretend to – to be your enemy. I'll finesse it. You can count on that. I don't like her. Yes, we are friends. Pinky swear."

They pinky swore and smiled at each other.

"Good. Have fun – but watch out for Haines!" Spence warned. "He makes Gordy seem like a Buddhist monk. And I will be glad to – consult – if – you have any concerns vis-à-vis..."

"Yeah – don't worry – you will be consulting...I'll talk to you tomorrow, before I go to Gordy's. Where do you live anyway?"

"On a wooded hillside just outside of Gresham. Just off the Springwater Bike Path, so it's a nice ride from downtown. We have made arrangements for a couple of families of homeless people to camp out in our yard, use the shower, store stuff. We help them out and – they watch the house when we are gone. I'll have you out for dinner soon."

"Great. I share a little house with a woman near Laurelhurst Park. Our neighbors think we are lesbians."

Spence looked surprised. Alison smiled, somewhat enigmatically, got on her bike, and headed east up Pine Street.

Spence headed the other way, toward the river. When he got to 3rd Avenue, he cut over to Oak, and then rode down toward the Eastside bike esplanade, turned left and headed south, up the river toward Sellwood. As he rode under the Morrison Bridge, he saw the square-jawed Mullet Head – again. Only now he was straddling what looked to be an expensive, royal blue racing bike, no helmet, of course stolen. Purple wife-beater and camo long shorts on a two thousand dollar bike? Mullet Head stared at Spence again as he rode by.

Spence knew that most of the people living on the street were just shit out of luck, many having lost decent jobs. No unemployment insurance. No food stamps; it had all ended nationwide late last year. And what was work anymore anyway? If you weren't staring at a computer screen all day, you weren't doing shit, financially. Some say that schools had failed to train people to do the only decent paying work that was available. But it was evolution that failed to prepare us to sit still and stare at electronically created symbols, not schools.

And then there were the refugees – mostly white refugees, 21st century Okies, who really were "internally displaced persons" (IDPs) whose homes were either destroyed or their environment had become unlivable. They just kept coming and coming. Unlike refugees, IDPs are not protected by international law because they are legally under the protection of their own government. But the Real-Prez (and later Temp-Prez) saw no difference between IDPs and refugees. It added up to millions of homeless people.

Spence pedaled past the Tilikum bike bridge and out of the city onto the bike path. The river was down, and it had been another bad year for snow in the mountains. As he came up on Ross Island, he looked down below the bike path on a wide area of wooded land that flooded most winters. Spence could see tents and lean-tos and even a couple of yurts set up. There was a chain-link fence along the edge of the path, but Spence passed three cuts in the fence where it could easily be breached. On the beach were two scows being loaded and a couple of cabin cruisers anchored just off the shore. A police patrol boat was coming up from the city, loud speaker suddenly blaring out.

"Attention. Camping is not permitted on any land adjacent to the river or on any of the islands in the river, within the city. Remove your belongings and leave the area now. Anyone found to be setting up any structure, permanent or nonpermanent, will be subject to arrest, fine, and imprisonment."

Spence looked out at over 100 people on the western shore of Ross Island, a former gravel pit which had recently closed all of its operations. The north end of the island was hollowed out by almost a 100 years of digging, and the pit that had been dug out of the middle of the island was now part of the river. To the south the Island formed a wide circular loop, like an atoll around the center where the pit had been. Just below where Spence looked down from the bikepath, was a staging and embarking area. On the river between there and the western shore of Ross Island a little Portland Police boat, with at most four cops, pretended they were going to arrest two or three hundred people down on the bank. No one was moving.

Spence rode past Oaks Park, weaving between the streaming gaggles of hangdog men, families, mothers with infants, carrying or pushcarting their bundles of blankets and other possessions. It was an endless stream of people. There was a perceptible fear of what was coming. The fires to the east and south had come so fast that people had had no possibility of gathering the things that might make life in the open bearable. A sad and frightening mix of anger and hopelessness reflected from their faces, especially the children.

Then, coming around the bend ahead of him, in formation, a phalanx of young stone-faced soldiers. National Guard? No, they all wore an eye-catching black and green uniform that appeared to be well tailored body armor suits. ICE – no – Now (V)ICE stood for Vagrancy, Immigration Control Enforcement.

The recently augmented, enlarged, and reconstituted Federal force had expanded their jurisdiction after several close, but definitive SCOTUS rulings allowing the "emergency funding" for (V)ICE. The House had voted down (V)ICE funding as well as the authorization to "interdict illegal vagrants as de facto illegal immigrants" by a huge margin, with 1/3 of the Rs joining the rejection. But Real-Prez laughed at the Speaker's ineptitude at the Rose Garden authorization ceremony.

Native born American IDPs – homeless people – were now illegal refugees.

The soldiers were all young, mostly white, but not all. Some black faces, but few brown ones. They were double-timing up the bike path – two abreast, shields out, batons and side arms on their hips. About a third were young women, hard faced, not unattractive, and fit. Spence silently counted until he got to fifty, then stopped.

His eyes hurt from the persistent smoke. The forest around Bull Run, the city's reservoir, was burning. The towns of Sandy and Estacada had been evacuated. Mount Hood was being denuded, and with it Portland's green protective barrier. The Coast Range was burning east of Gold Beach. The Sisters Wilderness was cinders, as was the entire rim of Crater Lake. In fact everything south of Cottage Grove was largely abandoned, and burning itself out.

The homeless were constantly being herded away from cities and high-end neighborhoods. It was no longer news, just monotonous facts. The administration refused to keep any statistics about the state of the refugees, who were now being labeled, in effect, as "illegal immigrants."

Spence finally left the riverside bike path. He rode into Sellwood, zigzagging through the neighborhood, which consisted mostly of old, two-story wooden houses built in the fifties and early sixties, with small yards up against each other. Not many people out. Spence smelled dinners being cooked. Yards bare and brown, some newly placed rock gardens. Men sat out on most of the porches, many with rifles or shotguns on their laps. Six months ago when the American migrants started coming, people would set a table out for people passing by to eat, and be invited to camp on porches or in backyards – but those days were over. Everyone was hanging on by a thread. "Foreclosure shootouts" – people not leaving their homes to the banks quietly – were now a regular occurrence, and SWAT-like teams were now often hired to deliver the final papers.

There was a scattering of homeless people walking on the streets, most now headed toward the path and the supposed sanctuary on Ross Island, hurrying away from something, toward something, what they didn't seem to know. Hundreds of people were camping on the flat spot across from Ross Island, and many more were on the way. Every couple hundred yards a pair of young (V)ICE commandos on black all-terrain bikes rode by.

Spence rode his bike through Sellwood, and then across the Milwaukie Avenue bridge onto the long continuation of the Springwater bike path out to Gresham. Once he passed 205 and crossed Foster Road, the scattered campers turned into a long ribbon of tents and pull carts. Children were everywhere, crying and darting across the path.

There were cops and uniformed workers from the city, with small mobile aid stations. It was forbidden to camp anywhere along the path, but people were just waiting for dark, to set up tents, or to move into the wooded parks in Powell Butte or Jenne Butte.

Crazy was beginning to seem like a communicable disease.

Even if you were normal as they called it, if you fell off the gravy train, for any reason, even for a little while, it could mean a permanent trip to poverty street, where hopelessness was too often fatal. The convoy didn't stop to pick up people floating in life vests.

Spence didn't pedal hard, but it was a gentle uphill ride, which you only really noticed coming downhill from east to west. His house, split level, built into the hill, was hidden in the trees, with a dirt driveway. He walked his bike along the footpath that wound through a wall of blackberries. His "tenants," who had been giving each other haircuts and drinking coffee yesterday were nowhere to be seen. By mutual agreement, the tenants, two couples, their three children, and the "uncle" (who was well armed, and handled "security"), slept in their large and well-appointed tents on the lawn. Spence knew this strange and extremely uncomfortable situation could not continue indefinitely. His tenants were being targeted as "rich" themselves. Summer was easy, but winter would come eventually.

It was an old house, in the midst of being repaired. Half of the siding with natural cedar shingles, the other half dark blue staggered shake vinyl. Who cared what it looked like? Their tenants worked on it in fits and starts, but only when they needed money. Margaret kept close watch on the accounts, as they couldn't afford much of an outlay.

Before the tenant arrangement, Spence had planted motion-detecting video cameras around his yard. The flashes gave it away at night of course, but the pictures were taken and used as chips in the struggle for peace with the never-ending people wandering through the yard, hundreds of people each week. Spence had turned it off soon after the tenants moved onto the lawn.

He wheeled his bike up. The yard was empty, the two big tents had been broken down, and he noticed the lawn was brown where they had been. He put in the code to open the garage and then he saw the tents stowed in the corner of the garage. His guests were off on a trip somewhere, maybe to a clinic or possibly to the riverside gathering he had just passed. They had done that before.

"Hey man, you got a pump? My tire is flat." Spence turned around and coming up the driveway was Mullet Head.

CHAPTER 12
CHUBBY RIDES TO G'S HOUSE

6:00 pm, Friday, July 17, 2020

CHUBBY HAD A FUNNY FEELING ABOUT THIS "TIGHTY-whitey wine and cheese party" too, and wondered what was really up. Even so, from the tone in Heber's voicemail, he had the feeling that things were beginning to close in, that maybe this meeting wasn't so routine. As has been said, Chubby hadn't smoked any pot since returning to North America. But now, he was uptight all the time, and began to doubt that the sharpness in his thinking was worth the anxiety that came with it. His dad's death, and G skipping out, as well as the high-pressure work building the *SwiftPad* business had stressed him out to the point where he just didn't want to be part of it anymore. He wanted to get stoned and stay there, but he knew he couldn't, and so far he had not, but it was a struggle, with no end in sight.

Which for some reason brought to mind Howard Hughes – Chubby figured he had more money, but did he really have any money? Heber had been the watchdog and gatekeeper, and that had been fine with him, but now, he was wondering – where is it?

But that wasn't the point. Hughes had Mormon assistants who isolated him from his money and everything else. While realizing his situation was not even remotely the same as with Howard

Hughes, Heber Young, a direct descendant of Brigham Young, was now his accountant, and his business agent. He had let Heber handle everything while he had been off on a drugged-out holiday, same as Hughes. Yeah, he thought, better take charge before he ended up the same way.

Chubby was a little ADHD, not like Hughes' OCD (which was actually the opposite). His ADHD – his tendency to get distracted, and jump around from thing to thing – was not rooted in technology, as it was with so many people. He had always been that way. The flip side was he could handle a lot of ambient shit that sometimes overwhelmed other people. He noticed the hum from the street outside and could hear the conversations in the store or the ringing of Ranjit's cash register, and could keep track of it and it didn't bother him. Late at night, some of the customers stood outside the store and talked or a car pulled up with the radio blasting. Chubby's apartment was on a side street, so there was not as much traffic, but to Chubby it was a metropolis of noise, a cacophonic city, and he heard every whispered word echo off the street, and knew all the stories behind them.

He could feel it all creeping up on him. I am a self-hating neurotic, he thought, needing to break out of the emotional trap he felt he was reentering.

He felt not too comfortable going to this *SwiftPad* board meeting. But seeing – G – no matter all the shit, it would be good to see her and Jim. He could do it, and he would.

Politics. It was to be a "Caroline for President" fundraiser. Kip liked Rosie, but felt sorry for Caroline for some reason that made absolutely no sense. Everyone knew her, and the Party biggies loved her and she had money. But she seemed helpless and vulnerable. Caroline was still out there campaigning, working at it, but not liking it. In spite of her open mike blurt before stepping out to speak to the AFL-CIO convention she persisted. Still, everyone heard her say, "You left my fucking meds where? Find them, you fucking cunt, God damn it!!"

Even so, she had her fans, who were with her to the end.

But what other choice was there? Turdashian? A paparazzi a-hole.

Rosie Snyder? She was solid in coastal Blue states, and a big goose-egg in the Reds. Rosie scared the money, which meant the big liberals on TV all were counting her out, before she even got started. Rosie looked like Golda Meir after six months on the Atkins diet. Portland was apeshit for her.

And Cadez – every week he was rising more and more in the polls. Once again America was enjoying sniffing its own butt hole. Cadez waited like the spectre of doom. He was relentless, and with the only other options Caroline or Turdashian, all the Main Street money was reluctantly going over to him. So yeah – Go Rosie! But upon further consideration he thought, we are so fucked. Again.

Chubby spent the rest of the morning reading the news on a loaner eye-pad at the Klam. Now that the original *SwiftPad* was part of the *Post*, the app was just another Stupid Totalitarian Toy. Microsoft had their own "alternative reality" app, which you could download at the App Store. GIP was looking at buying one, although, as usual, it did not fit their supposite business model. Google had an open source product that mirrored the Stock Market – it had "meta-stocks" like "General Health and Well-being" and "Environmental Progress" and "International Compassion," and people actually put money into those shares, and the price rose or fell based on what was happening in the world and how much people were buying or selling the stock, using real money, or even Bitcoin – phony money buying phony stock. People were talking about *SwiftPad* in the past tense now, as if it was one of those pioneering but alas no longer relevant one-offs, like Facebook. There were so many of them out there… It had all become sugary mind candy.

The gathering at Jim and Cynthia's place was to kick off at 7 pm, and since it was a beautiful day, Chubby decided to try out the new hybrid road-trail bike he had bought that afternoon.

He left about 6:30 and rode down MLK and over to the eastside Esplanade, along the river. The bike path hugged the east bank of the Willamette River for the next six miles past the Tilikum bike bridge. Hundreds of people were walking on the path, pushing and pulling wagons and carts. A man and a woman were harnessed together pulling a cobbled-together wagon with a young girl and an old man riding on top of old clothes and photo albums. The line was endless, but it was tight, and organically well ordered. But still Kip had to pedal slowly and carefully, avoiding people. They were walking south and as he passed Ross Island, he saw that a couple of sections of the chain link fence had been torn down, and people were pouring down to a wide level area that was usually flooded in the winter but now jutted out into the river. Someone had a fire going down there and he could smell some kind of stew wafting up. He stopped and walked down to the flat area by the river.

The kitchen and the distribution were being run some very harried and tired looking men and women, most in their forties or so. They were helping people, getting clothes for the kids, shoes, while volunteer doctors and dentists helped sort out the infected, the tired, the psychotic, and the addicted. It was a human staging area, covered by a long canvas lean-to. Supplies were being loaded on to five cabin cruisers anchored off the flat. On shore, a line of sick people were waiting to board. A woman was screaming, apparently going into labor, and a group of medicos was in conference about whether to put her on a boat that was in the process of shoving off, heading downstream toward the city. Another boat was arriving.

Chubby approached a man who was managing about five large cooking pots randomly set over the well-tended charcoal fire. "Who are you?" the cook asked, with a tired, irritated scowl.

"Nobody. Who is running this?"

"Just us. We are just trying to get them through the next couple of days. But it is hopeless. People coming by the thousands."

"What do you need?"

"More. We have plenty of volunteers – but we need – money."

Chubby gave him all he had, about five hundred in cash. He wrote down a number for the *SwiftPad* admin office. "Ask for Gina. Tell her Chubby sent ya. I'll let her know. Get somebody to figure out what you need through the fall. Work up a budget. Be realistic about how much you can handle. Tell them what you need and what you are doing. We'll get you the money as fast as you ask for it." Kip picked up a flyer about their organization.

"What's your name?"

"Joad."

"Grapes of Wrath!"

"Yeah, my grandfather wanted to change it."

"Tell Gina who you are and that you talked to me. We'll get you more money and help find you a better place than this. I promise."

Chubby decided, this is what he was going to do. He would give away money, the right way, directly, looking people in the eye. Change lives directly. Make them accountable. Pull it together – step-by-step. He climbed back up to the bike path, unlocked his bike, and rode on. When he got to Sellwood, he got off the path and continued down the streets to the Woodstock neighborhood.

CHAPTER 13
SPENCE ARRIVES AT HIS HOUSE

7:30 pm, Friday, July 17, 2020

S PENCE SAW MULLET HEAD AGAIN, AND FELT HIS
heart racing. Spence had seen him along the way, but not
noticed him after passing the phalanx of (V)ICE troops on
the bike path. He had followed him all the way to his house on
the bike ride in from town. Mullet Head was walking a royal blue
racing bike up the gravel driveway. The oversized purple wife-
beater sleeveless Tee, and saggy camo shorts made him look fat
in the middle with skinny arms and legs. He pushed the mirrored sunglasses up in front of the long, unnaturally black mullet.
Up close he seemed flimsy and fragile, not really that scary. His
freckled skinny and mottled arms didn't match his shade of hair.
He walked stiffly and seemed to be breathing fairly heavily – he
was an old man! This gave Spence a small sense of relief, as he had
been thinking about what he had in his garage that could be used
as a weapon – a shovel, a wrench, or even a golf club that he hadn't
swung in 10 years. None of it was really handy and if the old guy
planned to attack him now, Spence would have to fight with his
fists. Mullet Head's long shorts hung pretty flat, but he could be
carrying a small gun or knife. Spence was unworried but alert.

"Can I help you?"

The man looked behind him. Spence set his kickstand so he would have both hands free.

"Spence – is Maggie here?"

The voice – it took a few seconds to process, because it didn't match the face.

"No – shit!"

"Can I come in?"

Spence stared at Mullet Head for a few seconds, trying decide what to do, then muttered "fuck," and waved the old man into the garage. He closed the door with a switch on the wall and they went through the garage door to the kitchen.

The old man, the Mullet Head from outside the *Reigny Deigh* office, was the same guy he had seen on the Eastside bike path by the Morrison Bridge. He had apparently followed him from his office, and waited outside The Leaky Faucet while he and Alison had sloshed down beers.

Mullet Head worked his fingers around the inside of his toupee and pulled it off. Then he began to peel off what appeared to be a dimpled latex chin. It left some little white glue splotches on his grody gray beard stubble, but the transformation was complete – it was Nathan Schuette, once a famous author, his former mentor, and the man whose former girlfriend was now Spence's wife.

Spence was still speechless, partly from surprise, but mostly from suspicion and anger at the weird stalking. If he hadn't recognized him, Mullet Head – Nate – would have seemed like some kind of psycho, a possibility he didn't completely discount, even now.

"Who was that woman you were talking to at that bar back there?"

"What?" Not a good start to our reunion, Spence thought. "It is good to see you too, Nate," Spence said with dripping sarcasm.

"Is Maggie here?"

I'm surprised you haven't already cased the place, Spence thought as he stared at Nate.

"I just got into Portland this morning," Nate said.

Spence did a double-take at the answer to the unasked question. Not this again, Spence thought. "She won't be home until later. She is teaching a class tonight." Spence cursed himself silently for telling him that much. Did he fly in on a dirty carpet? They continued staring at each other. "Start over," Spence said. "I am very glad to see you. I have thought of you a great deal lately. In fact, your name came up today at *Reigny Deigh*."

Nate nodded, seemingly unsurprised, and looked around, as if he were waiting to get on with it.

"Why the disguise?"

"I didn't want to run into Gordy or any of his flunkies, or anybody who might recognize me. This is no time for the normal routine of life. The shit is going down! It is all slipping away. How long do you think you can continue this comfortable existence?"

Fuck, Spence thought. "I know. We are being overwhelmed, and most people would rather look away from..."

"Yeah – well. This coming election might well be the last. Anyway, to be honest, I didn't know what I would find – I wanted to be sure...just wanted to check things..."

"Come on in. Let's go sit down. Hungry?"

"I am."

"Make yourself comfortable – I can heat up a ziti casserole. Want something to drink? Beer? Wine? Vodka and lime?"

"Lime? real lime?"

"At about $30 per pound." Spence laughed.

"No. Just water. Squeeze some lime though. Maggie make the ziti?"

"I did."

Spence poured a glass of water and himself a beer. He cut a lime and squeezed half into the water, and grabbed a bowl of sunflower seeds and brought them into the living room.

When did Margaret stop being "Maggie"? For the first year after she left Nate, he had called her that. She had moved out and gotten an apartment in the attic of an old house in downtown Eugene. Spence would sneak over sometimes late at night.

Spence and Nate had once been close, closer than he was with Maggie. It was 20 years ago. Nate was almost old enough to be his father – or hers. Back then, when Nate was closing in on 50, he seemed barely 30. Spence met him in Eugene, playing basketball under the Washington/Jefferson Street 105 Bridge. Full court with metal nets, dry under the freeway during the rainy winter months, and back then you could jump into a high-level intense game on the weekends. University athletes would sometimes show up, along with a cadre of street ballers who could play.

Nate used to be a slick East Coast, hippie street baller, with a fall-back-baby Dick Barnett jay, in Cons and long red hair. He bragged that he had "handled" local North Eugene high school All-American Danny Ainge on the same court back in the seventies, before Spence even got to kindergarten. It was believable too, considering how he handled the young bloods as he approached a half century. He could match up with most everybody who showed up; it was bizarre how back then he hadn't seemed to age. It wasn't just his "fall back baby!" jumper, or wily "old man moves" under the hoop. It was a full bag of tricks on D too.

That was why it was so shocking to see him now, after removing that black mullet wig, revealing a wizened, sallow-faced, rummy-eyed old man. Nate was clearly exhausted from the bike ride. He sagged as he sat down. The last 20 years had not been good to him. Had it been Maggie who had kept him so young back then? If so, why did he, Spence, feel so old now, still a few years short of a half century, younger than Nate had been when he had met him?

In Eugene, 1999, Spence lived two blocks away from Nate and Peggy, in the Whiteaker westside neighborhood. Total coincidence, if you believe in that kind of thing. Maggie, as Nate called her, was a raven haired elven fairy queen, kept a beautiful hippie house, which was nothing like what she and Spence had now. Now their house was filled with aging nouveau-Ikea-lite furniture, and Salvation Army plates and dishes set out on a rickety pine table they had picked up at a garage sale.

But back then, the house she shared with Nate was an grotto of delights, with stained glass windows, chimes, incense, India print slip covers, bodhisattva statues, and lots of kitschy extras – little medicinal bottles of Vin Mariana Cocaine wine, a tiny jar of Bayer's heroin – knick-knacks from a 19th-century drugstore soda fountain. Margaret and Nate had a big-speakered stereo that was always blasting something provocative from their vinyl collection.

When she left Nate, she left all of that, and never tried to recreate it.

Spence, 26 then, often a visitor, sometimes would sit by himself in their living room, going through the albums, reading all the liner notes, and came to know the collection better than they did. Spence slowly began to worship Maggie.

It started slowly, and merely as a half formed thought. Maggie floated around her house, sometimes wearing a Saturday Market hand-made woolen blouse, with her tight, upturned breasts peeking in and out through the loose knitting, and sometimes in long silky dresses, and other times in weathered, ass-hugging denim jeans, that her long, lustrous, almost iridescent black hair almost reached. Spence pretended that he was suddenly just noticing her. She also had been 26 a year before the turn of the most recent century. Maggie had deep gray eyes like sparkling moonstones. A goddess, in Spence's moonstruck eyes.

Nate didn't seem to understand that Spence was an invasive infestation, an encroacher impatiently waiting for his chance to pounce. Maggie became a token of power for whom they desperately battled. On her part, she really enjoyed their mysterious, musky struggle for her love. She must have somehow egged on the battle for her heart, because it thrilled her in a way she could never admit, not even to herself. Nate pretended not to notice any of this drama.

She had been raised outside of Sacramento by her mother. Her father had stayed in the neighborhood and married her mother's best friend. Maggie got out of all that a week after finishing high school, and hitched a ride with a friend up to Eugene, where she quickly got a job as a waitress at the Excelsior. She had older and younger brothers, and had been raised to be a compromiser and peacemaker, but after high school decided she was going to be uncompromising in her search for happiness, even at the cost of peace, even if that meant breaking someone's heart. She just wanted someone to love, she told herself.

She had met Nate on a rainy Eugene afternoon when he impulsively handed her a floppy knit hat he grabbed off a craft-table at an outdoor arts fair she was sashaying through. Made her look dangerous, he said. That was how it started, and a month later they found a place together near 3rd and Monroe. He hinted that he still had some encumbrances, but never really explained them completely to Maggie. Outwardly this never registered with her.

It was an old house, built in the '30s, with high ceilings, tall windows, and a rickety balcony off of the big bedroom above the porch. It came with a dirt floored garage complete with an upper room. Maggie liked school, but loved finding little treasures to put into the house, making it her own, comfortable, inviting, and filled with little chintzy ornaments and trinkets that fit perfectly into her ironically bourgeoisie vision of charm and beauty. She was happy because she never allowed herself a moment to be otherwise.

Soon after Maggie moved in, Nate got his turn in the barrel as a flamed-out disgrace, suffering an internationally embarrassing "encore dumping" on the cover of *Der Spiegel* from his former girlfriend Dagmar – and then – this was the real turd plop and splash – he lost his book contract, and was branded some kind of plagiarizing fake, possibly a panty sniffer as well. Maggie never appeared to lose a minute of sleep over it all, was into her second semester, a popular undergraduate, studying psychology, and sailing through. She smiled blithely at his troubles, and seemed to try and cheer him up as he went through hell.

Somehow, they did get past all that, and for a few years, Nate and Maggie became a sort of a power couple, as those things went in a small city like Eugene. In spite of his troubles, Nate was after all, a fixture in town, a controversial fixture it is true, but sometimes those were the best kind.

Then one day, Nathan brought Spence home, both of them smelling like goats after playing basketball all afternoon.

Nate seemed to pretend not to notice that Spence was waiting for his chance, or if he did notice, it did not seem to worry him. Maybe he was even encouraging it? Was that what made it even more of a challenge, that Nate's lack of concern was a studied insult to him, a mocking of Spence's manhood? Was he not even worth worrying about?

Vickie had recently left Spence and he was broke, working for stock in Gordy's company. Spence was pissed at Gordy for fucking Vickie, and was trying to decide whether to move to Portland. He was getting stoned every morning. Nate visited Spence's tacky hellhole of an apartment a few times, sometimes bringing weed, and even coke once or twice. It was a sad abode, a little post-breakup, alcoholic-in-training barracks, and Nate did his best to cheer Spence up. They both liked getting loaded, which took the pressure off of their constant competition for Maggie, who took a puff of pot now and then, but not so much, and besides she had school and work.

She was not happy when Nate invited Spence to move into the attic above the garage, and gave them both the silent treatment for a long time after.

And once – how could Spence forget – one afternoon, right after Maggie left to study at the library, Nate opened up a mason jar and dumped out something that he said was mashed-up tree fungus, "Ur-shrooms," he called them, which Spence ate with a shrug, and after a queasy unpleasant come-on that at first seemed like the normal, natural lysergic acid experience, turned out to be much the opposite. No sparkles, no polyopian trails, no primary colors or pristine clarity, no unification of time, space, and spirit. It was a just a reality trip, in all its mundane griminess, direct, and not even based on Spence's own conscious experience, but something else, like a tedious replay of someone else's life.

It didn't feel "like" time was in flux – time really was in flux, as direct and concrete as only the most realistic of dreams can be. It took him back in time, all the way back to the spring 1970. As Spence lay on Maggie's horsehair-stuffed, upholstered couch, he entered a world that he barely interacted with, but only watched, an encore performance, years after the show had closed. It was a real, dangerous, historical experience from the early '70s, American, with all the tacky clothes and wiggy looking hair and Easy Rider insouciance, overlaid with Nixon's tape dialogues that changed scenery from basement drug dens to bare fluorescent offices, sometimes pulling him in like an early graphical, inter- active computer game. From a Midwestern campus to a tropical, Central American penthouse, each scene appeared much like some of the early *SwiftPad* simulcasts, that had infatuated so many as the world went to shit. It was what Spence would later call his stolen life, and what Nate would call the life that was stolen from him, by accident of his more recent birth.

So when Nate took off in '99 on what Margaret called "his annual winter trip," to somewhere in the Midwest, Spence put on his full court press. When Nate returned from somewhere in southern Illinois, tired and weakened, Spence and Margaret had not yet even fucked, and that made it worse for Nate, for now he felt guilty for standing in their way.

Maggie worked constantly, as a bartender, or on the doctorate she would never finish. Nate's China novel/memoir had run out of steam, and Nate had given up trying to sell the movie rights. Spence heard their whispered arguments about money, which usually petered out as he came into earshot. Spence was newly divorced, bitter, and demonically horny. He was in love with Maggie – and with Nate too.

On that day, two decades ago, while Maggie was out, Nate told Spence, with hushed, almost tragic overtones, that the fungus was dying, and the river bank eroded, and the most of the creekside oaks were dead or had been cut. Nathan described how they had walked to the river and found two oak trees covered in the pinkish ears, that clumped together like mussels on a jetty rock, but that was it. He and Elwood looked for two more days up and down the Kaskaskia River, but there was no hint of any more of the yellow tree fungus. "Elwood and – his girlfriend – need it more than me, so I am out," he said.

Nate pulled out one last ear of fungus, a huge ass-kicking, mind-bending dose, and shared it with Spence.

That evening, Spence had quickly pounded out 50 type-written pages of vomited consciousness about Nate's experience, which now was his experience. He had felt every ebb and flow of it, and later he rewrote it, embellishing it here and there, but mostly sticking to what he had "seen" and "felt" (or hallucinated as the case may be). Some of what he wrote he was pretty sure had not happened yet.

Over the next month, as the horrible physical effects of Nate's withdrawal from the Ur-shrooms began to appear, Nate and Spence would sometimes get stoned on sensimilla sativa, listen to music, talk about history, and books, and of course Nate's book about China. It was about that time that Maggie had moved out and got an apartment nearer the University. Spence worked hard at being a good friend to the man whose woman he intended to steal. It was then that Spence and Maggie started fucking, in a way Spence had never dreamed was possible, but actually was very ordinary and garden variety.

Spence never could admit his story was based on the Ur-shroom experience, because he could not separate his experience of "imagining" Nate's story from anything else he had ever written. Nate and he would argue endlessly on the nature of creativity – can an artist really steal another's soul?

Nate still insisted that it happened to him and that Spence had stolen it (even though, how do you explain that Nate himself had written "The Last One In Is a Rotten Egg" years before Natalie Wood drowned?). Spence understood the farfetched implausibility of his having written it without influence. But was still sure he had imagined it.

Why this was important to both of them was almost amusing, because the real bone of contention was Maggie. Nate was a quarter century older; didn't he wonder why Spence would sit for hours on the porch with her, watching the people ride by on bikes, playing a game – where are they going? Where are they coming from, and why? Spence and Maggie would spin little stories; sometimes about someone they knew or someone who they pretended to know, profiles of the people passing by, on foot, in cars, or on bikes. They would concoct little comic-dramatic vignettes about them, while laughing and drinking gin in the middle of the day.

It all played out after that with tacky, tawdry inevitability – Nate rapidly started aging, and Spence and Maggie finally started secretly screwing. She made Spence stop calling her Maggie, and Nate suddenly left a one sentence note telling her he was gone for parts unknown – and Margaret just as suddenly got pregnant with Kate. Spence and she moved together to Portland and Spence got serious about *Reighy Deigh*.

They never discussed exactly when she had stopped screwing Nate.

All that swirled around Spence's mind as he and Mullet Head – Nate – sat in his kitchen. He sipped his beer and Nate drank the lime-flavored water.

"How old is Kate now?"

"She is in Boston, at Northeastern, starts classes again next month I think." Spence looked up and counted on his fingers. "She's 20 in September. Couldn't wait to get away. She got married last month. Told us by a text. Not sure how she turned out so strong and independent."

"Sounds like someone I used to know," said Nate softly.

Spence laughed. "Even so, she and her mother are not that close," said Spence, perhaps trying to close off the topic or perhaps just confirming what Nate had said.

"That's too bad – about her not being close, I mean," Nate said. "But in my observations of how kids turn out, some kind of Newtonian 'reaction' occurs against what they see in their parents. The good ones will revolt against whatever their parents are."

Spence nodded, with a slightly forced smile. "Unless it's the parents who are the victims."

Nate frowned and shrugged. "What time does Maggie get home?"

"Normally in another hour."

"Well then I better explain what I am doing here, and then get out before she gets back. I think that would be best."

"No – stay – she will be really disappointed…"

"I have to go. Look – I have missed both of you terribly. Maggie obviously – but you too, Spence. For a while we were the three musketeers – or something – but well – anyway – I am happy because as you can see, I am an old man and you two have thrived. You have a child and a home. That is something I…" Nate trailed off.

"Your name came up at *Reigny Deigh* today," Spence said. "They want that story, a script – that – how shall I put this – that we uncollaboratively wrote."

"Those Ur-shrooms we ate, were not mushrooms. It was a tree fungus. Ur-shrooms sounds more psychedelic."

"I know, the Golden Fungus. You told me how you found them on a road trip from New Jersey to Kansas. There is a fantasy website with incredible artwork and crazy stories all about it. We have thought about using it in ad campaigns at *Reighy Deigh*. It offends everyone – as either exploiting a religious experience or promoting drug abuse. There is no middle, so we leave it alone."

"Right. Nobody really knows the truth of it. But you do. I know that experience inspired your screenplay treatment – You could not have stolen it in the usual way people steal ideas," said Nate.

"I am not sure I know what you mean," said Spence. "We need more to drink if we are going to have this conversation."

"OK. I don't want to have that conversation either. We don't have time. I want to get out of here before she comes home – for that reason. I saw Gordy come out of the building this morning. He doesn't look too good. I am not sure why…"

"Are you back for revenge?" Spence realized that could be taken in a number of ways. "I mean – over the *Sierra Sparks* deal?"

Nate laughed. "Revenge! Ah yes, there is that. *Sierra Sparks*! Please, give me a break! I hadn't thought about that – but, I did think you screwed me on the residuals."

Spence looked away and took a long sip of his beer. He was still a little looped from his drinking with Alison. "It never got syndicated. There were no residuals."

Nate looked at Spence for a bit and took a sip of water. "Anyway, I am happy you and Maggie have made it. A kid in college – still living under one roof. That's as good as it gets. No – this is way beyond that. Remember when we used to talk about bigger shit?"

"Yeah…" Spence waved his hand to change the subject and shook his head. "Actually, I was planning to try to find you again. Not like I did before. I mean tonight – I really was going to talk to Margaret tonight, and see if maybe she had been keeping in touch with you…"

"Why? Let me guess – first I can say that we have not been keeping in touch. She wouldn't have known where I was."

Spence smiled and shrugged. "So we both wrote the same

story because of the fungus telepathy? Is that what brought you here, like Satan suddenly popping up in Faust?"

Nate ran his fingers through his thinning reddish-white hair. "Yeah –we have a kinda Faustian bargain here, eh? *Reigny Deigh* is looking to grab the *SwiftPad* account – right? And they want to make a movie with my script, "The True Account of the Magic Mind Melding Machine." Right?"

"I didn't steal your script, and we would never use that title," Spence said.

"Excuse me – I meant our script."

"I am not stupid; I know it can't be a coincidence we both came up with the same story. I guess it must have been me that stole it, because that shit definitely couldn't have happened to me. I wasn't born then."

"So you now believe it was the Ur-shrooms? Or the Golden Fungus?"

"I guess. Either that or you are insane and invented your past to match my fiction – but to what end?"

"As you said, revenge."

"With that mullet, and phony chin, of course."

Nate smiled. "You experienced it just like I did. Because what is experience but another word for memory? And if you have the same memory that I had, then how is it not your experience too?"

CHAPTER 14
CHUBBY ARRIVES AT GG'S HOUSE

7:40 pm, Friday, July 17, 2020

THERE WAS STILL PLENTY OF LIGHT, WHEN KIP GOT to G's house. The Woodstock neighborhood had no nearby shops to sip coffee while waiting for other guests to show. Hired guards on bikes (that a *SwiftPad* story reported made very lucrative salaries) seemed to be everywhere. Two cruised by checking out Kip, but not approaching him. They were on foot too, dressed as civilians but alike, moving around and keeping lookout, and one of them stopped Kip, and asked him his business. Kip cooperated, rather than go into his usual flight of obstinacy. He noticed them all around, like hotel dicks, or secret service agents, staying half hidden in order to keep the neighborhood comfortable for its residents.

He felt like he had abeyant jet-lag, that his recent travels were only now catching up with him; at least that was his excuse to himself as to why he was suddenly so tired. He was sure that his internal biorhythm clock was dimly flashing "it's late, go to sleep."

"No more drinking," he told himself. "No pot, no nothing." He thought if he told himself that enough, he might be able to make it true, might be able to give it up without giving it up, to have a relaxed, cozy relationship with intoxicants, but still avoid them. It was just that he was dreading seeing her again, and the more he thought of it, the more he wanted to get high. He had been back from Istanbul for almost two weeks now, so he realized it was probably just anxiety at the thought of seeing her again. He had not had any pot for more than 10 days and his brain never seemed to turn off.

He was surprised when he saw the house – it was so normal. The neighborhood was pretty tony all and all; even the most modest of the houses ran an easy couple of million dollars in the current inflated market, but it still seemed very Norman Rockwell–like. Some of the houses had been built in the thirties. The streets, lawns, fences, and sidewalks all looked clean, trimmed, well painted, and repaired.

But it felt wrong. He knew Jim and G could easily afford a mansion overlooking Lake Oswego, or one right on the river, or a high-priced Frank Lloyd Wright–like architectural cathedral up in the hills, but he suspected this was some primal urge for a real "home" where people lived, a place with flesh and blood history. Jim had grown up in a two-room trailer with his mom, and he knew G came from a status-driven middle-class environment outside DC. So was this some kind of compromise that they came to?

When Chubby was a kid, he had always lived away from people, never in a neighborhood, as his dad had been a wealthy recluse, who was generally hated by everyone who knew him. So they lived in a big, old, drafty house a couple miles up a dirt road. Now Chubby liked living in the middle of the city, close to the street. He still missed his walk-up dive apartment on 11th and Stark. When his photo lab got ransacked by some puke whom he had probably befriended and then later forgot, it didn't faze him. He decided he would stay close to the street, close to people who really were struggling. He had never cared about anything that he owned. He never took care of his toys; he played with them until they bored him and then he left them in the yard to rust. His father would punish him and explain the importance of thrift and of maintaining what you have, but it never dented his behavior. It was all unnecessary shit. Things had never meant anything to him. And he didn't fear for himself; he lived every day like it was his last, and at the same time like he would live forever.

He was careless, but not with people; at least he tried not to be. Chubby drew strength from helping broken people who were hurting. It recharged him.

He would probably have fit in better in the Middle Ages in Europe where a rich guy like St. Francis could give everything away and achieve a fulfilled life. An ascetic who lived among the poor. Chubby loved the street. He looked for opportunities to step in front of bullies. Chubby patrolled the outer edges, taking on the little Al Capones, the bullies and grifters looking to take advantage of the weaker people, but as soon as the lights came on and the circus came to town, he was gone. He didn't like the spotlight. He stayed in twilight, watching. All this sort of went through his mind as he looked at where Jim and G had decided to live, and it made him realize that none of it mattered, we were all driven to do things by demons we couldn't control. He took some comfort in that.

He walked his bike up the driveway along the side of the house, parked it next to the fence leading to the back, and left it unlocked.

He reached over the gate, unlocked the latch, and went into the back. It was a medium-sized yard; in the far corner was a raised tomato and pepper garden recently planted with starters. An eighty-year-old oak tree billowed over the yard where the patchy lawn seemed verdantly alive but ancient. A couple of comfortable, well-cushioned lawn chairs and a recliner were haphazardly arranged around a cleanly cut section of a Ponderosa pine, solid, lacquered, perfectly flat, two feet high, four-foot diameter table. It glimmered in the setting sun like it was encased in amber.

"Hey, Kip." He turned around. There she was. Neither of them spoke, but just stared at each other. She was six or seven months' pregnant. After what seemed like a long time, G came over and hugged him. She pulled back and they stared at each other. They both smiled at the same time.

"Come on in," she said. "Jim is out picking up a few things – you are one of the first ones here." He followed her in the back door, then through the big kitchen, past a double-sided counter and eight-element gas range, a high doorway, and then into a spacious high-ceilinged living room. Wood floors, with a couple of Persian throw rugs, warm, deep-cushioned chairs and a big sofa.

A slim woman, early forties or so, with a silverish ponytail, gray sweater, and fashionably faded hip-hugging jeans was watching CNN. She looked at him with a wan smile and a sly wink. It was Paula. He had just seen her 10 days ago, and she had changed, but you would have thought it had been 10 years looking at what gravity had done to her, and the tiny wrinkles that had recently spread around her eyes.

The Republican presidential candidate Ben Cadez was haranguing a group of his supporters in Boise Idaho, and the CNN talking heads were in the upper corner of the screen droning on about delegate counts. G waved her hand in disgust at the TV and Paula reached over to the clicker on the coffee table and switched it off.

"Kip, this is Paula Flayer." G looked at them both expectantly.

"Hi." She stood, "I have heard so much about you."

"From who?" She looked different, more demure and soft, seductive even, as she seemed to cast an nonthreatening, slow mosey–like manner. Yet, something had definitely changed, she could no longer be mistaken for a young woman. She wielded less of an edge too, as if she might have recently turned 40 and embraced it. The vertigo Kip had felt in Georgia hovered nearby, under control still, but close. Apparently, he thought, Paula and he were supposed to pretend this is the first time we have met. He fought his suspicions and fears with a warm smile.

"Oh, I am a friend of Alice Hunt," Paula said.

"Oh, Well, cool. So you probably do know who I am..." This was ridiculous, but Chubby decided to let it play.

"Sort of. I know you and her son were best friends since you were boys. It's wonderful that you are still friends."

"Yes it is." Chubby looked at G, but she was looking away. Chubby stepped toward Paula and they shook hands and she smiled brightly. She is really playing this for the upper balcony, he thought. Chubby acted a little startled by her friendliness and seeming familiarity, because now he could feel G staring at him, almost suspiciously. The whole scene was making him apprehensive, but he saw no chance to buttonhole Paula and ask her what game she was playing, or even what had happened to her. Did she get made up to look 10 years older? Looking closely, that didn't seem – possible. G took his arm and sat him next to Paula, while she sat on his left. Is G trying to set me up? What would she think if she knew Paula's real age?

"Would you like a beer or something, Kip? The bar is pretty well stocked..."

"Not yet," he said. He suddenly realized that tonight was not the night to be announcing to these people that he was changing his name to "Cornelius 'Chubby' Welles." Or maybe it was the perfect time, but he didn't want to deal with all of the questions.

In an old SNL skit, Bill Murray was the talent agent and wanted Rodney Dangerfield to change his name to Chubby Welles. Was I the only one who realized the whole thing was a rip on Orson Welles, Kip wondered.

"How about a lemonade? Touch of vodka in it? G gave him a familiar, conspiratorial look. The last time he had seen her, she was headed through the gates at PDX, after a night of loud, unrestrained banging on his childhood bed, after an afternoon of slow passion in the cold flowing water of a nearby stream, after a picnic lunch on a nearby moss-covered rock. But all that was almost two years ago. She was insatiable back then, a sex machine, and now she was a madonna.

"Sure, just a touch," he said, immediately regretting it.

"Cynthia tells me you have been traveling in Asia," said Paula. "When did you get back?"

"I went over to the Republic of Georgia on the Black Sea," said Kip with counterfeit matter of factness. "I had some uh, business."

"Oh," Paula answered, while nodding seriously. G watched him. Business? For eight months?

"You know what sucks?" G said. "It sucks to give up normality. I should live in a condo downtown, where I could sneak out into the city anytime I wanted. I imagined it would be friendly anonymity here. Professorial. Soft cotton. Low impact nerdiness. But it doesn't take long for the word to get out. People look at me differently now..."

"Why?" Paula asked.

Cynthia gave her a 'be serious' look and giggled with embarrassment. "I buy my clothes at outlet stores. We drive a Subaru. But it doesn't fool people for long."

"The black Converse sneakers are a bit of a giveaway."

The three of them laughed.

"Yeah. I am almost done with punk. Almost, not quite. Still, call me Ms. Suburban Milquetoast. I am very ready for this little girl to arrive. After, I will settle and get serious. Can't now though, for some reason." G smiled.

Kip realized Paula could possibly have kids, even grandchildren. All he knew about her was she had had a pretty wild time in her early twenties, if Nate's story was true. That and the pretty wild time she had with him and Milana in that big feather bed. But now for some reason, that seemed ages ago.

They chit-chatted about the gentrification that had changed Portland, turning black people out of the homes their families had lived in for generations. It was déjà vu all over again for Chubby, having just had this conversation with Aldane. In 1946 the great Vanport flood washed away the homes of the recent black migrants who had been building "Liberty Ships" during the war. Most ended up in the Albina neighborhood, where Kip lived now above Ranjit's store. Gentrification had flooded the neighborhood with boutique stores, craft breweries, coffee shops, vegan restaurants, and young bicycle-riding hipsters. An even lighter shade of pale.

"Why didn't you get in touch when you got back? You could have crashed here while you look for a new place," said G as she handed Chubby a spiked Arnold Palmer.

Wouldn't that be cosy, he thought. "I already found a place."

"Oh. Where?" G looked at him intently.

"Above a convenience store, over off of MLK."

"Umm," she said.

He put down his drink. "I don't even know if I am going to stay in Portland. I almost stayed in Georgia. The Republic, not the state."

"Yeah, I saw that interview you did, and saw something in the Wall Street Journal," said Cynthia. "What is that all about? It seemed like you were still there."

"Yeah. I am still there, officially anyway. I am hiding. Did you not see the news? Gina down at the office helped me. I am trying to stay under the radar. I don't want to get back into the business. I have a new name. Well, old for you – Cornelius Welles. See?" Kip showed G and Paula his driver's license. "I shouldn't be here. Have you invited any press?"

"Absolutely not," said G. She looked at him with a strange mix of love and pity.

"Well, don't worry about it. I know everyone here will know it's me. Play it like it's just a one-off, back for the party, but otherwise, I am out of here."

"The *Reigny Deigh* PR people are here," G said matter-of-factly. "This is just a joke anyway right, Kip?" She noticed he put his drink down. "You don't like the Arnold Palmer?"

"No. Sorry – I am trying to climb on a wagon, but it keeps moving."

"Here – taste this," said Paula.

"Umm." He took a tiny taste without thinking. "That is good. What is it, a White Russian?"

"Kind of, except no alcohol. I added a special concoction, which I take for my – my complexion. And native lore says it's good for digestion. You can stay on your wagon now." Paula smiled. "Go ahead, I'll make myself another."

Kip took a healthy sip, and instantly felt warm inside, but then there was a mini explosion behind his eyes. He felt like he just stepped out of the cold surf into the sun. He drained the drink Paula had given him. He could feel it permeating through his body.

At that moment, a fakey, louche-looking guy came in, wearing green gabardine pants, black loafers without socks, and a purple camouflage print cotton shirt. It was Gordy, followed by Kayla and two young men in beards and matching black shirts, jeans, and white aprons. The young men brought in a large cake decorated with "Welcome back, Cynthia and Jim."

Heber went over and greeted them and directed the young men into the kitchen, followed by Kayla. Gordy moved to the other side of the room.

Kip looked at G, who shrugged. "This is a fundraiser, so Heber invited some hitters. That is Gordy Lobetts, who owns *Reigny Deigh* – you know – the big media company over in the Pearl. Heber hates him, but I think Hariet insisted on inviting him in order to tap his money. Do you know him?"

"No." Kip looked at G, who he felt was reaching out to him, feeling a love from her he had never experienced ever in any of their tumbles. He tried to think of something to say to her, but he couldn't. She looked away, and he was able to breathe again.

"*Reigny Deigh*. Yeah, OK, I think I know a guy there – Spencer – something – Stromborn. Yeah, Remember, I invited him to join the board back in the early days?"

"Of course I remember." Cynthia stopped and looked back at Kip. Kip was overwhelmed, but somehow fought to hold it together. "He turned us down. Aowch! Oh well." G made a funny painful face. Kip laughed, fighting back tears. "The woman who just came in the room – she works for Gordy. I am not sure what she does. Stanford Business School brat I think."

"So how was Georgia," asked Paula, apparently for G's benefit.

"It is a beautiful country," said Chubby, trying not to smile at Paula. He didn't know if G knew about Paula coming to get him. It appeared she did not. "A little dicey. I speak decent Russian and many educated people there do too..."

"Right – didn't Gorbachev's foreign minister come from there?"

"Shevardnadze. The West loved him. Very nasty man. Stalin was from Georgia too, and Beria, Stalin's last executioner. All real shits. But I loved it. I was happy there, the country is ancient, but still unspoiled, the climate is perfect– but things got a little complicated..."

G – Cynthia – feigned disinterest, but he could see the wheels turning behind her eyes. Then she smiled at him with a little twinkle.

Kayla, who had been greeting some people at the door, came over.

"Hi, I'm Kayla Holmes; can I call you Kip, Mr. Rehain?"

"There is no Mr. Rehain. My name is Cornelius Welles."

Kayla wore her dirty blond hair up, which made her cheeks look fat, and now they got red as well. She hesitated, then said, "Sorry...I thought..."

"Oh, I was just joshing you. It's nice to meet you. You can call me Chubby, in fact I would prefer it. But if you want to live, this conversation never took place. I am not here, capeesh?"

Kayla stared at him, frozen.

"You work for Heber, right?" Chubby asked.

"Well – actually, I was hoping that I would work for Kip Rehain. But..."

Kip smiled. "Just kidding. But keep me out of the press, OK?"

She broke out into a flirty smile. "Absolutely. Absolutely! Did Cynthia tell you?" She stepped closer, looking over at the door every 10 seconds or so. "We – *Reigny Deigh* – are submitting a proposal to manage the media relations for the *SwiftPad*

Foundation – you know – that was set up…we have an idea – we want to make a feature-length – well – it's kind of complicated – we can talk about it…"

"Foundation? Yeah, I recently heard something about a Foundation."

Kayla did a double-take. Kip could feel her trying to read him. Her thoughts were transparent somehow – it was weird – like he was able to read her – *What foundation! Was this guy for real? How could she get him? He wants to fuck me! Yes!* Something – he turned and looked at Paula, who had been sitting quietly. She was looking away from him but smiled as he turned to look at her.

"So are you going to discuss the company bio production tonight?" Cynthia asked Kayla, somewhat sharply.

"No, no – we will do that on Monday – my assistant Spence is working on the details now. There is so much work that needs to be done," she continued, slowly, "I just wanted to give you a hint – don't tell Gordy I told you – Pleeze!! We want to use the C2B neural interface. See if it really does work with your scripting language? Because – well – we are thinking of combining…"

"We? You and Spence? Or Spence?" Cynthia looked over at Kip, who was lost.

"I am hoping tonight we can… you know…get some ideas about it. I would love to sit down and talk about it. See if it is a fit."

That's nice, thought Kip. Get ideas. Make it fit. He smiled. Shit, this bitch is – so easy to see through. He nodded. If I can read her, then…

"I brought you a refill," said Paula, handing him another White Russian, "it's the last of it." She smiled at him. He took a deep sip and discovered he could hear and see thoughts and the rising and falling of emotional intensity coming out of every person in the room. Oh…and he felt strong, and desire, what powerful feelings! He could see clearly who wanted him too. He looked at Paula, whom he couldn't read at all. She smiled again.

Kayla leaned in toward him and said sweetly, "My geography

is weak, but isn't that area you were in dangerous? Wasn't it scary?" Chubby sat down next to Paula, on the couch. He relaxed and felt at ease for the first time – in so long.

"Scary things are everywhere, don't you think?" he said. He smiled at Paula, who had pulled her legs up under her and put her arm on the back of the couch, almost behind him, leaning in, coyly turning her head just a bit, so as to look at him slightly indirectly. Was she really that old? Of course she was. He understood now. He took a deep breath and could feel each oxygen molecule surging through his blood stream.

Kayla suddenly became nervous, as both Chubby and Paula turned and gazed at her. She nervously moved her hands and arms, while forcing a smile. The doorbell rang, and Kip could feel the relief flood out of her, as she walked away to greet the new guests. It was Jim, whose arms were full with grocery bags. Kayla grabbed the bags, almost dropping them but recovering, and took them into the kitchen.

Jim and Kip stared at each other and for an instant, some level of hostility flashed in Jim's eyes. Kip snorted. Even when they were kids, their friendship was unsentimental and competitive.

"Hey! Chubby, you're back!"

He looked at Jim.

"Jim." Kip got up and sized him up.

"Chubby, huh?"

Kip gave Jim an up and down look. "Yeah – that's right. It's Chubby. Kip is gone. Actually Kip is still in Georgia. And now Chubby's back." They did the bro-hug – the right-on, right-handed black power hand-clasp, with the left hand on the shoulder, held for two seconds.

"Yeah, I guess it's me now, huh? I mean, now I'm the Chubster," Jim said, as he leaned back and looked at his old friend. He had been dreading this moment, yet Kip could see Jim's happiness matched his own. All that was between them – Cynthia – suddenly united them again. Kip was happy to see him. "I put on a little weight," Jim continued. "But you look...you look almost ripped."

"He looks great, doesn't he?! I have never seen you so..." G carefully, hesitantly, put her hand on Kip's shoulder. All three were quiet for a bit. Paula was watching them all with narrow-eyed bemusement.

"Can I bring my bike around the back? I didn't lock it," Chubby said. They stared at him quietly, as he nervously backed toward the door. "I'll be right back." He smiled and walked out the front, half thinking to get on it and ride away, before it got too dark.

CHAPTER 15

NATE'S ACCOUNT OF EVENTS LEADING UP TO HIS KIDNAPPING

8:30 pm, Friday, July 17, 2020

S PENCE WENT INTO THE BACK OF HIS HOUSE AND returned with a stack of typewritten pages. Nate took the pages and looked at them. "Did I write this?"

"I think so. You said you did."

Nate leaned back and looked through the faded, coffee-stained manuscript, and shook his head.

"Go ahead and re-read it, out loud. Does it still make sense?"

December 1972

It was a month after Nixon had won reelection, and while everyone was slowly coming to grips with the reality of another four years of Dick, I was over it. I didn't know at the time how much rat fucking the Nixon campaign had done to spike McGovern's chances, so when Paula showed up dressed like a Junior Leaguer, in black tights and a plaid skirt, and with a check for my bail in tow, I figured I needed a change of scenery.

I had been charged with malicious mischief for throwing a rock through a cop car window back in the spring of 1970.

Bail was high, and I didn't dare call my parents, at least not until I really, truly had no other options. I suspected it was "secret testimony" that dragged me into it, perhaps from someone I knew.

Of course that probably meant Wally, my partner on that night run through the curfew gauntlet, but I refused to believe he would rat me out. Almost as soon as I was booked, though, a local drug lawyer, "Kid" Wendel, showed up with Paula Flayer, the woman who got me addicted to sex, and who I hadn't seen in two years. They posted bail for me. Paula was almost unrecognizable, dressed like a sorority girl. She had not owned a dress back in 1970, when I knew her.

Anyway, our sweaty affair was a distant memory. I was no longer an unfucked freshman, but about to graduate. On our way back to my apartment, Paula made it clear in a friendly way that she had a new beau, and that she certainly wasn't there to support the "revolution" anymore, but felt it her duty to keep me out of jail. And she had a business proposition for me. When I wondered why (I wondered a lot of things about Paula at that point), she said she felt she might have misled me back then in the spring of 1970, and she still felt a "connection" to me. And oh, by the way, her business proposition was that she wanted me to help her buy the ESP system that Elwood and I (but honestly mostly Elwood) had installed in his Kentucky Street house. She was working for some technology company that wanted it. She had talked to Elwood too, although, apparently he wasn't too high on selling. Elwood and I didn't have a clue what it was we "owned" anyway, or how much was his, and what was mine.

We advertised ESP, (Electro-Sensory-Pipe we called it) and invited participants to sign up to try it. By advertise, I mean we put up mimeographed signs on telephone poles and on bulletin boards in the Student Union and in Fraser Hall, which housed the Psych department. There were about five of us who had raised the money for the materials and built it. But only Elwood and I knew its real purpose. And my old dorm roommate Leone talked about it constantly during his radio call-in show for KUOK, the campus AM radio station run by the School of Journalism.

Elwood had discovered a yellow tree fungus next to a small river in southern Illinois during a car trip from the East Coast to Kansas. Elwood and Paula felt some level of "measurable" synchronicity of thought and feeling when they ate the fungus together. Elwood and I were trying to prove what was happening when we ate the fungus, after Paula disappeared after the summer of 1970.

But now, in December of 1972, Elwood had been going back every winter since that January in 1970 looking for tree fungus. It was still sort of a secret, although I am sure I had mentioned it in conversations, but it didn't elicit much interest from anyone. Even Wally, who was on the trip with us, and heard us talking about it, has never been interested. One thing Elwood discovered was that the tree fungus only grew in winter. He had become quite an expert in mycology, the study of mushrooms (and other funguses or rather fungi). So the two of us planned to head back across the country (in Elwood's car) and stop in Vandalia, and search for the fungus. I hadn't eaten any of it in over two years.

After I was released from my one-day sequestration in the Douglas County jail, Paula and I sat in my apartment, drinking wine, and talked about her "conversion" as I called it. She told me that her experience of acting as a courier for the Weathermen had proven to her that they were deluded, and in some cases, psychotic. One of them had tried to rape her, and none of them ever took a shower. Most of them came from money, and their "philosophy" really saw the poor and working class as props and ultimately as impediments to revolution. They looked to Che and Fidel, both rich kids like themselves, as their models. So she disappeared, to hide out from them.

"I got hired by Summa recently, which has a division looking at all kinds of psychological research. I was intrigued. More interesting than finishing my doctorate."

"So when did you start that?" I asked.

She suddenly seemed evasive. "Actually, only since last month."

"What were you doing before?"

Paula's face changed for an instant, like she had suffered a subtle shock. "I went traveling in South America last year," she said. "Until recently, actually."

"So, you are here to buy our ESP machine," Elwood said.

She nodded. I wasn't surprised she knew about it, although I should have been. Paula said she lived in Houston now, working for a strange psychometric institute called Summa. But there was a lot she wasn't telling me, I could see that right away.

Then it got interesting for me. She took my hand and leaned over and kissed me. It was pretty strange for me. Our previous romance wasn't really a romance; back then there was no doubt that we were going to fuck, so, why be coy? We just jumped on it.

Anyway, when I tried to get more romantic, she gently pushed back, and said, "We have all night. Let's take a walk in the snow." I didn't ask her about her boyfriend.

Finals were over, and most of the students had gone home for the holidays. But the snowstorm had covered Lawrence, Kansas, with a soft white blanket. It was quiet outside, no cars on the road, and the only sound I heard was my boots crunching the new-fallen snow. It was about 8 pm, and we ran into a group of people, a couple who I knew, KC suburbers who hadn't left town yet, sledding down 12th Street, between Ohio and Tennessee.

Paula and I borrowed a couple of cafeteria trays and went down the hill together, hugging and kissing.

"We don't know each other very well, do we?" I said.

"Well – I am still basically the same as back then." She nodded her head toward her old basement apartment, where I had barged in when running from the cops. It was two houses down from my apartment on Ohio Street. She made a face. I laughed.

Looking back it is hard to imagine how intense and serious the prospect of love with someone you had known before but haven't seen in years can be. And how desperately late in life 22 can seem, when you are 22.

"I still haven't tried the 'Electro-Sensory-Pipe.'"

The ESP ran between two sensory deprivation tanks, the size of coffins, in a garage in the back of Elwood's house on Kentucky Street. Elwood had built a platform around the sides of the tanks and tightly sealed to the edges a polyurethane sheet that was then nailed into the pine foundation planks. He pasted thick styrofoam all around the sides of the tanks. A little stepladder allowed entrance from the top.

"You've heard about the ESP apparatus, huh?"

"Well, I keep up with what is going on. Still occasionally think about finishing my doctorate. Somebody sent me one of your flyers. Actually..."

The tanks were kept at 98 degrees, and were filled with dissolvable salt that made it nearly impossible for a human body to sink. Sound was muffled and all light blocked. It was not done haphazardly, but was measured and monitored by Elwood.

"Actually what?" I pushed my hand up her plaid skirt and under her tights, but she pushed it away slowly, shaking her head, laughing.

Elwood had also designed a helmet that combined insulated electrodes with muffling earphones, an encompassing, black, completely opaque visor. The electrodes were positioned to attach to 28 points spaced around and on top of the skull.

"Actually, well – I want to see it. Maybe – try it?"

The electrodes came together into two bundled wires that snaked down into a box, which was connected to what looked like a small screen and printer that recorded the varying levels of the signals. Tank A received signals from Tank B. Or (flipping a toggle on a junction box) – A sent, B received. He also had small speakers and microphones in the tanks.

"I ate it a few times, but stopped because it made me sick. Elwood ate it almost every day," I said.

Paula and I walked over to the Kentucky Street house and just went in. Elwood was sitting at the kitchen table with a dark-haired guy, who looked Hispanic.

"Hey, Stew!" Paula separated herself and walked over and kissed him. Elwood was reading what looked like a business letter.

"Did you read this?" he asked me.

"No," I said, still confused, but having been abandoned by Paula before, I shrugged it off.

"It is an offer from Summa for our gear, and any notes on the research."

"Oh," I said. "Well, what is the offer?"

"$5000, plus a consultant's fee to help set it up."

"Where? When? Why?" I asked.

"We will discuss that when Elwood signs," Paula said.

"Nate is part owner too," Elwood said.

"Well," Paula smiled at her friend Stewart, "You two can work out the split among yourselves, and who is the main rep. We need an answer, today. Now actually."

Elwood looked at me, then said, "It says here something about a 'No compete clause.'"

"That means you can't rebuild it without paying us. We intend to patent it, which I assume you haven't bothered to do."

"No," said Elwood, looking at me.

I nodded.

"OK, we'll...have to think about it," I said.

Stewart stood up and was followed out by Paula, who didn't look at either Elwood or me.

"No – we need an answer now," she said.

"Or what?" I was a little pissed at her attitude.

"I am going back to my hotel," Steward said. Or whatever his name was. I looked at Stewart and he was shaking his head. "You two are making a serious mistake."

"Where can we get in touch with you?" Elwood asked.

"You can get in touch now. If you need to talk, go into your garage with the equipment. What is the issue? Money? Credibility? You can't do credible scientific research. You need to maintain a level of control – it will still be your baby – academically yours – use it for PhDs, etc. The $5000 is a bonus. Now you can hold us up with consulting fees – name your rate. But we need to know now."

I looked again at Stewart, who looked bored.

"Why the rush," I asked.

"We have a customer who is impatient."

"So what if we say no and a week from now, come back with a counter proposal?"

"This is getting us nowhere."

Paula unzipped her coat. "Stew, I am going to stay and try it out. Right, Nate? That is what we planned. How long will it take?"

"You want the whole deal? It will take some time to set up. It's midnight now. Don't want to wait until tomorrow?"

"No," she said.

"OK, I'll be back in a couple of hours. Do your thing, honey. You go ahead." Stewart seemed a little pissed as he opened the door. She turned one last time and looked at me, with a very strange look on her face. I shrugged and Stewart left.

Once he was out the door, Paula excused herself to use the bathroom. I asked Elwood, "Do you still have any of the fungus?"

"Does she know that it is the fungus that is really what we are testing? That the tanks and the ESP system are really just – lab props?"

"I don't know."

"There was that article hinting about something in the *Free Press*."

"Everybody thinks we are using psilocybin."

Paula came back in the room. "Nate and I want to get wired up in the tanks."

"OK." He got up and looked at me.

"You have any?" I asked.

"Yeah. We are going to get some more soon anyway, right?"

"So, Paula – we have some of the ergot – fungus. Remember from our trip two years ago?"

"So that is the telepathy?"

"You remember," said Elwood. "Yes. I have found that it perhaps causes an enlargement of the brain's capacity to perceive. I have been very meticulous in documenting it. But I – we – think you can read another person's mind. But I am not sure. Nate has tried it too."

"Yeah – it seemed to work, but I got a little sick. I'll do it again though, Paula, if you want to..."

Paula looked at me and smiled. "Really?"

I wasn't sure what her smile meant. Maybe she wanted to read my mind. I would rather that we just went back to my apartment and screwed, but then again this might be fun.

So Elwood brought out the dried yellow fungus ear that he had in a little plastic baggie. "This is the last of it. Enough for two, maybe."

"What about you?"

"It seems to wear out its effect if you use it regularly. We are headed back to Illinois this week to look for more. It only seems to grow in winter."

"How do you know?" asked Paula.

"I've been studying it for the last two years. I have been back to Vandalia a few times."

So Paula and I split what was left in the baggie, got undressed, together, both of us proudly and spectacularly naked. We put on Elwood's helmets and slipped into the tanks.

CHAPTER 16

THE BOARD MEETING CONTINUES

8:10 pm, Friday, July 17, 2020

CHUBBY WALKED OUTSIDE, THROUGH THE KITCHEN and out the back, and took a look at his bike. It was getting dark. He got on it, not knowing why or where he was going and coasted down the driveway, almost to the street, but then he changed his mind, or maybe he never really was leaving. He didn't know. He looped back and stopped before the gate and opened it and pulled the bike inside, shut the gate, and sat down on a lawn chair. He sat for about five minutes, breathing and looking up at the planet Venus as she rose in the east.

His head was clear, or getting clear, probably for the first time in months. Something had been triggered by the "White Russian" concoction that Paula had given him. He felt as though, on the periphery of his consciousness, he was seeing and feeling other people's thoughts. And he felt good, strong, alert, and very much alive.

He was going to get straight, totally. Whatever it was in the White Russian, it made him realize he wanted a clean, clear mind, from this time forward. Not starting tomorrow, but tonight. For good – well for the duration anyway. No more of any of that shit – take the world straight and true. One day at a time, anyway. Too much to do. He had wasted too much time as it is.

"Hey, Kip. I was afraid you might have left," said Jim, coming out into the back yard. "Man, I am glad to see you. Look what I got." He put a bong on the table and handed Chubby a lighter. Of course, put up or shut up, you weak fuck, he thought. Jim used to give him shit constantly, telling him that *he* smoked too much pot.

"It's legal," Jim said.

Chubby looked at the bong, shook his head, and laughed.

"What's so funny? Here." Jim handed him a lighter.

"No." He waved it away. "But thanks. I'm getting straight – starting," Kip brought his hand down as if signaling to count the basket after the foul, "– now!"

"But it's OK, professor, we're good citizens now. Pillars of the community. Noted philanthropists. Whale watchers. Sort of... would be anyway if any whales were left." he said, holding out the lighter.

"No. This – all of this..." Chubby waved his hand at Jim and G's house, "...is a message from beyond. It is a clear signal. Can't you feel it? No – no – I can see that you can't. Sorry, I'm – distracted."

Jim shook his head and appeared a bit worried about Chubby, but then shrugged his shoulders and fired up the bong for himself. Chubby's rush of transpersonal clairvoyance was fading. Whatever power and alacrity that milky drink Paula gave to his perception was evanescing. He watched the ember's glow brighten, then dim in the encompassing darkness, and listened to the gurgling of the water in the bong. He looked up. Venus had moved west; he could follow its position by comparing it to the upper branches of the oak tree in the yard. The Wheel kept turning.

"I guess we need to talk, huh?"

Of course, Kip thought. Jim moving in with GG. Knocking her up. Oh yeah, she used to be my girl. "Yeah, we do need to talk."

"About – Cynthia and me – right?" Jim said, looking a bit guilty.

Kip didn't answer him right away. Jim looked away.

"Don't be such a pussy, Jim. Yes. I am talking about you and..."

They stared at each other.

There it was. That was what it was. She wasn't GG or G any-more. Chubby couldn't call her that anymore.

"...Cynthia. You and Cynthia. Are you getting married?"

Jim looked at him. "You have been my best friend since..."

"Mrs. Allen's class. First grade."

"Yeah. I'm sorry – I never even asked – if you guys – broke up...I mean..."

"Don't be a dick, Jim."

"Yeah – no, of course. That is total shit." Kip watched him as he picked up the bong and then put it down again.

"Good. Glad we got that out of the way. We're good. So. What happened to Macy?" Pissed at Jim for being so obtuse, Chubby decided to fuck with him a little more. If this was going to be his last opportunity to torture Jim for stealing his girlfriend, he'd at least make him squirm by asking about *his* old girlfriend.

"Oh. Yeah – well – she found her ex-husband – Ming – the Falun Gong dude."

Kip sat back in his chair, looking up at the darkening sky, as he recalled his last night with his one-time girlfriend.

"Actually," Jim continued, picking up the bong, then putting it down again. "I only got to see her once and we hardly talked," Jim continued. "Ming – was in a prison in Zhejiang province – near Shanghai. Macy sat outside the prison for two weeks, every day from 6 am until dark. Sometimes with Charlotte." Charlotte was her daughter. "And amazingly, who knows why, they released Ming under house arrest. Charlotte already knows Mandarin like a native."

"Charlotte's a smart little girl," said Chubby. Jim picked up the bong again and took another hit.

"Macy made some comment about how I – 'should be with'– Cynthia – I have no idea why."

"Cyn and Macy didn't like each other very much," Chubby said and Jim shrugged. "So – what did you do?"

Jim grabbed the bong and started to light it again. It was all ash. He had a little tin of resiny buds in his pocket that he pulled out and refilled the pipe from, and fired it.

"What did I do?" Jim absentmindedly tried to hand Kip the pipe, who again waved it away. "Well – I toured the canals of Hangzhou. I visited the gardens of Suzhou. Took a train to Shanghai. I just moved from city to city. Qingdao – I stayed in Qingdao for almost – I don't know, a long time – and drank beer. That is where I gained all this weight. The Germans left a brewery there."

Jim took another hit.

"Then I got an email from Cynthia. She was in Beijing."

"When was that?"

"Shit, when was that...?" Light, gurgle, gurgle, exhale. "August? April? Not last April...the one before – sometime in April, I think. Anyway, I met her in Beijing and...we went to Tibet – Lhasa. Flew to Nepal. Me and Cyn. Hiked through the Himalayas. It was cool. I don't know. We just sort of...maybe we should go back in, you think?"

Jim left the bong on the table and went in through the back porch into the kitchen. Kip looked at the water pipe a second longer than he thought he should. He shivered with self-loathing and followed Jim in the back door.

Maybe I should start reading pamphlets from Alcoholics Anonymous, he thought. Kip looked around and everything he noticed, everything, every half-empty bottle, the six-packs in the fridge, and the smell of high-grade sativa buds, the hemp-fra-granced soap on the Rasta braids of one of the women – is that Hadley? (She waved and he waved back.) Kip's senses were alive to every intoxicant imaginable, as well as the thoughts and lusts of everyone he passed. Was that the way he normally was? It didn't seem "altered." But his head was exploding, for the most part in a good way. He realized he had to get out of the kitchen. When he finally made it into the living room, it was better.

"Kip!" While he had been in the back with Jim, a whole host of people showed up. Most of them were drinking wine, and already it was nearly standing room only. Cynthia moved next to him, and nudged him with her shoulder away from the door into a corner of the room. "I can't believe how skinny you are! We can't call you Chubby anymore." She wore a greenish-brown, ankle-length kaftan that fit her baby bump seamlessly, naturally, flowing over her body as if it had been woven to fit her at that precise moment. She had her formerly jet-black, now light brown hair up.

"Those moon eyes, Babe, I am..."

Cynthia looked away for a second. Then she smiled and touched him on the arm, which he thought was a mild rebuke. She must have put her hand on his arm like that a hundred times before, but he had never seen it for what it was. Until now.

He still didn't know why he had pushed her away. Maybe because he was afraid of all this, the house, the baby coming, people circling like vultures while politely drinking white wine.

"I'm so missing drinking," she said, as if reading his mind. "When I found out about..." she put her hand on her tummy, "... that was the first thing I thought – no more drinking. But, I'll get you one...?"

"No thanks," he said. He had to get used to this pretty soon, or he would have to go away, and let them be. She was no longer G. "Anybody ever call you Cindy?"

"All the time. My sister still calls me that. So does my mom. Not my dad though."

"OK – we'll start there. Cindy, we are going to be fine."

"I know. K. I'll call you K! Kafkaesque, no? I am so glad you are here, Kip."

"I prefer Chubby."

"OK – K. Too bad! I like it, so there! Does it ever occur to you that you have been calling me 'G' or 'GG' forever – I almost forgot what it stands for."

"Goth Girl," said K, with laconic languidness.

"I can't believe it! I guess that was me. Just between us though, OK?"

"We have HIJ between us then. G-HIJ-K."

"Ha. Yeah. G – K – alphabet soup!"

"And backwards – it's JIH," said K. H is N in Russian, he thought, but didn't say. So it's almost Jim between us. K felt dizzy, and needed to lean on the wall. Being straight for so long (i.e., the last several days) was discombobulating, and he wasn't even sure he was straight – but his mind had never been clearer. It was just a midst this battlefield-like attunement to his surroundings that he had some kind of flashback.

Paula was engaged in deep conversation with Arky, but she glanced at him at that moment and smiled and nodded. Cindy moved over to the group by the front door. K stayed away and watched without staring as she greeted people. She wanted him to join her, he could tell, but whenever she caught his eye, he pretended he didn't see her, or was looking at something behind her, or was too lost in his own thoughts to recognize she was looking at him.

K felt a very low-level, almost seething, contempt for the nouveau silicon richness of Jim and Cindy's little get-together. From the goat cheese and wild boar sausage hors d'oeuvres, the "artisan crafted" gin & ginger cocktails, the "homespun," found–in–a–thrift shop clothes, precisely worn and torn, mixed with superhero Batman/Flash ensembles, or just out-of-the-box prison work-release jeans, with wide quadruple folded cuffs at the ankles, paired with Jackson Pollock–style paint-stained canvas smocks, it all seemed so pretend and pretentious.

He thought about the stew the people were eating next to the river north of Sellwood.

He looked at Cindy – how did that nerdy, troll-like, geeky goblin-girl (as Aldane called her) become so fucking – elegant! In all of their time together, he never thought her elegant. Was that it? he wondered.

Not everybody was chic. The men on the Board wore basic muted, dull colored slacks and dark monochrome collared shirts. Hariet Miller, President of Cascade Sportswear, the grand dame of the Rose City, unpretentious, rich beyond imagination, an old lady "Shock Jockette," wore robin-egged blue pants suit and pearls. Her dirty quips titillated the handsome and beautiful paramours of the evening, while the regulars rolled their eyes.

Hariet was attended by the Stanford Business School suck-up, Kayla, on loan from *Reigny Deigh*. She kept Hariet's snack plate and wine glass filled. Kayla leaned in, talking closely to Hariet, pretending to be the true éminence grise. Kayla had a lacy look, with a black bra peeking out from her plain, white, loosely buttoned blouse, and jeans that fit her succulent and spherical ass like spandex. She was intently whispering to Hariet, but pulled back and away as K approached.

"Welcome back, Kipling," Hariet said, smiling.

K smiled, bent down, and kissed her on the cheek.

"So it looks like you are on the prowl again. Maybe I have a shot, huh?" She gave Chubby a leer. Hariet, 90, had been a widow for decades.

"Right now?" K asked.

"No – we'll need to schedule it. I don't want to mess my makeup."

"Hot date later tonight?"

"Pool boy with high standards." K clicked his forefinger on her white wine glass. "So what do you think, Kipling? Should we support Caroline? Any idea what she stands for? Or Rosie? She'll tax the hell out of us, you know."

"Taxes are the least of the problems. Look at the alternatives."

"Umm...I know, I know." Hariet coldly looked over at Kayla, who started talking to Jim, smiling and nodding, as he rambled on like a stoned fool. "You should get to know her."

"Who hired her?"

"Well – we were thinking of hiring her firm – *Reigny Deigh*. Not sure what I think, if you are wondering. She is new, and I am not sure I like her. Those ads for Cascade? You know the ones – with me scaling a giant tree – tested well in the right audiences. But Gordy has changed up his team, and I am not sure why...they need to bring in Spen or Sven something – I forget his name – about your age."

"I know him. Spencer Stromborn. We ran into each other quite a bit back before *SwiftPad*. I invited him to join the board but he passed."

"Anyway, he is quite creative, but he might be in the doghouse."

"Why do we need PR? We are over-exposed, if anything."

"Always polish the image. We need love, Kip. I've been in business almost 70 years, and I can tell you it is a constant process. You know, people think *SwiftPad* is too Big Brother. *Reigny Deigh* is thinking about a movie or something like a movie, about – and the whole – you know – well actually, now that I think about it, I am not sure what they want to do. Something related to *SwiftPad*. Or something..."

"Fuck."

Hariet made a face at his obscenity. "We – the rest of the board – we are all hoping now that you are back...that...we need your – leadership is not the word I am looking for...but..."

"What then?"

She smiled at him. "So how was it? What did you find on your adventure?"

"What did I find?" Kip laughed and she did too.

"You seem more – grounded."

"Maybe." Kip looked over at Jim. Hariet caught his glance and shook her head slightly. "He's got a lot on his plate. Maybe the bun in Cynthia's oven has him confused. It's not yours, is it?"

Chubby recoiled a bit and shook his head.

"Take it easy, Kipling, I'm just kidding." Hariet turned and spoke up louder. "Kayla, dear, join us, won't you?"

"Of course, Mrs. Miller," she turned away from Jim, who was in mid-sentence.

Jim then looked at K and lifted his half-empty drink, pantomiming a refill. They smiled at each other. Jim had it together, he thought. He was fine. Just taking a holiday. He deserved a break.

"Have you met Kip?" Hariet asked Kayla.

"Yes, earlier. Jim was just telling me about some of your mutual adventures. He makes it sound like you two were raised by wolves." She turned, but Jim was already headed for the kitchen to refill his drink.

K thought about Alice, Jim's mom, and Walt, his dad. Wolves? He shrugged.

Hadley, one of the original team members of *SwiftPad*, sidled up and pulled him away. She leaned close and whispered quietly. "Did Cynthia really bite off that bastard's dick that night?"

His eyes shifted quickly over to G – err – Cindy – then back to Hadley.

"Because it isn't easy to do – to bite it off completely I mean."

"How do you know?" K asked.

"Well, I know it can be done – but it isn't quick or easy. I took anatomy in college. And did some extracurricular research."

Chubby smiled, but then censored himself, and realized he could never go toe-to-toe with Hadley, because nothing fazed her. "Cindy did it," he simply said, shrugging as if to say "believe it or not, it makes no difference to me."

"Cindy...well..." Hadley looked at him, trying to see if he said "Cindy" with any ironic intent. "If you say so." She shook her head. "You know he wanted to take me back to his place? You know that, right?"

"Yeah," Chubby said. "I remember. Just before he killed that poor woman who owned the *Easy Girl Bakery*."

"Jesus." She shook her head again.

"He was one, sick, fucked-up..."

"But he was smart? Right?" Hadley said, looking intently at Chubby, and he could see that the thought of him, even though she had brought it up, was scaring her. "I mean he fooled you guys. He said the company – *SwiftPad* – was his idea. He did help you guys start the company, didn't he?"

"If Raleigh Highlooper was so fucking smart, how come he's so fucking dead?" he said.

"*Prizzi's Honor*? Yeah. Can you imagine if they had never caught him? He would be here tonight, flirting, trying to run things. And I could be fucking dead instead of him, and you all would be talking about poor Hadley...to Raleigh! Where is she? And he would be saying, yeah, I thought she might have had problems, probably ran off with some bad people...Shit. I am still not right. I have had constant nightmares for the last few years."

He nodded sympathetically. "Is that hemp oil in your hair?" he asked.

"Yeah – the real thing. Can you believe it? You can get high just smelling it."

"I know." K fanned his hand as if to push the fragrance away. "I am sorry. I am kind of ...you know – off of that."

"Really? Off of what? You! Kip Rehain? Not everything? I have some excellent mushrooms back at my place. Actually – I was wondering if you might like to come over...tonight?"

K looked at her, feigning interest. "Wow. Well – I am kind of on a wagon, of sorts, for a while anyway. I am cutting back..." He leaned over and put his empty White Russian glass on the mantel over the fireplace. *Hadley was visualizing him pulling her clothes off. He felt it as clearly as if it had already happened.* "It is going to be an adventure. I think I have been stoned or drunk almost every day...since..."

"...a minute ago..." she said, laughing while pointing at his glass on the mantel.

"Well – three – four days at least if you don't count – there was no alcohol in that anyway. But I mean it. I am going for total abstinence."

"What about sex? Theoretically, I mean."

"You mean hypothetically?"

She looked at him exasperated. "I'd wash my hair first..."

He sniffed her hair and pulled back. "Wow, Hadley, I mean it,

I can feel the buzz from over here. Yeah. But – I mean no, sexual abstinence is not part of my new regimen."

Before they could pursue that line further, the front door opened and Heber came in.

"Kip – you are here! Great. I see Paula made it on her own." Heber put on his tight corporate smile. "I thought you and Nathan were flying in this afternoon? You met Kip, right? Kip...?"

"Paula, yeah sure, we've met," said Kip a little too stiffly. "We met a couple of years ago at the tech conference I told you about."

Paula looked quizzical for an instant, then smiled and came over and shook Heber's hand. "Sorry, I came in yesterday. Nate didn't show, huh?" said Paula.

Heber shook his head, an overpowering presence with his cologne, dark suit, blue tie, graying at the temples hair, and square chin. "Everything OK?"

"Sure. He'll probably be here later I think," she said, giving nothing else away. Heber stared at Paula, who smiled like a beauty pageant contestant.

"I see Mr. Hunt is inebriated again," Heber said, changing the subject with a hint of disgust. He looked at Jim, who, feeling the attention on him, responded by letting his jaw go slack and his eyes roll up into his head. Heber's eyebrows furrowed.

"I am just kidding, Heb," said Jim. "I am sober, straight and seeing the world *au naturel*. It might be interesting, right, Chubby?"

Heber shook his head, and Kip gave Jim a look and they smiled at each other.

Heber signaled to Cynthia and Kayla, indicating it was time to get started. Kip stepped over toward Heber, who simultaneously retrieved a glass of club soda and moved away from Kip, without looking. Paula stepped away from the crowd, toward the back of the room, watching.

CHAPTER 17

INTRUDERS

8:20 pm, Friday, July 17, 2020

"OK – WE NEED TO GET STARTED..." KAYLA, SMILING tightly, stood in front of the fireplace, trying to get the room's attention. "OK..." she said a little louder. She feigned patience as the group slowly quieted and turned their attention to her. You could see she was experienced at herding small gatherings, and finally, everyone was quiet and looking at her.

"Welcome to the annual *SwiftPad* Board and Stockholders meeting. We will have plenty of time to chat with each other, and drink and eat some more. We can move to the backyard later for a Spanish style tapas meal. So I hope you all brought your appetite. We'll have an open bar too."

"That's what I'm talkin' 'bout!"

Silence, for a beat. "Tell it, brother!" Chubby shouted back at Jim and winked at Cynthia.

An amplified cough. They all turned to Kayla. "We really have a very short and simple agenda," Kayla said. "As you know, most of the shares are held by a few people. But in this case, the questions will be decided by a simple majority. Cynthia – would you care to make any comments?"

Cindy walked up and stood next to Kayla. In spite of Jim's spaced-outedness, the blitzed-out father of her unborn child was much in love with Cindy. And Cindy glowed in radiant pregnancy. She was still very shy, and not comfortable in front of people. But she had learned to face her fears. She smiled and breathed in and out, just short of hyperventilation, and then began to speak.

"*SwiftPad* is still a software company, and will continue to be. I am still in charge of development, but only nominally, because I have had other things on my mind lately." She touched her tummy and got a soft chuckle out of everyone. "Arky is really running things. Tonight we make it official. Archimedes Moropolis is now The Big Kahuna!"

More applause.

"Or something like that. Actually it means nothing because he's been in charge since we hired him, but we just weren't paying him for it." More laughter. "We always worked to the model that the best idea wins. I have not always followed that rule, and I wish I had. Arky was almost always coming in with the best idea first, so now – I hope the new title helps him keep coming up with the ideas."

"You aren't going anywhere, G," said Arky.

"We'll keep in touch. Number two – we continue our research on the 'neural-interface' or as it is being called in the press, the brain-link – the thing between the software and your brain. Normally you'd think that would be the big announcement, but well for now, let's call it – a new paradigm for communication. We have succeeded in building the internal command set to 'respond' to SP-Script commands. The goal being to build a programmable set of tools to push mental imagery into the neural pathways – to begin the steps for a total communication tool. It has the potential to program stories – academic subjects, fiction, news, directly into the 'reader's' consciousness. The potential for teaching and learning might well be transformational."

She stopped and looked out for questions almost as if she expected the room to start yawning in unison, but she still held everyone's attention.

"What? No allusions to dystopia? Should we show the movie *Brazil* instead? K – you love Philip K. Dick – nothing?"

Somebody hooted, "She said dick!"

Chubby shrugged.

"On other fronts, we are helping people, one at a time. More people – everyday more people – refugees from the dry regions are moving here. Yet," here Cynthia paused, "we – us – you all are getting richer and richer. It's all very hard to understand."

Chubby thought about interrupting her to tell them what was happening less than two miles west by the river. But everyone knew.

"We are doing something," she continued. "And we are trying – mental health counseling, drug treatment counseling, off-the-street coaching. It costs money – a lot of money, and it makes no sense from a business perspective, because nobody thinks that it really amounts to much more than a token gesture in the big picture. And they are right. From perhaps a – public relations perspective – is that a thing? If so, it is worth it because – this is our city. People are living on the edge, but – I believe we can do it, we can keep it together and get through this – as long as we don't panic, there really is no reason to bail out if we can just keep the peace."

An uncomfortable silence blanketed the room.

"A boutique homeless shelter? Really?" Heber had stood up and whispered the comment to Cynthia as he passed her, but the spot was mic'd and everybody turned and looked at him. Realizing they all had heard him, he continued. "Have you looked out there recently? Is that the best bang for the buck? Has anyone figured how much productivity we are losing and how THAT money could be put into better use?"

"Define better!"

"Is social welfare in our core competency? Sometimes what sounds good is just…"

"OK!" Cindy (GG) didn't look mad, just tired. "We will re-examine it. I know you make some sense, but Heber, people are hurting."

"But simple math tells you there is a limit."

"We will set up a working group that you can chair and think through it. Maybe you are right."

Heber made a face, as if to say, I should have kept my mouth shut. Then without adieu, he moved away.

Kayla stepped up on the stone hearth in front of the fireplace and tried to keep the attention of the room without raising her voice. An uncomfortable quiet filled the room.

"I want to give a special welcome home to Kip Rehain." Half the people turned around and looked at him, a couple clapped, one groaned, and the rest laughed or chuckled and then clapped enthusiastically. He gave a faint wave, like he was Queen of England.

"Fucking suck-ups," he said. Big laugh. So much for my Cornelius Welles identity, he thought.

"Speech! Speech!" Jim was yelling from the back of the crowd. Kayla smiled tightly, trying to deflect the suggestion.

"Yes, Kip, I think it would be good of you to report what you have been doing for the last – how long has it been?" Seb Madison, Nike exec (and former four-minute miler), seconded Jim's call. He and Hariet, fierce competitors, had once had a jibing though friendly relationship, but now eyed each other suspiciously.

K looked at Kayla, as her tight smile morphed into a dead-eyed stare.

"I have been away, exploring, a vacation, for lack of a better word. I was away longer than I intended. But I am going back to Georgia, soon, because..." He heard a loud noise from the back of the house, then a shout, which sounded like Jim.

Then a piercing scream, unmistakably from GG. He looked over at Paula...who was now standing off to the side, by the window...as she pulled a powder blue Beretta Nano 9mm out from under her gray sweater.

The front door burst open.

"Everybody! Down on the floor! Now!" One, then two guys, came in covering each other, one aiming right, the other left. The second man in scanned the group to his right, who were stampeding over to the fireplace. He took aim and fired. Gordy went down like a bag of wet cement. Screams, and now everyone dove to the floor.

From the other side of the room, K heard another shot. He saw the bullet go by in slow motion, then felt something wet hit his face and realized it was blood and brains from the lead man in the door. "Drop the gun or you're dead too!" Paula said with a loud but steady voice. Chubby tackled the second guy, who had shot Gordy, and took him down, and slammed his head on the hardwood floor.

All of the guests, prone on the floor, were screaming and moaning. From the kitchen entrance came a piercing wail, and another shot. Paula, her feet spread apart in shooting position, just sat down. K threw a roundhouse into the temple of the guy he had tackled, felt him go limp, and pulled off his ski mask. Blond hair, about 30, blood shooting out of his nose from his introduction to the floor.

Paula was down, sitting against the wall, stunned, but with her powder blue Nano 9 still steady and covering K. Another scream – GG. Another shot. K leaned away as it came, and felt it whiz by, seemingly inches from his ear. He picked up the Sig Sauer Luger from the unconscious thug's hand. Paula was down, leaning back against the wall and unsteadily pointed her gun toward the kitchen entrance.

In the kitchen doorway, with his arm around GG's neck, and his gun pointed at her jaw, a third masked invader emerged. G sobbing. Everyone was either on the floor or backed against the fireplace. Some were whispering on their fones.

Chubby pointed the Sig 9 at the third man. "Drop it." But he only tightened his grip on G's neck, and otherwise didn't move and said nothing. Dark sweater, ski mask, just like his two friends lying on the floor. The man on the floor stirred. Chubby pushed his head down, keeping a bead on the third masked man.

"Shoot! Shoot! She dead! Shoot now, motherfuckers!" Eastern European accent, Chubby thought. He glanced to his left toward where Gordy was moaning, blood seeping out around him on the floor.

"Fuck!" The guy holding G turned and fired, and the top of Gordy's skull exploded in blood and bone.

Chubby cursed himself for not shooting when he turned. But Chubby kept the 9mm Sig pointed at him as he led her toward the front door. He waved Chubby back with his Luger and kicked his breathing partner, who slapped at the foot and pushed back and slowly got to his knees. Chubby slid back, keeping the Sig 9 on the masked gunman who had G in a choke-hold. It was clear that the guy holding G was in charge.

"Him out. Now!"

With a profusely bleeding nose, and wobbly, he managed to stand. Big, with bulging arms, unsteadily, with hatred in his eyes, hair bleached, he picked up his dead buddy with ease and lugged him out the door, trailing blood across the threshold.

"We go now, else get dead bitch on lawn." As he listened, Chubby knew he was not Russian. "Two for one price!" He pointed the gun at her pregnant tummy, then back at her head. Was it Balkan? Not Serbo-Croatian. Hungarian? Maybe Albanian. Basque?

A blue Nissan Quest van pulled up to the curb and the back sliding door opened.

"Back in house. NOW!" They moved back, but as soon as it sped away, K ran out to get a plate number, but they were around the corner too fast. He saw a K and maybe a 5.

K ran back into the house. Heber was on his knees, trying to stanch Paula's bleeding. Then from the kitchen, came cries of distress.

CHAPTER 18
PEGGY COMES HOME

10:00 pm, Friday, July 17, 2020

S PENCE WAS ABOUT TO CONTINUE READING NATE'S tale of eating the yellow fungus and climbing into the sensory deprivation tanks when they heard the garage door opening. They both stared at the kitchen door to the garage. Spence stood up. They heard the garage door start to close as Margaret walked in.

"Hey, Peggy. Look who's here."

Nate stood up and Margaret stared at him, her face switching in sequence from questioning, to concern, to recognition within about three seconds. She dropped her purse and ran across the kitchen and hugged him. "Nate, it is so good to see you." They looked at each other and smiled, then hugged again. Margaret wiped away a few tears. Then they stepped away from each other. Nate looked closely and saw she was still the same as he remembered her, beautiful but in a strange, almost washed-out way, her features melded together in a manner that spoke of all of the ages she had lived since he had last seen her.

"How was your day, Peg?" asked Spence, pretending it was just the end of another day.

"Didn't you see the news? Over by Reed College? A home

invasion. People are dead. One of my students lived a couple of houses down."

Spence turned on the TV and turned to channel 12, the local FOX affiliate.

Men in ski masks, wielding guns, barged into an evening soiree in Portland's Woodstock District. There are multiple injuries and well as a reported gunpoint kidnapping.

Helicopter shot: Police cruisers, lights flashing, parked at oblique angles across the road, in front of a large gingerbread home. Two ambulances, up on the lawn. The mid July dusky sun was peeking from just below the horizon, blurring the aerial shot – about 8:30 pm.

"We are now hearing that two people are dead in that daylight home invasion into a home in the Woodstock neighborhood of Portland." A reporter, off camera, was reporting. "Neighbors report hearing several shots fired and of a brazen kidnapping at gunpoint. Reports say that a woman was forced into a getaway car."

Spence switched to KGW, the NBC affiliate. The view was of a ground shot of the scene of police cars, an ambulance and – then moving back as a cop pushed the crowd back with frantic shouts.

"... a crowded evening gathering of employees and associates of the software venture **SwiftPad**...at the home of Cynthia Oglethorpe and James Hunt...the prime creator of **SwiftPad** the social media application..."

Two stretchers carrying victims...ambulances that quickly sped away.

Nate tried his fone. "Fuck! Voicemail. She might have turned it off – if she is with somebody she will just power it off. I was – the woman I have been living with – for the last 10 years – in fact, Maggie – I knew her before I met you. Years before. She is there – at that party. We came to Portland together. Shit."

CHAPTER 19

AFTERMATH

9 pm to Midnight, Friday, July 17, 2020

SEB MADISON, WHO HAD BEEN PRE-MED BACK IN HIS running days, had taken over trying to stabilize Jim. The knife wounds were horrible. There was so much blood on the floor. Jim had smoked so much dope, it appeared to calm him. He was still conscious, smiling and shaking his head. He looked up at Kip and slightly shrugged his shoulders. His abdomen was one big wound and other than keep him breathing and try to stanch the bleeding, there wasn't much to do while waiting for the EMTs. His best friend was dying in front of him and there was nothing he could do.

Paula seemed in better shape; at least there wasn't as much blood and she was conscious and aware. She took a bullet in the rib cage. The ambulance arrived right after the first cops, and K just stood back and watched. A team went back into the kitchen, started IVs, pumped Jim up with sedatives, and got him on the stretcher. The cops were calling for a life flight and seemed to agree the Reed College Administration Building lawn would be the best extraction point – clearest area that was near for a chopper to land.

It was dark by then, and most of the people at the gathering were sitting around the living room, on the couch or in front of the fireplace, or on their haunches. Hariet, in her late 80s, appeared confused and speechless, and she was taken away in an ambulance as well.

Henderson showed up as the ambulance was being shut. He talked to a uniform, then looked over at Kip, and ordered him to stay put. Kip didn't have too much confidence in Ted Henderson, especially when things got weird.

In a few minutes though, when he saw the cops were ignoring him, K snuck away; even though he had been told to sit tight, he got on his bike and just rode, rode hard and fast, across the Sellwood Bridge, down Macadam and caught the last tram of the evening up to Pill Hill. He just sat in the waiting room, until Detective Ted Henderson arrived and immediately ordered two uniformed cops to take him downtown.

"Am I under arrest?"

"Do you want to be? If not, tell me you are agreeing to come downtown right now!"

"OK," said Kip. There was nothing he could do, and it was clear he would be leaving the hospital in any event. He was shoved into the back of a Portland cop car for the ride down to the station.

CHAPTER 20
NATE, SPENCE & MAGGIE/ PEGGY EAT ZITI

11:00 pm, Friday, July 17, 2020

NATE AND MARGARET SAT OUT ON THE ENCLOSED porch, next to one another on the link-chain swinging couch. "Your ziti smells good," Nate yelled toward the kitchen. No answer. Spence was in the kitchen, pulling the ziti out of the oven, making noises that sounded like a mashup of "Oh boy!" and perhaps, "Oh shit!" Nate and Peggy had their feet on the floor, and seemed to be working against each other, one pushing off while the other pulled in. Then they both stopped and the porch swing hung still.

"I don't know what to do. I am so exhausted. I was planning to get out of here before you got home, but…"

"What is her name, this woman?" Peggy asked.

"Paula. I am worried. She isn't well."

"You are always in the middle of things. First China and now this. Ever since you left, not much has happened to Spence and me. We married, had a daughter, got jobs, bought a house."

"Sounds like more than nothing to me."

"But it was all about you when we met," said Maggie, with a

hint of accusation in her voice. "You are still – didn't you ever just want a normal life?"

"I never thought about it," said Nate, looking hard at Maggie. "Well – that's not true, I know it has crossed my mind occasionally. You were the one who – No point dwelling on it now, Paula is the reason I am here. I have known her a long time. I guess to answer your question I would have to explain some very weird things."

"Like what weird things?"

"Paula has not aged since she was thirty."

"A lot of people stay fit and healthy," Maggie said, unconsciously pulling in her tummy and pulling her shoulders back.

"I am not talking about that! Anyway – we are part of the shadow government. We are starting – we are going to actively resist – all this – the (V)ICE, and the anti-human policies we have been living with. It is going to get ugly, but we are going to resist, fight it. Not just post anti-Prez messages on social media. Do you know what is going on up in Forest Park? Up in the hills above the city?"

"I have heard that the homeless camp up at the top of Northwest Thurman Street is overflowing with people. So many people, so many little camps, that the cops are overwhelmed. I see people moving up there, avoiding roadblocks and arrest sweeps, and setting up tents, almost like it was organized. Mostly refugees from the Southwest and from all the fires."

"There are more than a million people living in tents who have arrived in Portland and the area around in the last year. You notice all the Federal cops here?"

"Yeah, sure," Maggie said.

"All of this is the fault of the Feds – the Old-Prez is in all likelihood the one ordered that nuke strike that blew the Hoover Dam."

"How do you know that?"

"He wanted to start a war to get rid of – undesirables – people who – even poor whites, even though they were the ones who put him in power. He wanted an excuse to start a war with Mexico, but that is stalled in the Pentagon. The delay made him so pissed off that he decided to use the dam bombing as as excuse to 'cleanse' the country not only of foreigners, and the poor, but even the liberals who side with them. The Prezes, both temp and real, think the problems of the country can be solved by getting rid of inconvenient people. How do I know? Because every type of bomb has a unique radioactive signature and it was a US bomb that blew Hoover."

"I don't believe it. How do you know?"

"I have seen the data."

Maggie eyed Nate. "But he's gone, out of power, and his buddy Mr. Temp-Prez lost his primaries. They are toast."

"He's not gone," said Nate.

"How do you know?"

"He is still tweeting. No, I don't believe it for a minute. But I am glad you have heard things are happening up in Forest Park, and yet – you still know nothing! You have not put it together. That is great news for us. Because that has been the goal. It is about surprise. They are going to surprise Portland, by moving in, and we are going to surprise them."

"I still don't believe it," Maggie said shaking her head. "That is the kind of paranoid shit that has been circulating for years. It is what the so-called 'Real-Prez' was always saying."

"But now it's the shit the government is always saying," said Spence, joining them on the porch. "I am skeptical of stories too about an Underground Organization. From anybody, by anybody. Terrorists are under the bed! Fear mongering that is justifying all these stormtroopers on bikes and in the street."

Nate just looked at Spence and Margaret and smiled wanly. "There is an organization, and it is organized. I am part of it. It is national – East, West, even in the middle. You will hear from us very, very soon."

"Anyway," said Margaret, changing the subject, looking in vain at Spence as he retreated to the kitchen. "You think this thing on the news – invading the *SwiftPad* meeting – is part of what you are talking about?"

"Duh!"

"But why?"

"Why? Ever since Facebook, and then – this *SwiftPad* shit! All these liberal social media people are not innocent. In some ways it is the chickens coming home. Because SwiftPad now controls us – and that is what brought us to this, and it swung around and hit them in the ass."

"You were always so mysterious, Nate. I think that is what I liked at first, and then what I didn't like. It is frustrating."

"Here we go," said Spence, loudly, to warn them he was back in earshot. "You are hungry, aren't you, Peg? Nate?"

"Starving," said Nate. Margaret nodded, still a little angry at Nate's obtuseness, and leaned over to pull a small table up to the swing. Spence placed the two bowls in front of them. Nate and Peggy sat next to one another on the swinging couch, holding their bowls, while eating silently, looking away. They heard another siren. Even out here, they were always blaring. Spence went back to the kitchen.

"So..." Maggie turned to Nate.

"So indeed. Where did I go? I traveled. Some of my old residuals started coming in, so I had a little money."

"Unlike when we were together."

Nate looked at Margaret, but said nothing.

"I am sorry, it is just I haven't seen you or heard from you in – almost 20 years. And you show up, today...if you want to take a shower..." She fanned her hand.

"It's a disguise, Maggie, which I can explain...if you can get over it!"

"OK. I am over it, Nate. Over. But seeing you suddenly with no time to prepare, it's just... here you are?"

"Well, yeah, here I am. Hey, this swing is making me dizzy." Nate gave her a look.

"Me too," said Margaret, maintaining her sang-froid. They both put their feet flat on the floor and stopped the swing. Spence, carrying the bowl of salad, three glasses, and a bottle of rosé, looked at them and smiled. "Spence," she said, "I think we should take our plates and move into the kitchen. The smoke is killing my eyes." Spence pirouetted like an overwhelmed waiter and headed back inside.

The three of them brought their bowls and wine glasses into the kitchen and sat down to eat.

"So what do we do?"

"I need to go over to the northwest side tomorrow," said Spence. "Big meeting. I am not invited, but I want to be around – maybe help out a friend."

"Big meeting?" Nate took a big sip of wine.

"Yeah, Telly Haines is in town, and I think he is going to make a move on the company. I might just show up to fuck with people. I am not going to get run over anymore by Gordy or any of them."

"Really?" Nate looked at Spence..

"We have an extra room in the back, Nate," said Maggie. "Get cleaned up, sleep. You can't do anything tonight anyway."

Nate nodded. Spence turned up the TV, and they watched the coverage of the home invasion over in the Woodstock neighborhood.

CHAPTER 21
INTERROGATION

6:00 am, Saturday, July 18, 2020

"YES, DETECTIVE," SAID HEBE YOUNG. "THEY CAME in the front door."

K (Chubby) tried not to look at Hebe, but he caught the exasperation in his voice. Kip had no idea what time it was, but he had been sitting there for hours. He stunk. They had just left him alone in the interrogation room. Heber had come in and sat next to Kip just minutes before Henderson arrived, wearing casual street clothes now, his recently combed hair still wet. The detective sat directly in front of them at the cold metal table. Kip projected an exterior calm, hands on his lap, focusing on his *Ajna chakra*, his third eye, because he knew he had to get past this without exploding. He could see that the cops knew nothing, and would find nothing. Detective Ted Henderson, obtuse as always, was going over the story again, point by infuriating point.

Kip sat in aching silence as Henderson crossed something out on his pad, then wrote something else. "And then," the detective continued, "a third masked man came through the back of the house, stabbed Jim Hunt, and grabbed..."

"I didn't see him stab Jim. I assume that..." Kip trailed off in a subdued tone.

Henderson silently continued writing in his notebook. After a couple of minutes of scribbling, he stared at Kip for several dramatic seconds. He then said with florid emphasis, "He grabbed your business partner, Cynthia Oglethorpe – do I have this right? – grabbed her with his left arm around her neck, while with his other hand holding a gun to her head. Right?"

"He did the grabbing in the kitchen. I didn't see her until he came out into the living room, him holding her."

"Poor woman. She has a bad habit of getting kidnapped, doesn't she?" He looked up at K and Heber's blank stares. "Why does this story so sound familiar?" Henderson paused and looked directly at Kip.

"I don't know what you are trying to say, Ted, but that is outrageous, and you know it!" Chubby put his hands on the arms of the chair, prepared to spring. "There is no reason for..."

Ted Henderson had been the lead Portland detective investigating Raleigh Highlooper, the rapist/serial killer who had abducted Cynthia and dragged her through the thorny roses in the Portland Rose Garden, then into the adjacent grassy Amphitheater, where, somehow, his penis was bitten or lopped off. The official story was that GG (Cynthia) had bitten it off and spit it out, when Kipling Rehain distracted him, but Henderson had always doubted that sequence of events. He suspected Chubby (K) had cut it off after he had freed GG from Raleigh, and this suspicion seemed to be coloring the present interview.

"Sorry," said Ted. "Humble apology, kowtow, etc. Just reminiscing a little about the last time I interviewed Mr. Rehain here regarding Ms. Oglethorpe's previous abduction and her captor's loss of his – anyway. I was just – wondering – suspicious of coincidences. Occupational hazard. May I continue, gentlemen?"

Kip continued to stare off.

"OK then," Henderson slightly shrugged. "Unprovoked as far as I can determine, this masked man, who had his arm around Ms. Oglethorpe's throat, turned his gun on Gordon – Lobetts – the media executive – and shot him. Right?"

"Yes," said Heber. "Well, I was on the floor, but –"

"Yes, that is what happened. I saw it," said Kip.

"So he shot," here Henderson pantomimed the action, "he shot and killed the President of *Reigny Deigh Media* with the gun in his right hand, shooting across his body to his left, holding the gun right in front of Oglethorpe's face, who he had in a choke-hold with his left arm, in which hand he held a knife – right? And, this shooting, killing – it appeared to be premeditated. Right?"

Henderson looked at each of them for a protracted couple of seconds, then continued, "and then he turned all the way around, to his right, and shot and seriously wounded – a Ms. Paula Flayer, a security consultant from California. Is that right?"

Kip choked down his anger. "He did shoot Lobetts, but Gordon was already down. He was finishing him off. The guy that Paula shot in the head had already popped Lobetts when he came in the front door. The guy holding Cynthia finished him off. But I would agree with you. Premeditated."

"OK. OK. This woman was shot by the third guy holding Oglethorpe..." Henderson paused and looked up, quizzically at Kip. "Paula Flayer – correct?"

"Yes," said Heber.

"OK...OK. But she shot the first one in the front door. Correct?"

"Yes," said Heber. "I think so. It was her shot. In the head. After he – I think it was him, but I am not sure – had shot, wounding badly, whatshisname."

"You mean Gordon – Lobetts – OK." Henderson stared off for a few seconds. "Subsequently, this third masked man dragged Ms. Oglethorpe out the front door and into a waiting black Nissan..."

"Quest. A Quest van," said Kip.

"Right – a Quest van that had just driven up." He gave his notepad a satisfied tap with his pen.

The story in various forms was already showing up everywhere on social media.

"So this was a party or some kind of – high profile – fundraiser for –" the detective looked down at his notes – "Caroline Martin for President." Henderson made an unpleasant face and slightly shook his head.

Heber nodded to Henderson with an eye roll, acknowledging that it was indeed a fundraiser for Caroline Martin, and that he too was not that excited by the idea of raising money for the Connecticut Democrat.

"Why did Flayer have a gun? She had no license on her person to carry a concealed firearm."

"I think she's from California," said Heber.

"Well – this is Oregon…"

"Is that a question, Detective?" Kip shook his head incredulously.

"Let's review what we think happened…" said Henderson, staring hard at Kip. "This third attacker, who must have come in through the back door, where he…had possibly surprised Hunt, and stabbed him in the abdomen. Then, he came through the kitchen, and grabbed Oglethorpe."

"But he had a gun in his hand," K said to no purpose, not really thinking it mattered.

"That's right! Exactly, Mr. Rehain!"

"What do you mean – 'exactly'?"

"What hand did he shoot with?

"Right."

"We'll wait until the crime scene analysis and pathologist get back to us. They should be able to tell the direction the knife went in, and maybe which hand he used. And ballistics. Let's not get ahead of ourselves, Mr. Rehain. The other possibility we have to consider is that…maybe she was in on it? How could he have simultaneously wielded the gun and stabbed Hunt, and held her by the neck?"

K restrained himself. Then he thought – that is what Henderson wants – me to lose it and assault him. K went back to impassive – third eye, third eye.

"But that doesn't seem likely, does it? We'll come back to that when we get some specific evidence from the labs. Oh, yeah.

Speaking of evidence, guess whose fingerprints are on the gun – maybe the one that shot Lobetts?"

"Mine. Yeah. The Sig Sauer right? I picked it up, after I clocked the second guy in. Think about it, Ted," K said, trying to close the discussion of the GG-was-in-on-it theory, and also he wanted to bust Henderson's balls. "He probably didn't grab GG until after he cut Jim – probably with the knife in his right. Then he switched the knife to his left to get the gun."

"OK," Detective Henderson angrily blurted. K's face was blank, so he went on, "It's all preliminary, so let's stick to what you actually saw or did. He came out of the back, then, after shooting Flayer and – Lobetts – shooting – Lobetts – after Lobetts had already been wounded. He was holding his hostage, and told the second attacker..."

"Ordered," K said.

"Ordered – ordered the second attacker to drag the body of his partner out to the getaway car."

"Yes," K said.

Henderson looked down at his notes, then his phone, and hesitated, "...Flayer... she's now in surgery. I know that she showed up, said she was some kind of private investigator from San Francisco..."

"She was invited," said Heber.

"Why?"

"I told you...we didn't hire her to protect us per se – I didn't think...that the threat was this imminent..." Heber trailed off. Henderson again waited for almost a minute before he continued.

"What threats? This could be very..."

"Impersonal, general abuse type threats. 'I hate people like you.' We have a very high profile company," said Heber.

A uniform cop came in and whispered something in Henderson's ear.

"Thanks, Morgan. Interesting tidbit – the DA would kill me, but I will share it with you. Flayer doesn't even have a California PI license. Are you sure there was no other reason she was 'invited' as you say..."

Heber shrugged.

"Mr. Rehain – you attacked, punched, and disarmed the second attacker. Why did you do that? We are running the gun you grabbed from him now, but…"

"Excuse me, but that is a stupid question. Why did I do that? Jesus."

Henderson didn't react.

"What is Jim's condition?" Heber asked.

"Jim Hunt – from what I understand, it's not looking good – bled out pretty bad, stabbed. And his wife – were they married?"

Kip shook his head. "The driver had a face mask too…the boss, the third man who held Cynthia sounded eastern European," he said listlessly.

"Russian?"

"No. Maybe Balkan. Albanian, or possibly Hungarian."

Henderson gave Kip an incredulous look. "How would you know that?"

Kip slightly shrugged.

"We found the van, abandoned about a mile away." Henderson kept looking at Kip.

"Sounds like they planned it," said Heber.

"Ya think?"

"I never saw the dead guy, Ted," said Chubby. "It was the other one I clocked and pulled off his balaclava – heavy-set with short bleached hair."

"… you didn't check his pulse…"

"I was squeezing my sphincter, if that counts. Dumb me, I forgot to check his vitals. Jesus, Ted, I wish you would pay attention, this is the third time I have told you…" K said.

"Detective Henderson – understand? So cut the shit and tell me what else you know, or…"

"Sorry, Detective," K said. He tried to look sheepish, but Henderson wasn't buying it. "But, come on! Everyone there saw. His head popped, practically exploded. She shot him – after they forced their way in with guns drawn. If anybody had cause to shoot…"

"Why was she armed? Why was she there? Who is she?"

K looked at Heber, with no intention of telling him about meeting Paula by the Black Sea or visiting her apartment in Frisco. He had flown home with his Dudley Dureedy Canadian passport. No easy way to check connections. Still, if they started looking…

"She showed me her PI license paperwork before I hired her. It looked legit," said Heber.

"Did you check her out? Your outfit should have caught that. Aren't you some kind of lawyer…"

"We have a small staff, comparatively…"

"Mr. Young," Henderson took a deep breath. The power of Heber's thousand-dollar business suit seemed to hold him back – that, along with his $100 haircut and square Mormon jaw. Because Heber was no lawyer.

"What happen to the neighborhood guards? I saw at least four guys who seemed to be lookouts of some kind. Where were they?"

Henderson didn't answer right away. "They hijacked the comm system. Sent them on a wild goose chase."

K had to get out of there. Find her, he thought. There were holes in his own story too, Kip realized. He had to find her.

Then, like Hermes arriving on queue from Olympus, a courthouse flunkie came in and handed Heber and K each a sheath of folded documents – restraining orders to not discuss the case with anyone. Heber showed his to Henderson.

"Fuck – Feds – Fuck!" Henderson slammed his notebook closed and made a sign with both hands to shoo them away. "Get the fuck out. God damn it!"

CHAPTER 22

SPENCE HEADS OUT TO MEET ALISON

6:00 am, Saturday, July 18, 2020

SPENCE WAS ALREADY UP. HE SAT AT THE KITCHEN TABLE, drinking a glass of water. Peggy came out into the kitchen.

"Want some coffee?"

"I got to get going," said Spence. "I hardly slept."

"Wait up a little. Nate is leaving too, to head up to the hospital. We should think this through. They are shooting people, Spence!"

Spence shrugged. Maggie made coffee.

"Sleep, alright?" Spence asked.

"We just talked until he fell asleep. I didn't sleep much either." Spence shrugged again.

"Toast?"

"OK," said Spence. The two of them sat there, saying nothing as they munched on toast and drank coffee.

Spence's cell rang. He flipped on encrypt – it found the one-time cypher for the calling number. He texted. "Don't speak! This is my only burner – and it is toast. One-time-pad."

Ali: "Eastbay Girl says – Meeting still on – (V)ICE every-where – but at two – must use the OTP." She hung up. He decrypted – a map popped up and zoomed in.

"I have to meet – a colleague – Alison," said Spence in a way that caught Margaret's attention. "But not until later. About noon."

"I am going with you," said Margaret.

"No," said Spence. "I am going into the office, first. I need to check some stuff, check and see if our link into the SwiftPad test system is still up, go over my SwiftPad code for Nate's script, see if..."

"Is she going to be there?"

"Who? Oh, at the office, Alison. No, I don't think so. No."

"No?"

Spence looked at her and she stared back. Spence seemed to suppress a chuckle. "You know where Couch Park is?"

"On Couch?"

"No – it's in Northwest though, four blocks north of Couch, on 20th between Hoyt and Glisan. She will be there around noon. There are too many checkpoints. I want to get out of here early before all the people camping down by the river get up."

"I'm going!"

"Fuck. No. I will meet you there. You guys hang out here until then. Probably have some more catching up to do. I need to concentrate when I get to the office."

Peggy started to say something, but stopped herself.

Spence got up and headed for the garage. "About noon. At Couch Park. OK? We'll have lunch afterwards." They put their cheeks together, and Spence headed out.

Spence made it down the Springwater Corridor past all of the camps, where there were some people stirring as the sun slowly began to get above the horizon and the clouds hanging over Mount Hood. He pushed hard through the Sellwood neighborhood and turned north, staying on the eastside bike path. He wanted to see the camp, see if (V)ICE had let the people alone or had forced them out. He headed up the river past the abandoned remains of Oaks Amusement Park, which was fenced off like a medium security prison with razor wire and German shepherds patrolling.

As Spence rode north, the bike path funneled down to a tight stretch of about a quarter mile, where there was a pretty steep drop-off and a long steel fence between the path and the lake in Oaks Bottom Park. He was going back the same way he came, but going back always looks different than the way there. And now it really was different. There were about 50 (V)ICE commandos spread out straddling their bikes on alternating sides, in a sawtooth formation that forced everyone to slow down and weave through, where they took your picture as you rode. It was so fucking early!

Undoubtedly they were emailing all the faces as they took them to an ID database looking for – escaped inmates? Terrorists? Indigents? Tourists? Spence had never been arrested, had never publicly shared much beyond his final four bracket, and appeared to be unperturbed as he cruised through the gauntlet.

He rode at the speed of the young woman in front of him. She wore high-waisted jeans, braids, and granny glasses. She was slaloming on an electric scooter through the young, arrogantly posing, cold-eyed Federal (V)ICE cops without once seeming to notice them. Spence saw they were aiming their cameras with laser pointers, and saw the blue light hit her cheek. As he came up on the young gendarme who was pointing his phone at him, he reflexively turned his head away.

He got through the bike path gauntlet and speeded up. Along the edge of the bike path was an endless stream of refugees. They were mostly white, with some Latino families, all of whom who looked edgy and stressed. Spence sensed hopelessness, pain, and loss.

As he came to the entrance to the trail on his right that led up to Milwaukie Avenue, he suddenly encountered to two (V)ICE cops who zoomed out on their sturdy, black hybrid road-mountain bikes and cornered him, forming a V in front of him.

"Where you going?" The young cop's unnaturally blond hair was piled up under her helmet, cascading out over her ears and forehead. She raised her dark eyebrows while focusing her cat-green eyes at Spence. She had a slight smile.

"Downtown," said Spence in a neutral tone.

Her partner, whose short sleeves were rolled up a half turn revealing linebacker-like guns, and whose face was hidden behind a full brown beard and wrap-around mirror shades, pushed a button on his handlebars that set off a brief piercing siren. Spence stiffened into a slight flinch, and then had to put both feet on the ground to avoid losing his balance. Both cops laughed.

"Downtown? Really? At 6:30, on a Saturday? You're a busy beaver."

"How did you know? Yes, I went to OSU!" Spence tried to drain any sarcasm out of his voice or expression, but was failing miserably.

The linebacker looked at his partner with mock quizzicality. "You mean Ohio State?"

"No, Rakey. He means Oregon State! Beavers. Get it?""

"What a shitty university. What, couldn't get into a good school?"

"Wait," said the blond commando. "I bet you are meeting a friend? Right?"

Spence, who stood 5'10" and was a bit flabby in the gut at 210 lbs with his shoes on, stared off, patiently waiting to get going.

The cat-eyed cop read from her phone, "Spencer Stromborn, 47, OSU grad, currently employed at *Reigny Deigh Media,* married to Margaret Daniel. Other info address, blah, blah, previous addresses, social media posts – admittedly old posts – mostly pictures of dogs and colleagues, and basketball players. No *SwiftPad* profile either. Interesting... are you hiding anything, Mr. Stromborn?"

"You mean am I sympathetic to the real President? Or the ones who overthrew him?"

"Oh my – so you do have opinions! Well, it's a free country – believe it or not, we are here to keep it that way. You don't have to support anyone! But we have a responsibility to keep the peace and protect the country from people who would try and disrupt and undermine our peace and prosperity. We are going to ride up the hill to Milwaukie. See the turn-off for the path up ahead? Officer Rakoff is going to go first – you second, and I will follow."

"Am I under arrest?"

"That is up to you. Do you want to be under arrest? Or do you just want to talk to one of our detectives who is waiting for you up there?"

There was a shot, which came from down on the spit of land next to the river. Then another, then what sounded like automatic rifle fire, coming from multiple guns.

"Let's go, Stromborn. Up the hill!"

Spence froze as he heard screaming.

"Now! MOVE."

CHAPTER 23
BACK TO THE HOSPITAL

9:00 am, Saturday, July 18, 2020

HEBER AND K WALKED OUT OF HENDERSON'S OFFICE, took the elevator down to the lobby and into the bright mid-morning. Neither of them had slept last night.

"I guess we are not supposed to talk to one another about this…" Heber said as they walked away from the downtown Justice Center.

"Bullshit!" Heber grimly goffed.

"You think they're bluffing?"

"Yes. Pure, 100% bullshit!"

K gave his daddy's accountant a thumbs-up. Heber normally wouldn't say "shit" if he had a mouthful of it, but, K thought, the guy is made of steel in some ways.

As they walked out, Heber had put his hand on K's shoulder. Simple and unpatronizing. He remembered standing in front of his father's body, wrapped in a biodegradable shroud, and Heber had put his hand on his shoulder then too. It seemed weird to Kip that Heber would be around still. It is a big job, managing the money for a company like SwiftPad, and he handled it, better than any of us. We all bailed a little, except Heber, Kip thought. He had to trust him, even if he didn't understand what he was doing, particularly with the money. He knew Heber was a Mormon with a capital M, had probably voted Republican in every election since Nixon. Still, Kip trusted him.

"What time is it?" Kip asked Heber, who looked at his MTM Chronograph, while shading his eyes from the morning sun.

"9:10."

"Well, shit on a jagged stick! Fucking eight hours. Henderson is a fucking – I am going back up to the hospital."

Chubby and Heber were just crossing Main on SW 3rd Avenue, when a black (V)ICE cruiser turned into the Federal Building's underground garage, just down the street near 2nd and Main. Chubby saw a lone man in the back seat. He appeared to have his arms pinioned back, and he stared back at Chubby, then started to move back and forth, and lunged up and down as if trying to get his attention. The cruiser pulled into the garage and the steel door quickly shut behind it.

Heber, who didn't appear to notice anything unusual with the (V)ICE cruiser, said, "They are going to ask for a billion dollars ransom."

"Who? Oh, for Cynthia. Yeah, probably." This was the second time Cindy had been kidnapped. She had been a tech celebrity since she was a teenager, and now this was going to turn the world upside down.

"We will pay, of course."

"Right." Kip was in a funk about the guy in back of the cruiser. "Can we? How fast can we pull it together?" Heber didn't answer, or maybe he was still thinking about it.

"So why did you hire Paula?"

"I think you know more than me," Heber said, after half a beat. "It was Alice's suggestion."

"Yeah. Maybe," K said noncommittally. "How do you feel?"

"I am like most people in this country. And in this city too. Everybody in Portland pretends to hate the Feds, but most people are glad (V)ICE is here. People are scared of the refugees. They are afraid they are going to move into their homes, and take them over. People like me – I am seriously wondering who people like me are, if there are any anymore, to tell the truth."

Kip suddenly realized that he had recognized the handcuffed man under arrest in the (V)ICE cruiser.

"Anyway," continued Heber, "as far as Paula goes, we never talked about her being 'security' or anything. Just made that up for the detective. I just took Alice's word. I know she has a – whole other – thing. Anyway – I came here direct from the airport, so I wasn't packing. Won't make that mistake again. Darn – we should get back over to the hospital."

"Yeah." Heber would have to be fired, K thought, the sooner the better. Can't be fucking around anymore. He is not reliable, K thought. It's war. There will be no ransom demand, at least not a serious one, he thought. They aren't after money. They want it all, and if they break her, they can get it. The round-up is beginning. Hammer time.

Kip took a deep breath and shook his head. Can't fire Heber, he recognized. Take a year to unwind his accounting. Chubby was delirious and his brain was taking him all over the place, and he knew it. Paula's White Russian, whatever it was, was still working.

"Let's take the bus – we'll get there faster by the time we get to the parking garage. My bike is still parked up there." They walked up to 5th Avenue and caught the number 8 up to Pill Hill – OSHU.

K hadn't eaten yesterday or last night and now it was 10 am. Felt like he was going to melt, not belly hunger, just a bit faint, but only for the moment, and he quickly pulled himself together.

The bus made its way up the hill toward the hospital.

CHAPTER 24
GUNFIRE ON THE RIVER

11:00 am, Saturday, July 18, 2020

MEANWHILE, ON THE OTHER SIDE OF THE RIVER, PEGGY and Nate stopped when they got to the Sellwood Bridge.

"Why didn't you wake me earlier?" Nate had on one of Spence's Beavers T-shirts, with his droopy camo shorts, mullet and chin in place, and no helmet.

"Habit. I remember you biting my head off for waking you back – then."

"You're a real funny girl. I am different now, Maggie. Older men don't sleep as much."

"Hmm. Well, OK. I am worried about Spence too. Let's cross here, rather than down at the Tilikum bridge."

"You mean the bridge that looks like a slinky?"

"Yeah, I guess. If we cross here, there's a bike path into town, down through the park close to the river," said Peggy.

"Can't we ride on the street? We are more likely to be picked out if it isn't crowded."

"We can ride on the sidewalk, up ahead. Then we'll cut through the park for a half mile, then get back on Macadam."

Once across the river, looking back, they saw a huge crowd of people pushing along the river looking to camp at Sellwood Park.

And up the river even more people crowded in among trees close to the water.

"Some days," said Peggy, as she and Nate watched from the park across the river, "they are left alone, but sometimes, they get forced out as it is getting dark. Strange rumors about (V)ICE's 'outreach' – talk of registrants getting trucked off to 'rehab' camps. It is awful. They get herded away from Sellwood, then forced to keep moving. The Vagrancy ICE sometimes sends in food trucks, but the lines in front of them are very short; they force people to register before they can eat or take any food. They are singled out afterwards and get trucked off to the rehab camps. There is a big one about 15 miles west at Sandy River Park out past Gresham."

When they got to the South Waterfront tram station, they stopped. There was shooting from across the river. A lot of shooting.

"Oh my God – Spence could have been caught over there," said Peggy. Nate tried to look back across the river to see through the haze. He saw the automatic rifle flashes, followed by the sound of continuous firecrackers.

"The shooting is coming from boats. Look! But Spence should be at the office by now. Fuck, they are just killing people!"

"Jesus, Nate, what are we going to do?"

"Just – just – we have to keep going. I am going to take the tram up to the hospital and see if I can find out what happened – to Paula. I need to know if she is alright."

Peggy got off her bike and came over and hugged Nate. "I haven't seen you in almost 20 years, Nate!" She was crying. "I am so sorry and scared. Things are changing bad."

"Stop it. Look at me."

Peggy's eyes were filled with tears and she kissed him on the mouth. She lingered. They pulled back and looked at each other. "We haven't talked about anything – Spence's script and why they are after it, this *SwiftPad* crap, you, or me. It doesn't matter, though, looking at you now, it all washes away, and we are here, now."

"Yes," he said. "We are here." Nate pulled back, just a bit. "Be careful Maggie. If I can, I'll meet you at Couch Park. Have you met this friend of Spence's, Alison?"

"No. I think they are just co-workers."

"Huh?"

She shrugged, and smiled slightly. "They work together – I don't think they are..." Peggy trailed off, embarrassed.

"You know this park, right?"

"Yeah – it's on the other side of 405 – 20th and Glisan. Over in Northwest."

OK," Nate smiled wanly. "Got it. Wait for Spence there. I will be there as quick as I can. We'll figure the next move then."

"Yeah."

"I still love you – you know that. I just wish we could have..."

"I know." She kissed him again. "See you at Couch Park."

CHAPTER 25

GOODBYE

11:30 am, Saturday, July 18, 2020

TOTALLY EXHAUSTED, KIP MADE HIS WAY TO THE SUR-
gical waiting room. Alice was there and she came up and
hugged him.

"When did you get here?" K asked her.

"Couple hours ago. He is still in surgery. It is not good. Why,
Kip?"

"I don't know. I have no idea who those people were that...or
why..." And that was, after all is said, the truth.

They waited, and after a while started talking. Kip hadn't
seen Alice in almost a year. He told her about his trip to Central
Asia, and his romance, skipping the part about Paula. Alice was
struggling to stay positive, and asked questions about his trip.
They were both desperate to keep their minds away from Jim's
situation. She asked if he had met any religious people, Tibetan
Buddhists, Daoist holy men, etc.? He pretended he had, to take
Alice's mind off of Jim.

She was in shock, but still held out hope in a peaceful trance.
Kip didn't want to disturb it, although what she was going to
have to go through...he couldn't face it. He didn't think he could
get through it.

Finally, time arrived. Here and now. The doctor came out and told them Jim was gone. Alice hugged Kip.

"We are alone, Kip," she sobbed.

Some part of K knew he had to get through this and be strong. Alice shook in his arms. "Take us to him," she demanded of the doctor. Kip hugged Alice and he felt the hyper-awareness that he sensed he shared with Alice – he almost expected Jim to walk out and meet them and tell them it was OK.

"He is not ready to be..."

"I don't care," she said.

The doctor took them into the operating room. They were just finishing up detaching him from the IVs and instruments. His face was bleached out.

Jim twitched. Alice took a deep and startled breath.

"That is normal," said the orderly who was cleaning up the gauze and odds and ends of emergency surgery. "Neural electrical spasms."

K thought it was more than that, but let it pass. Was he still there, he wondered, taking his time, leaving slowly? They looked at Jim for a few minutes. They said good-bye and K told him not to wait around, just get going, he would catch up later. Alice sobbed. She held his face, and kissed him. She pulled herself up, nodded, squeezed his hand once more, and Kip led her out.

"We are going to get these guys. I promise. He was my brother."

They hugged.

"I am OK," she said. "You go ahead."

CHAPTER 26
THE GREAT ESCAPE

Noon, Saturday, July 18, 2020

PAULA SAT UP IN HER HOSPITAL BED. THE CROW'S feet around her eyes seemed to be spreading like roots growing in a time-lapse film.

"We have a plan, Paula. You just need to walk straight down the hall to the entrance. Some guys will help you into an ambulance. They will take you away from the hospital and move you to another transport and take you down to Benton County – to Alice's compound. Try not to falter. You got it. Walk carefully. The bandage only needs to hold until we get to the ambulance – you can lie down there. We have a great doctor who will ride with you. Can you do it?"

"Yep." A little out of it, she focused on each task. "Where's Nate?"

Chubby bent down and untied Alice's shoes, which were sitting next to Paula's bed.

"I am sure he is OK. Alice, you are going to have to bluff it out when they find you here instead of Paula." Chubby helped her take off her shoes and put them on Paula's feet.

"They fit close enough," Paula said.

"I will say – I got tired and overwhelmed. Jim – oh, dear Jim! I came in here and I fell asleep. I'll tell them, 'I am an old woman. I just lost my son! Leave me alone!'" She smiled through her tears, and Paula did too. Alice tied Paula's hair back and helped her pull on her own flower print dress and adjusted her sun hat. Alice settled into Paula's hospital bed and pulled up the covers.

"Ready?"

Paula nodded at Chubby. She stood, holding the railing at the bottom of the bed, took several deep breaths, and nodded. She walked toward the door, in front of Chubby, opened the door herself, and started striding down the corridor, with a determined and alert stride. Chubby walked slowly behind her, while Paula stayed well in front, walking steadily and freely.

"Excuse me! Sir! Yes – you – we need to talk to you." Kip looked unperturbed, but just a little annoyed, and stopped as they walked toward him. A trim, tall, blond man in a sharp blue suit, brown tie, and shiny brown shoes, accompanied by a similarly dressed black man, albeit in a beige suit, approached. The black guy showed his badge and held it open as Kip looked carefully at it, slightly moving his lips as he read.

"FBI? Mr. Small – Ron? Ho boy! You guys still in business? I thought you all got transferred to Homeland Security."

"Sometimes I wonder about that too." His white partner chuckled. "Be that as it may, we want to have a conversation with you."

"Regarding?"

"You are Kipling Rehain, correct?"

"Who?"

"Kipling Rehain? – software entrepreneur? – *SwiftPad*?"

"I am sorry, no. No, I am Cornelius Welles – some of my friends call me Corny – or Wellesley – and some call me Chubby."

"Were you just visiting the woman who was shot?"

"Oh, Paula. Yeah. I think she is going be OK. Still bleeding some, but it appears it is under control. She is asleep now." He nodded back toward the room. "No, no – I see what you are driving at. No. I am a private detective. Here's my ID." Kip produced his extremely high quality Cornelius Welles IDs: driver's license and Oregon PI ID. "I was hired by the *SwiftPad* crew – along with Paula – we were running some leads and I was just talking to her."

"You know it's a federal crime to lie to the FBI, don't you?"

"Sir, I am a licensed investigator. I think I would understand that, Agent Small. Of course, I will be glad to help, but can you give me a few minutes? I have to take a shit so bad I can taste it." Chubby squinted and moved his hips in a tight circle.

"Yeah, OK." The two G-men looked at each other, and Agent Small made a face of slight disgust and shrugged. "Sure, we'll be right over here."

Kip smiled and then walked stiff-legged with tight butt-cheeks over to the men's room, opened the door, then turned around quickly, glanced back and saw that the two G-men had turned away and were walking toward Paula's room. Chubby then sauntered to the entrance, not looking back. He got outside and saw Paula patiently standing down in the driveway, wearing Alice's dress, sun hat, and over-sized sunglasses. Chubby flagged Heber's private ambulance and using hand signals directed him to Paula. The uniformed paramedics put flashers on, pulled up in front of Paula, and got out to help her into the ambulance. Kip walked down the driveway.

"We are all set," the driver said. Kip smiled at Paula as she sat down carefully on the stretcher. She gave him a thin, exhausted smile back. He quickly stepped down the driveway toward the bike rack, unlocked his bike, and headed down the hill.

CHAPTER 27
WATCHING FROM THE SHADOWS

11:40 am, Saturday, July 18, 2020

N ATE BOUGHT A TICKET FOR THE OHSU TRAM, AND took his bike up to the top of Pill Hill. When he got out, he had a hard time maneuvering through the crowd. He asked a woman where the main entrance was, and she directed him around to the other side of the building he had just come through. Ambulances were parked around the entrance. They were backed up all the way down the hill. There was an endless queue of people arriving. Nate waited, watching.

After a few minutes, his eyes fell on a woman standing very unsteadily wearing a sundress and a floppy hat. Her face was lined and her eyes unfocused. Then a man with a not-so-closely shaved head and a Lucifer beard came out of the hospital, as if he was trying not to be noticed. He signaled across to what looked like a private ambulance (a Citroen), and it quickly cut off another car and blew its "Wah-Wah" European horn, scaring a pedestrian back on the sidewalk. It pulled over and the two EMTs got out and approached the lady in the sunhat and began leading her toward the back. Then she took her hat off.

Nate saw her, but he couldn't believe how much she had changed since earlier yesterday. He looked around and there were cops everywhere, and he stepped back behind a pillar to avoid their glances. She seemed alternatively alert, then unfocused, and did not hesitate as she got into the back of the ambulance.

As soon as she got in and the attendants closed the door, the man with the Vandyke beard and the stubble-covered dome began walking a bike fast down the hill, where he mounted it, and turned onto a path into the trees.

Then two men in nice suits came out looking frantically around – they just missed seeing the guy with the stubble-covered head and Vandyke. Nate watched them – one white, one black – pull out fones and start walking toward the parking garage.

As soon as they were out of sight, Nate got back on his stolen blue racing bike and tried to follow Lucifer Vandyke. He coasted down the hill and turned into a path about where he saw him turn in. It was rough terrain and Nate's bike wasn't made for off-road. He carried the bike down the nature path until he got to the lower road, hopped on, and then put it into progressively higher gears and started driving hard down the hill.

He came out on Barbur Boulevard, just up from the Under Armour Center. He saw Lucifer ahead, and caught him at the light just before going over the 405.

"Where are they taking her?" Having finally stopped, Nate was exhausted.

"Shit! Schuette? Where the fuck have you been?"

Nate, recognizing the voice, peered at Chubby. "Kip! You look like a shit-out-of-luck Fu Manchu!" He leaned over like he was going to hurl. "I saw some guys in suits come out after you who looked like they ..." He stopped to catch his breath.

"Speaking of trash – what kind of animal is that on your head?"

"We should start a band."

"We need to get off the street," said Chubby.

"Yes, we do."

"Listen. They killed Gordy Lobetts and kidnapped Cynthia

Oglethorpe. Principals of *Reigny Deigh* and *SwiftPad*. I saw another *Reigny Deigh* guy. He is the –"

"Shit – Spencer Stromborn."

"Yeah! How…"

"Long story," said Nate. "Where did you see him?"

"In the back of a (V)ICE cruiser. They were pulling into the Courthouse, earlier this morning."

"FUUUCKK! Shit, I should have gotten up earlier. Shit. They are starting to round people up. This is it."

"Yeah, yeah. Listen, I was there. So was Paula. She saved my life and got shot."

"How did they get all these ICY fuckers deployed so fast? It's a fucking invasion."

"They knew it was coming – it's a fucking Reichstag Fire. American style."

Another cruiser went wailing by. Nate, breathing hard, focused his solar plexus, trying to center himself. Can't quit, he told himself. "They are shooting people over near Sellwood. Just firing away with automatic weapons from a boat into a crowd of refugees."

"This is bad. I got a guy – he is going to pick me up down here – in front of the Econo Lodge. They executed my best friend. We grew up together. Closest…he was sliced open like a fish."

"I'm sorry."

"And Paula – she looked bad. Fuck."

"We still don't know…We can't…, we have to stay calm, and…" Nate stopped and tried to regain his composure. Kip was weeping. They stood there out in the open, straddling their bikes in the middle of one of the busiest intersections of the city. Nate was still struggling to get his breathing under control.

"And that douche from *Reigny Deigh* – Gordon Lobetts. Just executed him in front of all of us," said Chubby. "None of this is an accident. Fuck. We need to get out of sight and stay low. Otherwise they are going to get me. Probably you too."

"You have a burner number? An OTP?"

"Two. Use this one."

Nate typed it into his one-time-hash. "Here – copy my hash. Got it? I'll join you if I can. We should be safe to chat tonight with our burners. I have to make one more stop. You go to ground and wait."

CHAPTER 28
INCIDENT AT COUCH PARK

Noon, Saturday, July 18, 2020

AFTER PEGGY HAD WATCHED NATE'S AERIAL GON-dola rise up the hill, swaying back and forth, sailing over I-5 and on to Pill Hill, she rode hard through the South Waterfront's canyon of condos. In the city, the local cops left the small groups of homeless alone, as long as they stayed off the streets and the bike paths. Margaret, at the last minute, decided to ride down the path along Waterfront Park anyway. People who didn't appear homeless were out walking and biking there. Some were smiling and talking with animation. The Westside, with its major business offices, was heavily patrolled, mostly by the local cops. Peggy looked out on the river and saw patrol boats with big binoculars checking the shoreline. The faint echo of gunshots from south along the river continued sporadically.

At Couch, Peggy turned west, and rode up the gentle hill toward the northwest side of the city. It was becoming cloudy, but otherwise a beautiful, not-too-hot summer day. She crossed the 405 and at 19th turned north, staying on the sidewalk for the four blocks (riding against one-way traffic). She walked her bike into the park at Glisan, not bothering to lock it.

Peggy entered Couch Park, walking up a slight rise, slowly, looking around, trying to scope out the situation. She sat on the concrete circular benches around the little fountain, near a play structure. A woman with medium-length brown hair, thirtyish, who appeared tired and drawn, was watching her preschooler climbing on the modern art jungle gym that looked like a Picasso sculpture. For a Saturday afternoon, the park seemed strangely deserted.

Peggy smiled at the woman, who smiled tightly back. She was fidgeting nervously and then suddenly called her young son over, who whined about leaving. He was traversing the metal upper bars that were more or less parallel to the ground, and came down the toddler chain ladders. He fell as he dismounted the jungle gym, started crying, and was quietly hushed by his mother. She led him away.

Margaret was suddenly very depressed. She knew practically nothing about the woman she was to meet. She worked with Spence – and he seemed nervous when he told her about – Alison. Wow, don't forget her name, she thought. Margaret didn't know how old she was or what she looked like. She checked her burner, and expected Spence to be arriving soon, but because of the overwhelming (V)ICE commando presence and all the gunfire, she was very worried.

She was alone in the park. Peggy sat quietly on the bench next to the play structure, waiting. She was hyper-alert, aware of every bike or car that passed. A couple guys – college types with cargo shorts and Nike shirts – bouncing a basketball started walking over to the court on the far uphill side of the park. Spence should have been able to ride here by now, she thought – it wasn't that far from his office. She fought against her own thoughts, refusing to think about what might have happened.

Peggy watched the guys shooting baskets. They either ignored or didn't see her. One of them lit up what looked like a joint and sucked on it while his partner shot layups, rebounded and shot again, as fast as he could, until he finally missed after about eight shots. Then he smoked on the joint while the other guy shot.

Then, out of the shadows, a spiky-haired woman appeared with a green pullover, loose-fitting jeans, and large, round earrings that seemed to glow green. She stood in the corner with her hands up, waiting for a pass. The taller of the two guys standing under the basket fired a pass to her and with one smooth Ray Allen–like move she fired a jumper that swished. She moved to the side and took another pass and swished that. And another. And then another at the top of the key. She waved, and then she walked directly to Peggy, who asked, sotto voce, "Alison?"

Alison sat down next to her. "How do I know you?"

"Spence said he mistook you for a lesbian when he first met you."

Alison laughed. "I was all-state 10 years ago. Where's Spence?"

"He left early this morning to take care of some stuff at the office. I hope he comes soon. They were shooting people over by Oaks Park. I could hear the shots and people screaming. I am worried; he probably rode through there earlier and might have been hit. He should have been here already. I am not sure what – he said we needed to meet you here about a *Reigny Deigh* meeting."

"We were originally supposed to launch the *SwiftPad* C2B movie project with – the script. You know about that right?"

"You mean Spence and Nate's script?"

"Nathan Schuette? You know him?" Alison turned away from Margaret. They heard something coming up the path.

"Nate?"

"Maggie. Yeah." Nate had apparently parked his bike by an iron fence across the street. He was trudging along, shuffling, old man style, and breathing fairly heavily.

"Gordon, the *Reigny Deigh* guy, is dead. *SwiftPad* exec – Jim Hunt – dead. And Oglethorpe – the *SwiftPad* inventor – kidnapped. Who's this?" Nate asked.

"Gordy's dead? Shit." Alison slumped over and shook her head.

"Who are you?" Nate asked again, with an edge to his voice.

Alison gave Nate a long, smoldering look. "Alison. Alison Aykroyd. I work with Spence at *Reigny Deigh.*" Nate grunted. "You are Nathan Schuette – I know – I know about you."

Nate nodded submissively. Alison scooted over and the three of them sat on the bench, watching the hoop shooters.

"Also – Paula – was shot," he said. "She is the woman I was telling you about, Maggie."

"Oh no!"

"Yeah. She is alive. Some friends were able to smuggle her out of the hospital. They are taking her to a safe place. But she looks...not good..."

"Nate – I am so sorry." Peggy put her hand on his shoulder.

"She's strong." Nate looked up and noticed that the two guys had stopped shooting baskets.

The tall guy in cargo shorts looked back at them. "You want to play?"

Nate waved them off. "I'm too fucking old," he said in a soft voice to Peggy and Alison. "Saw you knocking them down – nice stroke. So?"

"The meeting is apparently still on – still at Gordy's condo. I didn't know he was killed though. Have they announced it yet?"

"No," said Maggie, who was searching her fone for news.

"We have a new face in the company, Kayla...and she is a – I don't trust her. I am sure she will slide right in with Telly Haines – maybe she already had before today – who knows? Apparently Gordy's death...has not caused her or Telly to have too many tears."

"Fucking Telly Haines," said Nate.

"Anyway – Kayla texted me about the meeting and told me some people were wounded, but...said nothing about Gordy being dead."

"So why doesn't she wait until..." Peggy said.

"Because Haines doesn't want to wait," said Nate. "Right?

This woman, Kayla, she knew he was dead. He was targeted. I talked to a guy who was there. He saw the bullet explode the top of his skull. Everyone there knows he is dead."

"I guess," said Alison, looking at Nate with respectful wonder. "Yeah. Telly doesn't want to wait. He wants to take over the company before people start asking questions."

"The script is dangerous, because it is true – it is the true history of the origins of Ben Cadez," said Nate.

"Right. I am sure they want to kill it or kompromat it."

"So…," Peggy asked.

"I don't know what to do with my version." Nate scanned the park, holding his hand up for a brief silence, listening with a worried frown. "Here – words are nothing anymore. Anyone can write – words. But now stories will be pumped directly into people's heads. That is what they want to control. And that might be the only way we can stop them."

"Listen to this," said Peggy. "This just popped up when I S-Peed *Reigny Deigh*:

Reigny Deigh Media has announced it will be producing selected *SwiftPad* content for use with the Gupta C2B. A new *SwiftPad* technique for coding narration and video together along with brief cuts to actors is a relatively cheap and effective technique for portraying a story. According to *Reigny Deigh* executive Kayla Holmes, this technique incorporates the *SwiftPad* feature of morphing, and mixing a finite set of episodic bites into an exponentially larger number of potential stories, hitting each *SwiftPad* user in a particular way, cutting through to their socio-political-cultural-economic sweetspot. "So the coding will personalize the content, Holmes said. "The scripting language takes input from most generally accepted novelistic and screen-writing techniques, and creates an individually targeted product that is different for each user who engages with the eStory. It will have profound and lasting effects on the *SwiftPad* users who experience the stories."

"Spence is really the only one at *RDM* who knows SP-script," said Alison. "It is so new. She is so full of shit, just mouthing words Spence wrote."

"So – you combine that with this new C2B technology and boom. Instant and total propaganda, direct and unfiltered by experience or consciousness," Nate said.

"One – encode the story. Two – add the variable and flexible *SwiftPad* narrative," said Alison. "Yeah. Basically, that is it."

"Three – encode and broadcast it as a C2B package."

"We need to get our script out in the world, and published on the C2B, so everyone knows what a ghoul Cadez is," said Nate. A ghoul, like me and Paula, he thought. "If we can get it to the technical people – the originals, not the Amazon staff – maybe they can do it."

"But which one?" asked Alison.

"For all intents and purposes Spence's version and mine are the same. He gets details wrong – names, streets, some sequences. But – as far as the basic money shots go – he had the experience too – in a different way. But we need to fix his errors or they will tear it apart – if part of it is wrong then all of it is, they will say."

"So you have a script too?"

"Mine is told – autobiographical," said Nathan. "Spence's is – second hand – an, 'as told to' via psycho-pharmacological enhancement. His might actually be better. More dramatic. Reality is messy, and inconsistent."

"But not as – true – right?" Peggy looked confused as she spoke.

"True?" Nate laughed, and leaned over to catch his breath again. "Who knows? Maybe his is true. Just because I lived it – supposedly lived it – doesn't mean I remembered it right. Maybe Spence was better at reading between the lines."

"Regardless, they want to own it so they can bury it – or rewrite it," said Alison. "Anyway, I have Spence's version." She held up her fone. "He gave it to me yesterday afternoon. But we still have to convert it to SP-Script, but – you don't code do you?"

"Fuck no," Nate exclaimed as if she was insulting him.

"Then – unless Spence shows up – we will need one of the *SwiftPad* people to do it," said Alison. "If they have any style or artistic sense."

"Art has nothing to do with it," said Nate. "The art happens in the brain of the person receiving it. Right?"

"Yeah. I suppose someday, when it is better understood how the script works, it might make a difference how it is built." Alison watched the two guys shooting baskets. "For now, all we can provide is just use cases, and highly defined deliverables. In the end, what comes out is uncontrollable."

"But still enough to control the country. Maybe we just have to shut down *SwiftPad*; the C2B is just brainfuzz without it," said Nate.

"With Gordy dead, things are going to change," said Alison, as now Nate noticed the two basketball players looking at them and whispering. "Not for the better."

"Alison, you have to go to that meeting with Telly – and keep in touch somehow. You have to join them, even help them – until we pull the pin."

"Pin?"

"The grenade – the no turning back point – that is coming. This will be incredibly dangerous. But if *Reigny Deigh* takes over *SwiftPad*, then we will need to control *Reigny Deigh*. Somehow."

Alison looked over at the basketball players. The two shooters, wearing cargo shorts and tee-shirts with Nike logos, fanned out as they walked toward them.

"Hey," the taller one said, "you guys want to come to a party?"

"No thanks," said Peggy.

"Oh, you should, really should." The shorter one started to pull out something from his back pocket. He was walking quickly toward them and racking a round into the chamber of a small Luger. "Put your hands up! Now!"

BANG! and the short guy was down.

Nate leaped up and quickly kicked the little Luger out of the short guy's hand, all the while keeping a bead on the tall one.

"Down on the ground now! Or you are both dead. Now." The shorter shooter was moaning. His left foot was covered in blood where Nate had shot him. Nate picked up the gun and handed it to Peggy. "Aim right at his head. If either one moves, kill him." Nate bent down and searched the tall one, who seemed to be shaking. Nate pulled out his phone and wallet, an identical gun, and a (V)ICE badge. He found a syringe in a little quiver in his back pocket. "What is this?" Nate pushed his gun hard into the taller shooter's neck.

Then – a muffled shot and an explosion of blood.

"He moved," said Peggy.

"Oh God! You killed him!" The taller guy tried to sit up, was kicked back down by Nate, and then began to cry.

"What's this? What!"

"Propofol," he sobbed. "We were only supposed to drug and..."

"And what? How did you know we were here?"

"Ahhh, no," said the tall one on the ground as he looked over at his dead partner. "We are looking for a dyke. Mr. Haines sent me! I thought it was her! No! We just wanted to talk. Please! You're going to kill me...please!"

"Take it easy, man. Just stay calm. No, I'm not going to kill you. Relax," said Nate. "It was just an accident," he turned away casually and took the short guy's gun from Peggy. Then Nate turned, leaned down, and pushed the barrel tight against the back of the tall guy's neck. The shot was muffled, and there was very little blood.

The three of them looked at each other and then Nate said, "Help me." He and Alison pulled the shorter guy's body over and stacked him on the other guy, unbuttoned their shorts and pulled them both down to their ankles, and positioned them homoerotically. "Let them think about that. They might get thrown off." He wiped off the kill gun and put it in the short guy's hand, then handed the other to Alison.

They walked to the gate, got on their bikes, and rode up the hill, away from the park, just past 21th Avenue. It was impossible to know if anyone had seen them, there were so many vantage points. They wheeled into the back of the Trader Joe's parking lot, under some trees.

All three of them appeared to be in shock, and were breathing hard.

"We…" Peggy was hyperventilating, "…fuck. Oh fuck."

"They are looking for me," said Alison.

"Seems like it. They know you work there and…" said Nate, "they might have nabbed Spence and if so then they must have his fone – didn't he call you?" he looked at Alison. "What did he say, in his call?"

"It was a text. Nothing…used an OTP."

"Sure?"

Alison nodded. "We traded hashes yesterday afternoon."

"Still."

"He kept nothing on his company fone. He was really strict about it," said Peggy. "He memorized the hash on his burner."

"He might have pulled his script off the cloud onto his fone," said Alison. "He showed it to me yesterday."

"Hold on," said Peggy. "Yes! I got into Spence's cloud. How do you delete…"

"Here, let me," said Alison. Peggy glared at Alison as she handed her the fone.

"Spence's trusts you with his could passcode?" Nate was smiling.

"Yes. I trust him too," Peggy and Nate stared at each other. Alison looked at them both.

"There is a function," said Alison. "here – Blastscram. It is supposed to be unrecoverable. Spikes the backups too. It will take another half hour, but if they aren't into it yet – it should be gone."

"They can break him, but it shouldn't matter, as long as he deleted the script after he gave it to me."

"What about you?" asked Peggy with an edge.

"Blasted it as soon as I read it."

"How much more do they know?" asked Nate. "The whole thing is over if they know we are onto Cadez. If they torture Spence – and they will, when they find these guys dead – we might have some time, but not much."

"Oh fuck. Dammit, Nate, why did you come back!" Peggy looked at Alison and felt angry at her too. "I wish you had just left us alone!"

"Why does everyone think I am a lesbian?" asked Alison, letting Peggy's anger bounce off. Both Nate and Peggy laughed.

Peggy looked around, "Is there a camera here?"

"I checked the poles and windows around the park; maybe, but I doubt it," said Nate. "Here? I don't think so."

"Let's get out of here," said Alison.

"What are you going to do now?"

"I have to go meet with those guys," Alison said. "It will throw them off the scent about these guys. Haines is in deep with the government. These were ICE – (V)ICE guys. Right?"

"They had the IDs," said Nate.

"So – If *Reigny Deigh* – Telly – is connected with killing Gordy, then..."

Nate looked at Peggy. "Yeah – it will be incredibly dangerous. Wait here. I am going to check for cameras up ahead."

"Spence will throw them off the scent," said Peggy. "For a while, anyway. He won't give you up easy."

"I know," said Alison. "We just have to hope we are clear for now."

Neither woman spoke, but just looked off in the distance.

"I am staying with Alison," Peggy said. Nate felt let down for a second, then nodded.

"Yeah – yeah. That is best," said Nate, looking at Peggy, shaking his head and holding her hand. "A guy is picking me up in five minutes. I have to get to the spot. Just – try to get in and out and find out what you can. Maggie – hide and watch. Alison, can you signal Maggie? Can you get to a window or find some way to signal Maggie if things start to go south?"

"It's at Gordy's condo. I've been there. I'll try and signal with my fone light from the top floor balcony if I can step away. We'll figure something out."

"I wish we hadn't killed those guys," said Peggy.

"We killed two cops – so...yeah...we know what that means. Alison, give the gun to Maggie. You have to be clean. Maggie – if it gets bad, just point and shoot. Don't let them take you."

"I was a soccer mom. Yesterday I was –"

Nate shrugged. "Sorry." He took Peggy by the shoulders and looked at her, with a slight smile. "As Bogey once said, the problems of three little people don't amount to a hill of beans in this world now. They have Spence, Maggie. Not maybe, they do. My friend saw him in the back of a (V)ICE cruiser pulling in to the Justice building." He looked at her hard. "I'm going to my safe spot," said Nate. "Ranjit's Kwikie Mart off of MLK on the east side, just north of Killingsworth – it is upstairs. Got it? If they get you, you have to keep that secret. We will be out of there by tomorrow." Both of the women nodded.

"Don't get caught. Life is going to take on a different meaning now. Alison. You just have to make magic, that's all."

There was nothing more to say. Nate held Peggy's hand, and she realized she was Maggie again; Peggy had left the premises. He squeezed her hand a little, and then rode his bike down the hill. He saw an open gate next to a house on 19th Avenue and quickly pushed his stolen bike in and shut the gate behind him, hoping the owners would like the $3K bike. He walked the rest of the way to the I-405 exit near 16th and Couch, where Aldane was right there, somehow, and picked him up in his tricked-out 1990 Cutlass Ciera.

CHAPTER 29
COMMAND POST ABOVE THE KWIKIE MART

2:00 pm, Saturday, July 18, 2020

Who would survive? Interesting questions. I would predict it will be convicts and file clerks... Imagine what will happen. A small group of vicious criminals will fight an army of file clerks for the remaining means of life. The convicts will know violence. But the file clerks will know organization. Who do you think would win?

Professor Groeteschele Failsafe

CHUBBY WAS ASLEEP ON HIS COUCH WHEN NATE AND Aldane trudged in. Aldane had stopped along the way for a bucket of chicken, which Nate carried up the rickety outside steps. As they walked into Kip's high-ceilinged apartment, Aldane took off his shoes at the door, and slid in his socked feet across the smooth, polished wood floors. Nate, trudging in behind, was munching on a chicken leg. He was pretty ripe, and Chubby picked up the scent from across the room. Nate looked every day of his 70 years. "How safe do you think we are?"

Chubby said he thought they were safe, for a little while anyway. His apartment above the Kwikie Mart was almost in plain sight, which is the best hiding place sometimes.

"We cool," said Aldane. "Took a long go around Albina, no followers."

"You got any pot?" Nate looked like a dog that hadn't been fed for a while. "Or something to drink? I need to take a nap," Nate asked.

Kip shook his head. An old stoner, how fucking pathetic. Kip felt the same urge of course, as he always did when he was stressed, or even when he was feeling good for that matter, but for now he was still "on the wagon." Right now, Kip thought, it would turn him to an inert pile of shit, and considering the current hostilities on the street, it might get him dead.

Jim was stoned when he died.

"We need to focus. We have to think and be alert, otherwise..." Kip sat on the edge of his recliner, facing old, bedraggled, bleary-eyed Nate, and wondered if he was anchored to a senile geezer who was going to get him killed.

"Yeah. I know." He did indeed. Just killed two cops, Nate thought, and I can't tell anyone. Compartmentalize. "I know. It's just – too much stress," Nate said. "Stress kills. Got to stay alive." Nate looked over at Kip to see if he cracked a smile, but he didn't. He plopped down on the couch, then leaned back, with his mouth half-opened and eyes half-closed. "I need to block it out. But no worries, I am cool."

"Block what?" asked Aldane, who made it plain from his expression that he had serious doubts about Nate.

Chubby stared blankly at Nate. He looked like death's ugly older brother. "If you want to take a shower..." Chubby pointed to Nate's crouch and staged whispered toward Aldane, "Urine..."

"Yeah – Fuck you Rehain. it's just – yeah, OK, let me do that..." Nate pulled himself up and limped toward the bathroom in the back of the sprawling apartment.

"So what's you gonna do?" Aldane was still standing by the door, watching his friend and this stinky old man who he had just retrieved off the street from the other side of the river. The old man started to the bathroom but turned and stood there as if he forgot what he was doing.

"I don't know," K said with a finality that seemed to physically chill Aldane. Kip had never seen Aldane worried, even when running through the Jamaican jungle from machine gunfire. "Paula is going to get to Alice's hippie village somehow outside the compound. I don't know if she will make it. She was fading."

"Half of (V)ICE is here or will be soon," said Aldane. "Some shit for sure going down in this town."

"It's already started," Kip said.

"Yeah? Where?"

"I saw a guy I know in the back of a..." Kip said, turning to look at Aldane. Nate, standing naked at the bathroom door, was listening. "A guy – he works for *Reigny Deigh*. They were taking him into the basement of the Justice Center downtown."

"You know him, old man?" asked Aldane.

"Yeah," said Nate, scratching his bare ass as he stood in the bathroom doorway. "A long time. Spence Stromborn...about 20 years ago he stole my girlfriend and married her. My life is a long series of relationship fuckups. I am beginning to think it's me..."

Kip shook his head at Nate, got up and looked out the window down toward the street.

"I just left her, Maggie, and another woman, who works with Spence at *RDM*," Nate said. "Kind of dykey in a sexy way. Alison something. I trust them. I trust Maggie anyway, and Alison seems OK."

Nate thought – Maggie and I killed a couple of cops while Alison watched us. Killing someone up close with accomplices changes things. Everything actually. Have to trust.

"Alison is meeting with *RDM*'s new boss," Nate continued.

"Telly Haines. If Alison and Maggie can get out – then I think they will come here. I gave them your address."

"You're shitting me?"

"No shit," said Nate.

"Those women are fucked if they don't get out of there. And we are fucked if they follow them here."

"I know. It's fucked. Too late to do anything about it now. Neither one can go back to their place – both are too close to Spence, and they will start digging. No choice."

Kip shook his head. "Fucking Telly Haines." Business partner of the old Prez, made his money in AM radio with Daddy's money. Daddy ran derelict ships, carrying illegally cut timber out of Borneo. Jersey scumbag with lowlife mob connections. Kip looked at Aldane. "You staying up in the Hills tonight?"

"No. They taken over my lady's house. AKs and rockets on their belt. Serious shit! I ain't goin' up dar."

Chubby looked at Nate, who nodded. "Yeah – he's right. We have moved a small army up there and nobody noticed it. It's coming. Maybe soon."

"Don't worry 'bout me," said Aldane. "I'll be back here tomorrow early. I got some shit to attend to. And a show – my band, we opening tonight for the Jean Katon Express. Dey doing the Moda tonight."

"Shit, that's right. That concert tonight! The Mane Shakers and the Jean Katon Express! How many people will be there?"

"Well, you know, she's hot. Filled up the Dome in New Orleans last month. I don't know, maybe five, six thousand. Just the city, with the shit going down, nobody gonna come out but the Stone Brothers of the 6th Dimension."

"He means people who listen to his radio show. It's a thing Nate."

Nate, still standing there with his old man nakedness flaccidly exposed, picked up his camo shorts and pulled out his fone. "A thing huh? Fuck, how many did you say?"

"Maybe six thou, maybe more, it's hard to tell. She sold 4 thousand advance."

"Fuck," said Nate, pulling up his camo shorts. "I gotta talk to some people." He went in the bedroom and shut the door.

"Some crazy shit. I be staying with Jean herself tonight, if I don't fuck up, like you always do, Kippy."

"Thanks. Good luck."

They heard Nate shouting into the fone.

"Maybe I can get you out of town," said Aldane. "Won't be free. But I can talk to Jean, see if I can get you a seat."

"To where?"

"Memphis. Jean Katon and her crew gettin' out tomorrow! G5 baby, super plane! Joan and me used to be tight – Ha! I saw her tonight after I heard about dem grabbing the Goblin girl. Flying back to Memphis. You heard 'bout Memphis? Stone cold bloods in charge! Colonel Hassan Coleman threw all the RedHat mota-fukers out! The Marcus Garvey Collective controls the river port up and down for a couple, three hundred miles. Fucker knows his shit. Air traffic is tight! No crashes yet! Ha! That what scares the shit out of me! I might be able to get you a seat. And of course – you gonna need a motafuken big box of hundreds!"

"Tomorrow I'll stop off at *SwiftPad* HQ. I have to clean out the safe, can't go into a bank. Too much to decide anything tonight. This calypso lady won't take my note? Can't you vouch for me?"

"She don't owe me," said Aldane.

CHAPTER 30
SIGNALS

1:30 pm, Saturday, July 18, 2020

ALISON PARKED HER BIKE ACROSS THE STREET FROM Sheer, the new "exclusive" wine bar on Northwest 23rd. Peggy, who was walking her bike, looked at the noir poster of a woman's stocking-sheathed legs. "This is new, isn't it?"

"It used to be the Easy Girl Café."

"Where they found that woman – killed by the *SwiftPad* executive!"

"Yeah. Walk your bike behind me on the other side of the street," Alison told Peggy, "not together."

They walked up Glisan, Alison going first, up the left side of the street, with Peggy a half a block behind on the right, both walking slowly toward Gordy's condo building. It was not hot and unusually quiet for a Saturday summer afternoon in Northwest Portland; hardly anyone was out on the street. The home invasion over in Southeast Portland had the city rattled.

Alison pulled out her SIM card, crushed and scattered it and then ditched her burner, so all she had left was her *RDM* company fone, which at that moment popped up with a video chat from Kayla.

"Alison!" Kayla was a consummate fake, and Alison sensed

the fear behind her perky greeting. Alison hit the green button and smiled.

"Hey, Kayla, I am just about there. Has it started?"

"Oh, Alison," Kayla said, breathlessly, "I am so worried about Spence! Did you know he was picked up by Vagrancy and Immigration Control?"

Alison did not look at Maggie, who had walked over and stood next to her to listen in. Maggie put her hand over her mouth to muffle her own sobbing.

"How do you know?"

"Well – the authorities have been in touch with the company!"

Gordy was dead and Spence, his long-time number two, was under arrest. Today was actually the end of Kayla's second day with *Reigny Deigh*. What exactly was "the company," Alison thought?

"Who's in charge?" asked Alison.

"Mr. Haines and some of his associates are here. They are asking – they say they own the company? Is that true?"

"Do they...?" Who am I kidding, she thought?

"Alison, they want to come and pick you up. Where are you?"

"Nearby. You are at Gordy's right?"

"His condo – on Park, just off of Vista – yeah."

"Tell 'em to sit tight, I'll be right there." She hung up. "Peggy – you know Washington Park at all?"

"Sure."

"There is a path up the hill, just on the other side of Burnside. Just cross over to the park down at the end of the street. It will take you up there. You can see Gordy's penthouse condo from just above the statue of Sacagawea."

"You mean the Lewis and Clark Memorial."

"Yeah! If you can get there and watch, its the tallest and newest condo. I'll try and get out there to signal you. One flash, I can get out, so head for Ranjits or whatever over on MLK right?"

"Got it."

"Two flashes – it means trouble. Just let me be, and hope for the best. I'll do what I have to do to stay out of trouble. We will play it by ear. I'll use the flashlight on my fone. Just take care of yourself, and let me do the same. I can handle this."

"OK. How do you know…?"

"I am just strange – OK? I ride my bike around a lot and notice things. Listen! One flash – I am OK and I will meet you at the address Nate gave us. Two – let me be, I can't get away. Got it?"

Alison headed up to 23rd street and then over Burnside toward Gordy's condo alone and Peggy rode south across Burnside and found the path.

CHAPTER 31
BRIEFING AT THE COMMAND POST

N ATE CAME OUT OF THE BATHROOM, DRIPPING AND wrapped up in a big towel. "I left my backpack in a locker across the river," he said.

K pointed toward his bedroom. "The clean pile is closest to the door."

Nate then returned to the living room, still wearing the towel, but carrying a pair of corduroys and a blue collared shirt. "I'm going to wear this tomorrow. OK?"

"Yeah." Chubby remained on the couch and didn't look up. "It's a good look for you. Be sure to wear the mullet."

There was a knock on the door. Kip answered. A native American woman dressed in Jean's, boots, and an ancient green field jacket was at the door.

"I am looking for Schuette."

Nate came out of the back bedroom. "Hey, are you from the Grennell group?"

"Yes, can I look around?"

Nate looked at Kip, who shrugged.

She walked into all the rooms, even looked in closets, and out the windows. Then spoke softly into her fone.

"Two men are coming up. Can we clear that table?" Without waiting for an answer she picked up some dirty food bowls and cups and moved them to the sink.

Four men came in, the two younger ones carrying what looked like Uzis, a white man about mid-fifties and a black guy in his forties.

Nate came over and greeted them. "Nate Schuette. Colonel, we met at Ishpeming."

Colonel Hassan Coleman stood 6'5" and had a sad, long ebony face and narrow, flat nose that displayed some heritage from that borderland south of Egypt, where black people of the Savanna met Sahara nomads. Senator Harvey Grennell was another story. A Republican Senator from Nebraska, who led a division in one of the recent Mesopotamian wars, he was slightly balding and had a round, everyman face that would have fit better on a harried father in a sitcom, or a car salesman. Back before the rise of "Real-Prez," he had been mentioned as a possible presidential candidate. He smiled easily on TV as he did now, introducing himself to Kip and Nate.

"We don't have much time so let's get to it." One of his aides spread a map of Portland out on the coffee table in front of the couch, and there Grennell sat, inviting Kip and Nate to sit beside him. Coleman stood behind them.

"Our intelligence all points to the fact that Portland is their objective. They are putting the equivalent of a division of (V)ICE into Portland with intent of declaring martial law, and – well – to shut it up. To shut down all resistance to the administration. I don't know whether this is being coordinated with the kidnapping of the Oglethorpe woman or not but it appears they are using that as a jumping off point, if you will. They have enough personnel here now to take over every institution private and public which they say poses a threat to them."

"The thing that is missing," said Colonel Coleman, "was a way to engage the people of Portland – Mr. Schuette – your idea to use this music concert will give us what we need – people power."

"That's right, Hassan. We have skilled fighters," said Grennell, "and great command and control, good intel, high morale, as far as it goes. But we only have fifteen hundred people in town. We have recruited another five hundred, but they have almost ten thousand (V)ICE here. So we can't match them openly. We have to divide them."

"Wait a minute," said Kip. "What are you talking about, the music concert."

"Let me lay it out for you, Mr. Rehain," said Grennell. "We have an opportunity to take out their Command and Control tonight – about 8 pm. The entire upper command of (V)ICE has reservations at a restaurant – Genevieve's."

"Never ate there," said Kip.

"It's on 23rd," said Aldane.

"So, if we decide to move now, step one," said Coleman, "is to – put something extra in the food that will take out the senior officers."

"Wow, that will fuck them," Kip said.

"Yeah – for a few hours," said Colonel Coleman. "But that means we are committed. All in."

"Next we will use your application – Mr. Moropolis, your company's technical guy, has set up a *SwiftPad* message board based on specific user profiles, messages that he says will only go to people we know are friends who are in the place we want them or need them – messages detailing where people should be, and when." Grennell looked down at the map, the stabbed his finger against it. "He claims there is a 99% surety that there will be no leaks. Some kind of psychometric mumbo jumbo, but-"

"Arky knows his shit. If he says it, its true," said Kip.

"But that is the key is to prime the pump," said Hassan.

"When people see a crowd going where they are told to go

via *SwiftPad,* it will make it easier for them to join in," Grennell explained.

"This is all or nothing. We have to go all out," Coleman added.

"Here, look at the map." Grennell smoothed out a topo-street map of Portland. "They are focused on the west side of the city, so we will too. Step two – once the senior officers have eaten, we need to create a diversion. It will have to be harsh. Our troops will find a way to ambush and either capture or kill some (V) ICE – up here." Grennell pointed at the general area around Washington Park. "We think that their junior officers – based on the orders we know they have and the training we know they have received – will send a large force up to find who did it. But there are only a few places they can enter – we expect them to send columns up this path here – and here," again Grennell stabbed the map. "A couple of thousand at least.

"It will fit into their overall plan – an excuse to start what they intend to start anyway."

"We are ready and can cut them up," said Coleman. "We expect them to attack at night, because of they have supplied their people with night vision equipment. Well, we have a surprise for them."

"'In your face laser tag,' we call it… it is our turf and we have been preparing the defense of Forest Park for months. But the problem comes when they start calling for reinforcements."

"We need people in the streets. We know where the choke points are, they will have to come out – here – here. And then depending – bring their reserves down from PDX either coming down I-5 from the north or from the east on 84. Once they commit, we can trap them on the highway. We can put barricades up, but what will really stop them is people."

"We don't think they will shoot into crowds," said Grennell. "but they might, if they see how desperate their situation is. If they do that, it goes viral – they don't want video out there of them shooting Americans in the street. It will hurt them."

"So you need a few thousand tethered goats," said Nate.

"Yeah," Coleman was smiling and nodding. "It's not a dinner party. We need people in the street to block their movement. It will give us time to neutralize their forces in the Park, then we can mop up, and defeat them in detail."

"So your idea, Mr. Schuette, to use the people gathered at the Moda to hear Jean Katon is really is the lynchpin. We know that the artists will support us, but we need to make a pitch to get them enthused, to get on the street. We need to interrupt the concert and convince a few thousand music fans to march out – to convince them we have a plan." Grennell nodded to Coleman. "And we do, we are ready. We give them vests – orange vests, green vests, blue vests – three teams. Then we march them out – two of the teams – hopefully a couple of thousand people – march them over the Steel Bridge. The other group will stay on this side of the river as a reserve to block whatever freeway (V)ICE decides to use to bring up their reserves. Easy access for either freeway is the Moda."

"It will be dangerous."

Neither officer said anything.

"When?" Nate asked.

"7:30," said Grennell. "Mr. Rehain –"

"Please – Kip."

"OK – you call me Harvey. Kip, you are famous in this town. You built *SwiftPad*. You need to fire up your people. We will have everything ready. You just need to get them to put on the vests and march out and follow our people."

Kip nodded.

"Anything else?" Coleman looked at Nate and Kip and around the apartment, but whatever he was thinking was not visible on his face. No one said anything.

"We are leaving. You can get to the Moda OK?"

"It is just down MLK. The (V)ICE cruisers have been staying out of this neighborhood. We'll be there."

Former US Army Colonel Hassan Coleman and retired

General, now Senator Harvey Grennell, stood and without another word, followed out their security detail.

Nate and Chubby sat on the couch, silently, thinking about what had just happened.

"So what are you going to do? What are you going to say tonight?"

"When Jim and I were kids," Kip said, "Alice would banish the men who visited her after one night. No relationships, just pack them out the door, early in the morning, and never see them again, or at least not until her next yearly pilgrimage to the Oregon Country Fair – Hippieville. Every summer she would disappear for a few weeks. Jim would stay with us at the compound – always in July. She was very secretive about her other life. She never told Jim much about it."

"That was where she met Paula," said Nate. "Paula, myself, and some others – we belonged to a group. We called it the Circle of the Golden Fungus."

"I always thought that was some hippie fairy tale. Fungus?"

"Yeah. Remember I told you we found the stuff in southern Illinois back in 1970? Well, after all the shit from the early '70s – the Weathermen, getting kidnapped to Nicaragua, Paula and I started eating the fungus every day. And stayed young. When I went to China, Paula sent me packages now and then – to a PO box in Hong Kong, herbal medicine. Anyway, during that time, some of the heaviest people on the West Coast – politicians, actors, musicians, writers – they all sort of converged, and took up the slogan, even though most had no idea what it really was. There were some assholes in the midst, but for the most part it was understood what kind of society we needed to build if we were going to survive as a species. Jim's mom was the one who kept it together."

Nate sat at the end of the couch, and continued. "Everyone trusted Alice – and liked her. Anyway, after the whole thing with Hughes in December, 72, Paula continued to hang out with Stewart Gent and ended up as part of Nixon's second plumbers unit. The unknown plumbers – that were never discovered and never really disbanded – but they just morphed. She knows too much, and now that they know where she is and that she is hurt, they will be seriously hunting her."

"Never disbanded?"

"Well, politics, parties, personalities, they come and go, but the money doesn't move much, it mostly stays put. There is continuity in all things, good and bad. The same fights, the same fears, the fear of freedom, and the need to dominate and crush, is part of that DNA too. The fights are about the same thing, all the way back, even if the labels and external causes change. Which side gets expressed and why? Fuck if I know! The need to eliminate anyone who just wants to live their life and enjoy the bounty of the earth, and leave something – that need is powerful too – look at the polls – Real-Prez stays at 35–40%. Maybe even more lately. It comes and goes in phases. Nixon resigning wasn't the climax of that particular cycle, it was just the fallout. The real fall was in Nicaragua in December 1972. That pretty much changed everything."

"Nicaragua?"

"Well that is the nexus point. That's where Cadez came from. He was supposedly a Nicaraguan Army officer's son who was killed in the quake. Raised by good Texas Christians. Not bloody likely. He has been on the scene forever. Like us. Why is he like he is? How do people come to be who they are and believe what they believe? Anyway, he got most of our stash of fungus. I understand he had his continuing dose synthesised in one of Howard Hughes's Houston labs. But Gent – Cadez – has to be 80, 85."

Chubby held his tongue. Nate had been the first to report on some of the biggest stories of the 20th century – the nuclear attack on Russian troops invading China, and the Old Testament carved on stone in Chinese characters from the 3rd century BC. Everyone had shunned him; every single respectable scholar or knowledgeable person called him a fraud, and yet…

"I don't know what the fuck you are talking about," said K. "Is this another of your historical exposés?"

"I was there, my friend. And so was Paula. Cadez was there then, and he hasn't changed since."

"1972? You would have been what – 21–22? And Paula..." Here we go again, the woman who never ages. Yet – somehow – Chubby knew it, there was something...

Chubby continued, "So, OK – so let's say that Paula is this mythical goddess-like woman who stays young and beautiful for 50 years. What are you trying to do, start a religion?"

"She is not immortal. You saw that when she got shot."

"She gave me something to drink at Jim and Cynthia's house," said Kip. "She called it a modified White Russian – milky. And for a while, I could see things – people's thoughts, and even a bullet in mid-air that I was able to avoid."

"That's the last of it then. That was the last little bit of tree fungus we found in Vandalia – 50 years ago."

"The last of it. Except for the shit made in the lab – that Cadez has."

"Yeah," said Nate. "That lab shit will fuck you up though. You can't control fungus – nobody can. His shit makes you psychotic and homicidal. I never understood how Cadez – actually del Gente – of the people – what a joke – how did he eat the shit and still believe what he does? We know it is happening to Cadez. We just have to figure out how to show his condition to his followers and the world. They all think he is some kind of Latino Baptist pastor."

"So you don't really believe that Thomas Pynchon mumbo jumbo about a special underground that controls the world, do you?" Chubby asked.

"Believe?" Nate widened his eyes and stood up. "What a strange word. Belief is just wishful thinking. But when things happen – like encountering you – it's the only framework to hang it on. Belief is a contradiction to reality. I believe what happened, but that isn't belief. It's memory and perception. Belief is tied up with the laws of probability, which tell you anything is possible. The Circle of the Golden Fungus is not some West Coast New Age mysticism – it is an ancient, naturally forming, and perhaps inevitably forming conspiracy that your fucking software – *SwiftPad* – has primed – activated – or is awoke more accurate? OK?"

Fuck, Jim is dead. All this magic fungus and people who never get old – didn't help Jim.

"I need a drink – I have to think – to say something to these people to get them to risk their lives." Kip brought out a newly opened bottle of Willamette Valley Chardonnay (2015). "I am trying to quit drinking and – well all intoxicants, in spite of my slip-up with Paula's fungus White Russian and – I want to be straight. But it is not easy. But a glass of wine – well, that doesn't count, does it?" Kip poured himself a small glass.

"Thanks, no, anything less than two doesn't count, by definition," said Nate as he held his glass out.

"Really?"

"Yes – let's drink to the end of the good life here in North America. In other words – the end."

"How? Why?"

"You guys made it – you unleashed *SwiftPad* on the world – it is kind of up to you to unmake it."

"But now they've got GG," Kip said. "They! We don't even..."

"We can't fix that now," said Nate, leaning over to help himself to another glass. "But we will. We have to plan and we have to keep from getting caught. Oglethorpe must be smart, right?"

"Fuck, way beyond me."

"And she is valuable and she knows it. We have to trust her that she can...keep her head."

A siren. It was coming from the south up MLK. They both held their breath, hoping it would pass Ranjit's store.

"Paula lived on the stuff. You know how?"

"No." Kip looked closely at Nate and saw that he had slight

tremors, almost imperceptible – more like vibrating rather than shaking.

"She used to go back to Illinois couple a times a year. Elwood? Oh – that is another story! But – the thing was – he loved her too and he would give her the fungus. He moved there, and tried to cultivate the stuff. He worshiped the fungus. Lost his soul, I think. Studied mycology, mushrooms and fungi, and ate them too. He is still alive, all six foot eight of him. Moves every couple of years so people don't wonder why he looks so young. If I had been 6'8", and ate fungus everyday, I could have played with everyone from Bill Russell to LeBron. I guess she would have short periods where she didn't eat it – didn't have it, didn't want it – but for the most part she ate it every day. And she never changed."

"So – she is really Alice's age. 75, I think."

"Yep. Older actually, I think."

"I saw her at the hospital," said Kip. "Her face was starting to crack apart. I swear she aged 10 years in a couple of hours."

"You talk to her at the hospital?"

"Yeah," said Kip. "She was concentrating on just walking straight, a little out of it, but that was because of the sedatives, I am sure. I figured you must have followed me from there."

Nate forcefully smiled. "You asked me what I was doing in Portland. Alice had Heber invite Paula – and me – for that gathering, where Oglethorpe was kidnapped. Getting Heber to take the bait was easy. We were ex-intel types, or so Heber was led to believe – he figured he needed professionals…"

"When Paula covered me with her Beretta yesterday at the house, and got herself shot in the process, that was all I needed as far as proof to trust her."

"We need an exit strategy from here, from Portland, and off the grid. Otherwise, we are dead men, my friend. It is going to get brutal after this."

"What do you want to do, Nate?"

"The Circle of the Golden Fungus is meeting up with our

allies in the East again in Michigan on Lake Superior. We had a meeting last December, but I don't think any of us thought it would get this bad. One of us needs to go and tell them what is going on. We need command and control, planning. I need to report on what happened here."

"You mean tell them what happened to Paula and Oglethorpe."

"Yeah – and figure out how to get GG back. But Portland is really the key – it is clear that Temp-Prez and his bosses want to break this city."

"Bezos, Gates, Ellison, Cuban – most of the tech guys are under house arrest." Kip showed him the headlines on his tablet. "See? This has been in the planning stages for months. They have no intention of giving up the White House. It doesn't even matter if you had been on *The Apprentice*."

"So you know you are on their list too," said Nate. "They targeted the *Reigny Deigh* guy, right?"

"Gordon Lobetts? Yeah, they were targeting him alright."

"I never understood until today..." Nate mumbled, fading, barely keeping his eyes open.

"Umm. What?"

"You know, immortality. Time, decay. I kept telling Paula that she was missing the best part of life...the slow decline, to eventual oblivion. Now it is happening way too fast; civilization seemed like it would live forever, and it's like the fungus died and civilization is dying at the same time."

"It's not just the fungus that is dying."

"No. It's not. Anyway, living forever young is no way to experience life. She must be in incredible pain. I know she was down to her last few days' supply, that she only brought a little bit up to Oregon. Which she gave to you, so you could see, if only for a moment. It is the last of it. We have to look for more, which is another reason to head for Memphis. It seems to grow around the mid-Mississippi region. But it might be all gone from there too.

We need to find Elwood. If Aldane can get me to Memphis too, I will snake up the Mississippi Valley and look for him."

"Let's ride over to the Moda,"said Chubby. "I know what I am going to say."

"Aldane is going to be pissed at us messing up his show with Jean Katon."

"Yeah," Kip laughed. "He is really going to be pissed."

CHAPTER 32
JOHNNY LOVES YA!

3:45 pm, Saturday, July 18, 2020

Ben Cadez, the junior Senator from Tennessee, was often mentioned as a possible candidate for President. According to his official biography, he was raised by Dorn and Gabby Perdew in Addison, Texas. His biological father was claimed by Mrs. Perdew to be Colonel Adolfo Cadez, a military aide to General Somoza. He was purported to have died in a plane delivering supplies to Nicaragua after the 1972 earthquake. Ben's mother, once a famous child evangelist, has said that she conceived Ben "in a night of unbridled passion" with Adolfo Cadez just before he left on that ill-fated flight.

Gabby Delmont, a long-time C-list celebrity and reality show regular, who was often seen at WWF matches, has been a long-time and very visible supporter of conservative causes and candidates. Her marriage to Dorn Perdew was televised on the CBN, with Pat Robertson performing the nuptials. Young Ben was heard crying in the background. Home schooled from kindergarten to high school, Ben Cadez served as a missionary in Brazil, where he was involved in a disputed and fatal incident in an Amazonian native village. His escape was the subject of a made-for-TV docudrama. Three days after his return to the Dallas area, his stepfather was found to have hanged himself in the chapel of the Heavenly Pavement Gospel Megachurch near their home. After the funeral, Cadez enrolled in SMU as an undergraduate, where he completed a degree in political science in two years, with honors.

Cadez attended Stanford Law, graduating Cum Laude, and after his stint clerking at the Supreme Court (Justice Thomas), he moved to Tennessee, practiced law for about 10 years, then ran for Senator, and won. His following across the country was intense and devoted. His bio claims that he has never lost a case, although the ABA has unofficially censored him for this disputed claim. The most famous of his clients was Ezra Fernwillow, the notorious killer of a doctor at a Nashville Planned Parenthood office. Fernwillow, now free, often appears on webcasts, and occasionally even on Fox cable news shows, and is actively supporting Douglas Turdashian, who is seen as Cadez's only opponent on the Right.

Cadez is extremely charismatic on camera, but there were reports that attest to his psychic instability, and uncontrollable temper. His good looks were often compared to that of the recently retired soccer star Ronaldo. At his boisterous rallies he often revs up the crowd by introducing his adoring mother, who will grab the microphone and deliver vicious right wing attacks on various liberal media and political figures.

From "The Fall of it All – The History of the Big Dump"

A LISON WALKED UP TO THE ENTRANCE OF GORDY'S

condo. As she passed the guard at the desk, he looked up from his phone without moving his head, then shifted his eyes back down again. She got to the elevator and took it up to the penthouse, and as she stepped out was immediately beckoned down the hall by a hard-eyed, tall, stoop-shouldered man with a gray crewcut and a shiny green sport coat.

"Hey, sweetheart. You Alleeson. Yeah? We have been waiting for ya. Come on in, Telly wants to meet ya."

Alison entered and walked through the hallway. Sitting at a counter on a barstool she saw the Senator, Ben Cadez, who appeared to be listening to a joke. The man telling the joke turned around and looked at her. He smiled like a crocodile getting his tummy rubbed.

"Alison!" Alison turned to her right and saw Kayla, whose face looked photoshopped with pancake makeup and lip gloss. She was dressed in tight jeans that fit her ass like a tourniquet, a green silk blouse, and green platform pumps. She click-clacked toward Alison, while looking over at the Crocodile, who was smiling and nodding for no apparent reason or immediate effect.

"Alison, this is Telly Haines. Telly, Alison is one of our top producers. She is bigly responsible for *RDM*'s fan base. Can I say, Alison, that your work is 'data driven'?"

"Sure. You can say that. I don't exactly know what that means though..." There was an instant of uncomfortable silence, followed by Telly laughing uncontrollably.

"I like this one," he said looking around, smiling.

Alison counted the people in the room (five, including a woman in the far corner, wearing a short skirt and striped blouse, intently reading a *People* magazine), checked out the doors, and the windows. She looked at Kayla and realized Kayla was completely at sea, trying to figure which way the tide was running.

"Oh, I mean your material always resonates," Kayla continued. "You never bomb, Alison. There must be a reason..."

Kayla was talking out of her ass. They had only met the previous morning, and Kayla didn't even know her name then.

"Well, Gordon used to say I wasn't threatening enough," said Alison deciding to be gracious. "He hinted my stuff was too 'audience-friendly.'"

Kayla laughed and mimed disagreement.

This shocked Alison, (and everyone else, judging from their

suddenly sadpuss faces) into some kind of proper grief. "I can't believe – what happened? Were you there, Kayla? Where is his body?"

"Lew?" Telly asked.

"Autopsy," said a roly-poly guy eating a sandwich, wearing heavy dark-rimmed glasses and an unbuttoned three-piece pinstripe blue suit, with visible sweat stains on his off-white shirt.

"Has anyone called his family?"

"Does he have family?" asked the girl reading the People Magazine, without looking up.

"I don't know," said Alison. "I think he is originally from Florida."

"Didn't somebody tell me," asked Kayla, "he knew someone named Johnny?"

"You never met Johnny?" The eavesdropping Crocodile stood up, walked over to Alison, and put his arm around her shoulder, while smiling conspiratorially at her. "Lew – bring Johnny in. Alison. As you might know, I own 51 percent of *RDM* – my attorney, Lew, will verify. Hey, Lew – you got the papers?"

"Sure, Telly." Lew was nodding his head while he finished chewing. "Right here!" He got a big laugh that became a chuckle when he held up a briefcase.

"But I want to say, you are so, so right, Alison. I am devastated. Unbelievable! We are forgetting the most important – the absolutely most important reason I am here and my friends and partners are here is to remember Gordo, and help *RDM* heal from this terrible thing – this is so unbelievable! Gordon was like my brother. Brilliant man!"

As soon as Telly's grip on her shoulder loosened, Alison slowly moved back from the Croc, nodding seriously, then smiling, refusing to give in to an overwhelming feeling of fear and disgust.

"You call me?"

"Johnny! Come on in. Did you meet Alison?"

"Oh, yeah. We did some major smoogling out in the hall. How ya doing?"

"Great," said Alison, wondering to herself what "smoogling" was. She reached over and aggressively shook Johnny's hand. The greeting seemed to confuse him.

"Johnny – hi, I am Kayla," Kayla said, taking advantage of the breach created by Alison's handshake. "I heard that Gordon used to run a lot of his ideas by you."

Johnny laughed and looked around the room. Everyone was smiling. "I'd drop by now and then and me and Gordo would talk about stuff."

"Talk about stuff. You could say that," Lew broke in.

Johnny looked at Lew, who shrugged and waved his hand.

"Why did he like my ideas? Telly, why did Gordo like my ideas?"

"Johnny, because you are a fount of persuasion!"

"Yeah – I got a fount – right here!"

Lew looked around, offended that Johnny was stealing his lines.

Alison laughed and pretended to fire a finger gun at Johnny. Telly shook his head with faux disappointment and signaled Alison over to the kitchen counter. "So Alison – this is our – *Reigny Deigh Media*'s newest – and most important – client – Senator Benny Cadez."

Alison saw a withdrawn, almost reticent emanation pulsing from Cadez's closely shaved face. He looked as if, in that instant, he had just stepped out of the Star Trek Transporter, and had barely finished materializing. He stood up to shake her hand and he was tall – at least 6'4". He had dark hair that flowered out of the top of his head, and overflowed down the sides, layered around the white-walls above his ears. He had a bit of a widow's peak. She tried to look him eye-to-eye, but his wide-open, almost bulging, probing orbs gave nothing away.

She saw his eyes were light gray, and seemed out of phase and mismatched with the rest of him. He was looking closely at her, and it almost hurt. He also had a thin dark mustache that followed the lower border of his upper lip from corner to corner. The guy spent a lot of time with his razor.

"Have you ever converted a story to a *SwiftPad* script?" he asked.

So direct, she thought. What does he know about *SwiftPad* scripting? "I have worked on projects – it is generally a collaborative kind of deal. There is a lot of trial and error involved. I am not a coder, but I understand the structure – psuedo-coding its called. Its not trivial or something that can be knocked out quickly. Without an SP-holoscopic interpreter to do debugging, it is…"

"So what's that?"

"It is a 3D interpreter – makes simple holograms. It shows bare, stick-figures, with stark audio, combined into holographic interpretations of the script. Very limited, the trick being each individual will fill in the blanks in their own mind, with their own particular stories. It doesn't reference profiles or do any of the background interactions with the Xpers, or anything like that. Just sort of vanilla conversions…you don't need an SP-holoscopic interpreter to encode an SP script – but…"

"Xpers?"

"Oh, short for Experiencers, the readers, viewers or the 'mind-readers' who used the beta wave transfers of mental images into a virtual reality."

"And you want one. One of those holy scopes."

"The only one I know of was built by Archimedes' team."

"The *SwiftPad* app's guru," said Cadez.

"Yeah. I remember reading an article where Arky was talking about the TET – Total Emergence Technology, and what it would take to make it 'commercially viable'…the goal is to use the off-the-shelf Elon Musk neuralink virtual reality devices as receivers. But then Gopesh Gupta came out with the C2B interface, and that blew Musk's product out of the water."

"OK," said Cadez.

"I like it!" Telly slapped Cadez on the arm, who seemed not to feel it.

"The holoscopic interpreter that I saw was very rudimentary, but that was a while ago. As for scripting, I have only done it the 'old way,' punch it out minute by minute and run it through the secondary low wattage system, and plug it into myself; I interpreted the output. It is not easy, because you have to separate your subjective impressions from the story you are trying to tell, and it is exhausting. And it is just so damned slow! It can take months to do the conversion."

"Kayla," said Telly, who had been pretending to be preoccupied, "You know this Archimedes guy?"

"He was there last night – standing a couple feet from Gordon when he was shot."

"Jesus!" Telly looked at Johnny, who shrugged.

"We have a project – big contract – gonna have to bust a nut on it. You game, Alison?"

"I don't think I can do it alone. Like I said…"

"If we can get you this thing you need? This holy thing…"

"What will the story be based on…"

"We are working on that…listen – we'll talk business tomorrow. Where are my manners! This condo – it's yours! You and Kayla – me and the rest of the team – we are out of here tonight – gone!"

"I am staying at the Marriott downtown," said Cadez.

"Somebody should stay here," said Lew.

"Yeah – Gordo's not going to need…"

Johnny's abortive quip was quickly cut off by a look from Telly. "Johnny will drive you down to your hotel, Senator." He continued to stare daggers at Johnny.

"Thanks, I have a driver and a van waiting for me outside." Cadez quickly walked out of the main room with his phone to his ear.

"What I meant was," said Telly, looking at Alison, "this is a terrible, terrible thing that happened last night. But – your little business – *Reigny Deigh* – has actually been mine for about six months. I bought it from Gordo for $1.2 billion – actually he owed me a lot of money and – in any event, I bought it and we kept it quiet, and Gordorino continued to run things – didn't want to kill the goose, right? But – I own it – right, Lew?

"Yeah, Telly. This place, too – this entire floor – including the roof just upstairs – it's beautiful – you can see the mountains and everything!"

Alison looked out the east-facing window.

"Things in town are a little dicey – you know with all the disturbances going on..."

"You mean arrests and..." Alison responded.

"Yeah – it is not good – any of it." Telly lifted both of his hands, but then dropped them to his sides as if they had moved involuntarily. He seemed nervous, thought Alison. "We just need to get through this. Clean up things. What are we supposed to do otherwise? Anyway – stay here and get this done. There will be even more money when you finish."

Alison remained stone-faced and silent.

"It's a new game, Alison, in every way. To start, I am tearing up your current compensation package."

She stared off into the distance, glancing at Telly, then looking away again, troubled, and thoughtful, and a little bit resigned. But inside she was seething. Government agents were kidnapping and murdering people in the street, in Portland – and an hour ago, she had helped to kill two of them. What to do? She was on the lam, she realized. Inside the Belly of the Beast? Breathe, she thought.

"Maybe you are right," she said.

Telly looked at her hard, then slowly began to smile.

"Stay here for a few days while we get you set up – we are kind of in a hurry – we need the Senator's *SwiftPad* promo piece to hit the day the Convention starts. You know why – we moved the Convention up to next week – we need to blow away this Turdashian character – who is worse than – anyway, this brain-scanning virtual reality – we want everyone who has neural VR interface to get to know the Senator in a good way."

"They sold over 10 million units in the last year alone, Telly," said Lew.

"That includes everyone that matters – including the delegates. So it is important that you bring this in – well..." Telly looked around at everyone else – then he picked up a "To-Do" notepad off of the counter and wrote on it and showed Alison.

"Yours – guaranteed. Starting now."

"Wow. Really? That much?"

"It's just a start, sweetheart. Lew – here, update this immediately – you do direct deposit? By tomorrow, Lew. Six months in advance, too, to show we aren't fucking around."

Alison stared at the note. "The person who really knows how to crunch a *SwiftPad* script is Spence Stromborn. If you want this done in a hurry then – can we can get him on board? I have been trying to contact him, but..."

"Well – we'll see." Telly looked around the room. "I understand he is in some trouble."

"I'll see if I can find out what his situation is," said Lew. "Maybe we can file an appeal to get him out."

"Yeah – I like this," said Cadez, who had returned and had been listening intently, "Let's try and get the premise solid – in the meantime. Kayla. That is your job."

"Got it."

"Wow – OK," said Alison. "We can start tomorrow – I can come back – I have some – personal business to wrap up, if you know what I mean."

"Sorry. You are staying. It's too dangerous out there."

"I am staying too," said Kayla. "It will be fun."

"I didn't bring my night clothes though...?"

"We are almost the same size! I have lots of clothes." Kayla was beaming.

"Alright." Alison forced a smile at Kayla. Play it to the hilt, girl, she thought. "But – I am not the maid or anybody's girl. You got that?" Alison turned and looked hard at Telly, who put his hands up and nodded vigorously. "And nobody comes in without knocking – no cutesy surprises – I mean it!"

"Great! Absolutely!"

"I agree with her, call first," said Kayla.

"100% 100%! You guys hear that!" Telly turned to Cadez – "Didn't I tell you!" Then to Johnny, "You understand what she said?"

"Yeah, yeah, sure."

"Food! Absolutely 100% organic. You a vegan or any of that shit?"

She shrugged. "Not really. But no hamburgers or hot dogs or any of that processed meat."

"Johnny, get one of those caterers to help you. First-class food delivered every day, starting tomorrow morning. Breakfast – eggs, bagels, Jewfish – the works. And get some decent coffee! Buy the beans. Get the good shit!"

"I am going out on the balcony and smoke pot," said Alison. "Please – leave me alone for a while."

"Hey – we're family – go get inspired, kid."

CHAPTER 33
LIVE AT THE MODA!

7:30 pm, Saturday, July 18, 2020

CHUBBY AND NATE STOOD IN THE WINGS, LISTENING the Mane Shakers do Peter Tosh – "Get up, stand up, don't give up the fight!" Perfect. Nine thousand standing – a big standing O.

"I think now is a good time," Kip said to Jean Katon, who stood next to him.

Jean walked out onto the stage. The place erupted. She hugged Aldane, and waved, but they kept clapping. Finally, they stopped.

"It's time to shine, Portland!" Another standing O.

"I know what you want, but how can we be singing when right outside – right out there, where you live. They are treating you fellow Americans like trash, to be thrown away, like garbage. This is your city! I ain't out here to tell you anything good. It's bad. Outside – outside, they are killing your brothers and sisters – right outside!" Silence.

"Is that right?" – NO!

"Can you live knowing that?" – NO!

"Git up. Git on up! Git up, git on up! Git up, git on up! – Come on now, sing with me, Git up, Git on up!"

Everybody was on their feet, singing along, clapping. Finally, with a crescendo from the band, it subsided.

"Now I want you to put your hands together for Mr. SwiftPad – Portland's own – Kip Rehain!"

Kip walked out to mild applause – tepid, compared to what Jean had roused.

"As you might know," pause, silence. "I got lucky and met GG – Cindy Oglethorpe. They took her yesterday. Just grabbed her – her and her unborn baby – like they were so much meat. They cut up my friend – killed him."

Kip paused again. Not a whisper, dead silence.

"And another man was shot down, Gorden Lobetts, cold blood. Shot him dead. I was there! Ten feet away."

A pigeon in the rafters flapped its wings, and it almost startled the crowd, it was so quiet.

"Now they are tramping through your streets! Soon they will be taking what they want – soon enough. If you open your mouth – well – they have some camps out in the desert – just for you. Seriously the contracts have been let – Halliburton is making a killing on them.

"We used to just laugh at each other's political ideas, they just didn't matter all that much to most of us. Now, we have fallen into – hard lines. We used to drink with each other, play softball together – now – not so much. We have divided ourselves up.

"I know a lot of different people love Jean Katon – and you are here to hear music. So seeing me can't be too pleasant. I understand.

"But – as Jean said – it's time to shine, Portland. It ain't gonna be easy. Any RedHats here? Any supporters of the Prez? It's OK. It's OK. This is peaceful ground. You are safe here. No. Sorry. I am stealing – stealing Jean. You paid to hear music. Well the music is over. I am sorry. I am sorry.

"But the rest of you – I am a little pissed! Tonight – they are moving in. You must have noticed them, right? In your town, and I am not hearing a lot of complaints, frankly. You heard the shots on the river yesterday? I suppose some thought – well – they were refugees. It is terrible – but it is different than shooting people in town. Well it isn't. The RedHats are taking over Portland – tonight as we sit here. If it makes you uncomfortable, don't worry – it is almost over. They are moving in, taking over the TV stations and Mayor's office, and all of the city's organizations. You will have to answer to them on the street tomorrow, but for most of you, it won't be that bad.

"But – by next week – many of us will be under arrest. They have lists and they will be coming – maybe to your door. I know they will be looking for me. What about you? Your friends? Your family? Think they are coming for you?

"Right now, we have a chance to change history. Most people don't get that chance – but we have it! We can do something about it. We have friends – people who have come to support us and help us through this. People from places you would never expect would stand with us. But they are standing with us, risking their lives to keep these fascist scum from taking our city. We can stand too. We have to stand. Stand up to them. Stand! Stand! Tonight. Now. Now!

"Someday, years from now, when we finally have our country back, maybe a little child, maybe even your grandchild – who knows – They are going to ask you – because we will teach them, we won't let them forget like we have forgotten – we will teach them – and they will ask – What did you do to save America? Tonight – you can give them that answer. Tonight you will be talking to your grandchild and all the future Americans who will look back at this day and say thank you – thank you people of Portland for standing up to the cruel, greedy bastards who tried to steal our country!"

Chubby looked out and everyone was standing, clapping. They were looking at him. Yes.

"See the men and women in the vests walking in. If you are with me, if you are with freedom and with you neighbors then stand up and join us! Stand up to (V)ICE, put them on. Put on the vests they are handing out – orange, green, and blue. Stay with your color. You are part of something. There is a plan, I promise you! Three teams. You will be the Wall that Protects Portland. I am asking you – put on the vest and march out to protect Portland. He wanted a God-damned wall! Well we are going to give him one. We are the wall! It stops now! Be the wall! Be the Wall!

Jean came out, "Everybody! WE ARE THE WALL! WE ARE THE WALL! WE ARE THE WALL!"

"Orange Team!" Kip put on a vest. "Up! Let's go!"

Then – Jean began to sing the "Battle Hymn of the Republic" with a quivering French accent that would have sent chills down the spine of an arctic narwhal. Everybody joined in and they were in tears as they sang.

"Green Team!"

"Blue Team!"

With Kip at the head, the Orange and Green Teams headed out of the Moda Center Plaza, over to and across the Steel Bridge. The Blue Team stood in amorphous formation in front of the Moda Center, singing, and waiting for orders.

CHAPTER 34

PEGGY SPARKS A FIRE

7:30 pm, Saturday, July 18, 2020

PEGGY FELT FOR HER GUN FOR THE THIRD TIME SINCE she started riding up the macadam path toward the Lewis and Clark Memorial. It was scary as well as a little slick – a leaky sprinkler puddling on a turn. She felt the bike slide a bit as she braked and swerved to avoid a hand-holding couple ahead who could not decide on which side to walk.

Part of her wanted to just go to the cops and confess everything, and try to make a deal – turn in Nate, Alison, and anyone else involved, anything to get Spence out. Soccer mom, a decent job and a boring but reliable husband, a house, decent circle of friends – and now – a fugitive, conspirator, and a cop killer. Her husband was in jail. All within a few hours. She wanted to sit down and cry and hope somehow she could make it all go away. She stopped and took a breath, and felt the gun again, in her leather bag. She continued up the hill, passing the statue of Sacajawea and baby Jean-Baptiste. There, up the rise, just above the ten foot high bronze Indian woman and her baby, was the phallic memorial to the men she led across the country.

She climbed up a little rise until toward a stone obelisk and looked down on the seemingly peaceful almost sleepy city.

She saw Alison crossing the street below, and going into Gordy's condo. Peggy sat down on the grass, partially behind a tree that hid her from the main path to and around the memorial. She could see the balcony of the penthouse. She thought of Nate again, who came back into her life today. What a fucking day!

Twenty years, and – he's back. Peggy was cried out. Sometimes, in her daydreams she would remember that the happiest days of her life were with Nate. Nate knew everything, took care of everything, and all she had to do was...

She waited.

An hour, then two hours. It had been years since she just sat and did nothing. Rather than make her anxious the time just sitting and waiting cleared her mind. She breathed and focused. Some people came up the steps of the memorial, and walked down into the park, but didn't see her. She felt invisible. She stood against a tree and stared at the top of the condo.

Then on Gordy's penthouse balcony – the lights – two flashes – 15 seconds later – two more flashes. Alison was trapped. Or maybe she was doing the trapping. Nothing Peggy could do now, just have to see how it was going to play out. So now it was get down the hill and over to Ranjit's Kwikie Mart on MLK, on the other side of the river.

She stood up and just at that instant, she saw two (V)ICE troopers walking up Park. She stared at them for a couple of seconds, and then, SHIT! They saw her. She stared back at them, in some kind of trance almost, then realized they were quickening their pace, walking toward her. She got on her bike, coasted down the rise, and headed up the hill, around the old reservoir then turned into the entrance to the Rose Garden, running and carrying her bike up the steps. She found herself at the top of the Washington Park Amphitheater. It was secluded and for some reason she felt drawn to it. As everyone in Portland knew, the stage of the Amphitheater was where Chubby had saved GG from the sadistic serial Killer Raleigh Highlooper and cut off his dick.

Peggy walked down and sat in the second row of the Amphitheater, looked out at the empty stage, and thought she felt the spirits of the women Raleigh had murdered. Why had she pulled the trigger? It wasn't an acident, she realized. She had murdered those two young cops in the park.

She needed to get across the river to Ranjit's market. Wait until it starts to get dark, she thought, and then head out. Then she heard someone coming, from the left out of the rose bushes. She stood up and thought about going back, but it was too late. Uniformed cops – (V)ICE had split apart and were stalking her.

Peggy really hoped that an idea, any idea, would eventually occur to her, because as she looked blankly, and listened to the shooting echoing up from down river (pop, pop, popping almost constantly for hours now) she started thinking about how she would get down out of Washington Park, and through town and across the river to eventually make it to the apartment above the convenience store on MLK that Nate told her about. Coming up the hill had not been a good idea, she realized. She knew she had to do something. They were slowly moving toward her with the clear intention of confronting her. She was scared, and briefly saw herself getting shot and dying, like those two young guys they had killed in the park. She pretended to ignore the two young men, who were strutting, in their (V)ICE uniforms, coming down the slope of the hillside. They didn't say anything, but her stalkers moved apart as they approached, seemingly to have better angles on her. She saw no one else in the park, and the (V)ICE boys were walking faster now toward her, and it was no longer possible to ignore them, or pretend that they weren't focused on her. They didn't call out to her, and she felt rooted to that spot, not knowing if she should begin walking away or toward them. She began slowly to turn and walk unhurriedly down toward where she left her bike. That was perhaps her worst move, and she immediately knew not to change her mind now or it would be even worse.

"Hey, where are you going?"

She stopped, but didn't look toward them. They were about ten yards apart from each other and thirty yards from her. Wolf-pack style. It was too late, and now they were too close. She should have brought her bike up here.

The second (V)ICE man called out, "Hey, miss, are you alright?"

Decide now, girl, run, or bluff it out. I got what I need, she thought; Alison is on the inside, so I need to get back across the river and find Nate. I am part of it, and this is the situation. Report. Breathe. Now smile.

She looked at the two (V)ICE men, thinking, be cute, a little pro-miscuous and slutty, act drunk and say she was waiting for a lover who never showed, now looking to party with anyone. And if they don't bite, then come on pissy and lowbrow with a big-assed atti-tude. Leave me alone! Loud, like she knew what hurt really meant, and nothing these badges and guns do could make her life worse.

None of this actually happened though; she just stood there, looking out over the city, ignoring them, too scared to act.

"Hey – girlie. What are you doing here?"

"Officers! Hi. Beautiful night, if only the shooting would stop, don't you think?"

"There's a curfew out, ma'am, you're not allowed to be out here. It's dangerous."

"Like you said, ma'am, there is shooting tonight."

They stood there, one on each side, hands free, one with a small automatic rifle slung over his shoulder, composite stock, and carbon-fiber barrel, like a cyborg gun.

"K, sorry, I just – why do you call me ma'am? Do I look like a ma'am? Do I? Oh, never mind, you don't understand, it's hard for women! You don't you know, please, please, you don't know!" Peggy started sobbing. "Give me a minute, please!"

The three of them stood there, the two cops playing it very cool, waiting. "I have a resident card," she said. "I am not an illegal."

She walked up to them, getting close enough to force them to backup a half a step, and they looked at her and one of them called it in, giving location and description of her, "We got somebody here, let's let's let's let's let's let's" – it all became blurry to her, and she reached for her gun, but went to the wrong pocket and pulled out her phone instead, to show her ID. The two young commandos froze for a second, then they moved in close, no room to move now, and they were looking at it, and nodding, but not checking it, but checking her, it's OK, and seemed like they were concerned for her safety and well-being. One of them was shooting her ID with his camera.

She didn't really know what her next move was or what she should do.

"We are just concerned, ma'am. That you are OK. Are you OK? We're looking for a couple of people that caused some problems earlier. You shouldn't be here. We can take you in, for your own safety."

"But – maybe as a woman, I have to say, not all sex is assault. Right? Maybe we were lovers? Is that even possible?"

"Ma'am, were you assaulted? Are you OK, ma'am?"

"No – I don't know, he said, he said," she said.

"What did he say, ma'am?"

"Ma'am, tell us your name."

"Margaret. Margaret Stromborn." One of them looked at his phone. "Sometimes I go by Peggy. I am OK. I am OK. Just a work thing. We are friends, I'm Peggy Daniel, or I was. Just fun, it keeps you young, right?"

Peggy, smiling hard, tried to pull back, but they slowly closed in on her, and she brought her arms up, defensively.

"I can walk back to my bike and then home, no problem," she said, but it was gradually escalating, though they were still not touching her, and had not changed their seemingly friendly expressions, trying to make it seem ok.

"You from here?"

"Well, yes, I am from Eugene." Inside she was shaking with rage and fear. Would they frisk her? The gun was in her bag, not her pocket, she remembered.

"It's a shitstorm down there. Is your family OK? Do you have a family?"

"Yeah – it is like here. A lot of homeless people."

"Are you soliciting to sell sex up here?"

"What? You think I am a hooker?"

"No, ma'am. We just need to ascertain your intentions."

Keep your cool, girl, she thought. "I am not homeless. I have a legal address. I just drank a little tonight. I am not driving."

"Yes. Exactly. We will note it, 'Peggy was not driving!'" The other VICE guy laughed. "Ma'am, to put it simply, there are too many homeless – or to put it in plain American, fucked-up illegals, people who didn't take care of business, and are now looking to steal and get something for nothing – right? Am I right?"

Peggy looked at them. Should she agree? Should she continue her hysterical drunk act? She hadn't actually talked to someone who thought like that in a very long time.

"Matt, that's – we don't agree, OK."

Peggy perked up. Good cop – bad cop? Was it an act?

"Just living in Phoenix was enough to make you homeless – you can't live without water." He looked at Peggy. "Fucking terrorists!"

"And you know who they are," said Matt. "Fucking Eco-terrorists!"

"Where did they get the bomb they used?"

"Air Force terrorists," said Matt, laughing unnaturally. "Need to clean out that snake pit in Colorado Springs."

"My partner and I don't agree about many things," said Caleb. "It is bad luck. I guess I wonder, though, if we all need to subsidize 'bad luck.' Right? Eventually we have to deal with the real enemies. Unfortunately Portland is ground zero. That is why we are so suspicious, Peggy. Isn't it better to keep the country – you know. We will turn into Mexico if we…"

"Exactly, Caleb! It's about Preparation! Some of us are prepared. You prepare by planning…"

"And with prayer," said Caleb.

"Sure. If you don't think ahead – boom – it hits you before you know it. You make your own luck! Right, Peggy?"

"Where are you from?" Peggy asked Caleb, who kept reciting the Boy Scout motto.

"Loveland, Colorado, ma'am. We have our problems there too, especially in Boulder. Mostly stoners, easy to handle. We are still OK out there. A little dry this year. But it's OK. Both me and my brother joined the Interdict and Control Emergency Service. That's what we call it now, internally of course. It is still about immigration – just internal immigration."

"A long way from border security, isn't it?"

Caleb was getting info through his ear piece. He grabbed Peggy by the arm. "Search her!"

Matt found the gun immediately and Caleb threw her on the ground and put his knee in her back. Matt got down with him and his hands went everywhere, into her pants and even into her vagina. Caleb cuffed her with a zip tie, and they both pulled her up.

"Bag the gun."

They started marching silently back up to the tennis courts. Peggy was looking out, suddenly aware, seeing everything. Out of the trees, she saw a black man with mud-covered jeans and nylon jacket, and a raging afro, limping toward them. He had a dirty bandage across his right eye that appeared to be bloodstained.

"Hey, you guys have any food in that cruiser? Donuts, potato chips?"

"Get down on the ground, homey!" Matt stepped away from escorting Peggy and jogged toward the tramp, with his gun out, pointed away.

"Homey" stood his ground. "Never mind! Keep your donuts." He turned, and with a cattywampus limp, slowly began moving back toward the trees.

"Halt!" Matt was closing in on him.

Suddenly from behind the cruiser, a full-bearded guy in camo with a night vision helmet and a laser sighter stood up, put a spot on Caleb's head, and shot him dead. Matt turned, firing without aiming, ricocheting off the cruiser. Two more muffled shots from different directions, and Matt spun before falling, clearly dead before hitting the ground.

Peggy stood still in the middle of the parking lot. The black hobo came running up to her, with no trace of a limp. "Come with me if you want to live!" Peggy heard laughter from the shadows. He picked up the bagged gun. "I always wanted to say that," said the homeless-looking black guy, lifting up his bloody bandage, winking lusciously, while cutting the zip ties around her wrists. "We do gotta move fast though."

They ran through into the trees, passing the teched-out camo guys, who silently nodded with thumbs up. At the first bend in the path, Peggy stopped and looked back. The two guys were gone.

"Come on, we have to move."

They skirted around the Japanese Garden, crossed a couple of lanes, and got to Burnside.

"I don't have my bike."

"Forget it." They squatted, looking. "Down!" There was no traffic, for 10, 20, 30 seconds. A cruiser sped by, then braked, slowing down. The hobo, now without the bloody bandage, eyes now bright, and watchful, cautiously chambered a round into his Smith & Wesson 9 mm luger. "Here." He handed Peggy back the gun the (V)ICE guys had taken. She looked at it. Snub-nosed 38 revolver, still had five rounds.

The car continued on.

"Now!"

They ran across Burnside, staying low, climbing fast, the hobo checking Peggy frequently, who had no trouble keeping up. They stayed in the shadows, passing behind the Pittock Mansion, then into more trees, up, up. Moving fast. Into Forest Park, and up to the Stone House, the old resting spot built in the '30s.

Twenty people, a third women, green camo, armed to the

teeth, lounging, nervously checking weapons, sharpening knives, and checking each other's gear.

A fit, wide-eyed, craggy faced man walked around, pointing out little things, calmly pointing out where people needed to blackout reflective streaks on shoes and jackets with shoe polish, snapping unsecured equipment. He looked about 45, a watch cap covering up what appeared to be a skinhead, face darkened with black war paint, occasionally looking down at a tablet.

"Here she is, captain," Mosley said.

"Ha! That bait! How you feeling? They will be here soon. Looks like they are going to be attacking tonight, instead of waiting. Coming from both directions. Get her out of here, Mose. Everything square?"

"Yeah. She is good. You OK, right? We have to keep going up the hill. This is a prime target."

Peggy nodded, realizing now was not the time to ask the million questions that were popping into her head, one after the other. Who were these people? What were they planning?

Peggy and Mosley started up the hill, off the trail, zig-zagging, stopping every hundred yards or so. People in camo with sawed-off shotguns, Heckler & Koch assault rifles, rocket launchers made out of PVC pipes, Uzis, scoped rifles, and the ubiquitous Kalashnikov.

They came to an outcropping of rock which concealed the entrance to a ladder that led down 15 feet to a large enclosure, and saw about 15 men and women, all but two of them working furiously on computers, talking intently into headsets.

Peggy and Mosley sat in the corner and were joined by a thick-set woman, with deep eyes and her long dark hair tightly tied back. She handed Moseley a cup of steaming broth.

"What happened, Reg?" She was looking at Peggy though.

After intros, over the next 10 minutes, Peggy spilled everything – her husband Spence, what he did for *RDM*, now in custody, Nate, and the *SwiftPad* psychodrama, Alison, what she knew about *RDM*, and of course the two dead (V)ICE plain clothes in the park. She held nothing back and when she finished, both Reg and the woman stared ahead silently.

Mosley led Peggy over to a woman who was sitting in front of a laptop with a map of Forest Park. "Over here," she said, "more of our bait sheep, the homeless camp in Balch Creek Gulch."

Mosley said, "You, Peggy, are a prime target of course; they will be coming after you. Your name will be on the news tomorrow morning, probably all over the world. But – we have an entrée into their..."

"Mose," Clare interrupted, without looking up from the laptop.

"Yeah, sorry, we have good intel, coming and going, let's leave it at that. For now, they think you are someone else. It is temporary, but it gives us a couple of days to keep your people off the radar."

"People supporting this government are, in many cases, just scared," said Clare. "Support is real, but they have slipped over the edge to actively suppressing voting, and well, lying about what is happening. There are some morally bankrupt techs, for sure, who will join the kleptocrats, but basically most of them don't even understand the technology that props them up. Frankly it is our job to make them aware there will be war crimes trials, and collaboration trials when this is over."

"The only reason we think we can pull this off is that the Air Force has grounded itself, even though SAC is still flying missions up in the Arctic Circle, watching the Russkis," said Mosley. "In fact though, ICE, with the V, has occupied a number of airfields. But they can't fly the planes, or run the support systems, so they are keeping them in the hangars. But so far no missions against the homeland."

"OK – here – we changed your whole on-line bio," Clare signaled Peggy over to look at a screen. "They think the woman in Washington Park who killed two of their commandos is an Eco-terrorist, a tree occupier from Washington State. No family. Eventually they will probably catch up – we can keep muddying the water for a while. So there is time to get your friends and family to safety."

"My husband was taken in – a few hours ago. My daughter is in Boston."

"Well – we know that – and there are a number of things in motion to get him out. But it will get worse first. We already contacted your daughter – she is one of us anyway, so that was easy."

Peggy expressed no surprise about her daughter.

"Here." On the thermal map they saw a long line of trucks and cruisers coming up Thurman. "Two thousand people are camped in Macleay Park. Cops has been harassing them for weeks, but they just fade into the park when it gets heavy. Here. We have been slowly infiltrating the camp, moving out mothers and children, getting ready. They are also coming into Washington Park and will be sweeping up, following the route you took to get here. We have occupied most of the private houses along Fairview Blvd and Kingston. Even out by Germantown Road, because they will try and get behind us there. We know their plan. They are committing two, maybe as much as four thousand of their young (V)ICE commandos to the Forest Park operation. These kids have had virtually no combat training. They think they have an advantage with their night goggles, but if they wear them, they are going to be blinded for a few days tonight. They went right from the political rallies to putting on their sharp black uniforms. They are adept at intimidating unarmed crowds of refugees, but have never faced determined organized armed resistance."

"We will lose people," said Mosley, "But we will not retreat. We can take them out, we can retake the city, temporarily at least. This is a propaganda operation. We know they will come at us with everything. And more tomorrow. Messages from Washington are ordering all homeless camps removed without delay. They are planning to make an example of Portland. So if we strike first, well – we will see if we can push them into a mistake."

"What about Cynthia Oglethorpe? Who took her? Where did they take her?"

Clare looked up, and hesitated. "We have nothing yet."

"They lost four tonight, and that is the reason they will use for the operation. This will be a vicious fight, but we have been planning for a long time and have so many traps waiting for them. The hard part will be 'losing ground' early and convincingly, so they commit and chase us. It appears they aren't waiting until morning. They don't want us to "escape". They are coming into the park. Well, we have night vision too, that will work, not brand a white light on our retinas. So it couldn't be better! We are ready. We are going to cut them off and kill all of them."

"Do they know how prepared you are?"

"No indication they understand the scope of our occupation of the park. They know we have some guns, and probably think we are just a little group of disgruntled ex-military. That is why they are throwing everything they have at us. We are more than a little group, as you can see."

Peggy was amazed at the extent of the resistance. "You have done a good job keeping it a secret up until now."

"Six months – small work parties, digging, laying power cables. We have been given access to many homes of the rich people up here in the West Hills, ever since the Thanksgiving Decrees were announced last fall."

"Do you have enemies living up here in the West Hills?"

"Oh yeah! But by tomorrow we won't." Clare ran her finger across her throat.

"Peggy," Mosley got up. "You stay here and watch the action. I am going to check and make sure our Stinger battery is in place and ready to fire when they put up the helicopters in a few hours."

"Make sure they know we are waiting until the bulk of their troops are inside the park perimeter. No premature ejaculation!"

"Never been a problem, Clare!"

Clare smiled and gave Mosley the finger as he climbed up the ladder out of the cavern.

CHAPTER 35

AIN'T NOTHIN' BUT A REVOLUTION

After Midnight, Sunday morning, July 19, 2020

"YOU SHOULD BE PROUD OF YOURSELF," SAID NATE.
"Why?" Nate and Chubby sat on the steps overlooking Pioneer Courthouse Square, looking out at thousands of Portlanders occupying the whole center of downtown Portland. All around the square surging crowds were cheering. Nate and Kip had a good view. Down in the center of the square about two hundred of (V)ICE's finest were sitting and squatting morosely, disarmed and guarded by two young women, who casually let their assault weapons hang against their thighs. The crowd, which was on all sides of Pioneer Square and seemed to stretch all the way down to the river was chatting "ICE OUT! ICE OUT!"

"Grennell just sent this out – The West Side in the city is secure. Still mopping up in Forest Park. The bridges are all under control. The airport is still contested, but nothing can land, so they can't be reinforced – tonight anyway. Grennell's command center is the train station. Over two thousand just surrendered on I-84. They are putting prisoners on the train to move them, south where they are refurbing a refugee camp for POWs." Nate reported.

Chubby was grooving on the chanting, taking his mind off of GG, for a few minutes anyway. "So – you said you met Paula a second time when you were at school. I still can't picture you as 18 years old."

A young man brought them a water bottle. "Compliments of Colonel Hassan Coleman," he said. Nate gave him a cock-eyed salute.

"OK, let me tell you how that went down. It is somehow appropriate in these circumstances."

Spring, 1970. Kent State – the war came home. National Guard troops – mostly kids who didn't go to college, but also didn't go to Vietnam – gunned down four kids just like me. I was 18. The University's Student Union nearly burnt to the ground – somebody sent a Molotov cocktail to the top floor in an elevator. I saw the fire start from my dorm window, across the campus. I wasn't particularly political at the time – but this, and the events still to come – woke me up.

By spring, I had forgotten about Paula – remember, I told you about the road trip back to school? I saw her once on campus and waved, but she ignored me, if she even saw me. It was springtime, and I went to class, halfheartedly did the reading, but mostly I was locked up in the dorm room, listening to Hendrix, Ten Years After, Jeff Airplane, Led Zeppelin, Buffalo Springfield, Quicksilver, the Moody Blues, Allmans, the Dead...you get the picture.

Anyway – after the Student Union burned, Wally and I – Wally – the guy from the car trip, when I first met Paula earlier – decided to run across town from campus to eastside of Lawrence, where we had heard most of the "action" was taking place.

Wally and I ate a tiny bit of LSD, maybe an eighth of

a normal dose, and decided to cross over, to join with our black comrades in East Lawrence, and see if we could get into some real action. We left through the back door of the dorm and hid in the bushes on the fringe of the parking lot and watched a patrol car slowly roll by, crushing loose gravel into the asphalt. The beam from the cop's hand-held spot lamp tracked relentlessly along the edge, but we were well hidden. Then the red and yellow bubble gum light spun and flashed, the siren wailed, and gravel spit like jet exhaust as the patrol car fishtailed out onto the street. We sprinted across the parking lot, carefully avoiding the illumination of the street and park lights. We ran around the edge of Potter's Pond, and then got down behind a tree as a formation of National Guardsmen appeared, marching down into the grass, across the side of the Campanile Hill.

The acid was leaving palinopsia trails everywhere. The night was spinning and yet was perfectly still and pregnant with a multidimensional wholeness, kaleidoscopic and vibrant. Plato suddenly made sense to me – everything that existed had a perfect model that existed outside of time and now that ethereal plane of existence was on full display. It was all there, right in front of me.

Anyway, when the soldiers had passed, we ran the rest of the way, crossing Mississippi Street and up those old Depression-era red brick steps toward the north side of the top of Mount Oread. We watched another National Guard unit march across the Campanile hillside. We had somehow slid between the two groups of soldiers without being seen.

As I watched the marching soldiers, one by one, they became pennies, and the formation became an old penny collection that I had started as a little boy. The pennies were getting up out of their ordered, neat blue cardboard folder, and marched back to where they came from, under seat cushions, behind furniture, into the pockets of long unworn jackets, into piggy banks shattered long ago, pancaked into copper razors next to abandoned railroad tracks, wedging into the top of loafers.

This numismatist nightmare, this twisted parody of Gresham's Law, wasn't just bad money chasing good money. It was the entropic falling away from all ordered things to disorder. Those poor suckers playing soldier, chasing us, playing freedom fighter, at the same time trying to escape from the order they walked in, the orders that made them do it...while we did the same.

Whoooah...even now, 50 years later, I remember how stoned I was that night. Wally lit up again. He took a hit and passed it to me. The soldiers marched slowly, no longer in step but not breaking formation, up the Campanile.

There was another gunshot. The marching soldiers stopped, brought their rifles to the ready, then continued. Wally killed the joint. A humming engine, a car was coming down from the campus, slowly.

"Here comes oink, oink!" said Wally. The spinning bubble gum machine was clearly silhouetted. My stomach gurgled. The static of the squad radio got louder and louder...

I got ready to throw. Wally stood up and threw straight down. I remained squatting behind the ancient rock wall and lofted my flat-ended rock up high, while barely looking. Wally's rock hit the hood a second or so before mine smashed through the front windshield – and the squad car squealed to a stop.

The two cops were instantly out of their car, one of them bleeding from the head. Their guns were drawn. We turned and ran up to the top of 13th Street.

"Halt!" A fat man in a blue blazer, running, if you could call it that, was right behind them, gun drawn. Where did he come from? We ran through a frat house lawn. Another police car pulled into the driveway. Two more cops and more blue-blazered fat guys, also guns in hand.

"Freeze!" Wally vaulted onto a chain-link fence. A black cop came out of nowhere and peeled him right off the fence with a full bodied sack tackle. I jumped and was over it, while Wally was pounced on by a second cop. "Go!" he yelled. A warning shot, please fire a warning shot first, I thought. I… was lost…into an alley…headlights appeared at the other end…down a muddy slope. I ran between two houses and was shielded from the alley. Sirens from different directions were converging…jumped into a dug-out space about as deep as a bucket in front of a cellar window and squatted down.

Suddenly, half blinded and scared shitless, I saw a light switch on the other side of the window, inside the cramped cellar efficiency apartment – a woman –curly dark blond hair fell to her eyebrows and shoulders. A red strike fist was stenciled on her tight yellow tee-shirt. She looked at me with piercing blue eyes from a couple of feet away, over her rimless granny glasses. It was Paula! I desperately made a pantomime, as if I were flicking off a switch.

She turned off the lights and opened the window.

A car door slammed. I held my index finger to my lips.

I heard them talking. "I think he went down…" There was a loud splat and someone laughed…someone else snapped, "Quiet…get up!" The walking continued toward the cellar.

Paula propped open the window, took my hand, and guided me inside to the basement floor from a rickety bookshelf. The police were continuing toward us. Without closing the window, or saying a word, the woman pulled me by the wrists to her bed. She flipped back the covers and with a matador's move pulled them over both of us. Just as we settled, a flashlight shone in, slowly working around the room toward the bed.

"Hey look! You! Down on the street. Halt!" The flashlight swept away and there was running.

"Thanks," I whispered. Paula looked different two inches away.

"Wow! It's you!" She took off her glasses and giggled. "You must have been bad."

My mind was racing. I still hadn't been laid, and my second semester in college was almost over. I was pretty sure she had forgotten my name, but I felt – this was it! More scenes of frustrated desire rose and tumbled in my memory. Each time it had been yes and then no. There was more muffled shouting from outside the window, and then a shot. I started laughing. She felt my crotch and opened her eyes in mock surprise.

"I am tripping..." The faint light from outside the cellar window reflected off a poster of Tommie Smith and John Carlos raising their hands in protest at the Olympics two years earlier. White plaster was painted over the dirt walls. Most of the rest of it was covered with album cover art and R. Crumb–like political posters. Half-opened books and reports lay everywhere. I saw it all from the bottom of a vortex.

She laughed and kissed me on the mouth. "You're the guy from New Jersey, right? Nate! Take off your shoes," she said. She hadn't forgotten! But then we had spent three days in freezing hell together.

"What happened tonight?" Paula threw her jeans out from under the covers. I sat up and leaned back against the wall next to the bed. What had happened? They got Wally.

"I threw a rock through a pig's windshield." I tried not to sound like I was bragging.

"All right! I can't believe tonight," said Paula. She lit a joint and gave it a very self-satisfied toke.

"Oh," I was starting to level off – the acid wasn't so strong anymore – of course, I only took a tiny bit.

"You'd never guess who left here not 10 minutes ago."

"Richard Nixon," I said. She had a coughing, laughing fit,

with pot smoke coming out of her nose. She took a moment to compose herself, started laughing again, and pulled the half-smoked joint away when I tried to reach for it.

"Abbie Hoffman."

"Wow. Far out! He's still in town, huh?"

Paula nodded with continued self-satisfaction. I didn't know what to say. As Paula leaned toward me, her perked-up breasts pushed into my face and her arms wrapped around my neck. I rolled on top of her. "I want you to lick my pussy first," she demanded gently.

I put my knee down between her legs.

"Unh-unh. Come on."

I put my foot down between her ankles.

"No! Come on. Eat me first..."

I was embarrassed and confused. I didn't want to put my mouth where I assumed that Abbie Hoffman had just had his dick. At least I thought that was what she was implying. But, fools rush in, and tonight was finally going to be the night. Paula closed her eyes and was rocking back and forth. I slid my head down her body. I stopped at her belly button and lingered. Here we go, I thought. I poked my tongue out of my mouth, and put it to work. I threw myself into a frenzy and then, tasted something salty, and then something different, something that smelled like diluted bleach. I had jerked off enough to recognize the smell; it was cum.

I stopped and sat up. So did Paula. I suddenly realized what I was giving up on and pulled her down again and she opened her legs. But my cock was no longer hard. What happened? I got up and went to the bathroom, to rinse out my mouth.

"Come back to bed," she said to me as I was leaning over the sink trying to find my nose. "We've got all night."

The next morning I woke to see Paula was already up at her desk, with pen in hand, writing. The sun was up and she was ignoring me, so I got up, pulled on my pants and shoes, and mumbled some "see you later" shit, which she acknowledged with a smile. Then she got up, gave me a hug, and kissed me, and then she said, "Go down to the sheriff's office – it's downtown, one street over from Massachusetts – and find out if they have your friend. Find out how many they arrested, if you can. Get their names if possible. If you can, tell them to be strong, stay silent, and we'll have a lawyer there before noon."

I was working for the movement now. I nodded. She kissed me again. "I'll see you later," and gave me the smile that promised another visit to paradise. I left Paula's basement apartment.

I finally had done it, had been fucked, and I finally knew the afterglow of glorious and transforming sex. I was flying, and I wanted more, I wanted to fall into her arms again. First, I had a job to do.

As I was to discover, Paula was the brains behind the demonstrations taking place on campus and would be out firing up the crowds on campus later in the day. She was an amazing speaker, so laid back, and well, being beautiful didn`t hurt either. She gave me a job – an assignment – a direct order from the Revolution. I went from a young Wildling of the night to a Knight of the world-wide revolution – I was a made-man.

I walked downtown, tracing the steps Wally and I had intended to make last night. When I got to the county jail, I went right in the front door and was greeted by three hard-faced, glaring cops sitting near the front desk.

"What do you want, hippie?"

I looked at the faces, hoping that they hadn't been the ones who chased me last night. They laughed as I gave them nothing but puke-ass cool. I didn't say anything to incite them, just stood there and dared him to arrest me.

"I said what do you what?"

"Wally Cherry. I need to see him." I asked.

At that instant, they all went quiet because a man in his mid-thirties walked in just then. The cops knew him. He was the definition of Midwestern haberdashery self-abasement, Henry Kissinger horn-rims, flat-top hair, conservative 1950s summertime slacks and shirt (which contrasted against my long hair, Grateful Dead tee-shirt, and dirty mud-splattered bell bottoms). But this guy had some kind of power that turned off the red-necked attitude in the desk sergeant. Hung around his neck was a World War II vintage Graflex Speed Graphic camera.

As I stood in front of the station sergeant signing in, he took my picture.

That picture ended up in *Life* Magazine later that summer. It was a black and white contrast of rebellious youth versus grizzled authority, with the crew-cut desk sergeant staring down at me with what looked like hatred as I filled out the request. It became one of the iconic pictures of the protests during that spring of 1970, and would give me a status way beyond what I deserved. For the next three years I was a little bit famous in Lawrence, and was feted by students, professors, and the community. Totally unearned, bogus and without merit, the picture was my ticket into parties, occasional good grades I didn't have to work for and – well – lots of sex, which was my main preoccupation. But more important than all of that, it gave me the cred I needed to do what was coming next – which was fronting the EEG tests off campus.

I saw Wally and delivered the message, found out who else was locked up. I told them to wait for the lawyers, stay strong. And they did. That event pushed me further into the spotlight, put me on all kinds of subversive lists, which eventually ended up with Nixon's secret unknown Watergate crew, those working on the Huston Plan. I have not been able to get out of all of that notoriety ever since. Then my book on China came along and that sealed it.

~~~

Anyway, that is how it all got started.

Chubby listened silently to Nate tell his story about his sexual/political adventures as a freshman in college. "So what happened to Paula? Did she join the Weathermen? Bomb apartment buildings and go underground?"

No – she went the other way. Completely. Flipped. Became one of Nixon's people. Plaid skirts, Peter Pan collared blouses. It still doesn't make complete sense, but she became – she lent her talents to the enemy. At first she intended to be a double agent against them, but it soon became clear that the resistance had deteriorated into madness – bombs, paranoia, and just rank criminal behavior, disguised as revolutionary action.

I stayed in Kansas that summer. We ate what she said was the last of the tree fungus she and Elwood had collected back on our January trip across the country. As I told you, they had disappeared for an afternoon when we were stuck in Vandalia, Illinois, and I always assumed she had decided to fuck Elwood of all people. But I guess they had eaten the quantum tree fungus – how Elwood knew it was trip candy and not deadly poison – who knows? He eventually got his PhD in mycology, trying to understand the fungus and figure out how to grow it in a petri dish. Which is another story that will have to wait. But by the spring of that year, 1970, I had experienced enough to know that this was something different. Just before Paula left campus for Ann Arbor, Michigan, to meet up with the people who would eventually become the Weathermen, she and I went for a walk around campus after eating two whole fungus ears. At the time I thought that we were just sharing hallucinations. I had been reading about

Quantrill's raid on Lawrence in 1863, and thought I saw bush-whackers with six-shooters standing in front of Fraser Hall. She saw them too. And they saw us! We saw other things – I saw her fall into a crevice that opened up right in front of us. I got down on my hands and knees to pull her out, but there was no hole, and I looked up and she was standing there with a frightened look on her face. She said, "I don't think it has happened yet!"

The fungus opened our minds up to the quantum world – space and time were obliterated and we existed outside of the normal false trappings of reality, and in the true universal, where matter can exist in many places at once. After a while, we saw that the world around us had changed.

But the fungus made me violently ill; I thought I was dying. I felt like my insides were going to explode, I didn't stop eating it, but I skipped days, and I don't know, that probably wasn't very good for me. Stopping and starting sometimes seemed like a Groundhog Day experience – you know, waking up and thinking – haven't I already done this? I came to see where it would make people suicidal."

"Not you though, huh?" said Kip.

"Me? Naw, I am too much of a masochist to kill myself. But Paula never did get sick. I don't know why she was able to do it – but she did, and well – she has hardly changed. She once told me that the past is as alive for her as now it is for us, but I am not sure what she meant by that.

After that, Paula got swept up by the national anti-war move-ment, and a month later, she left on a radical organizational tour – Madison, Wisconsin; Berkeley; New York – some kind of Yippie roadshow, with Abbie and all his buddies. I think the grand poobahs just wanted her hotness nearby.

After Cambodia, and the demonstrations that spring, the War was beginning to wind down. We were still killing Vietnamese of course, and fucking up their country for generations with herbi-cides, but American soldiers were leaving the battlefield.

But the Movement tried to live on, with the Weatherman. She was totally disgusted by the sexist hedonism of that crew. More important, she saw that their tactics had no chance of working without a bloody revolution, which they would lose. So she decided to infiltrate the other camp, figuring she could do more by pretending to be a double agent. Really it was to get away from the morons, the psycho Weathermen. It was easy – she got dressed up, put on a bra, stockings, and with almost no questions asked, she was working with a pretty boy PhD named Stewart Gent, a.k.a. Stewardo del Gente. He reported to Gordon Liddy for a while. All of which fit perfectly into the paranoid mindset of Nixon's crew.

Anyway – I was out of money and I had a burning sensation in my dick, so I went back to New Jersey for the summer, got treated by the family doctor, and didn't see Paula again until December of 1972, when she and Stewart conned me and Elwood out of our EEG machine.

CHAPTER 36
BUGGING OUT

2:00 am, Sunday, July 19, 2020

TWENTY MINUTES AFTER TELLY AND HIS CREW LEFT Alison and Kayla, they were back. They all looked freaked out, their casual wise-guy attitudes gone.

It was true; the rumors of a revolt were true.

"We gotta get out of here, Telly," Lew was looking at his fone and Telly was listening to the shooting, which was very close.

"These fucking scum. Our guys will handle it, don't you think?"

"Telly, it's bad out there. Cadez couldn't get to his hotel so he is coming back; his van is outside. We have to make a run for the airport, and the only way is by chopper. We have to meet the chopper at Wallace Park in 15 minutes if we want to get on the last fucking plane out of here. It is a total shitshow in this town," Lew said.

Alison was out on the balcony, watching the fireworks up in Forest Park. Johnny was there too, smoking a cigarette. Did Peggy get my message, see my flashing fone light signalling I was stuck here, she wondered? Did Nate make it across the river? And Spence, what about Spence?

Lew came out on the balcony.

"What the fuck is wrong with these people, Lew?" said Johnny. "I would understand it if this was a shithole city like

Newark or Baltimore. But these people are living like fucking kings in this town. Maybe it's 'cause the broads all dress like men – hey no offense, Alison, but I don't know how to explain it? It would be even better if they would keep the vagrant scum out. Fucking libtards. The old Prez should never have quit, you know? This new guy has fucked things up royally. Where did they get the guns? Jesus, I would get it if this wasn't such a rich white town. Must be outsiders, don't you think, Lew?"

"Johnny, I am only going to say this once – watch it with all that Real-Prez is the Real-Prez talk, OK? Telly don't like it. We work for Cadez. Alison, we are leaving now, let's go."

"Lew? Can..."

"STOP! I don't know what you were going to say, so let's leave it there. Sorry, kid, but Telly needs you. We are setting up a new show – new *SwiftPad*, new *Reigny Deigh*, the works. You have to come. None of it will work without you. Telly and the Senator are counting on you."

Johnny finished his cigarette, glared hard at Lew, and they went back into the suite.

Kayla came into the living room and smiled. "Can someone help me with my bag?"

"Leave it, kid; we are going to be tight as it is," said Lew.

"But –"

"Shut the fuck up!" Telly glared at her, and she hung her head like a whipped dog.

"Senator's down in the van waiting," Lew said.

"You don't think these guys are going to actually take over Portland? The city is full of (V)ICE commandos." Actually Alison was delighted and was having fun pretending she wasn't. "How's it possible?"

"Fucking cocksuckers! Let me tell you about these fucking Portland people and the so-called 'foodies,'" said Telly. "Big dinner, celebrating the crackdown on the scum coming into the city. The top officers of (V)ICE – twelve of the top officers were together at this so-called haute cuisine dump down on 23rd. Every fucking one of them got as sick as a shit-eating dog! Poisoned. Not only were they sick – but they were drugged – all out of their fucking minds off on some kind of drug trip. This hellhole of a city ain't even in America. It's like Baghdad or some such shithole. No, Portland is toast, the President is gonna bomb this place to dust!"

Alison looked away.

"So – I need you. I don't need you dead. Come on, the car is here." Alison took a deep breath, and followed them down to the elevator. Got out at the parking garage, and the van was waiting. In the back seat was a man, his hands locked behind his back, wearing a canvas bag over his head.

OK, Alison, girl, she said to herself. Showtime. She got in first and sat next to Cadez, who was sitting behind the Crocodile. Didn't look at the man in the bag. She pushed up against Cadez to make room for Kayla, who was sobbing and shaking.

Alison turned to Cadez, and smiled. He smiled back and patted her hand. She took his hand and pulled it into her lap.

CHAPTER 37
AT THE RAILWAY STATION

8:00 am, Sunday, July 19, 2020

KIP HEARD SOMEONE COMING UP THE OUTSIDE STAIRS to his apartment above Ranjit's Kwikie Mart. He got up, on two hours sleep, and began searching around his bed for his pants. He was pulling them up when the knocking began. It was a firm knock, not angry or demanding, but not faint either.

He walked out of the bedroom and saw Nate, clad only in his tight, high-waisted blue underpants, his flaccid old chest bare, thin straw hair matted, but face set, determined, standing completely still next to the door, his 7.62mm Luger held with both hands. Kip walked to the door, glanced at Nate, nodded, and put his hand on the handle.

"Who is it?"

"Soldiers of righteous Jah be coming for your fat, white ass!"

Kip opened the door. Aldane came in and looked at Nate, who had not yet moved.

"Damn, look at old stony, all up an' ready!"

"Morning Cums Electric," Nate said as he lowered his gun and reset the safety.

"I tink you mean dat de motafukin' Iceman come. You ready?"

Aldane was on high alert, scanning the apartment he had left a few hours ago, as if expecting (V)ICE to jump out of the bedroom.

"What's the plan?" Kip was pulling on a tee-shirt.

"Jean Katon's plane was able to land at Aurora airport south of here, but we ain't getting there. 99 closed and I-5 is definitely not gonna happen."

"Sorry about fucking up your show last night."

"I finally – finally – get my shot – opening for the Queen of Haitian Reggae herself! And who fucks it up? My ol' buddy Kippy. Yeah, that's about right. Shoulda figured," said Aldane.

"You be sure to mention that when the historians interview you when you're an old man. Tell us about the Battle of Portland, oh wise one!"

"They never believe any of this shit."

"I am going over to *SwiftPad* headquarters. Get some money. You guys wait here. I'll be back."

"Good – I am going to crash out in yo tinky bed," said Aldane.

Nate was looking at Chubby's eyePad on the couch. "Good plan, Kipster. I'll wait here in case Maggie and Alison show up. Keep in touch," he said without looking up.

Chubby pedaled down MLK past shuttered shops and restaurants. There was very little evidence of the fighting until he got to Broadway.

The first thing he saw was a blasted (V)ICE cruiser. The black and white Ford Sandcat was burnt and two dead uniformed (V)ICE commandos lay on the road next to the cruiser, burnt black.

Chubby continued rolling down Broadway toward the bridge, and witnessed similar scenes. At the bridge a woman in a bicycle helmet, orange vest, and camo stretch pants armed with a short-barreled machine gun stopped him.

"I need to see General Grennell," he said, giving her his real ID.

"Fuck me! Kip Rehain! They are playing your little talk at the Moda last night everywhere!"

"I need to get to *SwiftPad* HQ!"

She pulled out her fone and turned away, to talk. When she came back, she said, "Ride across, stay in the middle, bomb squad is busy, so don't stop. Somebody will meet you in front of the train station."

There were more wrecked trucks, on both sides, and covered corpses lined up along the side. He turned off at the bottom of the Broadway Bridge into the train station parking lot, which had turned into a huge staging area. He was met by a couple of middle-aged guys, with hand guns on their hips.

"You Rehain?" He nodded. "Come."

He came into the main waiting area, which had been cleared of the most of the wooden benches and turned into an interrogation area, with a couple of hundred young (V)ICE commandos, packed together, all hands bound behind with zip-ties. Some visibly sobbing, others staring blankly into space. They were being pulled up one at a time and taken out to the train platform. Outside on the platform next to the tracks, he saw more groups. Then a burst of machine gun fire. Cries from the (V)ICE sitting on the floor. No one else looked up.

"Over here!" Chubby went into one of the offices that used to be a ticket booth. Senator (General) Harvey Grennell stood up, no hat, wearing jeans and a camo pullover.

"Senator," Chubby stuck out his hand.

"Mr. Rehain, we don't have much time, please sit. Nice work last night."

"I didn't do anything." Chubby looked at Grennell.

"You probably have heard of the Ishpeming Group, which is my controlling authority. I report to the resistance committee. I will say right now, I didn't care much for your city here when I got here two months ago to help pull this together."

"Why?" asked Kip.

"Well, I didn't think it really stood for anything – just self-involved, epicurean navel gazers. Most of the men and women you see with guns – from both sides – are not from here. Some are, but we have been arriving in small groups with the refugees over the last three months."

"So everybody – you and (V)ICE – came to fuck up our city."

"Don't get me wrong – we have been recruiting locals – and have had no big trouble. A couple of restaurants took out a lot of officers last night – drugged and poisoned a bunch of them, which fucked up their command and control. They took a tremendous risk. People in the south hills gave us their houses, and didn't blink. Twenty of those beautiful architectural wonders overlooking the city. Two or three of them are destroyed – shot to pieces. But – nobody even ratted on them. Kept up their routines while we mounted rockets and machine guns on their balconies. Let us store ammo in their garages. And they joined us. The street people – we made soldiers out of a lot of them. The best thing I can say about you Portlanders is – we were able to keep the surprise. I never thought that would be possible. There were leaks of course, but the stupid fucks didn't believe it. They thought if it was coming, then it was from the refugees down at Sellwood – that is why they shot most of them. We deliberately sent signals confirming that our people were coming in that way. False flags all worked perfectly. It is terrible – paid a horrible price to keep the plan secret. This whole situation is going to be fucking brutal."

"They are going to come back. You know that."

"Oh we expect it. They are putting up a tough fight around the airport. We need to get control there before the day is over to keep air transport out. And open it up for us, too. But they will get here – yes. Eventually. They got a few choppers out last night – rats leaving the ship."

More machine gun fire.

A blond with long hair braided into two pigtails came in. "Just two more, and then that is it, Sir."

"How many total?"

"Nine, only the ones brutalizing the kids or who we could positively ID doing the shooting over at the high school. We matched the killers with the prisoners. The rest of them are tied up on the platform. What should we do with the bodies?"

"Pack 'em on the train with the prisoners. Make 'em ride together. Burn 'em when you get there. The bodies, not the prisoners." Grennell gave Chubby a wry smile.

"What about the one's we ID'd shooting into the crowds – We have thirty dead out on I-84 who stopped the reinforcements from getting to town."

"Pack 'em all up and get the train out of here. Save the evidence. Make sure to keep them separate so they don't get meshed in with the others. Have we intel on the camp?"

"Fifty guards; the stockpile seems not to have been disturbed. We'll be there in two hours or so; Intel is pretty sure they won't put up much of a fight. We have people there ready to smooth things for us."

"Recruit as many as you can."

"Twenty thousand people. Sure – we will get a lot of recruits. What do we do with the rest of them?"

"Set up a council, have elections, tell them the truth and let them decide what they want. Let them know, if they oppose us, we will kill them. Make sure they see the bodies before you burn them. Otherwise, let the rest go."

"Sir!"

"Even if we win," said Kip, "it is going to take decades to fix this, isn't it?"

"Maybe, if ever. We will never be the same. You have to get your software company on board. Democracy is going to be a hard sell I am afraid. Frankly that is the other reason we are here, to protect and gain operational control of the social media package, *SwiftPad*. What's the status on the company?"

"Well – it was decimated yesterday. Cynthia Oglethorpe was kidnapped. Jim Hunt was killed. I don't know where our Chief Technical Officer, Arkie Moropolis, is either. I have not heard from him since yesterday afternoon. Other than Heber Young, the money guy, that is the leadership."

"And you."

"Only nominally. I have been gone for the last eight or nine months. I wasn't technical anyway."

"I see."

"Look, I am useless here. I need to find Cynthia Oglethorpe. I don't give a shit about anything else. I have resources, money, maybe. I need to get to our Headquarters."

"Last report, we control the *SwiftPad* campus, such as it is."

"We have about 45–50 data centers worldwide – I don't know – fifty, sixty thousand people. We only have about two hundred employees at the office – I think. It's all fluff here, the hard stuff is elsewhere. Heber decentralized the finance system, thank somebody's God. So we can keep paying people through this, I hope. I haven't been to the headquarters since –"

"That was our first objective actually. We expect that the Feds will be shutting down the app in areas they control. After today, there will be no more Internet – just various unconnected branches. We are going to encourage people to stay off, except for business, and use direct lines or OTP encryption. It will be a seismic shock for the country. Our suspicion is they kidnapped Oglethorpe to rebuild their end of it."

Another quick volley of machine gun fire from out on the platform.

"Glad that is finished. If we lose, I will certainly be brought up on war crime charges. There was a horrible massacre at Lincoln High School last night. They murdered 80 kids who were staging a protest. We have video. It is awful – they tortured some of them, in front of everybody, before they shot them. They didn't even cover their faces or wear masks."

"(V)ICE doesn't think they can be terrorists. We are creating propaganda that says otherwise."

"Is there other fighting still going on?"

"It's mopping up. The thing we are worried about is we have a fire going up in the hills. It is spreading and if Forest Park goes up, we aren't sure we can stop it. I hope it rains."

"Is the Army going to support the Temp-Prez?"

"Temp-Prez! I laugh when I hear that. What a joke. I am not sure. The only good thing is that these (V)ICE troops have been folding like three-ring binders. Their main training is political. We'll see."

"I need to get to the *SwiftPad* campus. Then – somehow find Cynthia."

"We'll get you to the headquarters."

CHAPTER 38
MOPPING UP

6:00 am, Sunday, July 19, 2020

PEGGY WOKE UP ON A CALIFORNIA KING, ENSCONCED in silk sheets. The soothing sounds of the Cetacean voices came on at 5:50 am, and lasted five minutes. The couple who owned the house had welcomed the Ishpems in weeks ago, and had moved into a friend's house over in Raleigh Hills, and no one had disturbed anything in the house, including the music settings on their sound system.

Mosley lay sleeping. Peggy opened her eyes, and an involuntary mental inventory quickly booted up in her head. Two days ago (or was it decades ago?) 6 am bike into town, to the gym, stretching and lifting, then biking across town. Teaching her 8 am psych 101 class at PSU, followed by coffee with a student she was advising, an hour break reading in her tiny closet of an office, lunch, seminar with five graduate students, then waiting around for three hours before her "The Future of Psychology" night class. Then arriving home to find an old lover,(actually, she realized sadly, the only old lover) casually talking to her husband. She hadn't seen Nate in 20 years. Dinner, horrible news on TV. Back on the bike yesterday, across town, and – oh, yeah – she killed a man, shot him in the head when she panicked. That was new. But her husband was in jail, not her, and not Nate either, more riding, up the steep hill to Washington Park, meeting the woman her husband was seeing on the side – no, she didn't know that. Then standing inches away, two cops shot dead. Into the woods, to a murderous firefight that lasted all night, and now – in a million-dollar bedroom overlooking the city with a hard, young soldier. So hard. She stiffled a giggle, and looked at the time on her fone on the teak wood night table next to the bed. It was 6:10 am. About three hours in bed, with some sleeping. And what did you do yesterday?

Well – she skipped one thing. About 2 am they had stormed into Gordy Lobetts' condo. It had strong doors and locks. Mose had some C4 and boom, boom, they were in.

Peggy went up on the balcony where she had seen Alison's light. She had expected to find her body, but nothing, only the residue of a hasty exit. A gum wrapper was on the floor. She opened it up, hoping somehow it might have a message, but it was blank. She looked through each room, looking under cups, in the medicine cabinet behind the mirror, everywhere. No clue, no sign of anything other than a bunch of people had been there, drinking coffee, eating pastry, and a deli plate filled with baby carrots, empty bottles of scotch, food left out, already beginning to smell, and they didn't wipe their feet either.

Mose told her, carefully, hesitantly, that another team had broken into the Justice Center and freed almost one hundred people that (V)ICE had been holding. But no Spence, although one of the prisoners remembered seeing them take him away. Mose had seemed surprised at her reaction, but later she would have no memory of how she felt when she heard the news.

She didn't feel bad about where she had ended her day. She didn't believe it, but as she searched her brain and listened to whatever popped up, and it was clear, she really didn't feel bad. Yesterday, it must have been because of yesterday, she thought.

She had developed a hardened fatalism about life in the last

12 or so hours. It was the most natural thing in the world to fall into bed with Mose, after last night. They had wiped out most of a squad of (V)ICE commandos, and left the prisoners zip-tied together around a huge Douglas fir. Then were ordered to "hold" the nearby section command post, and that was what they were doing. It had nothing to do with Spence. Or Nate either, not in the slightest. She had never experienced anything like last night. She wondered, would Nate be proud of her? Why would she even care? The thought disturbed her. He had left her in an incredibly dangerous situation, but she had come through.

"You awake?" Mosley asked.

"Yeah." Even with so little sleep she had never felt more awake.

"We gotta get going. Siena said we had to get down to the *SwiftPad* HQ by 9 am and relieve the guard. I would rather do that than clean up. Bodies, blasted trucks –"

"And fire, can you smell it?" Peggy sat up, revealing her breasts. "How old are you, Mosley?"

Mose laughed. "Twenty-three."

She pulled the blanket up, to cover herself. Not much older than her daughter.

"You get up first," she said. She waited for Mose to ask her that question, but to her immense relief it never came.

"Have you ever read anything about the Six-Day War – Israel back in the sixties?" Mosley got up out of bed from a flat sit, no hands. His naked ass – she couldn't believe it was so beautiful.

"No," she said.

"Apparently it was an orgy in Israel after the war. At the time they weren't sure how it was going to go. The idea that Egyptians and Syrians might end up occupying Tel Aviv was not out of the realm of possibility. They were sure it would be a long war at best. But when it was over, and they had taken the Golan Heights and Sinai – well – everybody was fucking. It was like a patriotic duty. Israeli women let it all hang out for a week. That closeness to death is an incredible aphrodisiac."

"What's your point?"

"I don't know. I'll – get dressed out in the – out there. See if I can find something quick to eat."

They walked down the winding road along the ridge. People were coming out of the houses and applauding them. They were soon joined by other Ishpems, as the rebels were becoming known. They walked with weapons at ready, on the shoulders of the road, covering their side, trusting the colleagues had the other side. Where had she learned that? Peggy had read books on war, and on the psychology of combat. It had fascinated her, and some instinct for battlefield survival had somehow emerged in her last night. She stood her ground, even when the man next to her went down. Didn't faze her. Where did that come from, she wondered?

Their orders were confirmed by fone to make haste to the *SwiftPad* HQ. They were on Cornell Road. As the crow would fly, the industrial district was straight through the easternmost section of the park, but it was burning. Luckily there was no wind. It had been a late spring, and while it wasn't very dry, the undergrowth was dense. She looked up and saw dark clouds moving up from the south.

They hiked down and picked up a ride in front of the Audubon Society Center. Mosley told them where, and they were taken directly there.

The industrial district looked like a town hit by a rogue tornado. Some buildings were untouched and some were shot up and in a couple of cases burned. The *SwiftPad* HQ was in the former category. There were two sentries posted on the front corners of the perimeter, but they looked relaxed. Peggy jumped out of the truck and went into the former mostly wooden warehouse.

She walked in, her AK slung over her shoulder, and was greeted by two older men, who looked beat.

"Where have you been? We had to stay here all night," one of them said.

"Sorry," said Peggy. She smiled and gave them a flimsy salute, which caused the two guards to shake their heads in mild disgust. She was followed in by Mose and a couple of others, who took over debriefing the two guys who had been relieved. She walked into the main "foyer," if that was what it was. It didn't look anything like what she expected a tech HQ to look like. The walls were raw, unfinished plywood. There were wires lying on the floor, held down by gray duct tape. Old couches and big pillows that looked right out of the 1970s were spread around the vast space. It smelled a little mildewy. Surrounding and above were conference rooms, again, cheap furniture and mismatched chairs. In the back, up on the balcony that overlooked everything, she saw the top of a man's head, chin in his hands, listening to someone whom she couldn't see. He looked familiar.

She and Mose climbed up the raw wooden stairs to the balcony and saw a man with a head covered with a two-day stubble, and a goatee that was morphing into a full beard. He was talking to a woman about thirty, white, in a dashiki smock, hair bushed out, like it was recently released from imprisonment, sitting in front of him, with her legs askew.

"Hello, how goes the battle?"

"Not bad, but not quite over," said Mose.

"Aren't you – Kip Rehain?" Peggy was squinting, not exactly sure she was right.

"That is what everybody keeps telling me."

"My – uh – friend Nathan Schuette said he was going to go to your place last night."

"Who are you?"

"Peggy. Margaret Stromborn."

"Holy shit. Maggie! We waited for you. Wasn't there another woman with you?"

"Alison, uh, she works with Spence, my husband." Peggy realized she had no idea what her last name was. All State in basketball 10 years ago, she did remember that. "I think she was kidnapped by the guys now running *Reigny Deigh*. They might have been able to fly out."

"What is the status of your company, Mr. Rehain?" asked Moseley.

"Mr. Rehain? Shit, everybody calls me Chubby. This is Hadley. She knows more about that than I do."

Mosley didn't see any chub in "Chubby," but an almost skinny, clear-eyed guy of about 45 or 50, with stubble on his scalp, and a goatee gone to seed.

"Internationally, not bad," said Hadley, who was filling out a tight, black body suit in a most attractive fashion. "But we lost connection to almost all of our US-based data centers last night. The main link to BC Canada is still up, and that is giving us pretty good international coverage. Otherwise our network is 'blinking' 12:00 o'clock. But the interesting thing is – China opened up their firewall to *SwiftPad*. We gained 180 million new users in the last four hours. It is all relayed too – we have no data centers there so it is piggybacking on Korea and Vietnam's links," Hadley reported.

"Just got a message from our CTO, Arkie," said Chubby. "He is working from an 'undisclosed location.'" Kip didn't mention it was the compound down in the Coast Range. "We expect there will be a reaction from the Feds to all of this, and we need to co-locate system management down there for redundancy."

"The Ishpeming Committee is concerned about – the direction your company might be taking in the wake of Ms. Oglethorpe's – kidnapping," Mose said.

"I'll be in touch with them soon. I am leaving for the Midwest tonight. If they took Cynthia there, I need to go and find her. I don't give a shit about anything else right now. Arkie will run things on the West Coast for now."

"Don't forget my husband. Or his colleague."

"Alison Aykroyd and Spence Stromborn. We are doing every-thing we can to track them," said Mose.

Aykroyd, thought Peggy. Of course.

"No, I won't forget," said Kip. "I plan to make my way up to Michigan, to see the Committee. I am going to go through RedHat country, get the scoop on the situation. I think I can pass as one of them. Any word on security in Ishpeming?"

"They are fine. Seven thousand new troops are training there. A Great Lakes Coast Guard squad defected, so no one will sneak up on them from the water. It's battle stations all over the country, especially after last night."

"What's in the backpack, Mr. – uh – Chubby?"

"Five million dollars in hundreds. Over a hundred pounds of paper. "

Mose was the only one who laughed.

"Want a ride? Want to go see Nate, Peggy?" Kip asked.

"Can I go?" Peggy looked at Mose.

"Yeah. You are relieved." Mose looked at Peggy, and smiled. She stepped over and planted a kiss on his lips.

CHAPTER 39

GOIN' SOUTH

Noon, Sunday, July 19, 2020

"**J**ESUS, MAGGIE, YOU MUST BE EXHAUSTED," SAID Nate, back in Chubby's apartment.

"I'm tired. Yeah."

"No word on Alison or Spence?"

"A chopper took off from Wallace Park around two and dropped off six people at PDX," said Peggy, looking at her "resistance-issued" fone. "There were two private planes that left at the same time – around 2 am – one actually filed a flight plan – for Nashville. It had six people, two women, three men in suits, including one who was obviously a prisoner. His head was bagged and he was bound. The other plane – nothing – no report on occupants, nothing. No flight plan."

"Aurora is way south, isn't it?" said Nate. "Why can't we leave from PDX?"

"Shut down," said Peggy, with her eyes half closed. "They will be tryin' to bring in more troops. That would be where they would try to land."

"So if Ishpeming controls PDX, why do we have to go to the Aurora airport?"

"They have trucks on the runway. They are trying to set up defenses there."

"So the invasion can come from Aurora?"

"Or Hillsboro. Smaller runways – big transports are iffy for either."

"The G5 is waiting," said Aldane. "Let's go if you want out of here."

Peggy sat on the couch, barely awake. Nate continued to get dressed.

"We got one seat, you got the cash?"

"Yeah – how much?" Kip asked.

"Fifty K."

"K," said K.

Aldane shook his head.

"Let's get going. You coming?"

"Might as well," said Nate, who was in the kitchen, spreading butter on an end piece of bread.

"Good, you drive my car back, ol' man," said Aldane.

Peggy opened her eyes, but didn't say anything.

"Nate should go too," said Peggy. "Don't you have to report to HQ?"

"I am staying. Try to get to the Rehain Compound. So far Comm is good there."

The three of them shambled down the rickety, wooden, outside stairs, piled into Aldane's 1990 Cutlass Ciera, and headed south on MLK. They turned left on Ainsworth, then over to 15th and turned right, heading south again. Sunday early afternoon, no traffic, the reports of the sporatic fighting in the West Hills apparently keeping people inside. Northeast Portland, the Alberta and Irvington neighborhoods, dense residential areas that were usually bustling with activities on the weekend. Most of the front yards had vegetable and flower gardens, and on an early Sunday afternoon in July, normally you would expect people out doing gardening before it got hot later. But the streets were deserted.

They crossed over the 84 Freeway, and traffic was light but stopped in both directions.

"They got roadblocks out, stopping and searching," said Nate.

Aldane was looking at his fone and driving. "We clear for a while up ahead – maybe. Dis app is a wrong piece of shit."

They continued, staying off main streets, crossing under Highway 26 onto Milwaukie Avenue. "Let's stop and have something to eat. Listen a bit. Maybe somebody knows what's going on down south. Too many cops out."

They parked the Cutlass on the street and went into the The Back Story Café, which was crowded. There were no small tables, only long picnic-style benches. They sat next to a pasty guy with a beard, tee-shirt, and cargo shorts, who was smiling too much, and a slinky, hollow-eyed young woman with short, disheveled black hair wearing a candy-striper blouse and muddy pajama bottoms. Pasty immediately recognized Aldane.

"Bro, I know you! You with the Mane Shakers! Wow. Hey – Wow. Some shit last night huh? Jean Katon had the place smokin'!"

"Wasn't all that was smokin'," said Peggy.

"So, Bro," asked Aldane, "Did you join the march?"

"Fuck no! I went home. I hear Real-Prez is coming back now. About time."

"Yeah, right," said Peggy.

"I'm Sequoia, this is Darmie," the young woman said, jumping in nervously.

"Darmie?"

"Short for Darmonious," said Darmie. "I've seen you somewhere?"

"Probably at one of Dane's shows," said Chubby.

Darmie didn't look too sure that was it.

"Did you hear about what is going on up in Forest Park?"

"No, I don't believe we have," said Nate, deeply intent and serious. "What have you heard?"

"I was camped up in the Park, last night," said Sequoia. "Wow, was it incredible."

"She means Forest Park," said Darmie, "Macleay campsite, off of Thurman Street. Bunch of dirty refugees."

"You weren't there!" Sequoia glared at Darmie. "It was just before dark, hundreds of (V)ICE rolled up in trucks, just drove right in; I just made it out of my tent when a truck rolled over it. I heard people screaming horribly. They all had night goggles on and these blinding flashlights. A lot of screaming, too, especially from the ICYes. We had to spend the night sitting outside – in the grass. Trashed our tents, looking for people or something. And – the rest of them went up the hill from the Park. Gunfire all night. We couldn't leave – people were shitting right in the open, in the middle of everybody, crying, then the (V)ICE guys come down, looking fucked up, some with no guns. They kept telling us if we moved or made a sound they would shoot us. Then Bang, Bang! Two of them go down, there is yelling and out of the woods practically falling off the side of the hill – real steep if you don't use the path up there – these camo dudes come down, with some (V)ICE dudes tied up and said we were free – but had to leave, no waiting. My bike was fine, but my shit was gone, and the (V)ICE dudes fucked up my tent. I tried to get as far away as I could."

"That's when we hooked up," said Darmie, "again."

Sequoia looked at Darmie. "Yeah," she said.

"You know what I mean, right?" Darmie smiled at Chubby, who didn't smile back.

Peggy stirred her coffee, looking closely at Sequoia. Aldane ordered scrambled eggs and toast, Nate a bagel, and Chubby and Peggy a piece of quiche.

"Did you guys hear about the kidnapping? You know *SwiftPad* right – well GG Oglethorpe – she like – made *SwiftPad* right? Well some RedHat dudes kidnapped her and killed a bunch of people. You heard about that, right?" Darmie asked.

"I heard something," said Chubby.

"Well, you know *SwiftPad* is trying to take over the country, man – you control *SwiftPad*, that is the ball game, right? That's what it's about, man."

"Social media is only one factor in the equation," Aldane said, assuming the Thurston Howell the Third persona he used when he talked to his fans, just to fuck with them. "You have to balance that with other institutional forces and the historical realities as well as regional and demographic considerations."

Darmie nodded intently. Nate smiled slyly at Chubby.

"So where do you think they took her, Darmie?" Nate asked.

"Oh – no question – back east – RedHat country. Missouri, Arkansas, somewhere. Maybe Lake of the Ozarks. That fat dude on the radio, always talking shit hinted they were in Cape Geraldo. That's where he's from, you know," Darmie explained.

Sequoia was looking at Chubby's toast, so he slid it to her.

"Yeah – well maybe she is there," Darmie said.

"How do you know?"

"It's all over, man. Don't you listen? Music sucks anymore so I listen to talk radio. They sayin' they're gonna set up a 'fair' *SwiftPad*."

"Have you heard anything about the roads south of here?" asked Aldane.

"Hmm," said Darmie. "99E down to Canby is blocked."

"How do you know?" asked Aldane.

"It has been blocked both ways since last night. Nothing coming in from the south. That big camp by the bend in the river got shot up yesterday. Lot of people trying to get out of there. After all the shit up above town in the park, they are blocking everything."

"So what are people doing?" Nate had been getting the eye from Sequoia. She was a scared young girl trying to find some shelter.

"I live with my mom. Maybe try to find a job. Anything is better than staying in those camps. I just need to meet some people, and show what I can do. It's harder for a guy. A girl like Sequoia can write her own ticket. Isn't that right?" Darmie said.

"You mean like – what? – For twenty bucks?"

"And breakfast," Darmie broke up laughing. "Don't forget breakfast!"

"Oh, fuck!" Everyone at the table looked up at the TV in the corner, which one of the cooks had just turned on. The room went silent.

It was Real-Prez filling up the screen. He hadn't been seen since last November.

"I want to thank the Vice President for filling in for me these last months, while I recovered. A lot of bad things happened. Some bad people. We are taking care of it. Believe me."

Temp-Prez was standing off to the side, looking worshipfully at Real-Prez, applauding along with some number of people off camera.

"I have a few announcements," Real-Prez continued. "First – the Party's Convention is next week. I don't know why I wasn't on the ballot this spring, but it's a disgrace. Unbelievable! Totally unfair. How can you have a primary, a fair election without the President? People tell me it's the first time a sitting President was not on the ballot! But that's OK, that's OK...the delegates know what happened. I am not worried.

"We don't want the socialists to take over – nobody does! It looks like Senator Scaredy Cary-lion is probably going to be our opponent. Unless they lose their minds completely and nominate Rosy – Rosy Rosy Rosy. Can you believe it? There is a piece of work. Can you imagine having to roll over and see that in the morning? I don't know, it's bad, so bad – bad people, unbelievable. So we have to win. Have to win. The delegates know that. And Ben and Doug – well let's face it neither one is too bright – can I say that? And their crowd sizes – you can fit them in a high school gym! Not popular. At least Doug the Turd Herder – it's true – he worked in a shit water treatment plant in college. You know what that is – herding Turds! It is funny because his name – what is it Turdmanojian – Turdmasian. See what I mean? Anyway, at least he is getting some crowds. Nothing like my crowds – but some crowds. Some crowds.

"What about that Senator – Ben CaDAZ. KayDez – am I saying that right? They say he went to Stanford. Some say it really wasn't him – people tell me the real Ben Cadez is a fake. He's a fake – not even real. He replaced the real Cadez. Was he killed in Brazil? Is it true? I don't know – people are saying it. Ben Cadez – Ben Cadez. He's a real winner.

"But I am going to be there next week at the Convention. Down in North Carolina. I will be there. Lot of people love me there. Nobody like the people in Carolina.

"Number two – and I say number two, I mean it, number two is a real pile of shit if you have ever seen it! I am talking about that horrible horrible place, Portland Oreegone. That's right – I call it Commie town. Nothing but Commies. Well they had a little dustup in Commie town. Bad bad people. Unfortunate, but not my fault. I was out – but I am back now! Sneaky sons a bitches! Ambushed our wonderful wonderful men and women, young men and beautiful women. Went to that shit city to help them. Shot in the back. Well, that is over, believe me. I am back and Commie town is going to learn a lesson quick! Come out here – come on."

Eight young men in what appeared to be Air Force uniforms came out and stood at attention behind Real-Prez.

"What do you fly?"

"Certified on F-16s, sir."

"F-16s! Beautiful. No more staying on the ground, no more 'recusing yourselves' from the fight. Are you with me?"

"YES SIR!" the eight pilots yelled, snapping to attention.

"You're next, Memphis. Since Ben KAYDAZ of Tennessee can't seem to control his own state, we are going to have to do it for him. Have you seen the pictures? Can you believe some of those 'Bad Dudes'? I call them bad dudes, but you know what I am saying, you know.

"So I will just say, Portland, if you're listening," laughter and more applause, "Portland – we are coming. We are coming." More applause. "Thank you everyone."

The cook turned off the TV, and turned, and nobody objected. Kip looked at Nate.

"I'm done," said Aldane.

"Let's go," said Chubby. "You want to come?" Sequoia nodded. "Get away from this fucking creep?" Nate was looking at Darmie.

Sequoia got up. "Thanks for breakfast."

They all climbed into Aldane's Cutlass. "So Dane, where we going?" said Kip. "We got to find a way to get to Aurora."

"Turn up here," said Peggy from the back seat, between Sequoia and Nate. "Cross the Sellwood Bridge."

"Fuck, then we are on the wrong side of the river," said Kip. "The only other bridge is I-5, and we sure aren't crossing there."

"It's not the only way across," she said. "Trust me."

They crossed the Sellwood and went down 43 along the river. It was all wooded, hiding more wealthy houses, but there was no traffic. They got to Lake Oswego and the downtown was a mess. Most of the stores along the road – burnt or shot up. A cruiser, shot up with its passenger door open, was stopped crosswise in the road. Aldane had to go up on the sidewalk to get around it.

"Turn up here – we'll go up Stafford. So Sequoia, where are you from?"

"Kingman – but I was going to school in Tempe – System Engineering -when the dam broke."

"It didn't break – it was blown."

"I know. Terrorists! It was a mess. Nothing at first, but then the water shut off. People still stayed figuring it would come back soon, but then – after a month – well it got ugly. Grocery stores ran out of bottled water. They trucked it in, but it was expensive. I hitched a ride to LA – it was almost as bad there, then I heard that Portland was the place to go. But the fires in Cali were awful – all the way. I ran out of money, and hooked up with these guys." She stopped talking and stared out the window. Peggy put her arm around her. She was almost holding back her tears. "Finally made it to the camp – well near where we are going. They had food and water, and a place to sleep at least. Weather was nice. And it was safe – a lot of single women were there and we stuck together – but then I met Darmie – he was supposed to be doing some kind of volunteer work – he sang some, played the guitar. He invited me into the city, we went all around to get in, he had residents' ID and said I was his wife. When I got there, he got weird, so I left him and moved up to the camp where I told you. But then I went back. He bought me breakfast at least. Where are we going?"

"Aldane and Kip are going to try and get on a plane, then we are going south – to a good place. Can you work?"

"Yes. I can do anything. I know computers and networking. Really, I really do, I just need a chance. Ask me about the IP stack. Or spanning tree."

Stafford Road was crowded going north, but no one was headed in their direction. The bridge over the Tualatin had two guys in camo sitting in a truck and another in the back holding an AR-16, but they were not stopping traffic. Then they crossed the bridge over 205 and saw a nightmare scene. From the bridge they saw five or six burned-out cars that had been going north. There were corpses on the road.

"I heard they sent a chopper with a fifty cal strafing these motafuks – fuck!"

They took a left at Mountain Road and swung around through more McMansions, some burning, most abandoned. Past the golf course, down the hill to the river.

Unbelievably, the Canby Ferry was still running. It was a raft that held about six cars max, with a diesel engine half exposed out of the housing. The river wasn't a hundred yards wide at that point. The ferry cost six dollars. Chubby gave him a hundred, with a keep-the-change wave. On their way across, a body, looked like a young teenaged boy, floated down the river.

It was another five miles through farmland to the airport. Aldane drove right up to the edge of the runway, next to the hangar.

It started raining.

In the hangar Jean Katon was waiting. She hugged Aldane, and smiled.

Her keyboard player, Adele Humpkin, the wife of Gary "Leone" Humpkin, the unofficial "Speaker" for the Ishpeming Committee, came over.

"Hello, Nathan."

"Adele."

"How's your spooky girlfriend?"

"She is sick," Nate shook his head as though it was the first time he was admitting that fact to himself.

"Love is a strange thing, isn't it?"

"Tell me about it."

It was really coming down now. Umbrellas were out. Jean came over to the car, where Kip was getting his backpack out of the trunk. She held the umbrella over him while he pulled out five stacks of hundreds.

"Fifty K?"

"Welcome aboard."

Chubby hauled the heavy backpack up. Aldane threw the keys to Nate. "Take care of my baby, old man."

"Have a good trip. Good luck." They all hugged, and then Kip, Aldane, and the rest of the Jean Katon Express boarded the G5. Nate, Peggy, and Sequoia, windshield wipers clapping, headed south for Alice's compound in Aldane's 1990 Cutlass.

To Be Continued...

COMING ATTRACTIONS

THE FINAL VOLUME IN THE *SWIFTPAD* SAGA IS coming. Follow Chubby as he travels the globe to search for GG, while the Real-Prez fights his party to get his job back. The Ishpeming Resistance is under siege. Will Portland survive the coming onslaught? Can Nate save Paula? What happened to Alison and Spence? Will America break its social media addiction? Will America find its soul? Will Chubby find GG?

www.ingramcontent.com/pod-product-compliance
Lightning Source LLC
Chambersburg PA
CBHW071137100726
47908CB00008B/2630